Grays' Plutonium

Grays' Plutonium

War, Technology and God: A Multi-Galactic Odyssey

John W. McSherry

iUniverse, Inc.
New York Bloomington

Grays' Plutonium
A Multi-Galactic Political Analysis for all Self-Proclaimed gods: How to Indenture Science and Technology for Greed, Power and Oppression

iUniverse books may be ordered through booksellers or by contacting:

iUniverse
1663 Liberty Drive
Bloomington, IN 47403
www.iuniverse.com
1-800-Authors (1-800-288-4677)

ISBN: 978-1-4401-5339-6 (pbk)
ISBN: 978-1-4401-5338-9 (ebk)

Printed in the United States of America

iUniverse rev. date: 8/5/2009

Contents

Foreword

Grays' Plutonium explores the political, scientific, and theological concepts common to all civilizations, regardless of their technological advancement. Civilization can be broken down into four concepts: truth, politics, war, and propaganda. The concept of truth stands alone, while politics, war, and propaganda come under the heading of "advice."

Truth is not a relative concept, but a foundational reference built on honesty, integrity, and reverence, where our creator in itself is truth. Imagine there were two people. One believed in only accepting advice, and the other believed in God. In the biblical book, Ecclesiastes, a dying man examines all life's meaningless lessons, only to conclude that God was the answer all along.

What does it mean to take advice? When an individual decides that another's advice is better than his own, then can truth be found in that advice? What drives the need for financial sales, only to see the economic climate collapse? The same goes for politics or war. Advice is inherently false because it is power driven. Who is the beneficiary when advice is purposely fraudulent, when opportunists walk on the backs of the fallen who believed the advice they received was gospel?

As life's vanities result in calamitous catastrophes, who is the beneficiary when that advice falls short? Economic frauds and schemes depend on those who would rather seek that advice than depend on themselves. It is on the backs of the fallen that the sinful heroes emerge, fulfilled that "their" version of the truth rose victorious. Higher they climb, as if in a race to collectively share in the martyrdom that despises the one truth that is God's.

Imagine this landscape: a mountain that is truth, and a swampy bog that is advice. Advice is as unpredictable as swampy footing, until you find yourself trapped. The bodies of inconsequential advice seekers continue to pile up, until advice itself becomes a monument of propaganda.

Those who seek God's truth can depend individually on the solid footing and foundational understanding of stewardship, responsibility, and fellowship. Freedom is an individual concept in which God's truth rewards those willing to climb. Advice is freedom sacrificed, where individual greed and power become the common denominator that destroys all humankind.

One of the Machiavellian horrors posed by the democratic socialistic party is eminent domain—alternatively what I call forced colonization. Colonization is a politically driven term meant to justify idealistic survival, not human survival. The Greeks, the Romans,

Napoleon, Hitler, and other all superpowers sought to push their sphere of influence through colonization. Even in the galactic world of stellar colonization, the eminent politics of territory, power, and greed continue to challenge the one foundational truth that God's influence is the ultimate judge.

To deny that colonization is its own warfare means that colonization is as benign as a bullet to the head. The constitution's second amendment rightfully allows a counterbalance to those who would employ conspiratorial colonization. Denying the right to self-defense is the same as committing treason against America's right to exist. College students who consume this fraudulent propaganda find themselves as pawns or sacrificial lambs in someone else's revolution. As governments dictate through oppression and colonization, technology and science are the first to be indentured, inciting cultural and political corruption and greed.

To encapsulate my ideas, I chose the science-fiction format to demonstrate the dynamic of multiple hypocrisies. Archeologists have documented several multiple civilizations where the stellar night sky spawned its own reason for living—faith in something greater than themselves. If UFOs do exist, then the militarization of space is irrelevant. China and the U.S. have already militarized space by targeting wayward satellites. If we assume that Earthly governments have the power to dictate policy despite the existence of UFO technology, then who is in charge? To deny the truth is to assume that we are being milked at a price beyond what our governments can pay.

I remember watching the moon landing, knowing someday that our generation would be next. We were content with slide rules, determination, grit, and the desire to do the impossible. Look at us now: incompetent, lazy, and willing to negotiate surrender at every turn. I present this truth that strategy and politics ultimately renders science irrelevant at the hands of a more controlling technology. We, as the chattering class, understand that technology can never substitute individual freedoms when the government tells us otherwise. There is a race to destroy America where the government demands nationalization, absolute control, and concealment through governmental propaganda. The government's role is to give fraudulent advice as a means of building monuments to the vainly martyred.

I have a question for all the UFO enthusiasts: have you seen a young or baby Gray? No. Stem-cell research is immortality through stasis regeneration. What is stem cell research when God becomes irrelevant, and where the assertion that political perversion rests in the discriminatory miracle of stasis immortality?

The government's role is not to alter the fabric of scientific or technological research. The government's desire to propagandize Big Science is meant to corrupt scientific purity, and to contaminate the public's image that science is individualism and inherently evil. Big Science again represents fraudulent advice meant to manipulate the masses into submission and universal agreement. Science, in its purist sense, is the individual's ability to conquer nature's obstacles, but Big Science is the ability to create fabricated obstacles, which in the end corrupts all inquisitive thought.

Do I believe in little gray aliens? I would to approach this questions from a different angle. Are advanced civilizations really advanced? The mark of an advanced civilization is not in technology or arrogance, but in the wisdom of its citizens to preserve what is civil based on freedom's inalienable rights. In the phrase, "might makes right," we are witnessing an radically liberal government hell-bent on socialistic oppression, only to justify what is correct in their own mind. Big Science preaches the hypocrisy of advice. If the Grays are not milking us, Big Science certainly is.

Would our socialistic government willingly forfeit such alien technology for individual research? Obviously not. Our socialistic government would rather advertise fraudulent advice than reveal the truth. Though this sounds conspiratorial, we have allowed ourselves to accept inconsequential fodder of fraudulent advice without question.

I remember a prominent Democratic president saying, "If you talked about a problem, then you fixed it." Never mind actually fixing the problem, because advice is a far better weapon against individual stewardship than solving the people's desire for security or representation.

Science cannot be dictated by man's arrogance. Unfortunately, technology is malleable enough to assimilate man's destructive and manipulative desire for power. In that regard, technology reacts in contempt if science proves otherwise, it is always science's fault when manipulation does not mirror man's political agenda.

Grays' Plutonium is a parable typifying today's changing world, and of the struggle between war, technology, and God. Because the elite see themselves as an advanced civilization, it is not enough just to be secular or civil, but to understand that civilizations can never stand on arrogance alone.

John W. McSherry

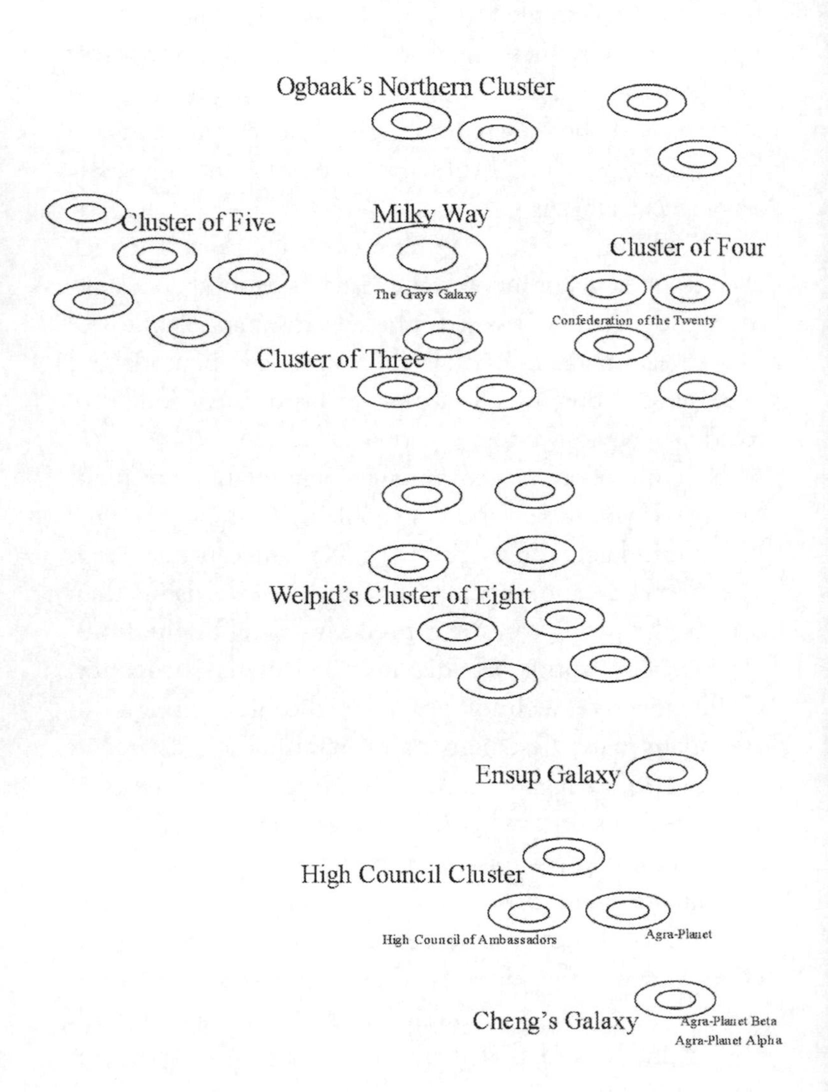
Ogbaak's Northern Cluster
Cluster of Five
Milky Way
The Grays Galaxy
Cluster of Four
Confederation of the Twenty
Cluster of Three
Welpid's Cluster of Eight
Ensup Galaxy
High Council Cluster
High Council of Ambassadors
Agra-Planet
Cheng's Galaxy
Agra-Planet Beta
Agra-Planet Alpha

Chapter 1

Wayne Ceroi

The Ceroi family lived in the rugged Dakota butte region, east of the Rocky Mountains. Wayne was in junior high when his parents died in a car crash involving a drunk driver. Wayne, now in high school, continued to live in his parents' house. As with many kids at age twelve who lost their parents, many misunderstand the real psychological damage behind the tragic loss of loved ones. Unfortunately, subsequent bouts of depression only becomes worse later in life when real relationships need the most attention. Wayne had time to reflect, time to gaze at the stars, and time to walk the same road where his parents died.

Since his parent's death, the folks in town called Wayne "that kid" who lost his parents. Wayne discovered the harsh reality of being the only child and thus, the only surviving child. It was this reality that forged his character as a young adult.

Wayne did not have a letter jacket or a girlfriend, nor was he a member of a high school association or club. Wayne was anything but average—he enjoyed the outdoors, astronomy, physics, science, and mathematics. Many of his high school teachers knew his parents. It was not easy for them to have Wayne in their class, but Wayne's love for science seemed to bridge the gap between them. Wayne often found himself at the chalkboard deriving math equations or physics formulas. It was not that the teacher could not do it, but the kids seemed to learn better after Wayne's misfortune. Wayne hated English and social studies, but he tolerated physical education and after-school sports. Wayne loved to play chess, but was not interested in military tactics. Wayne had built a small runway in his backyard to fly remote control airplanes. Many of his friends came over to engage in aerial dogfights in the clear Dakota blue. Wayne grew to admire many of his friends who proudly displayed their pilot's licenses because of Wayne's backyard airport. Wayne did not see flying as an end, but as another clue in the mystery of science and physics.

Wayne was of average height, with an average appearance and an average personality, but he tried his utmost to be different. The Ceroi ranch was a five-hundred-acre spread along the high prairie bluffs adjacent to a long country road. His parents were not very interested in agricultural or cattle ranching. They wanted to provide a playground for their only child. His parents built the house some twenty years earlier when they purchased the property in the 1980s. The house itself was an ordinary ranch design, but Wayne modified the layout based on his interests and hobbies. The master bedroom was a huge soldering lab. He repaired discarded radio equipment, frequency generators, and an old magnetron. Wayne had two part-time jobs, one at the local radio transmitter, and the other repairing Instrument Landing System, or ILS, radar from the regional airport. In the second bedroom, Wayne set up his dual wall chalkboard for math and physics equations. If Wayne had a single passion, it was the relationship between gravity and energy. Wayne refrained from science trivia or science fiction, because he believed science fit into three categories: science propaganda, Hollywood science, and mathematics based science.

The third bedroom was his private sanctuary, which he shared with no one. The living room and side kitchen he kept fairly tidy and organized, with the dining room as his private study hall and library.

If there was one day Wayne regretted, it was graduation day. One month earlier, Wayne had submitted his senior project, "Calculating the coincidence between gravity and infinite energy." Wayne's physics teacher had submitted the paper to a friend of hers, a doctorate candidate currently working on her paper in electro-mechanics.

Wayne broke his paper into three concepts: first, if infinite energy exists next to infinite mass, then is gravity infinite? The second concept explained the fission-fusion energy cycle based on the plasma frequency of the heaviest fissionable material used. The basic concept of fission is the sudden release of energy and the degradation of subatomic particles from heavier unstable radioactive elements. The basic concept of fusion is the rebuilding of those unstable radioactive elements and reconstituting the original radioactive atom. Wayne's third theory was the function of gravity at a black hole's entrance in relation to the negative gravity coefficient at its exit. See appendix 1 for Wayne's complete senior project.

Wayne returned home alone after graduation. He felt more comfortable conducting science experiments or reading physics journals than entertaining guests or attending parties. Some of his friends came over after graduation, but Wayne did not feel like socializing. He greeted the rowdy graduates from his rustic front porch as their tightly packed sedan pulled into the driveway.

Wayne said, "Hey, guys, go on without me."

Voices of objection and some calling him a "party pooper" blended with the loud music as the car pulled back onto the gravel road.

Wayne sat down in his favorite rocking chair and watched his friends drive off in a cloud of dusty loud music.

Wayne waited for about ten minutes, then went into the house, changed clothes, grabbed his car keys, and drove off to the big city some hundred miles away.

Wayne felt sure no one would recognize him there. He drove up to the parking lot of a small strip mall and parked his car. Wayne picked up his high school diploma, transcripts from both high school and community college courses he attended, and walked into the Navy recruiting office. Wayne said, "I want to take the nuke test."

It is not often a Navy recruiter has a kid fresh out of high school wanting to take the nuke test. The recruiter said, "All right, we have a test here. Let me see your transcripts." Wayne handed over the freshly typed transcripts and the freshly printed diploma and sat down at the computer with the test already booted up to the first question.

Normally a nuke test takes a couple hours. Wayne said, "Finished." The recruiter looked at the wall clock and it had only been thirty minutes. The recruiter slipped in a VCR tape saying, "This is the nuclear program, the toughest academic program the Navy offers." Wayne sat down in the lounge chair while the recruiter retrieved Wayne's score from the computer. Wayne turned around as the recruiter jumped out from his seat saying, "Wayne, you aced the test!" Wayne went over, turned the VCR tape off, and said, "When do I leave?" That was all it took. The recruiter had all the necessary paperwork and the qualifying test score, so off they went to the military entrance processing station, known as MEPS.

Then next day, Wayne's schedule was jammed packed with medical tests, security screening, nuke paperwork, and finally, his orders to go to boot camp in Great Lakes, Illinois, followed by a two-year nuke school in Charleston, South Carolina. Wayne signed all the necessary paperwork, finished his medical screening, then later in the day was sworn into the Navy.

When they returned to the recruiter station, Wayne's recruiter said, "You have two days before boot camp. Take care of any necessary business before then. I will pick you up on Friday for final MEPS processing, then we'll get your plane ticket to boot camp."

Wayne said, "Thanks for everything, I will see you Friday". Wayne left the recruiter's office and drove straight home.

Wayne needed a house-sitter while he was gone, but who?

Wayne remembered his physics teacher, who constantly complained about her old, rundown apartment. Maybe she would consider moving. Wayne spent that whole day and night cleaning up the soldering stuff from the master bedroom and taking down the two chalkboards. He painted all the bedroom walls and cleaned the hardwood floors until they shined. Wayne cleaned up the living room and kitchen, moved all his books from the dining room to the garage, and cleaned the yard the best he could.

After nearly twenty-four hours of steady cleaning, he called his physics teacher and said, "I need a house-sitter, this is your chance to get out of that old apartment."

Wayne felt her enthusiastic pause, and then she said, "Wayne, I accept." She continued, "Where are you going?"

Wayne said, "Nuke school in South Carolina with the Navy."

Wayne understood the tension with traditional high school teachers and their obvious distaste for the military. He could hear her teeth digging into her lips as she said, "Wow Wayne, that's nice."

Thursday afternoon, Wayne gently relaxed on the porch in his favorite rocking chair. He could see a car slowly approaching along the old gravel road. He watched his physics teacher gently pulled into the gravel driveway with stuff, some of which stuck out of the back windows. Wayne walked to the driveway as she drove in.

Wayne said, "Welcome to your new home!"

She opened the door and got out, obviously taken

with the house, even though it was only for six years. It was a vast improvement from her nasty apartment in town.

Wayne approached the car and said, "I'll help you with your things."

She said, "Wayne, I want you to have this before you go."

Wayne looked the manila folder titled, "Senior Project, Wayne Ceroi."

She said, "A friend of mine who is a doctoral candidate studying electro-mechanics had a chance to examine your work. Even some professors at the university looked at it."

Wayne interrupted her and said, "I know what you are doing, and I appreciate it. I need some real hands-on science, but not from a lecture hall. I am only obligated for six years and will have plenty of time for school once I get out. This is my time to breathe and finally put my parents to rest. I hope you understand."

She humbly nodded and said, "Can you help me with this stuff?"

Friday morning rolled around. The recruiter drove up bright and early in front of Wayne's house just as Wayne walked on the porch, all bags packed.

The recruiter said, "The other car, you have a friend?"

Wayne laughed and said, "One of my old school teachers is house sitting for me, she's asleep, and I didn't want to wake her."

Wayne got in the recruiter's car, and off they went. It would be six years before Wayne would see the house again.

Three years later, Wayne stood over the skeleton and keel of an aircraft carrier sunken in a massive dry-dock. Now a third-class petty officer dressed in his crisp, dress whites. Wayne had finally received orders to his first active command, the newest aircraft carrier still in its early stage of construction.

A chief walked over to the smartly dressed third-class and asked, "You have order here, son?"

"Yes, Chief," Wayne said, showing his orders.

The chief said, "Come with me. We will get you checked in."

Wayne gazed in amazement at the amount of activity. like Welding sparks, busy ironworkers and hundreds of pallets packed with supplies carefully organized on the pier. The chief escorted Wayne to the personnel trailer, where a yeoman promptly checked him into the command.

The chief said, "Can you weld?"

Wayne said, eager to learn, said, "No, but I'm dying to try."

The chief smiled at the kid's enthusiasm, saying, "See that big guy sitting at the picnic bench? His name is Roy, the best welder we have. He's a nuke welder, and he needs an apprentice."

Normally the nuke welder's school was nearly a year long, but Wayne had enough of school. Wayne was ready to get his hands dirty after spending the last three years in training and in school.

The chief said, "Once Roy feels you're ready to go solo, he'll qualify you on three projects. If you pass his demanding criteria, you will receive your nuke welder's card."

The yeoman issued Wayne his berthing room at the plush barracks built specifically for the workers and his meal ticket to the base's chow hall. Wayne took his duffel bag and headed off to his room to change clothes.

Over the past two years, Wayne managed to keep a 99 percent test average in nuke school while taking both correspondence courses and university courses through the Navy's educational program. Wayne graduated top of his class while taking five additional university math courses, four university physics courses, and four university chemistry courses, all successfully completed with a 95 percent GPA.

Wayne's educational advisor said, "You need ten more graduate and doctorate courses to earn your PhD."

Wayne was shocked at his progress. If only his high school physics teacher could see him now. Wayne changed into his blue work overalls, excited over his next demanding challenge, nuke welding.

Wayne ran over to the adjacent dry-dock, where Roy was waiting with a brand new set of welding leathers.

Wayne said, "You must be Roy. I was told you needed an apprentice, and here I am!"

Roy was a huge man, the son of an ironworker from Pittsburgh, Pennsylvania. Roy had lost his mother when he was very young. Roy's earliest memories were with his dad, and of the oxidizing smell of freshly welded metal. As a young boy, Roy watched his father work from the safety of the supervisor's trailer.

Roy received his first welding mask and torch when he was ten years old, and by the age of twelve, was helping his father with contract work. Roy was a gruff man with massive forearms and gorilla-sized hands. His matted, brownish hair was dented from the head straps on his welding masks, and had a vocabulary that only Tarzan could love.

Wayne said, "What are these? They look like motorcycle garb."

Roy said, "Dese ar'welding leathers. Protect you from sparks and splat'r. If'en you want to work here, y'se got to wear dese. Now put 'em on!"

Wayne did not question Roy's insistent behavior, and he did not want to get off on the wrong foot, so he quickly donned the leathers and said, "Now what?"

Roy already prepared three types of welding machines used at the job site. Roy said, "Dis is oxyacetylene, dis is MIG, and dis is TIG." Roy looked around for a couple seconds and said, "Come with me." Roy took Wayne over to a pile of discarded metal bulkheads, sheet metal, and angle stock. Roy said, "What's wrong with dis bulkhead?"

Wayne looked at the ordinary piece of metal, figuring this was an important quiz. Wayne studied it and saw something odd. Wayne said, "The weld joint broke along the seam."

Roy was surprised at the lad's correct answer. Roy said, "Congrats, you correct! Why?"

Wayne again studied the metallic bulkhead. The seam still had a factory protective glaze where someone tried to weld over top of it. Wayne took a chance and said, "It wasn't properly cleaned before welding."

Roy slapped his new apprentice on the back, almost knocking him down, saying, "You passed!"

Wayne thought it could not be this easy, and then

he heard Roy say, "We reuse dis piece of bulkhead. You grind the seam to a bright metal col'r."

Wayne grabbed the awkward, industrial-sized metal grinder, put his safety glasses on, and touched the grinder to the metal. A brief fountain of sparks shot behind him as Roy laughed, saying, "Lay into it, boy!" Roy handed Wayne some ear guards and a hardhat, saying, "Get to it." Wayne picked up the large circular grinder and started in. The sparks were flying in all directions. The bone-chattering vibration resonated through every joint, every muscle, and every tooth in his jaw. Day after day after day after day, Wayne hit the grinder as he followed all the architect's drafting and witness lines.

Wayne began to understand that a good weld depended on a precision fit and a well-prepared surface. Wayne fabricated inner-hull bulkheads, doorway passages, watertight integrity bulkheads, ballistic bulkheads, and learned how to fit doorways made of one inch metal.

After six weeks of constant grinding and preparing Roy's stock, Roy said, "We try MIG welding today, lay down bead here." Wayne could not be happier. Wayne had watched Roy weld hundreds of times using various techniques and with different welding machines. He learned about the physical properties of metal, whether it was forged or tempered, whether it was micro-crystalline or brittle, or whether it followed a grain.

Roy gave Wayne a small piece of metal stock and said, "Go over to the metal-bending table and make me a square." Wayne had made thousands of metal squares for medicine cabinets, head cabinets, or berthing racks, and he had become an expert in fabricating anything off a bending table. Wayne brought the square metal box over to where Roy was standing as Roy said, "Now weld it to dis bulkhead stock."

Wayne tried not to panic as he rolled the spool of wire until it extended about half an inch from the business end. Wayne donned his new welder's mask and insulated gloves and got into a comfortable position above the project. He lightly touched the metallic brazen wire to the interface between the bulkhead stock and the box with one tack weld. He moved down about one inch, made another tack weld, and continued down the line on both sides.

Wayne stopped, raised his welding mask, switched the welding machine to standby, and said, "How is that for a first try?"

Roy said, "Why did you tack it?"

Wayne said, "Tack it so not to overheat the metal."

Roy said, "Good, now finish it smooth."

Wayne turned on his machine, put his welding mask back on, and proceeded filling in between the tack welds until both sides were smooth. Wayne was pleased with himself as he raised his welding mask and secured the machine.

Roy picked up Wayne's first assignment and threw it across the work area onto the pier some forty feet away. It landed with a crash as it bounced and ricocheted off the various pallets and onto the cluttered concrete pier. Roy said, "Did it break apart?"

Wayne had lost sight of it, thinking it had fallen into the water on the other side of the pier. Roy and Wayne walked over, and there it was behind a large pallet. It did not break!

Roy said, "We try TIG." Wayne listened as Roy

explained all the various switches and knobs and the power and amperage settings, and then said, "Dis a 440-volt, three-phase electrocution machine. it will kill you dead if'en you not careful."

Wayne put on his insulated gloves as Roy handed him the handgrip. Roy clamped two pieces of ballistic stock together, each piece one inch thick. Roy said, "This is a butt joint, start with tack welds where two pieces meet at middle and work out to edge."

Wayne jerked his head to drop the welding mask over his face as he angled the welding torch and lightly held it just above the metal, letting the arc do all the work. He applied one tack, then another, until several tacks extended from one edge to the next.

Roy picked up the assignment piece with his mighty arm and let it fly as he yelled, "Heads up!" Wayne froze in anticipation as Roy tossed his twenty-pound welding assignment some thirty yards. It came down with a solid crash, bouncing around until it came to a rest on the pier. Roy walked over and said, "You passed!"

The final whistle blew, ending Wayne's first real day of welding qualifications. Wayne knew it was a good day—his first day at welding! It was his first step in the very long process of putting this aircraft carrier together.

One year later, Wayne and Roy had become welding friends, working mainly mid-ships and on the bow structure. Wayne was still under apprenticeship probation, so any inspection work went to the project manager or Roy for final approval. All qualifying paperwork identified both the welder and who inspected the work. It would be another six months before Wayne would receive his welding license, then be reassigned back aft to the reactors to finish his nuke-welder's qualification. Wayne was happy that Roy would accompany him to the reactor room to complete his training.

Another year passed. Wayne had received his welding certification and was now working back aft, doing grinding and fitting work for the company that was installing the nuclear fission unit. Due to the precision involved, Wayne spent days watching the engineers and technicians measuring load, torsion, and torque tests of the surrounding superstructure. Wayne helped on the coolant system, routing piping and installing flange grommets through the engineering complex. Roy told Wayne that another contractor received the final coolant system, which only allowed qualified pipefitters because of enclosed containment regulations.

Roy and Wayne went to work on the island structure and the mid-ships hanger-deck complex. Roy and Wayne split up; Roy went to the hanger deck, and Wayne became part of a fabrication crew to build the island a couple of piers down.

Wayne never had a brother or anyone closely resembling a father, but Roy was becoming a close friend. Because Roy as a civilian, Wayne had to obey all restrictions pertaining to civilians, like on base privileges and security protocols. Wayne never entertained after work hours, because he was too exhausted at the end of the day. Sometimes he would collapse on his bed without taking a shower.

Another year passed, which marked Wayne's fifth year in the Navy and one year to go before his discharge date. He could see the light at the end of the tunnel after an incredible journey. He dressed himself in blue coveralls, carrying his most prized possession, his welding leathers. The aircraft carrier was 90 percent completed, with much of the welding assignments already signed off. The final phase of construction shifted to the massive job of wiring, installing electronics packages, painting, testing, and evaluation before leaving dry-dock.

Wayne felt a growing emptiness as Roy's contract was about to expire in a couple days. Roy's union had signed another military contract, building a maximum-security outpost in an undisclosed location. Wayne kept busy with engineering tasks like control-room wiring, monitors, coolant valve inspections, relays, and an overabundance of engineering publications.

Roy wanted Wayne to meet him after work to celebrate with some friends. Wayne, even on the weekends, rarely went out because he was either too sore or too tired, but he agreed to accompany Roy for a final night out.

Roy walked into a busy nightclub, with Wayne following like a lost child. They sat at a table by the bar as every interior wall was devoted to a large-screen sporting event. Clouds of hot-wing pepper dust and the smell of day-old beer and sliders off the grill filled the air. The place was packed as Wayne listened to every conceivable conversation over the shouts and cheers after touchdowns, field goals, or bone-crunching tackles. Wayne noticed some nice-looking girls, but his life was already too complicated. Roy said in his Tarzan voice, "Waits here." Wayne looked back as Roy walked around, apparently looking for something or someone, but after losing interest, he returned to the Nebraska college game, which was nearing half-time.

Wayne heard a bang in the back. He looked back as

he watched Roy slap someone against the wall. Wayne knew trouble was only a few minutes away when Roy grabbed a girl and escorted her toward their table. Wayne expected the police to arrive at any moment when Roy put this girl in front of him and said, "Do you want to meet my sister?"

Wayne remembered those immortal words throughout high school. If only he had a nickel for every time he heard that phrase, "Hey, do you want to meet my sister?" Wayne started laughing as the phrase stuck in his head. Wayne quickly said after seeing Roy's obvious agitation, "Yeah, I want to meet your sister, but now the police are on their way. Let's get out of here!"

Wayne was laughing as he held Roy's sister's by the hand. Roy went to the rear of the bar for some more punching lessons as Wayne shouted, "Roy, forget it, the cops are coming!" Wayne and Roy's sister continued laughing as they left the bar in a mad dash, realizing Roy had taken an alternate exit.

Wayne stopped in an adjacent park, nearly out of breath, saying, "Hey, my name is Wayne. Roy is my welding buddy. I am very glad to meet you."

Roy's sister said, "My name is Sarah, and so far I've had a pretty good evening. Roy is such a blockhead. I have seen him throw a two-hundred-pound man some twenty feet, but he means well as my protector. Right now, I'd like to relax in a good restaurant."

Wayne saw a nice restaurant on the other side of the park as they slowly acquainted themselves in the autumn evening air.

Sarah was a couple years older than Wayne, but he did not mind. Wayne wondered if his mother would like

Sarah, with her shoulder-length, dirty blonde hair, high cheekbones, deep blue eyes, and amazing smile. Sarah was a child psychologist specializing in the comparison between inner-city kids and destitute rural kids. She spent all last summer in Appalachia, but was now finishing an inner-city evaluation in metropolitan DC. Sarah was not very fond of her brother or her father, and living without a mother deepened her need for attention. Her only desire was to help other kids with similar circumstances.

Their first evening together passed without notice as the restaurant closed its doors for the evening. Wayne needed to get back to the base, and Sarah had some case studies to finish up. Wayne said, "Roy has been the father I never knew, but when I heard Roy was being reassigned, it would be a rough adjustment without him. But now I have something even better, Roy's sister, Sarah."

Sarah felt the same way, but she needed another evening to be sure. Sarah said, "How about tomorrow at the wharf, say about six o'clock, I know a charter captain that can take us around the bay."

Wayne said, "I would like that very much."

Wayne and Sarah got up from their seats as Wayne paid the restaurant bill and the tip from his freshly minted credit card. Wayne helped Sarah from her seat, and together they walked onto the busy street to her parked car. Wayne had the perfect evening, and with less than one year left on his obligation, Dakota was calling him home. Sarah gave Wayne a little kiss on the cheek, saying, "See you tomorrow." She got in her car and drove off, leaving Wayne still in la-la land.

The next day, Wayne saw Roy gathering up his stuff as if it was just another day. However, it was not just another day, because the two welding friends who had been inseparable for three years were about to say goodbye. Wayne just stood there about twenty feet from where Roy was packing his equipment. Roy looked over, and Wayne could see the large shimmering tears welling up from his eyes.

Wayne said, "I really like your sister. I am glad you introduced us."

Roy smiled and said, "If you marry her, then we can be best buds forever."

Wayne laughed and said, "I really like to see you in a rodeo, I bet you could punch out a bull with one fist!"

Roy laughed and said, "Just don't name one of your kids Roy."

Wayne said, "I like Bud better." They quickly walked toward each other reaching out in a manly embrace of true, lasting friendship. They were friends to the end, as each pledged their eternal bond of faithful camaraderie.

Roy gathered his stuff, loading it into the utility pickup, and closed the rear gate. Wayne waved in a silent goodbye as Roy, still teary-eyed, got into the truck and drove off. Wayne could not bear losing his best friend, but his important date with Roy's sister was only hours away. That date was the most important event in Wayne's life right now.

Wayne spent all that day trying to keep busy by helping unwind wiring, splicing huge wiring bundles, and checking the continuity of each sensory connection between the reactor housing and the control room's instrument panel. At last, the four p.m. whistle stopped all work. Wayne signed off all the necessary paperwork for work done and checked in his toolbox, making sure all tools were accounted for. Wayne could not escape fast enough from the dry-dock as he headed to his barracks to change into some nice clothes.

Wayne saw that it was only five p.m. He started walking over to the wharf, quietly rehearsing the evening in his head while enjoying the sounds of waves against the shore. As Wayne nearing the dock's parking lot, he noticed Sarah's car. Wayne hurried to the wharf's boardwalk access ramp, and there was Sarah, quietly enjoying the calm, salty air. He nervously walked toward her, and she noticed that it was Wayne who was also one hour early. Both laughed at each other's desire to get there first as Wayne said, "How was your day?"

Sarah said, "A boring subject. How about we get a snack before the boat launches?"

Wayne took Sarah's hand as they strolled down the wooden pier to the concession stand.

Sarah knew in her heart this was no accident, but Wayne was trying too hard to be helpful. She said, "Roy called me today."

Wayne took a deep swallow and said, "Ugh, what did he say?"

Sarah laughed and said, "He said he liked the name Bud."

Wayne and Sarah passionately reached for each other in an emotional display of tears as each said, "I love you."

Wayne never imagined this would happen to him, but in his heart, he felt the empty void of childhood slowly filling with Sarah's affectionate presence. They relaxed their embrace, still gazing at each other, and smiling at each other's red eyes and tear-drenched faces.

Wayne said, "We have about thirty minutes before the boat takes off …"

Sarah stopped Wayne midsentence, saying, "Let's go shopping!"

Wayne, obviously confused by the change in plans, said, "Okay."

Sarah held Wayne's hand as they returned along the boardwalk toward the parking lot and to Sarah's car.

Wayne watched through the passenger's window as Sarah pulled into a shopping mall and stopped the car. Wayne had no idea what was going on, but he realized he was obviously missing something. Sarah parked the car and shut off the engine. Sarah smiled and gave a slight chuckle, saying, "I have never been as happy as I am now. Wayne, I love you."

Wayne quickly said, "Sarah, I love you." He stuttered, then said, "Sarah, will you marry me?"

Sarah wrapped her arms around him, saying between the tears, "Yes Wayne, I will marry you!"

Wayne suddenly realized why they were at the mall: the ring. Wayne saw the sly fox in Sarah's motives, but maybe that was what marriage was like—the joyful game of tag.

Eight years passed. Wayne sat in his favorite rocker, gently going back and forth as two kids suddenly erupted onto the front porch, slamming the screen door against the siding. Carolynn was seven, and Bud was five. They had just finished lunch and now rushed to their favorite small, motorized four-wheelers. The yard was trashed. Ruts and tire tracks gouged the open grasslands in front of Wayne's old homestead. Wayne laughed as these two energetic miracles blessed Sarah and Wayne's incredible lives together.

Sarah worked as a college professor in child psychology and served as an intern at the local pediatric ward in town. Wayne went back to school, received his PhD in physics and math, and was now teaching at the same college alongside his wife, Sarah. Wayne and Sarah recited their wedding vows no more than three weeks after that incredible day in the mall's parking lot. The aircraft carrier was still going through integrity and sea worthiness evaluations when Wayne was discharged from the Navy. Wayne brought Sarah to the Dakotas, but was a little nervous about her reaction. Once she saw the small, rustic house and felt the prairie calling her name, she claimed the house for her own.

Sarah named her first daughter Carolynn after her mother, who she never knew. Sarah admired Carolynn's light complexion, her shoulder-length, silky black hair, and high cheekbones. Her long legs and delicate arms were the jewels of Sarah's heart. Carolynn was everything she could have asked for. Bud was small, still under forty pounds. Bud was a fast runner, but not as fast as his sister. Bud had light brown hair and a much browner complexion after being in the sun all day.

Roy made several visits to the farmhouse as he crisscrossed the country from one assignment to the next. Roy especially liked western brisket barbecues and watching rodeos from the judge's booth. Roy was not able to make this year's county fair and rodeo, which just finished up. Carolynn played with the calves and lambs as Bud watched the tractor pulls. This was Sarah's fourth year as a professional pediatric psychologist and her fourth year sponsoring the inner-city rodeo invitation, where busloads of inner-city kids came and visited the rodeo. Sarah was impressed with the rodeo clowns as they divided the kids into groups and let them participate in the various events, like calf-roping, pig-chasing, cow-milking, and cattle-branding. In the cattle-branding booth, each kid received a one-square-foot swatch of genuine cowhide. Each kid had the choice of using three real branding irons, the Lazy E, the Sleepy Q, and the Rowdy X. The clowns helped each kid apply the hot branding iron against their cowhide patch. The kids wrinkled their nose at the smoke and smells of burning leather. At the end of the day, Sarah stood by the buses as the teachers lined up the well-behaved kids, all holding their decorated patches of branded cowhide. Some wore cowboy hats, some wore little chaps, and some were dressed up as Native Americans. Sarah had everything she could ever ask for.

Wayne sat on his porch, watching Carolynn and Bud shooting muddy rooster tails as they revved up their four-wheelers in a game of cat and mouse. Sarah was at the college and due back by supper. Since Wayne did much of his teaching from the Internet. He was home most of the time with the kids. Wayne did all of the laundry, the cooking, and the basic cleaning of the house, while Sarah did much of the shopping.

Wayne never was a churchgoer growing up, but with Sarah's encouragement, the kids needed to grow up respecting God. They found a little church about five miles out of town. The kids liked going there, because most of their friends from school went there, too.

Wayne got up from his rocker and yelled out, "Come on in, the sun's too hot!" Carolynn and Bud parked their four-wheelers in the shed by the house. Wayne said, "Take your shoes off before you go in the house." Wayne went into Bud's room to get another shirt, because Bud's was covered with mud. Wayne sat in the chair by Bud's toddler bed as Carolynn was laughing at Bud's dirty shirt. Carolynn and Bud were chasing each other through the house as Wayne shouted to Bud, "Get in here and change your shirt!" Carolynn and Bud came in laughing as Bud struggled to take the dirty shirt off. Wayne helped the little guy as clods of mud stuck in his hair. Wayne asked Carolynn, "Why is Bud's hair a mess and yours so clean?"

Carolynn laughed as she shrugged her delicate shoulders.

Wayne said to Carolynn, "Where are your locator beacons?"

Carolynn said, "Here is mine." The ringing locator beacon linked up with her father's which he kept in his pocket.

Bud said, "Mine is on the front porch."

Wayne was about to put on Bud's clean shirt when Carolynn screamed. She pointed to some sparks coming from the air behind where Bud was standing. Wayne pushed Bud to the side as Bud saw the sparks grew in intensity, creating a two-dimensional amoebic window of fire. Wayne was horrified as Carolynn continued to scream. Bud ran over to hide behind Carolynn. Wayne instinctively pushed the fiery window away as Carolynn and Bud watched their father disappear into the fiery window and vanish.

Carolynn held up her locator beacon to find her father, but it had fallen silent.

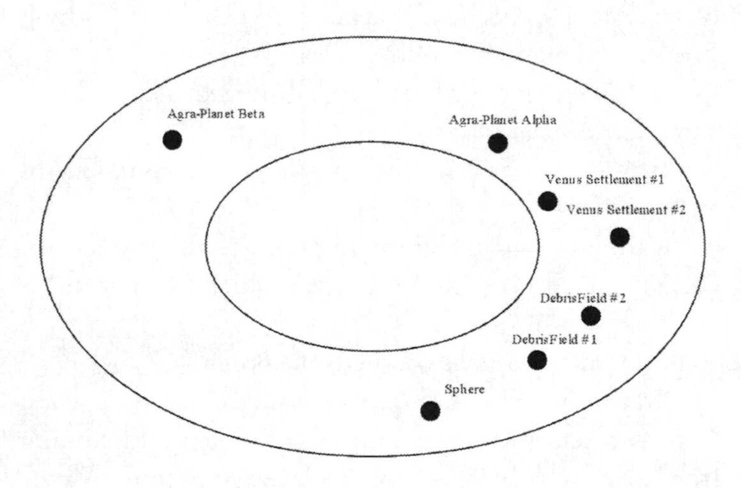

Cheng's Galaxy

Chapter 2

Sarah

"Carolynn, Bud! Carolynn, Bud!" Wayne repeated with heartbroken anguish. "Carolynn, Bud, Carolynn, Bud!" Meaningless screams were sacrificed against an unforgiving darkness.

An hour passed as Wayne's throat collapsed in torturous pain. Tearful pools of a father's agony moistened his hands as he tested the surrounding darkness. "Carolynn, Bud, Carolynn, Bud!" he shouted because nothing else mattered.

Another hour passed as Wayne dropped unconscious from exhaustion.

Wayne later woke up, unable to see, unable to hear, and unable to get back home. The air had an odd smell—a stale, synthetic aroma. He felt along the floor. He felt the slight curved wall behind him. It was smooth and uniform to the touch, almost a slick glaze, and flawless in every way. The air was still, with no noise, no vibrations—nothing but the constant echo from his breathing. Wayne shouted, "Hey!" to test the room's echo, and sure enough, he was in quarantine, encapsulated in an undefined container.

Wayne noticed a slight illumination from overhead as hundreds of stars appeared from nowhere. Wayne did not recognize any of the star patterns, if they were indeed stars. Wayne realized he was in a large spherical room about fifty feet across, with no apparent entrance or exit, and no apparent upper hatch or lower access panel, just a smooth flawless interior.

Wayne continued to wait and listen. Finally, he heard something like electronic servos and mechanical gears off in the distance, similar to a remote-control tank. The robotic noise grew stronger as a small doorway magically opened, allowing a small, robotic machine to enter. Once the robot had cleared the opening, the doorway immediately closed and disappeared from view.

Wayne tried to see, but the darkness limited any detailed contrast. The robot remained silent and stationary as two reddish, circular lenses protruded from the robotic body. A softball-sized access panel on top of the robot's housing swung open, releasing a silvery translucent orb. The sphere floated effortlessly above the robot. Wayne watched as the orb slowly moved from the robot to where Wayne was sitting. The orb was devoid of any exterior texture and had no visible internal components. The orb floated, almost scanning Wayne, and he was careful not to make any sudden moves against it. Then the orb descended to about one foot off the floor and began transmitting a series of bluish green holographic images about a half-second apart. The images were not recognizable. After about five minutes, the orb discontinued the holographic displays, actuated three small landing struts, and landed on the platform floor. The orb remained motionless on the floor as it began emitting a sequence of blinking lights. Wayne saw a bright reflection off the floor that caused him to look up. Protruding from the ceiling was a probe that appeared to mimic a modem transceiver exchanging data with the silvery orb.

The download sequence terminated as the orb again elevated itself off the floor and retracted its landing struts. Again, the orb continued projecting another sequence of holographic images, still unrecognizable. The orb again stopped, deployed its landing struts and landing on the floor to link up with the probe. Wayne patiently forced himself to sit through multiple sessions as the orb tried to coax out of Wayne any recognizable reaction.

Wayne felt comfortable with the downloading process, but had no idea what the little orb was trying to communicate. He remembered an ancient adage when dealing with electronics: "Never assume anything when building a communication baseline." Wayne took a chance; he reached out his hand while the two components were downloading. Suddenly the link between the orb and the ceiling probe broke as the orb drifted toward Wayne as if to receive an urgent message. Wayne took his finger and drew "001" on the floor. On the floor in reddish script was "001." Wayne inspected the floor more closely, realizing it was heat sensitive; the metallic floor responded to infrared imprints. The sphere was able to scan the floor's reddish heat signature, but Wayne needed to continue. Wayne drew "011," then "101," and finally "111," as if written with reddish infrared blood.

The orb hovered over the circles and lines, unaware of the basic machine language of zeros and ones. The orb tried to downloading something as Wayne continued to write. Wayne wondered if he made a mistake using prime numbers. He wrote down "001 A" as Wayne said the letter, *A*. Then he wrote "010 B" as he said the letter *B*. Wayne continued until he scripted "11000" for the letter *Z*. Wayne was not sure how the orb would respond, since the orb's audio-sound driver was probably incapable of duplicating human sounds, or if humans could hear what the orb was transmitting.

Wayne watched the orb return to the robot's upper access panel, disappearing into the robot's internal cavity. Wayne pressed his back against the spherical wall, even more depressed and heartbroken about his kids. He could see their horrified expressions as their father disappeared into the fire. Wayne could not imagine leaving his kids alone at home, but now he would give anything to be back there with his family. Wayne curled up in a little ball and cried himself to sleep.

Wayne slowly woke up. His chest and throat ached from the constant convulsive crying. The tiny pinholes of light emanating from the ceiling did little to encourage any emotional promise. Wayne felt relieved by the robot's benign attitude—at least they wanted to communicate.

Wayne wondered why the first robot was still there. Then he heard another robot with tank-like tracks thumping toward the sphere as the secret door opened. Wayne strained his eyes to see. This time it was a smaller box robot with a cathode ray tube monitor attached to its top housing. After a couple of seconds, the bluish white monitor came on—it was an oddly calibrated oscilloscope. Wayne said, "Hello," and watched his voice modulate across the screen. He took a closer look at the scaling and incremental calibration. It was set to the megahertz range. Wayne said, "That's not right." Wayne wanted to change the frequency settings, but the knobs were missing. Wayne watched as the oscilloscope repeated the waveform, but with no sound. Wayne said, "Yeah, I can't hear myself because you are recording it in the megahertz range—well beyond my audio range."

Wayne was getting frustrated. The notion of a biochamber popped into his head. One might assume that being a potentially biological hazard required both observation and quarantine. The sphere's technological method of downloading information seemed antiquated by alien standards, but the premise of first contact was not to assume anything.

Wayne continued to watch the monitor's silent waveform. Wayne sat there disgusted with the ordeal, saying, "Useless robots, I needed a live biological entity with some creative insight to fix this problem."

Wayne slouched against the wall, and the secret door opened once again. This time something very unusual passed through the darkness and hovered about ten feet from where Wayne was sitting. Wayne squinted, but could not make out the shape. He looked again, realizing the shape was in a constant state of flux. This was beyond bizarre anything real or imagined; it defied all biological classification. The unknown entity continued to levitate some two feet off the ground while its bodily shape pulsed in oscillating ripples.

Wayne continued to peer through the darkness without much luck. The entity motioned toward the monitor's input controls. The dark, amoebic entity created a small appendage that altered the inputs to the oscilloscope. Wayne watched as the waveform elongated as the entity turned the dial's frequency increments, but still no sound. Wayne sensed the entity's frustration with both the bot and the oscilloscope.

The brownish charcoal amoeba escorted both bots out of the sphere as the secret door closed behind them.

Wayne was intrigued. The entity's desire to communicated was encouraging. It seemed plausible that the entity communicated electronically or at such a high frequency.

The secret door opened, with the entity entering first, with the levitating silvery orb following as if it was a heeling dog. The silvery orb floated about one foot off the floor, then commenced displaying the same zeros and ones Wayne had etched earlier. Wayne felt he needed to change the format, maybe to an alphabetical dialog instead of machine language. Wayne put his finger to the floor and etched a twenty-six square grid across the infrared sensitive floor. In each square of the grid, Wayne placed a letter of the alphabet, starting with A and ending with Z. Wayne watched as the silvery orb mimicked the same information by displaying the same grid on its hologram. After Wayne was finished, he started making words by first identifying himself. Wayne wrote the letters *W A Y N E* on the floor as he pointed to himself. The entity seemed to respond to this new vocabulary lesson. Then Wayne wrote the letters *O R B* and pointed to the silvery orb. Then Wayne wrote, *S P O T* as he pointed to the entity. Wayne looked over as the entity danced a little jig, believing Spot was making some headway.

Wayne pointed to the word, *SPOT*, then said the word, *Spot*. The entity apparently watched Wayne's mouth move, but was not able to respond because the modulated frequency was too low.

Wayne had always wondered if first contact depended on the actions of the abductees or the abductors. One would assume that the abductor was capable or had sufficiently researched the abductees' characteristics. Apparently, this was not the case. Wayne felt he was the recipient of a tragic accident.

Wayne felt satisfied with the initial functional database baseline. Unfortunately, the words, *Spot*, *Orb*, and *Wayne* did not represent how Wayne felt. He wanted to go home!

Wayne watched as the entity and the orb retreated through the secret door. Wayne wanted to go home more than anything else, but to say that progress was being made was an understatement. Wayne wondered why Hollywood or UFO fanatics persisted in believing that all alien beings were humanoid in shape. Wayne saw that this entity was far from any biological or evolutionary experiment. It appeared that life sought refuge within an energy medium instead of a biological one.

Wayne felt his stomach growl. He thought it humorous that he had not included food in this three-word repertoire. With Spot being energy based, any understanding of biological nourishment would be an extreme alien concept. The secret door opened, with Spot pushing along another strange-looking box. The entity stopped with the box nearly below it. Wayne could hear something modulating like a phone modem when the small box opened up, and out emerged a small, plastic, hermetically sealed package. The sealed package suddenly morphed into a six-legged mechanical caterpillar crawling in his direction. Wayne said to himself, "This is the part of the movie where the sad sap dies."

The sealed package was about the size of a three-pound tube of hamburger. The cylindrical package was a dark, modeled gray color. Wayne watched the robotic gray caterpillar approach to about three feet away, then suddenly settle to the floor, retracting its appendages. The upper linear seam began to separate, revealing a hinge-less opening. Another tube popped out from inside the caterpillar's carcass, in a manner similar to toothpaste. Wayne looked up to see the entity motion, "Take it." Wayne picked up the gray tube and gave it the smell test. It was nothing he could identify. He tried squeezing the tube until a clear syrupy fluid oozed from its opening. Again he conducted the smell test; it was not sweet or bitter. He put his finger in the clear pasty fluid and gave it a taste. He said, "Glucose!" Wayne immediately put the tube up to his mouth and squeezed for all his might until the tube was completely empty. He began rolling up the flat end of the tube, pushing any remaining glucose toward the front. Again he gave it a mighty squeeze until he sucked out every drop. Wayne looked at the entity with the tube still wedged his teeth. The entity looked confused and puzzled that the biological unit would behave this badly toward a tube of glucose.

Wayne gave out a boisterous belch, unconcerned about whether they could hear it or not. Wayne became increasingly annoyed with the sphere's lack of illumination.

Since Wayne had gotten food just by thinking about it, maybe if he complained about the lighting, they might turn it up. The entity motioned for the mechanical robot to exit the sphere, and in a single-file formation, Spot and the mechanical caterpillar politely left.

Wayne understood that any vocabulary database must include similar encounters. He could name the probe and he could name glucose. Maybe he could also name the doorway or vortex that brought him here.

The secret door opened with the entity and the silvery orb floating into the sphere. Wayne put his little experiment to task by identifying the probe and the glucose by writing the letters *P R O B E* and *F O O D*. Then for the word *vortex*, he drew a fiery opening. The entity watched as Wayne's finger glided along the infrared sensitive floor, illuminating a circular cyclonic image with fire along its perimeter. The entity immediately became erratic, then left the the sphere leaving the orb behind.

The orb remained motionless, suspended in the air, apparently deactivated. It was still quite dark, but Wayne noticed that the entity left without closing the secret door. Wayne wondered if this was a test. He sat patiently until suddenly two entities floated into the sphere. Almost on cue, the interior lighting came on, forcing Wayne to hide his eyes. Wayne put his hands over his eyes, shielding them from the intense glare off the metal floor. Wayne said without thinking, "What in the hell are you?"

The entities were floating amoebas. Their bodies were in a constant state of flux, with no apparent mode of locomotion. The entities were a dark, charcoal translucent color, with no appendages, no visible eyes, no head, and no visible internal organs or chemiluminescence. They had no visible static aura or audible tones. They were just floating amoebas.

Wayne could not tell the amoebas apart. They were identical.

One of the entities activated the small orb, which started transmitting several holographic images against the sphere's curved wall. Wayne watched as images of vortexes consumed hundreds of spacecraft, leaving debris fields drifting in the aftermath. Images of scuttled, broken-up, and sometimes intact spacecraft drifted with the gravitational tide of the system's sun. Then there was another set of images where another vortex opened up, engulfing the entire debris field like a starving, carnivorous black hole. The sequence continued as the black hole suddenly appeared then disappeared, creating a gravitational implosion causing the entire solar system to collapse in a massive nova. The resulting cascading maelstrom erupted into a majestic expanding nebula. The last image was that of several entities trying to equalize the black hole's fiery turbulence, but the damage was already done.

Wayne realized these amoebas were inhabitants of open space, but was not sure about their relationship between the vortexes and black holes. Wayne watched as the orb continued another series of images that resembled alien "mug shots." It was unclear whether the aliens pictured in the mug shots created the black holes, or if perished in the destruction. Due to the less-than-quality holographic images, Wayne was not sure of the entity's intent.

The orb displayed several of the surrounding galaxies along with the mug shots of neighboring aliens. Wayne did not recognize any of the galactic shapes or swirling patterns similar to the pictures he had seen of the Milky Way. The orb continued as Wayne said, "Look." The holographic slide show suddenly stopped as Wayne drew what he thought was the Milky Way. His finger etched as the infrared floor illuminated two graceful swirling arms with a symmetrical, circular bulge in the middle. Then Wayne pointed to himself, saying, "Milky Way." Wayne realized that the Milky Way was not the official alien classification, but at least they might recognize the shape. The orb responded with images of known galactic shapes. Wayne watched some two hundred images, all unrecognizable. Wayne had no idea what the Milky Way actually looked like, and he felt stupid trying to identify his home galaxy from a slideshow of images.

Wayne wondered why none of the mug shots included grays or humanoid-like creatures similar to what Hollywood portrayed as UFO aliens. Wayne again put his finger to the floor and drew a stick man—a body, two arms, two legs, and a head. He wrote "uprights" because this is what humans or humanoids were, they stood upright. The orb searched through its alien holographic database, but no humanoids were listed.

The orb displayed a galactic weather map. The map was an overlay of contoured isobar lines that extended through thousands of known galaxies. Then the orb displayed a deep-space vortex with an overlapping isobar map. Wayne could see that the contoured isobars represented gravitational lines of flux. In the normal vacuum of space, the isobar lines were equally spaced and uniform. When the entities introduced vortexes or black holes, the contour lines immediately became compressed and distorted. Wayne understood that black holes exerted tremendous gravitational forces, powerful enough to prevent light from escaping. Wayne could see that the entities were depended on gravity, but was unclear if they needed equilibrium or to create violent wormhole-like storms.

Then the orb displayed a blank square, almost like a mug shot, but without the face. Maybe the entities knew of the vortex's creation, but were not sure who made it.

Wayne had little reason to doubt the entity's honesty. It appeared that they were looking for the aliens responsible. Wayne was a victim of an unfortunate accident; he represented an incredibly primitive species who offered little value to the investigation. Wayne understood all too well that politics worked the same way. It was the government's role to convince the public they were incredibly primitive next to the elitism of the ruling class. The greatest threat to any paranoid government was an obstinate chattering class.

One of the entities motioned as the orb displayed an ordinary region of space. The orb projected a sequence of gravitational isobar images demonstrating how to bend space to accommodate faster space travel. The degree of spatial distortion was dependent on the intensity of the gravitational gradient based on the generated energy that created an interconnecting wormhole. The orb's images seemed to caution this idea; if the extreme flux of gravitational contours contacted each other, the resulting electromagnetic arc could upset the relationship between subspace and normal space. In Wayne's case, an alien species attempted a research experiment on gravitational subspace when a catastrophic accident occurred. As a result, a vortex or an electromagnetic arc captured Wayne and threw him into a completely different dimension.

Wayne had a difficult time telling these two entities apart, but one obviously possessed a greater knowledge of alien misconduct and detecting gravitational anomalies. He wondered if home was a foregone conclusion. He wanted to convey that he was not responsible for perpetrating either the spatial distortion, or the vortex. Wayne was not about to accept responsibility, but understood he needed the entities' help if he wanted to escape this madness.

The two entities turned and left the sphere with the orb following close behind. Wayne saw they had left the sphere's access doorway open. Wayne remained motionless, not risking the appearance of being guilty. After a couple of minutes, one of the entities appeared from outside and motioned Wayne to follow. After what seemed like days, Wayne finally got to his feet and looked down at the floating entities. Wayne had always seen the charcoal-colored amoeba from the sitting position, but now that he stood up, his perspective changed, and so did the entity's color. The first entity was a brownish charcoal color, and the other, who appeared to be the supervisor, was a yellowish charcoal.

Wayne exited the confines of the sphere's interior, only to walk into another dimly lit space. The brownish charcoal entity, the one Wayne named Spot, slowly escorted him to the left about forty feet. As Wayne followed Spot, the canopy's darkness gave way to a huge, brightly lit circular auditorium. He stood there, looking at the enormous casement of windows two-hundred-feet high, bordering the auditorium's circular walls for about a mile, meeting up at a dark, ominous ceiling. Wayne could barely comprehend this colossal image as he tried to estimate the auditorium's diameter. The auditorium stretched out across one massive floor with a diameter of two miles. There were no columns, no chairs, and no tables, just an enormous, empty space.

Wayne noticed in the distance the supervisor entity, returning with the orb in hot pursuit. The supervisor entity stopped some distance away and began discussing something with Spot while the orb displayed a couple of holographic images. It was the same blank square, the mug shot without the alien's picture. The supervisor entity motioned for Wayne to come over and look. Slowly a face materialized. Almost immediately, he recognized the familiar face of a "Gray," the most recognizable face in all UFO countercultures. The supervisor entity instructed the orb to display all the possible galaxies from which the spatial anomaly originated. The orb displayed image after image for about an hour. Nothing seemed recognizable.

Wayne needed a bathroom break. His fear and anxiety had consumed much of his body refuse, but now he needed to go. Wayne didn't have access to the holographic alphabet matrix to spell out the work "bathroom" but he pointed to a small airlock on the exterior wall instead.

Spot drifted toward to a small airlock attached to Wayne's encapsulated sphere. The airlock was about one foot off the floor, maybe one foot in diameter. This was inconceivable; Wayne was not about to contort himself, especially with this painful bowel movement. Spot opened the airlock, and hundreds of little roaches avalanched onto the floor. Immediately the insects crystallized upon exposure with the atmosphere. Two robots promptly rolled over and began cleaning up the mess. Wayne could not stand it any longer. He bent over, resting his back against the bulkhead, and immediately relieved himself over the frozen insect as they crunched beneath his shoes.

Wayne felt better, but the insects were a question for later.

The supervisor entity departed in its quest for more information as Spot motioned for the orb to continue displaying images. This time the images changed to gravitational gradient physics. Wayne watched as the orb displayed a sequence of twelve stair steps, the lowest step being normal space, and the highest step being a vortex. The steps represented the incremental increase of energy needed to penetrate the gravitational dimensions of subspace until a black hole is formed. Each incremental step in the sequence required a proportionate supply of power to sustain each gradient step. Every gradient step represented a mathematical variable separate from the previous step. The orb displayed a spacecraft transitioning between gradients. Although the jump between each incremental step looked proportional, the orb displayed two prerequisites for each consecutive step: more dimensional subatomic particles and a greater shield containment force.

Wayne understood the concept of a shield generator, but was not entirely clear on the dimensional gradient stuff. The orb displayed a spacecraft descending through the gradient process from subspace to normal space. Once in normal space, the potential energy stored at each gradient immediately converted over to kinetic energy, requiring an immediate discharge.

Wayne thought about his high school science report on gravity and energy. He understood that ambient gravity was reasonably constant within normal space, but each gradient represent a dimensional ladder through subspace, until critical gravity created a vortex or a black hole.

The orb displayed two more images: a spacecraft and the twelve incremental steps toward a vortex. A ship's dimensional capability could only sustain the fourth step. Then the orb displayed an image of a planet over the eighth step, and then over the twelfth step was a region of deep space bent to absolute maximum tolerance.

The orb displayed two aspects of gravitational gradients. In the first subspace acts as a cloak, but to use this cloak, all engines must be off. The second aspect represented a gravitational or dimensional propulsion system where subspace allows the craft to travel faster than light speed in normal space. Wayne was not sure how that worked, but it looked complicated.

The supervisor entity motioned Wayne toward the windows. Wayne could see a large spacecraft some distance away against the blackness of empty space. The orb then displayed an image of the first gradient as Wayne watched the spacecraft from the window. The craft began to glow a turquoise aurora, then disappeared from view. Wayne was impressed. The whole ship had just vanished. There was no visible anomaly or shadowy image—it was gone.

Then out of nowhere, a whole squadron of entities descended on the cloaked ship, causing it to erupt in a fiery cloud of reddish yellow debris. Wayne quickly backed up as debris from the explosion ricocheted off the windows. The supervisor entity seemed amused by Wayne's reaction as it motioned for another demonstration. A second ship repeated the transition from normal space to the first gradient as Wayne was looking around for the entities. The supervisor entity motioned to the orb to project a contoured gravitational isobar overlay over the cloaked ship. Wayne looked in amazement as the tightly compacted gravitation lines of flux radiated out like a magnetic field around the ship. Then the orb displayed an image against the surface of the window showing that the ship was going to the second gradient step. Each of the gravitational contours condensed themselves closer around the ship as the gradient's intensity distorted the surrounding space into an anomaly. Wayne could see the potential hazards of distorting whole regions of deep space by manipulating gravitational fields just to accommodate faster space travel. Wayne noticed that the supervisor again motioned for his entity friends to attack the ship. This time the ship vaporized in a cloud of debris due to the sudden release of potential energy as it exploded before dropping back into normal space. The orb tried to demonstrate what happened by displaying the ship's position along the gradient steps. Since the ship was operating in the second gradient of subspace, the correct procedure in returning to normal space would be to descend and stabilize on the first gradient before proceeding to normal space. Once in normal space, the spacecraft needed to discharge all its kinetic energy. The premature release of potential energy destabilized the subspace continuum, creating a subspace implosion or shockwave destroying everything around it.

Wayne had enough. His head was pounding as the

orb discontinued the presentation. Wayne motioned to the supervisor entity, asking if he could privately use the orb in his own research back in the sphere. The entity agreed, and the orb followed Wayne back into the dimly lit sanctuary. Wayne walked back to his original sitting position and relaxed himself against the curved wall. Somehow, his only secure connection between his kids and this side of the sphere was here against the wall, trying to plan his next move. He motioned to the orb by drawing pictures on the infrared-sensitive floor. The first picture depicted the stars and star clusters. His next two drawings were of the entities and their relationship with the other alien species. The orb hesitated. Wayne noticed the probe on the ceiling transmitting data to the orb as it maintained a static hover. After a few moments, the orb started transmitting several holographic images. Wayne watched as the greenish blue laser light paint image after image of star charts, alien species, and entities. Wayne realized that, if he touched portions of the orb's image, the orb would zoom in or zoom out according to Wayne's wishes. Wayne wanted to determine the frequency of alien societies along with their rise and fall, or the frequency of alien races absorbing neighboring space due to wars or conflict. The orb began displaying some species until Wayne interrupted and drew a box on the floor depicting the database of mug shots. The orb then incorporated the various aliens under surveillance by the entities to the aliens' rise or fall to power. In most instances, there was a relationship between the mug shots and the change in alien political power. Whether it was alien-on-alien conflict or if it was the forced entity intervention, the fact remained that alien history fluctuated with the ebb and flow of political vacuum left by previous species. Wayne was not sure if the entity's mediating influence created stability or aggravated the conflict among the alien species. Apparently, those species who better managed their technology survived. Even archeologists got into the act of salvaging ancient technologies for profit, because what goes around comes around. The profitability of those less fortunate never goes out of style.

Wayne wondered if the Grays accidently destroyed the Milky Way by some wayward dimensional experiment. UFO enthusiasts rarely portrayed alien spacecraft as benevolent visitors asking permission at every turn. They behaved more like suspicious observers engaged in abductions and clandestine maneuvers, posing more of a threat to Earth's inhabitants.

If the Grays' vortex was so unstable that it caused a fracture in Earth's time continuum, Wayne asked, "How did I get here?"

Unless the guardians conveniently omitted some critical information, the Grays must have known that a security breach had occurred, causing the experimental vortex to destabilize. Wayne said to himself, "Then who is the enemy here?" If the entities caught Wayne in mid-vortex, then they must have known who caused it.

The supervisor entity returned to the sphere while Wayne still observed the orb's imagery database. Wayne looked up and saw that the entity had some kind of keypad or touchpad computer. The entity handed Wayne the touchpad and motioned to the orb to display some pictorial instructions. Along the touchpad's margins were ship's systems, ship's classifications, ship's weapons, waveguides, fiber optics, schematics, star charts, dimensional systems, and installations manuals. Wayne suspiciously looked at the entity, wondering why this was important now. The entity again gestured for Wayne to take something: a hot-dog-sized, hermetically sealed silvery metallic vial. Wayne reluctantly reached for the vial, and the entity motioned for him to open it. Wayne held the vial at arm's length as he punctured the white hermetically sealed membrane with his thumb. At first nothing happened. Then, as Wayne held the vial with his arms extended, a small entity emerged from the vial's curved flange.

Wayne, admiring the little critter, said, "a baby entity." But before Wayne could get a closer look, it jumped on his arm and began burrowing into his skin. Wayne threw down the vial, trying to dislodge it before it vanished under his skin. Wayne jumped in horror as the entity worked itself through his arm, across his shoulders, and into his chest cavity. Wayne nearly attacked the supervising entity, worried that he had fallen victim to an evil scheme or had become an alien zombie. He fell to the floor, screaming, as his entire body convulsed and quivered. After about a minute, the pain began to subside, but Judas had already struck! Wayne knew that the enemy was in his midst, and he had now fallen under its spell.

The supervisor entity motioned over to the computer touchpad, asking Wayne to pick it up. Wayne was not about to pick up the touchpad, fearing something evil. Then Wayne heard a synthesized version of his voice from so long ago coming from the touchpad, saying, "Hello." Wayne looked over and picked up the touchpad, and a synthesized tenor voice said, "Hi, Wayne, can you hear me?"

Wayne looked up and said, "Who is this?"

The touchpad said, "Who? What is a who?"

Wayne hesitated and said, "What is your name?"

The touchpad replied, "Name? What is a name?"

Wayne realized he was making too many assumptions about an alien's sense of identity or the use of proper names. Wayne thought that maybe if he assigned a name, the entity might respond. Wayne said, "Cheng, I will call you Cheng." Cheng was the name they gave the chief engineer in charge of Ship's Engineering.

Wayne pointed to himself saying, "Wayne, I am Wayne."

The touchpad said, "Wayne, who am I?"

Wayne said, "Cheng, you are Cheng."

The touchpad said, "I am Cheng." The touchpad continued, "We do not have names, because we are of one body. We were drawn to this dimension when we discovered the vortex and found you trapped inside."

Wayne held up his touchpad and asked, "Can I communicate with other alien species, or can I only talk to you?"

Cheng said, "How many sentient beings do you believe exist?"

Wayne said, "I have no idea, but can I communicate with the aliens who brought me here?"

Cheng said, "No, they are outside our realm of understanding, yet were prominent enough to attract our attention. Your job is to discuss that with them."

Wayne did not understand Cheng's response. "What is my job exactly?"

Cheng said, "Find the aliens responsible."

Wayne asked, "How am I going to do that?"

Cheng motioned to the entity Wayne named Spot and said, "Follow my complement."

Wayne looked to see Spot floating off to the side. Wayne turned back to Cheng, but Cheng interrupted, saying, "Good-bye. I will contact Spot directly, but Spot is to follow your advice and direction."

With that, Cheng departed the sphere, leaving Spot hovering and Wayne alone. Wayne looked over at Spot and said, "What is your name?" He wondered if he had to name that one, too.

The touchpad slowly said in an oddly familiar female digital voice, "My name is Sarah."

Chapter 3

Debris Fields—An Explorer's Playground

Wayne fell to the floor, one hand holding his head while the other pressed against his chest because of Cheng's vile little pet. He exclaimed, "Sarah?"

The female synthesized voice from the touchpad said, "Yes, my name is Sarah. I'll share some secrets Cheng apparently didn't reveal, but right now, we have a spacecraft to refurbish." Wayne trusted Sarah more than Cheng. Also, calling this entity Sarah gave him some comfort, but not enough to talk about his real Sarah.

Sarah led Wayne to an airlock access doorway with a keypad on one side. She manipulated some push tiles on the airlock's keypad, causing the access door to open and revealing a long passageway. Sarah proceeded down the passageway while Wayne held his touchpad, flipping through the ship's manuals for airlocks. Suddenly the touchpad yelled out, "Get over here!" Wayne realized he was being tardy, and he hurried through the airlock while Sarah waited at the end of the passageway.

The passageway looked like a long, circular capsule. There were no windows, no airport-designed carpet, and no pictures of exotic planets. There was just a gray wash of painted metal. Wayne saw another open airlock up ahead, but he lost sight of Sarah's amoebic cloud. Sarah floated over the airlock's flange into a large chamber, again a gray wash of painted metal. Wayne lifted his leg to clear the airlock's flange, then proceeded into the auditorium. On one side of the chamber were three heavily reinforced windscreens with a control module in the middle. Everywhere else was only structural steel and metal braces along the chamber's circumference, all painted a drab gray.

Sarah positioned herself at the main console, saying, "You better grab onto something." The airlock door closed, followed by a loud bang as the locking ring disengaged. Sarah slowly engaged the shuttle's aft thrusters and exited the docking station.

Wayne went to the rear of the shuttle, grabbing onto the thick vertical metal brace. Wayne examined the ship's ceiling structure, which was multiple joists radiating like spokes from a wheel, each secured to the deck with extreme precision. Wayne gazed out through the front windscreen and saw only darkness. He sat down the floor, forcing himself into the corner between the metal brace and the interior bulkhead. Wayne waited for a sudden thrust of acceleration, but sensed only a gently nudge of forward momentum. Wayne said, "Where are we going?"

Wayne expected Sarah to answer, but instead, Cheng's

digital voice came over the touchpad, saying, "Your task is to select a ship for repair. Spot will inspect the hull integrity, the ionic engines, the hydrogen fusion reactors, and the dimensional system, if it has one, and weapons. Your job is to familiarize yourself with the bridge."

Wayne said, "How do I know which ship is the best?'

Cheng said, "Spot knows."

Wayne gave Sarah a puzzled look wondering, why Cheng continued to use the name Spot.

Cheng continued, "Spot has already loaded a contingency of bots onboard the shuttle. Once a ship is chosen and satisfied with the integrity inspection, the bots will be brought onboard to make repairs."

Wayne says, "That's a lot of systems to manage and maintain all by myself."

Cheng replied, "Spot and the bots will remain onboard until your mission is complete, then you will return the ship to us. A detachment of entities will escort you, ensuring all gravitational anomalies are neutralized and all threats disabled."

Wayne thought of the possibility of having his own spaceship, and now has to give it back. Maybe things might work out to his advantage.

Wayne walked over to the front windscreen and put his hand on the thick, reinforced window framing as he watched the universe pass by. The black canvas of infinite space was utterly breathtaking! Vast swaths of sparkling luminescence, majestic clusters of nebula clouds, and countless twinkling of tiny suns all beaconed with the invitation of adventure.

Wayne stood there for hours. It was like gazing into

a campfire, pondering the mystery of fire. Now he stood in awe, challenged by the mystery of all that was before him. This was a childhood dream come true. As a child, he could only glimpse stars from afar, but now he had a front-row seat, and the view was spectacular.

Sarah's rough, feminine digital voice echoed from his touchpad. "Look to your starboard. You should start seeing it."

Wayne peered into black void, but it was too dark, without enough contrast to notice anything. Wayne strained his eyes, saying, "See what?"

Wayne's eyes pierced into the black emptiness for any contrasting shapes or colors. After a few moments, he noticed something far off in the distance. It looked like a small asteroid field—little specs of dirt or dust against the black void.

Sarah was trying to position the ship closer to the debris field, yet maintain helm and navigational stabilization. Wayne could not see anything. He began to distinguish the changing background as the shuttle came about. Wayne noticed something in the distance: a salvage field of dead and dying spaceships. Wayne could not locate a whole one anywhere. They were all broken up, some still venting atmosphere. The drifting, mangled fuselages bore little resemblance to spacecraft—more like rustic relics of the past. Sometimes he could see occasional showers of sparks as alien welders cut away various sections of a hull.

Sarah said, "I'll be back."

Wayne watched Sarah dissolve through the hull to the other side as she sought to find anything resembling an intact spacecraft.

One of the problems involved in space-docking or salvage operations was judging distances in close proximity to debris drift. Accidental collisions, or "bumps" between large metallic superstructures was not only costly, but might result in catastrophic hull breaches.

Wayne heard Cheng's digital voice on the touchpad. "Spot has terminated her search, and she will be coming onboard to scout out another debris field." The transmission ended. Wayne was not seeing much, other than drifting scrap iron. Sarah effortlessly penetrated the shuttle's hull and appeared on the bridge.

Wayne said, "That was an amazing trick, going wherever you want."

Sarah spoke from the touchpad. "Yes, it is because of that ability that we must distance ourselves from all biological units."

Wayne asked, "Biological units?"

Sarah answered, "We are energy units. Aliens are biological units."

Wayne said, "Then how do you recharge when you consume energy?"

Sarah tried to explain, "As Cheng said, we are of one body. Because we are one body, we allow a certain amount of energy to exist as nourishment. We feed on the naturally occurring anomalies, where the forces of gravity and energy coincide as one. When alien technology advanced to the point of creating alien-made gravitational anomalies, the entities were excited, because it gave us another energy source. However, as the anomalies grew, so did the entity's greed for consumption. Many entities saw the overabundance of energy as more of a threat and decided to attack the anomalies. Unfortunately, some splits within the entities' hierarchy wanted the anomalies to continue. Several competing aliens attacked each other's anomalies while petitioning the entities into friendly negotiations. Several groups of entities repaired these anomalies and tears in the space-time continuum until we decided, no more."

Sarah positioned herself behind the main console as the ship maneuvered away from the debris field.

Sarah spoke from the touchpad. "This will be a two-day trip, so sit and relax." Wayne picked up his touchpad and walked to the rear of the shuttle. He sat down, nestled himself against a vertical brace, and started studying.

The touchpad offered several options: ships, systems, weapons, alien amenities, tactics, engineering, and dimensional systems. Wayne did not know where to start, then he thought of the mug shots. Maybe if he followed the most wanted, maybe they would know which ships were the best.

Wayne must have searched through hundreds of mug shots, their ships of choice, and their tactical strategy, then a common theme started to develop. The basic fundamental principle of all biological units was to propagate faster than their enemies. Faster propagation meant more planets to settle. More planets meant more industry. More industry meant more ships, and more ships meant a greater territorial influence. Wayne searched for any indication or notion of contentment or divine mystique between technology and power, but there was no such evidence.

The touchpad indicated which ships to avoid. It was not because they were flawed or lacked a technological edge, but because they were built in the last days of a dying empire. Due to the lack of quality, these ships represented the final sacrifice or "last-ditch mission" to rejuvenate an alien's dying breath. Many of these ships were equipped with huge dimensional systems, but lacked any discharge capability. Wayne thought about the burning ships or the "fire ships" meant to cause confusion along an enemy's assault line. These alien ships were very similar to the sacrificial fire ships.

Wayne studied waveguides, radar systems, and subspace dimensional drives that represented the newest advancements in engineering technology. Wayne pushed the touchpad's icon for subspace dimensional drive and waited for the data to boot up.

One light year in normal space is one million times greater than that in subspace. Therefore, if a ship travels one light year, it will only take one-one millionth of the time to reach that same destination in subspace. This is why dark matter or dark energy escapes from a black hole. Because of the proportional relationship to gravity, and as gravity accelerates beyond that of light itself, more black matter or black energy infiltrates into that dimension as a function of density and energy.

Wayne started to get a headache. He put his touchpad by his side as he tried to get comfortable against the hard, metal floor. Wayne's mind turned to his kids and his wife, Sarah. Wayne's horrible dreams and deep depression started to invade his most valuable memories of home. Wayne's only real mission now was to get back home, no matter how long it took. He finally fell asleep.

The touchpad received an audio message as Cheng's voice announced, "I hope you are studying while en route to the next debris field. My scouts are out looking for the Grays' galactic home world and came across some other interesting alien cultures though; downloading data now."

Wayne was half-asleep, deliberately disregarding Cheng's message or suggestions. He started to stir as he felt his shoulder and back ache from the oppressively hard metal floor. He opened his eyes to see Sarah at the controls and noticed a message on his touchpad from Cheng. Wayne closed his eyes and rolled over, trying to twist into another comfortable position. He was not cold, his back and shoulder just ached.

He reluctantly opened his eyes and sat up, stretching his arms and back. With few healthy yawns and some neck twists, he stretched both arms until his chest popped. He slowly got to his feet.

Sarah spoke from the touchpad, "Look down near you." Wayne saw the same nauseating tube of glucose he had grown to despise. Sarah said, "Biological nourishment is as varied as the number of aliens in the entire realm of space. Some are toxic while others can kill you outright. Just to be on the safe side, stay with the tubes."

Wayne twisted his mouth in contempt and he said, "Thanks for nothing." Wayne continued, "How long before we get there?"

Sarah replied, "About four hours. Salvage operators patrol these debris fields for fresh inventory, but apparently, this one was recent. We might find something interesting."

Wayne said, "Are the aliens hostile?"

Sarah said, "Debris fields are always hostile. It depends how hostile you want to be in return."

Wayne said to himself, "Strategy or tactics seem

worthless here in open space. It is like the old cowboy movies on the open prairie—full assault at high noon."

Sarah said, "A good salvage scout will have several frequency-monitoring devices. Each scout has a list of detectable frequencies it wants to measure. Uranium has a plasma frequency of fifty gigahertz, Plutonium is a slightly higher plasma frequency, and hydrogen also has a plasma frequency."

Sarah continued, "Once a salvage merchant claims a ship, all the power and plasma conduits are removed, then the magnetic segments and the waveguides. They remove the hydrogen fusion reactors, then the dimensional particle accelerator and amplifier, and finally, the entire weapons arsenal. The older computer cores are discarded because of non-compatibility. Each system has its own computer interface or recognition protocol, which must be loaded onto the main computer before the computer will recognize it."

Sarah continued, "A good salvage scout will also have a gamma-ray detector, used in detecting fission stockpiles of uranium or plutonium. Any minor radioactive material like silica, strontium, lead, etc., will be collected for sale to a contraband fusion replenishment facility."

Wayne walked over to the front windscreen and noticed many of the same galactic features from two days before. As Wayne pointed, he said, "How far is it to that nebula?"

Sarah said, "Based on the normal light year, it would take ten light years."

Sarah also said, "As far as the hull goes, the highest-priced hulls are made of uranium carbide. This is a very strong material, and it blends nicely with the dimensional stability characteristics of fifty gigahertz. The disadvantage is that a uranium-carbide hull is expensive and requires extensive maintenance. Hulls composed of an alloy of boron, aluminum, and magnesium are the strongest for the cheapest price. The least favorite hulls are composed of stainless-steel graphite composite. The problem with steel hulls is magnetism. Due to the sensitive frequency characteristics of dimensional plasma conduits, any magnetic interference could arc or electrically short both the waveguides and the plasma stream, resulting in a cascading explosion."

Wayne looked down at the touchpad and saw that Cheng had left a message. Wayne listened to the message, remembering he heard something when he was half-asleep. Wayne was too excited to study now; he wanted to see the debris field.

Wayne could tell from the galactic backdrop that the shuttle was changing direction and maneuvering into position. He noticed the absence of stars and a more open territory than before. After a few minutes, Wayne caught sight of some sparkling glitter, like sand grains, on the horizon just off the port bow. The shuttle slowed to a steady approach until the outlines of enormous ships came into focus.

Even Sarah said, "Wow, look at the size of those ships!" Sarah continued, "From my perspective, I calculate these ships to be between fifty to a hundred and twenty miles long."

Wayne shouted, "What? No! That cannot be! That's impossible!"

Sarah said, "Maybe by your standards, but never

underestimate the desire for power, especially out here in space."

Wayne watched as the shuttle slowly closed in. Many of the damaged ships were intact with lateral fractures, some venting atmosphere. As an object flashed across their bow, Wayne said, "What was that?"

Sarah said, "I need to back up. We've stumbled into a minefield." Sarah carefully put the shuttle in full reverse while jockeying the port and starboard thrusters for stability. Sarah said, "Wait here."

Wayne said, "As if I had a place to go!"

Sarah looked back, somewhat annoyed, then dissolved through the hull to look for a salvageable ship.

Wayne lost sight of Sarah leaving the shuttle's exterior hull. Many of the ships were obscured by drifting debris, but Wayne noticed a ship off in the distance that appeared to be more stable than the others. It was as if the ship was stalking, looking for an opening to ambush any unsuspecting victims. The surrounding darkness made it almost impossible to determine its hull integrity, except for the mists of venting atmosphere. Wayne thought, *At least these aliens value atmosphere.*

Wayne continued to monitor the suspicious craft as it slowly weaved in and out between the floating debris. Sarah rushed into the bridge and took command of the main console. She maneuvered around below the debris field, pursuing the ship Wayne had been watching. Wayne, still at the windscreen, looked back to see Sarah trying to outmaneuver the craft. Wayne turned back to the windscreen as the shuttle was closing in, nearly colliding with some drifting metal. He could see the sun's amber reflection off the ship's aft fascia and the enormous "turkey feathers" on each ionic-drive afterburner. Wayne counted twenty engines, each large enough to engulf their entire shuttle. The metallic turkey feathers had a dull black finish against the dim sunlight from years of heating and cooling.

Sarah commanded in a high-pitched, synthesized voice, "Computer, prepare to dock to aft airlock on my mark." The shuttle engaged its docking radar. Wayne watched as the shuttle slowly approached the docking ring and each ship began transmitting docking data. He caught a glimpse of a large keypad and approach lights, much like the old ILS radars he worked on as a kid.

The shuttle's synthesized computer voice began radiating from the main console as the shuttle gently nudged into place: "Docking in seven, six, five, four, three, two, one." A rush of compressed air secured the docking bolts. The computer's digital voice again said, "Airlock pressurization enabled, passageway pressurization enabled, security protocol, unknown."

The computer warned, "Airlock secure and responding, passageway airlock secure and responding, opposite airlock not secured."

Wayne said, "What does that mean?"

Sarah said, "It means that the opposite airlock was left open or was breached. I need to find out for sure." Sarah dissolved through the airlock's thick, ballistic membrane and entered the connecting passageway between the two airlocks. Wayne looked through the monitor as Sarah slowly approached the opposite airlock. So far so good.

Sarah inspected the aft airlock, which closed and secured, but some of the keypad's wiring on the other side was arcing and sparking as if damaged. Sarah passed through the airlock's flange door, trying to figure out what happened. Finally, she got the door to open, and the touchpad commanded, "Wayne come on through."

Wayne slowly opened the shuttle's airlock door and suddenly, a rush of air hit his face. Wayne said, "Whoa! What's that smell?" The horrible aroma of mildewed burlap, rotten musk, and soured milk exploded in his nasal passages. Wayne held his breath as he pushed the door open and walked through the brightly lit passageway. Wayne immediately noticed the walls. They were ablaze with colors, images of flowers and insects. He slowly inspected the artwork. Many of the insects looked familiar, but some totally bizarre, as if someone cut and pasted various images to make one creature.

Wayne passed through the ship's airlock, only to see a conglomerate of mass carnage. Wayne nervously remembered that he left his touchpad back in the shuttle. Wasting no time, he ran back to the shuttle's windscreen ledge and picked it up. Almost instantly, he heard Sarah's voice say, "Get up here!" Wayne ran back through the shuttle's airlock and down the passageway, again stopping at the massive display of bloodied corpses.

Wayne shouted, "I don't have a weapon!"

Sarah rushed back to where he was standing and said, "Pick one up, there are plenty of weapons here!" Sarah then returned to survey the damage as she transmitted the authorization code for the bots to come onboard. Wayne could hear a flurry of winding servos, gears, and motorized tracks slowly approaching from behind him as he tried to look for a weapon. Wayne picked something up, "What's this? It looks like an ox horn!" Wayne waved it over the touchpad hoping it would scan the object. The touchpad came back, saying, "Queen facial spike."

Wayne said, "Queen facial spike?" He put the horn in his pocket. Sudden fear and anxiety ripped through Wayne's soul as he yelled out, "I don't see a weapon anywhere!" Wayne looked and studied the bodies. A rainbow of bluish and yellow streaks covered the floor. Wayne looked but could not find a weapon of any kind.

Wayne went back to the passageway to study the painted pictures. In between the tranquil scenes of vegetation and trees were clusters of half-insect and half-Venus-flytrap-headed monsters. The flytrap head looked like the exotic carnivorous plant attached to huge, round, lengthy neck connected to a long, wingless insect body. The body had eight legs, six of which were on the ground. The forward pair had pincher like hands. The body was long, bullet-shaped, sleek, and aggressive. It was slightly hairy and non-segmented, with a stinger on its rear.

Wayne looked closer at the head. The greenish red dual-hinged flap looked exactly like a Venus flytrap, with large spikes protruding from each lobe to imprison its prey. He tried to find the eyes, then discovered they were on the forward part of the abdomen—two on either side of the neck. The large, oval-shaped eyes were sunken into the body with eyelids and surrounded by a protective sheath of keratin armor.

Wayne tried to imagine how any alien species, especially this one, could ever evolve from a hodge-podge of biological disasters, yet manage to come out in space. Biology does not determine survival, but how it adapts on the battlefield.

Wayne proceeded back through the ship's airlock.

With each step, bluish yellow ooze of thick, globular paste blended with orange and gray guts covered his shoes. Wayne noticed similarities between the individual bodies to those in the passageway paintings, many scarred from weapons fire. These were monsters. Their lobed, Venus-flytrap faces ranged from five to six feet across. Their necks were maybe four feet long, and their insect bodies were fifteen feet long or more. The legs were short but powerful, with bulging thigh muscles, wide, insect knee joints, and ankle joints.

The bodies were scattered in this huge entrance foyer forward of the airlock, some two hundred yards wide and a mile long. The brightly painted walls depicted playful children and adults mingling in the lush garden landscape. This was a vibrant culture where children were close members of the family. This was an organized society, where generations existed as one powerful force, each depending on the other, much like ants or bees.

Wayne could not find a weapon anywhere, but took out the ox-horn-shaped facial spike from his pocket and rescanned it across the touchpad. The touchpad said, "Queen facial spike."

Wayne said, "Touchpad, scan for queen." Wayne watched as the touchpad brought up an image of a large queen some thirty feet in length. Wayne just shook his head, saying, "I'm dead."

Wayne began walked further up the foyer away from the airlock. He noticed a junction of three corridors up ahead. Wayne could see Sarah waiting at the center corridor, which forked again up the center corridor some fifty yards. The corridors were more like avenues spanning about fifty feet wide. Wayne continued to search for a weapon as he ran up to where Sarah was floating. He listened, but could not hear anything. Sarah spoke from the touchpad's digital processor. "Take your touchpad and interface it with the airlock's computer terminal."

Wayne shoes were already soaked with bloodied ooze. He felt the slight irritation of athlete's foot as biological acids and enzymes penetrated into his socks.

Wayne ran back to the airlock, trying not to slip, and stopped at the computer's interface terminal. Wayne looked all over the touchpad for some kind of connection.

Sarah yelled out from the touchpad, "Just hold it up close. It should automatically link up. Watch the download light."

Wayne held the touchpad to the interface terminal as he looked around, making sure nothing was sneaking up behind him. He watched the data-transfer light flicker for a couple of seconds, then stopped. Wayne said, "That was fast." He tried it again, making sure he scanned it correctly. Again, the light flickered for only a few seconds as the touchpad vibrated from Sarah's irritated voice: "Get back here!"

Wayne ran back through the bloody obstacle course, splashing ooze and slime all over his pants and hands. The center corridor led to a junction of three other corridors. Sarah said, "Look." She pointed to a wall pictorial directory. One of the pictures looked like a subway or rail tram. One of the pictures was a gear along with the traditional drawing of an atom with three orbiting electrons. The last drawing on the third corridor was a picture of a shuttle and a docking ring pointing back where they came from.

Sarah said, "Get on the tram which will take you to the bridge."

Agitated because he had no gun, Wayne said, "Where are you going?"

Sarah said, "I need to inspect the hull and engineering, then I'll work my way forward through weapons and the dimensional systems and finally meet you on the bridge." Sarah looked down and said, "Where's your gun?"

Wayne yelled in protest, "I can't find one, there aren't any on the floor!" With that, Sarah expressed her impatience as she dissolved through the passageway's bulkhead, leaving Wayne all alone.

Wayne was not about to walk through that bloodied soup again. Wayne remembered the old rodeo saying, "You and the horse you rode on."

He listened for the pitter-patter of scurrying insects. Wayne was still amazed at the level of sophistication and benevolence of the frolicking young monsters that ran across the beautiful murals—the scenes of majestic mountains and lush, green gardens as Venus-flytrap-faced aliens danced in the meadow. He noticed that the sky was a reddish color with two suns and a huge, orbiting moon just above the horizon. Wayne said in an arrogant tone, "That's just wrong."

Wayne cautiously stepped along the passageway until he noticed an opening up ahead. He noticed that the air against his face was beginning to thin out, no longer smelling of rotting vegetation and mildewed burlap. He remembered being on the aircraft carrier down in engineering when the winds would blow through the passageways as the inside air pressure tried to equalize itself with outside barometric pressure. This was the same feeling; this huge ship was alive, breathing as pressurized environmental sensors tried to equalize.

He continued until he reached a huge subway station. The subway station was colossal, an enormous space some four hundred yards long and two hundred yards wide. The same mural paintings and images decorated every wall. The ceiling was some fifty yards above the floor, with recessed lighting and surveillance cameras. Wayne stood there, studying the cameras, but they appeared to be off. Waiting at the loading platform was a one-hundred-foot-long hot-dog-shaped tram suspended on a magnetic track system. Its door swung open as if it detected Wayne presence.

The metal floor was a greenish color, almost resembling grass in spring, and the walls documented everyday life in the land of biological monsters and evolutionary chaos. The heavily decorated tram was ablaze with bizarre graffiti resembling smeared insect claws, facial-lobe prints, and stinger impressions. The tram had a couple of sets of windows and no seats, but a command console up forward containing, several dashboard buttons and switches.

He slowly entered the tram and walked toward the console. He peered through the front windscreen, only to see the dark tunnel ahead. Wayne studied the pictorial buttons and switches that littered the face of the console's dashboard. He recognized a picture of an old ship's steering wheel, a bomb, a gear, and an atom with three orbiting electrons. He tried to figure out the fifth one. It looked like a dinner plate—maybe the cafeteria. The last button he could not figure out. It must be the dimensional complex.

Wayne hesitated, then pushed the ship's steering-wheel button, still terrified that he did not have a weapon. The tram's door retracted as locking bolts engaged along the shuttle's fuselage. The magnetic pickoffs from the tram's monorail tracking system lifted ever so slightly and started to move. The tram silently glided down the long subway station, and Wayne watched the passing wall paintings.

He took his touchpad and looked for Sarah's icon. Wayne pushed the button, and a few moments later, Cheng's digital voice said, "Spot is in weapons. I need you to interface the touchpad with the main computer's database, network, and biological scanners. When you get to the bridge, there should be an interface port connection. The download should take around ten minutes, so be patient. Once the download is complete, I will have complete control of the ship."

Wayne looked around for somewhere to sit, but there was not a chair or bench anywhere. He sat on the floor, figuring it was going to be a long ride. Wayne noticed some additional icons on his touchpad after he downloaded the data from the airlock terminal. On the first screen, one icon displayed, "Current location." He pushed the button, and an image came up with floor-plan schematics of the airlock, the foyer, the passageway, the three corridors, the subway, engineering, and the shuttle bay. Wayne said, "Is that all I got?" Wayne flipped through the touchpad's database for ships with twenty aft engines. The ship was long, but bulky in the mid-ships and back aft. He noticed some ram intakes along the port and starboard superstructures, like two massive angles on a carrier's flight deck.

The tram ran for some eight hours, stopping at the weapons subway station and the dimensional station. The stations looked identical. The bridge station was coming up next.

Wayne detected a slight deceleration in the tram's velocity. Wayne felt an overwhelming anxiety—what if those creatures are waiting for him at the bridge's subway station? Wayne looked on the dashboard for a kill switch. Maybe he could get out and walk to the station. He noticed a dim point of light up ahead as the tram continued to slow down. He could see the two tram tracks, but they were in darkness. They appeared to be suspended on air. Wayne could see a small pinhole of light off in the distance. Wayne knelt down, hoping to avoid detection. He could see the ambient light from the station filtering through the black void.

Finally the tram entered the bridge's subway station. Wayne looked around the loading platforms and the connecting corridors—all clear. The walls were alive with evolutionary madness as Venus-flytrap-faced children wrapped their heads around terrified groundhogs, feasting on the horrified rodents.

The tram finally stopped and the door swung open. Wayne listened for something to break the silence. All was quiet except for the slight echo from his labored breathing. He slowly crawled on his hands and knees past the tram's open door and onto the loading dock, looking for anything and listening to everything.

Cheng's voice suddenly broke the silence. Wayne quickly crawled back into the tram and grabbed his touchpad. Cheng said, "I noticed you downloaded a partial segment of the ship's schematic. On the touchpad's second display there should be two icons. One is for bio-signs and the other is camera interface. The bio-signs are like a motion detector that has a range of fifty feet, and the camera's icon can interface via a communications link to all existing camera units."

Wayne took his touchpad and selected the second display. He found the two icons, bio-signs and cameras. He pushed the touchpad's camera icon, but the touchpad's screen remained dark. He brought up the bio-sign icon and selected it. An image started to appear, but the orientation was all wrong. He moved the touchpad all around him, trying to align it with the subway station. He realized the dark blip in the middle was himself. Wayne tried to cancel out his own bio-sign from his touchpad, and then finally the blob in the middle disappeared. Again, he moved the touchpad all around for any detectable targets.

Wayne stood up, holding the touchpad chest-high as he slowly walked to the left toward an entrance to a distant corridor. He noticed on the wall a picture of the ship's steering wheel, with an arrow pointing down the corridor. The touchpad's motion detector remained clear as he slowly walked toward the corridor's entrance.

The tram's door suddenly retracted and closed shut. Wayne turned around, fearful that something else was in the tram. Wayne picked up the pace toward the bridge while the touchpad's display remained clear. He wondered if the bridge had a small-weapons locker. Wayne could see a brightly illuminated opening ahead. The air remained quiet. He slowly approached the opening and stuck his head around the corner. It was the bridge.

This was a massive space shaped like an amphitheater with three levels. The amphitheater's stage formed the backdrop where four huge, elevated windscreens peered into the dark void. In front of the amphitheater was a sunken sublevel with a small box in the middle. The bridge's main level curved around the sunken sublevel and composed most of the bridge's deck. In the rear of the bridge, closest to where Wayne surveyed from behind the corridor's corner, was an elevated circular platform. On the elevated, circular platform was a black, metal altar or table.

Along the curved main-bridge level were smaller computer consoles that monitored the ship's systems and diagnostics. Along the bridge's bulkheads were crown-mounted cameras, small access boxes, and computer-access terminals. Wayne saw a larger computer terminal attached to the altar on the upper platform. Wayne also discovered a small-weapons locker with the picture of a gun on it on the far bulkhead.

The bridge's air was still and quiet. The monitors were all off, and the touchpad's motion detector scan showed clear. The painted walls continued to depict the carefree Venus-flytrap-faced aliens' lifestyle. Wayne slowly proceeded into the bridge from behind the corridor's bulkhead when alarms started to go off and the motorized cameras pointed in his direction.

Wayne yelled out, "Oh Crap!" He ran to the weapons locker, but it was locked. He ran over to the altar trying to link the touchpad with the computer terminal. The touchpad's downloading light started flickering, but the alarms continued to scream as the cameras followed his every move. He found a pole leaning up against one of the bridge's windscreens. Wayne swung the pole as hard as he could up against the weapons locker. Repeatedly he smashed the weapons locker, but it would not open.

The alarms and cameras suddenly shut off. Wayne turned around as a Venus-flytrap-faced alien emerged from behind the corridor's bulkhead. Wayne rushed the creature, holding the pole like a lance and thrusting it into the creature's facial lobe. Wayne quickly retracted the pole from the bloodied carnage, and another scurried toward him. Again, the pole disappeared as it easily penetrated its soft outer skeleton, causing both eyes to rupture from their sockets. Bluish and yellow blood gushed out like a fountain, onto the walls, onto Wayne, and onto the floor. Wayne noticed a weapon in the creature's hand. He took the pole and whacked it across its, arm breaking it in two. He pried the gun from its sharp, insect-like claws and prepared himself for another assault. Wayne could hear the creepy scurrying sound coming down the corridor. Holding the gun, he went to the weapons locker and gave it a quick plasma blast. The door swung open, revealing three types of weapons: short, medium, and rifle-like plasma rays.

Wayne turned around, readying himself. These were large creatures, with five-foot lobe-span, three-foot necks, and thirteen-foot insect bodies.

Grabbing the medium-sized weapon, he examined his first two kills, their bodies still and lifeless. He ran back to the corridor bulkhead where a creature had stopped maybe five feet from where Wayne was waiting. He suddenly jumped out and gave both weapons two good blasts. The insect immediately exploded in a vaporous cloud of flying blood and debris.

Wayne kept firing as if in a shooting arcade until the

avalanche of creatures stopped coming. The bulkheads were awash with slime, blood, and ooze, covering the once-bizarre wall paintings. Wayne tried to regain his composure. The air was thick with bug guts, mildew, and the sounds of bubbling blood from the keratin carcasses.

Wayne looked over to the touchpad, but it was still downloading. Wayne scouted the bridge's layout. There was only one entrance, and that was the corridor. He counted fifteen dead aliens, but he could hear more coming from somewhere else. Wayne thought about an elevator or another lift-type access from inside the bridge. He went back inside and walked the entire perimeter of the bridge complex. Standing next to the altar on the elevated platform, Wayne noticed a recessed plate off to the left. The sounds of attenuated scurrying came from behind the recessed plate and from down the corridor. The sounds grew louder and louder. Wayne figured he could hide behind the altar and still angle himself for a wide-angle shot. He crouched down on the main bridge level with the altar shielding his face. Wayne took cover and waited. Wayne thought about the motion detector, but the touchpad was still downloading.

Wayne thought that a grenade might be helpful. Tactics told him that he was going to be rushed. He took off his shoes and threw one toward the corridor's entrance. Wayne watched as one of the creatures backed up out of the corridor into the bridge's entrance, his ugly face away from him. Wayne threw the other shoe over the creature's back, toward the corridor. The creature immediately turned around and Wayne blasted it into a rainbow of flying ooze. Wayne saw that the access panel was opening up as aliens down the corridor stormed the bridge. Shot after shot, Wayne blasted with both weapons angled off toward the advancing aliens with a flurry of plasma blasts. Wayne noticed that none of the creatures had gotten off a shot. The congested bloody corridor ceased all attempts to ambush the bridge. Wayne ran over to the weapons locker, threw down the older, small weapon, and picked up a fresh one. The battle subsided to an eerie pause, and the air was stiff with the smell of excrement and vomit. He could see small puddles of blood flowing from the bridge deck down to the lower recessed substructure, turning it into a lake of ooze. Wayne looked over at the touchpad. It had stopped downloading. He picked up the touchpad and headed toward the elevator.

Wayne found himself walking barefoot in the slow ebb of alien blood, carefully stepping over mangled insect debris as he went. He stepped inside the largest elevator he'd ever seen. Wayne estimated that it was some forty feet across, forty feet deep and twenty feet high. He found an access panel off to the side with several control buttons. One button was the ship's steering wheel, or the bridge; the next button was an oval-shaped symbol; and the third was a dinner plate. Wayne pushed the button with the oval drawing on it. Wayne watched the large access doorplate close into position, then lock. He felt several floor clamps disengaging as the elevator slowly descended.

The elevator continued downward for some five minutes. He felt the same floor clamps securing themselves with a grabbing metal-to-metal sound. The large access plate disengaged its floor lock and started to open. Wayne wedged his body into the corner, ready to fire if something jumped out. The air was still and quiet. He looked at the touchpad's motion detector—no movement. Wayne looked around the corner as he gazed toward a huge foyer area with three interconnecting corridors joining about a hundred feet away. He moved and looked to his side, seeing another corridor. He looked around for an oval-shaped picture like the one in the elevator. He could hear scurrying further off toward the other three corridors. He inspected the corridor immediately to the right of the elevator. It led to an elevator maintenance room. The access-security keypad next to the door was red, meaning it was locked. He went back to the elevator and looked around the corner toward the three corridors. The sounds of scurrying persisted, but too far off to be of any concern.

Wayne had one small weapon in his pants pocket, the medium weapon in one hand, and his touchpad in the other. The touchpad's motion detector displayed some targets, but they were going away from him. Wayne found the oval-shaped wall picture with an arrow pointing to the right corridor. The other two corridors were unmarked. He proceeded toward the oval-labeled corridor for about a hundred feet until he came to a large foyer with an open access door. The scurrying sounds had fallen silent.

Whatever this place was, it was huge. Wayne stood there at the chamber's entrance, trying to figure out what these oval things were. They were grayish plastic, silky-looking oval objects scattered all over the floor. They were about three to four feet long. Throughout the entire chamber were drapes or ropes tethered from the ceiling and hanging close to the floor. Some of the drapes or ropes held these oval things like hammocks, but some of the oval objects were on the floor, broken and bleeding. Wayne suddenly realized he had found the queen's egg depository.

The place was a mess. It looked like it had been broken into, sabotaged, or vandalized. Whatever happened, Wayne never knew of an insect species that would deliberately kill its own egg population. Wayne could not count the number of eggs, but they all looked damaged or destroyed. Wayne started to turn around when he heard something from inside the chamber. It sounded mechanical. Wayne waited for a second, then slowly walked further past the chamber's entrance, pushing the grayish dirty white eggs and hammock lanyards out of the way. There it was again, that mechanical noise. Hoping the touchpad had integrated itself with the computer's universal translator, Wayne said, "Hello." The mechanical noise picked up. It almost sounded stuck as motorized gears moved back and forth, trying to free itself.

Wayne never liked the notion that bots needed to be more like humans. Just the name "mechanical entity" conjured up connotations that the bot's creator had a crippling identity crisis. Wayne wondered why he had not seen other bots running around—why only here? Wayne was continuing to look around when the bot again twisted its gears. Wayne saw something off to the side, but was not sure what he was looking at. All of a sudden, he saw an enormous, red engine-hoist robotic stand emerge from its hiding place. Wayne could not see the base. It had two actuated rams: one on the upper hinge and another connected to its base. Wayne noticed wires or hydraulic lines running the full length of the bot's hoist boom. Wayne was not sure what the bot was doing. It looked like it wanted to attack, but then he saw that it was stuck in the lanyard webbing.

Wayne wanted to free it, but was not sure how it would respond. With each cautious step, he walked closer, hoping it would calm down. He saw the tangled and twisted jungle of egg hammocks wrapped around its motorized tank track. Wayne grabbed onto one end and pulled with all his might. He could hear the lanyards compressing together as the bot maneuvered its base back and forth, as if they were trying to work together. Wayne adjusted his grip while trying not to slip from all the ooze on the floor. He gave another good tug, then another and another. Wayne dropped the stringy mess, then walked closer to the bot and picked up another loose end. He grabbed on tightly and pulled as hard as he could. The bot's base started to come into view as the grayish white wrappings pulled away. Wayne could see a set of cameras about a foot off its base. The bot applied maximum amperage to all its gears and motors. They almost spun out, but broke free instead, nearly toppling over from being so top-heavy.

Wayne backed up, giving the bot room to maneuver. He watched as the bot retracted its enormous boom, which reached some fifteen feet high. The bot gently rolled toward him, but said nothing. Wayne talked into the touchpad. "What is your job?"

The bot remained silent.

Wayne then heard the scurrying noises were backtracking and heading right for him. He ran up to the corner between the foyer and the chamber's entrance and waited for the aliens to show themselves. Wayne put his touchpad on the floor and bought up the motion detector display. There were ten targets waiting at the junction near the other corridor. Wayne stood up and shouted, "Hey, you!" He looked down at the touchpad; the targets were on the move again. Wayne still hid behind the corner as one alien emerged into view, and then another. Both stopped in unison. Wayne looked over to see the hoist bot move around the chamber's entrance, and the aliens started to lose interest. Suddenly Wayne jumped from his corner position and landed in the middle of the corridor. He watched as three of the aliens flashed their huge flytrap heads from side to side, but refused to move closer. Wayne jumped back behind the corner, but still they did not charge. Wayne again jumped into view, shouting, "Hey!" The creatures again flared their massive heads, and then one attacked. Wayne held up his gun and sprayed its guts all over the passageway. The remaining monsters quickly accelerated to scurrying speed as Wayne blasted away.

It only took a few moments until all ten aliens were dead. The carnage seemed one-sided, but Wayne liked it that way. Wayne looked over to the hoist bot as it tried to fix some of the damaged eggs. Wayne now understood the bot's protocol: to protect the eggs.

Wayne called to Sarah from the touchpad. "I need you here—first stop on the bridge's elevator."

Sarah said, "What's wrong?"

Wayne said, "I found this bot, maybe it could help us."

Sarah bolted through the corridor's bulkhead, surprised that Wayne had found a bot. Sarah stopped and looked at this very strange robot. Sarah tried to approach it, but it backed away toward Wayne. Sarah was surprised that a bot would react that way. Sarah looked over at Wayne and said, "What happened?"

Wayne said, "This is an egg bot. When the queen lays her eggs, this bot hoists them up on these hanging nests. Someone vandalized the eggs before I got here. I found the bot tangled up in the netting and set it free."

Sarah again approached it, but it moved toward Wayne again. Sarah said, "I guess you found a friend. Certain alien species program their bots to perform certain tasks, and then destroy the bots after a couple months because they become overly social. This bot devoted itself to protecting and raising the queen's young, probably on a permanent basis."

Wayne tried communicating with the hoist bot. "Go with Sarah," Wayne said as he pointed to Sarah. The bot looked at Wayne, then looked at Sarah, and then slowly moved toward Sarah as she passed her body through the bot.

Sarah spoke from the touchpad. "Because we are energy based, I can alter its battery memory to obey only entities, but in this case, I programmed the battery to acknowledge you as the primary and me as the secondary."

Wayne said, "Wow, what a neat trick!"

Sarah said, "I can use this bot down in the plasma conduit, lifting the heavy magnetic rings." Sarah gave the bot some coordinates, and off it went toward engineering.

Wayne said, "Does it know where to go?"

Sarah said, "This bot probably knows the ship better than anyone." Sarah continued, "I'll be in engineering, I need you on the bridge to talk with Cheng." With that, Sarah dissolved through the passageway's bulkhead.

Wayne stood there, amazed at the whole situation as he watched the bizarre robot go off to engineering. Never had he seen a bot so devoted to its job. Wayne certainly understood the fatherly connection to his own children, Carolynn and Bud. However, to assume that a machine could respond as a biological unit meant that science had taken a very dangerous leap toward replacing life itself.

Wayne started walking back toward the elevator. He wondered why a salvaged ship still had a crew onboard. What about the queen who was killed and the bodies dragged to the shuttle bay's airlock? What provoked the rogue aliens to ransack the egg chamber? It almost felt like a conspiracy, but why? Then he thought about his own species, man. To assume that ruthlessness only pertains to aliens only exposes the hypocrisy of man's own consciousness. Even when man first walked the earth, murder was in the eyes of Adam's own kids.

Wayne boarded the elevator, pushed the button for the bridge, and watched the large door-access plate close.

Chapter 4

The Spider Ship

Wayne sat comfortably on the bridge's altar when Cheng's voice came over the touchpad. "I see that you have been busy. Go back to the subway station and keep watch. I will fly the ship from here."

Wayne grew increasingly agitated at the thought of being ambushed from behind. Wayne had little choice but to follow Cheng's instructions as he nervously walked back to the subway station with two weapons and his touchpad. The tram was gone, and as far as he knew, it could arrive at any time. If Cheng was flying the ship remotely, it was at least a two-day trip back the entity's base.

Wayne had just gotten comfortable when he heard Cheng's voice on the touchpad. "The ship just docked, take the elevator down to the cafeteria. Once you exit the elevator, you will see two corridors branch off. Take the right, or starboard, corridor and look for a flashing light. The flashing light will enable the ship's airlock. Proceed through the airlock, down the passageway into the large auditorium with the windows. I will be waiting by the sphere."

Wayne shouted, "What, we're here already? It hasn't been five minutes!"

Wayne took his weapons and the touchpad and headed toward the elevator.

Wayne followed Cheng's directions. He went down to the cafeteria, took the right corridor, and saw the flashing light. He pushed the illuminated security button, opened the ship's airlock, and proceeded through the passageway to where Cheng was floating.

Cheng's digital voice came over the touchpad. "Even though we are entities, we often take advantage of dimension travel ourselves. Sit down, Wayne, I have a lot to explain."

Wayne sat on the sphere's entrance ramp as he watched Cheng's dark, amoebic body.

Cheng said, "Every galaxy has the ability to create or destroy multi-dimensional rifts. We call it gravitational cleansing."

Wayne interrupted, "Did I miss something? Was Spot suppose to help me back there, or was it your intention that I confront those aliens myself so you could fly this ship back yourself?"

Cheng said in a calm voice, "We have seen countless alien societies come and go, seemingly oblivious of history's valuable lessons. We delegate out of respect. We judge species by their honor and analyze them according to that honor. Your responsibility was to secure the bridge, and you accomplished that task. Responsibility by no means mission complete, but responsibility is how we judge resourcefulness, creativity, and determination to see the mission through. Some aliens assume that by expressing weakness or humility, though honorable, see martyrdom as a better solution than burdening their conscience over the guilt of killing. Honor is also valuable—not to the point of sacrificing honor by surrendering, but escaping to fight another day. Wayne, you accomplished the mission, and your honor was vindicated by protecting others who were not as brave. Alliances are the quickest way to determine honor or dishonor. Just as death dishonors, life honors. The aliens you killed were a dishonored species, and they received their just rewards. I have seen countless alien governments or institutionalized despotism rise and fall, all originally created with the best of intentions. Unfortunately, the noblest of causes become sacrificed when subsequent generations consume themselves with greed and power. We seek out dishonorable governments and destroy them to protect the galaxy's natural processes. Alien societies who harvest dishonor at the expense of another's harvest demonstrate the greatest of contempt when they are not the ones starving. Wayne, I want to thank you for your bravery and creativity. You and you alone brought this ship back. Spot could have done it all, but what would you have learned? Remember, if you see someone else kill, you feel dishonor, but if you kill with justification or self-preservation, you see it as honor. Perspective always destroys alliances, but real honor comes in protecting those who are too feeble to fight. Never protect those who are capable of destroying you in the end. That is why we did not protect you, because we knew you were capable. Now let's fix your ship."

Wayne did not know what to think. He stood up and looked through the massive mural of windows and there it was, his ship.

Wayne said, "What needs fixing first?"

Cheng said over the touchpad, "Spot is in charge of all repairs, maintenance, computer protocols, operational testing, and final evaluation. Your job is to master all bridge's functions, consoles and the main computer." Cheng gave Wayne a health nod of approval and dissolved through the floor.

Wayne stood there with new purpose. He looked back at his ship, completely taken by what was entrusted to him. Wayne knew this was another step closer to seeing his family. It all hinged on doing what Cheng told him.

Wayne made his way back to the bridge, happy to find it completely cleaned up. He noticed a group of five bots working on the individual consoles and computer interface terminals.

He could not get the queen conspiracy out of his head. Normally, if the queen dies, the colony dies as well. What species would kill their own queen and her eggs? Then Wayne thought, where were the young? Where was the queen's chamber?

Wayne picked up his touchpad and brought up the bridge's construction schematic. The elevator stopped on the egg floor and the cafeteria. On the schematic, there were two more floors at which the elevator should have stopped. The second level and the fourth level had a large chamber area. Wayne sat and analyzed the blueprints, trying to find access. Then he remembered the small elevator maintenance room in that corridor.

Wayne jumped into the elevator and descended to the egg level. He hurried around the corner toward the corridor and the elevator's maintenance room. The maintenance room's keypad-security light indicated red. Wayne called up the schematic for the egg level and found the access code for the maintenance door. He waved the touchpad across the keypad, changing the door's status from red to green. The access door swung open, revealing a small, closet room with an elevator access panel and two additional buttons for the nursery room and the queen's chambers. Wayne pushed the button for the nursery, and he heard the elevator's floor clamps disengage as the elevator descended to the fourth deck.

The corridors were narrow. It was almost like a drop chute. When the eggs hatched, the infant dropped down the chute to the nursery. The elevator stopped on the fourth floor as the large access door disengaged its locking bolts and opened up. Wayne passed through a small access panel from the maintenance closet into the main elevator itself.

The air was stale. The smell of something dead hid in the shadows. Wayne quietly made his way from the elevator to the main foyer corridor and to a large open chamber. The dimly lit chamber contained the same bizarre wall paintings and colorful murals. Walking closer toward the chamber, he could hear the distinct sound of dripping fluid. Several of the feeding stations were broken into, and there were hundreds of dead alien infants. Then he heard a bot's servo engage and the sound of motorized tank tracks rolling along the floor. Wayne said, "Come on out, I am here to help." A smaller version of the hoist bot slowly emerged from behind a pile of debris. The little greenish white bot was about five feet high with its boom extended and had two little cameras attached to its lower chassis. Wayne could hear a random crackling noise, almost as if the bot was trying to communicate.

Wayne called for Cheng on the touchpad. "Found another bot in the nursery. Whoever vandalized the egg chamber also killed everything in the nursery."

The touchpad came back with Cheng's digital voice. "We found various parts of a dead queen two levels up. In addition, we found one drone. It appears very suspicious."

Wayne said, "The nursery bot is trying to communicating with me, but I can't get this translator to work."

Two seconds later, Cheng floated down through the ceiling. He briefly blended with the bot saying, "You are correct." Cheng grew a small appendage, which reached inside himself, pulling out the silvery orb. Cheng remotely connected the orb with the bot's battery memory cell.

Wayne watched as Cheng's portable orb began to conjure up an image. The orb displayed the bot's memory log, taken from the downloaded data.

The touchpad continued with Cheng's synthesized voice: "This little bot teaches communication skills to the baby aliens. It apparently contained a preprogrammed language protocol. The data indicated that the ship was hijacked. The queen attached to this ship represented her planetary colony. The ship, the queen, and her entourage were killed on their way to the queen's home planet."

Cheng's portable orb discontinued the bluish

hologram and he put it back inside himself. Cheng said, "I downloaded the entire bot's language protocol to the touchpad. Return to the bridge and talk to the computer—find out what's going on."

Wayne returned to the elevator's maintenance room and pushed the button for the egg room. Wayne returned to the bridge, but this time things were different. He noticed that all the cameras were moving and pointed directly at him. He sat down on the altar table and the lower bridge's deck box came on. Wayne gazed in amazement as red lasers began emanating from the box until a complete hologram of a majestic queen said in a computerized, synthesized crackling voice, "Who are you!"

Wayne was more curious than frightened, saying, "Search data file on nursery. Who killed the queen, her eggs, and her young?"

The computer paused the hologram program, speaking in a poorly digitized, garbled voice, "Queen Sora had her assassins attack this ship and kill the queen."

Wayne asked the computer, "Was the queen attached to this ship good to you, or are you glad she is dead?"

There was an troublesome pause. The computer replied, "She was a good queen, but she had her faults."

Wayne asked, "Then you played a part in her death?"

The computer replied, "Yes."

Wayne asked, "Did this ship have another mission other than to visit queen Sora?"

The computer replied, "Our mission was to destroy the entity's home world."

Wayne said, "I was an entity's prisoner, but I escaped.

I found this ship in a salvage debris field. I breached the security protocol when I came on board and neutralized the crew. I managed to connect your nursery drone to the main computer, then interfaced the symbiotic entity the entities gave me to this altar, allowing me to communicate to you. My name is Wayne."

The computer, in a poorly synthesized voice, asked, "Why are you with the entities?"

Wayne replied, "The same reason you killed the queen. Sometimes you have to make friends long enough to kill them." Wayne could hear the computer snickering. Wayne continued, "What now?"

The computer said, "Without the queen, the ship cannot be piloted."

Wayne thought, then said, "The real queen or a hologram one?"

The computer asked, "What do you have in mind?"

Wayne said, "If you keep the queen's hologram but let me pilot the ship, we can divide the spoils. What was this ship's alternative mission?"

The computer replied, "We recently terminated trade with another alien species who sold us contaminated feedstock. Many of our young died, but it was only recently we made the connection. We have orders to destroy their planet."

Wayne asked, "Would you continue on the mission if all your kind died from food contamination?"

The computer said, "Yes, but we haven't all died. They would not attack knowing we still existed. If they discovered we all died, and then our planet would be defenseless."

Wayne said, "Let's radio a message that your species

are all dead, but have a force of spider ships waiting to destroy their fleet in their eagerness to pick your bones. How many spider ships do you have?"

The computer offered, "How about this? You take this ship to the agra-planet and tell them the good news. I will forward a message to our home world to prepare for the ambush. The queen mother will be most pleased."

Wayne said, "Then let's go!"

Wayne knew that Sarah and her bots were still onboard, conducting repairs, but since it was a minor, low-impact mission, it would not be a problem.

Wayne commanded the computer, "I need a weapons and shield generator diagnostic. Also what is your enemy's weapons frequency?"

The computer replied, "The frequency is seventy gigahertz, why?"

Wayne asked, "What is the frequency of our shield generator?"

The computer replied, "The ship is based on the fifty-gigahertz wavelength of uranium and can't tolerate any weapons fire above fifty gigahertz."

Wayne said, "Yes, I know. We need plasma with a frequency of seventy gigahertz or greater to boost the shield generator's strength. I know it might create some dangerous harmonics, but it should reflect their weapons fire back on themselves, like a mirror."

The computer said, "How about this: we were testing something more dangerous than uranium. The theory is to emit a cloud of radioactive particles toward an enemy ship. Any ship exposed to the radioactive cloud, whether in subspace or normal space, will explode."

Wayne asked, "Do you have any of this special

radioactive material onboard? Can we plasma that material for use in our plasma cannons?" Wayne could sense this was an evil computer.

The computer replied, "Yes, already done."

Wayne said, "Plot a course, and let's go."

Wayne figured this little diversion might give Cheng some time to defend his own home world and maybe look for the Venus-flytrap-faced alien's planet. Wayne returned to the bridge's subway station and selected the Sarah icon on the laptop.

Sarah answered, "What's going on? The ship is pulling out of dock."

Wayne said, "Meet me at the bridge's subway station and avoid detection."

Sarah met Wayne at the station while he filled in all the details. Sarah agreed. It would be a good diagnostic exercise to see what this ship could do. Sarah said, "The ship was in excellent health. Most of the damage resulted from plasma blasts during the hijacking."

Sarah was surprised that the computer neglecting to disclose the contents of the radioactive material, because bulk radioactive material is considered contraband. Sarah explained that the entities were energy-based, as biological units were carbon based. The entities considered all radioactive substances elixirs of good health and ionic purifiers. Sarah took off on her quest to find the radioactive material and bathe in the fountain of subatomic youth.

Wayne maintained watch on the bridge, monitoring the radar scans for any enemy ships. The intended target was Agra-planet Alpha, which once represented about three hundred agricultural planets throughout the galaxy.

Unfortunately, due to alien disputes over territory, conflicts over food rations, and accusations of hording, only four agra-planets remained. The Venus aliens found that controlling only four agra-planets was easier than the three hundred once existed. The Venus aliens were not concerned at the lack of galactic food; it was only when the people were starving were the rich and powerful governors actually happy.

The four remaining agra-planets represent a massive galactic co-op catering in animal meat, grains, milk production, herbs, medicinal products, water, coffee, and an endless variation of natural and synthetic narcotics, along with beauty creams, soaps, and petroleum-based grease for robotic lubrication.

Each agra-planet has a client database, which represents a meticulous focus on quality. The Venus aliens had already picked up a previous order of biological ooze, enzymes, proteins, glucose, and keratin. Wayne suspected that the Venus aliens were attempting to play the agra-planet as fools. He knew that the contaminated food was not responsible for the infant's deaths, but there existed a deeper plot to conceal the real conspirators. What was amazing was that either outcome would prop up the queen mother's political standing.

Wayne continued to watch the radar monitors. There was no invasion force; there was no attempt to conquer the queen mother's home world. The computer insisted that the main force had gone around, maneuvering into flanking position, but Wayne knew better. The standing order was to discuss the contamination issue and see what happens after that.

Sarah sent Wayne a text message on the touchpad.

"Within communication range of Agra-planet Alpha. We are still one week out, so I prefer to keep a safe distance for security reasons."

Wayne commanded the computer, "Open channel to Agra-planet Alpha."

The computer said, "Channel open. The chancellor is on visual."

Wayne was about to greet the chancellor, but instead, said, "Holy crap!"

Wayne assumed that a chancellor's role was to look and act with a certain degree of intelligence, but the chancellor was anything but that. Wayne had not gotten over the fact that humanoids were at the bottom of the alien food chain.

The chancellor had a froggish-looking head, which protruded from a ram's-horn snail shell as bubbling ooze drained from holes along his foot muscle. The chancellor's greenish yellow frog face was more like a hairless squirrel's face, with a more slender nose structure and two bulging tusks from either side of its narrow mouth. Wayne watched the chancellor's tongue wiggling in and out between his tusks as spit slimed the viewing monitor.

Wayne said very politely, "Greetings, Chancellor."

The chancellor's digital voice appeared garbled, like the computer's translator processor, saying, "Can I help you?"

Wayne said, "I am an upright".

The chancellor asked, "What does upright mean?"

Wayne said, "An upright is aligned more vertically off the ground. I see your species is keenly aware of agricultural environments and the best conditions for a profitable enterprise."

The chancellor said, “Yes, we understand that an ecosystem is a delicate balance of water, soil, and growing conditions.”

Wayne said, “I found this ship adrift. Whoever owned it said their planet was dying and could not defend themselves. Some of my salvage friends see great opportunity in a new fleet of reconditioned warships. Do you wish to invest in such an enterprise?”

The chancellor shook his narrow frog face, almost toppling over from his top-heavy shell, and said, “No.”

The computer went berserk as the queen’s hologram suddenly came on, cutting Wayne’s picture off the monitor. The queen’s hologram yelled out, “You killed us! You contaminated our food, and we will destroy your planet!

Wayne called over the touchpad, “Cheng, attack now!”

Cheng called out, “Look above you. You can watch what happens to those who harvest dishonor from those who try to harvest honor.”

The computer shouted in its garbled voice, “No!”

Wayne saw Sarah bolt onto the bridge’s lower platform, short out the queen’s holographic display, then proceed to the main computer.

The computer yelled out, “No! No!” Then the computer’s voice growled to a halt.

Wayne noticed that all the computer monitors went black. The radar scans ceased as the ship started to list from a lack of navigational control.

Wayne said, “No wonder aliens destroy their computers after a couple months. This computer was way overdue!”

Wayne watched as the night sky erupt in a maelstrom as thousands of ships dropped out of subspace engulfed in fire and nuclear explosions, popping off like brightly illuminant popcorn.

Sarah suddenly appeared on the deck, then quickly left again as she dissolved through the ship's hull.

Cheng voice came over the touchpad. "All entities to the Venus' planet."

Cheng transferred an isobar gravitational map of the Venus's planet onto the touchpad screen. Cheng's voice again said, "The entire planet has wrapped itself in subspace." Wayne watched as the heavily concentrated gravity flux rapidly equalized into normal space. The Venus's home world was now a nebula of debris and rock.

Wayne remembered what Cheng had said: "When other people kill, you feel dishonor." Wayne did feel a sense of dishonor but realized that justification was in the eyes of the oppressed who found their freedom once again.

Cheng made his victorious entrance on the bridge where Wayne was still watching the fireworks from the bridge's windscreen.

Cheng said, "Wow! That was amazing! I anticipated something completely different. You managed to convince the computer that it was the agra-planet who would attack and not the entities. We picked up the computer's message traffic about their plans to set up spider traps close to your position. When we saw the chancellor say no, the computer immediately sent out a warning that it was a trap. The spider ships then broke ranks and moved against your position.

Wayne said, “I thought you would be mad.”

Cheng said, “No, that was brilliant. Once the computer interrupted your transmission with the chancellor, we realized how dangerous the computer had become. The chancellor was a little concerned when his night sky erupted, but we made sure none of the Venus ships penetrated their air space.

Spot emerged from the floor saying, “Computer is in reboot mode; the core has been erased.”

Cheng turned to Wayne and said, “Spot and I have decided to redesign the bridge network. Spot and the bots will replace all consoles with a single main console. We will add another computer core along with new system and diagnostic protocols.”

Wayne said, “Can I keep the queen’s hologram program here on the bridge?”

Cheng said, “Yes, but why?”

Wayne replied, “The first impression is nine-tenths of a successful negotiation.”

Cheng felt entertained at Wayne’s twisted sense of humor.

Spot motioned to Cheng, and Wayne heard the touchpad announce, “What the computer said about the radioactive material was true. That stuff is onboard.” Cheng said, “Spot has assigned several bots to clean up the mid-ship’s radioactive cargo hold.”

Wayne asked, “What is the material called and what can it do?”

Cheng said, “We do not have names for radioactive material; we use it as a cleansing agent. I know of two particular alien societies who pushed huge chunks of this material into each other’s solar system. The chunks of radioactive matter descended as dangerous comets as the star's gravitational force brought them closer to the orbiting planets. Each comet affected the other's sun. Due to the characteristics of the radioactive material and the star's fusion processes, each star expanded beyond its normal diameter. Engulfed in the ever-expanding solar fusion, the suns blossomed into the surrounding planets, destroying them. Each of the stars tried to equalize their expansion, but in a catastrophic burst of energy, both went nova. Obviously, the two alien societies perished. The irony was, in the glorious nebula that proceeded, a few of the smaller rival societies pillaged what elements they could find and started a completely new alliance from neighboring cultures. Sometimes the consequences of war benefit the unlikeliest of benefactors."

Wayne said, "What about Spot?"

Cheng said, "Spot will continue in your mission and ultimately become your galaxy's new leader. Spot is in charge now." Wayne jumped in surprise as Spot flashed onto the bridge from above and danced all around the complex.

Cheng laughed and said, "My work is done. Oh, what is an upright?"

Wayne laughed and said, "We are standing upright. However, we are humans. We respect life and individualism, and we have a fascination with war, intrigue, and politics. It is because we lack this technology that we survive to argue another day; otherwise, we would have destroyed ourselves long ago."

Cheng said, "It is only through war do you understand which cause was just, but war for the sake of war is an expression of dishonor and distrust. In the end, when a society attempts to wage war as a justification to perpetuate greed, power, religious intolerance, or malice, it only propagates what it cannot afford. Biological units never seem to understand that the wages of war can never replace the price paid in lost innocence." Cheng exited the bridge, never to return.

Wayne sat down on the altar and looked around. Many of the bots were already disassembling the bridge's many consoles. Wayne shook his head at the wiring nightmare. This was no ordinary wiring, it was fiber-optic cable. Integrating the entire bridge into one console seemed like an impossible job, but the bots were enjoying the challenge. Wayne watched Sarah helping some of the bots, and she looked over at Wayne.

Wayne said, "Why does Cheng insist on calling you Spot?"

Sarah said, "Being feminine or masculine is a biological term. Because we are energy, our ionic differences enable us to be whole. Only in special circumstances can our creator assign us proper names. Right now, we have a bridge to reconfigure, and it will not be an easy job."

Wayne said, "Can I have a bathroom? And what were all those insects?"

Sarah said, "We can put a bathroom in the subway station. All biological units have an excrement-access port build to their biological needs. The port you saw was a keratin recovery port. Insectoids are classified as either planetary or deep-space. Planetary insects can only survive in the presence of atmosphere. The deep-space insects are anaerobic organisms that crystallize in the presence of atmosphere. The anaerobic insects are keratin-based and consumed for exoskeleton replenishment."

Wayne asked, "Then the sanitation issue is more trouble than it's worth?"

Sarah replied, "All biological units are more trouble than they're worth."

Wayne said, "I still need a bathroom, and did you creator give you the name Sarah?"

Sarah knew she had revealed too much and left for engineering.

Wayne was concerned about the queen's hologram. He was not sure if Sarah might react negatively if another competing feline was on the bridge. Anyway, Wayne needed to explore. He had been on the bridge far too long. Wayne said to other bots on the bridge, "I'm going to check out the weapons department."

Wayne slowly walked to the tram, reflecting on the past few days. Wayne looked at the touchpad and brought up the icon of Sarah. There were only three listings: position, bots, and work assignments. Wayne touched the icon bots. He was curious how the egg-hoist bot was getting along. The touchpad brought up a listing of ten thousand bots under her command. Wayne shouted, "Ten thousand?"

The echo bounced off the subway walls. Each was listed according to its battery number. Wayne already had a headache. He put the touchpad in standby mode and boarded the tram.

It was nice getting away. He walked to the tram's dashboard and selected the button for weapons. The tram's door closed, the magnetic amplifiers engaged, and the braking clamps released. The tram slowly exited the bridge station. Wayne was on his way to rest and relaxation.

Wayne sat down on the floor, picked up the touchpad, and spent some time studying dimensional weaponry.

The tram slowly decelerated as it approached the subway station for weapons. A small light broke through the darkness, and the tunnel became more illuminated. Wayne had never ridden on a subway before, and so far, it had not been a good experience.

He could see the subway station opening up. The walls were covered in the same cheery, bizarre painting of little Venus children chasing terrified animal and stuffing their faces.

The tram stopped, the door opened, and Wayne stepped on the loading platform. The weapons armory had a two-corridor access: one from the subway and the other from the shuttle bay. The shuttle bay's corridor extended for about twenty miles below decks. Wayne noticed a theme change in the wall paintings and murals along the subway's corridor. The paintings depicted the little Venus alien kids throwing grenades at other aliens and blowing them up. Wayne wondered if the Venus aliens understood the term *conscience*. Wayne conceded that humans had problems conceding their consciences, too.

Wayne could see a large access door at the end of the corridor. Over the access door was a painting of an explosion, a torpedo, and a small gun like the one he used on the bridge. The passageway was about twenty feet across, whereas most corridors were fifteen feet across. Next to the door was a keypad, an intercom panel, a red and green warning light, and a closed-circuit camera recessed in the door's ballistic framework.

Wayne took his touchpad and requested the weapons

locker be unlocked, but the light remained red. He tried pushing the green light, but nothing happened—it remained red. Wayne then tried to find the keypad's access code from the computer's security database. He found two possible codes and began entering the first one. Nothing happened. Then he entered the second code. The light flashed green, but an alarm from inside the armory started to go off. The locking bolts from within the access door began retracting, one by one, until the door's hydraulic system engaged. Wayne had trouble grabbing onto the two-foot thick door, which had four huge hinges connected to the bulkhead's door jam. He finally got behind it and started pushing it open. The door stood about twenty feet high and fifteen feet wide. He could feel a rush of dry, stale air from inside the armory, because it was humidity controlled.

The corridor's ambient light only illuminated the first couple of feet inside the armory's main entrance. Other than that, it was pitch black. Wayne looked around for a light, but could not find one. The armory's alarm was still going off.

Wayne managed to retract the door far enough. He looked inside, trying to find the alarm shut-off switch. The constant ringing and buzzing was quite annoying. Suddenly the alarm shut off without warning. Wayne had just entered the armory's foyer when he heard the distinct sound of servos and motorized gears. Wayne knew that Sarah had visited the weapons area, but she never mentioned a bot.

Wayne listened, and from the darkness came another mechanical sound, this one much louder and stronger.

Wayne said, "Hello." Wayne took his touchpad and called Sarah.

Sarah said, "What do you want?"

Wayne said, "There is a bot down here in weapons. I haven't seen it yet, but it sounds really big."

Sarah said, "I was just down there, and I didn't see a bot."

Wayne said, "Well, I am about to encounter one right now, I really need your help!"

Sarah said, "On my way."

Wayne slowly walked inside the dark chamber as the sound of mechanical servos and motorized tracks began to move forward. Wayne's eyes strained to cut through the darkness, but even the dimly lit corridor did not help.

Wayne took another step forward, followed by a corresponding motorized track rotation. Wayne judged the bot to be about fifty yards away, and he could hear a distinct echo when the robot made an advance.

Wayne took another step, followed by another corresponding motorized advance. Wayne counted on his fingers all the mechanical oddities he discovered on this ship: the sad hoist bot that lost its eggs, the slaughterhouse nursery bot, and the belligerent computer who sought revenge against the conspirators. Now there was a weapons bot.

Sarah silently drifted up behind him, saying, "What do you see?"

Wayne jumped back, scared half to death, yelling out, "Whoa, what's that?" Wayne yelled, "Damn it Sarah! Don't do that!"

Sarah did not say anything, but she was most amused.

Sarah drifted into the darkness and disappeared from sight. Wayne listened for any mechanical movement, but heard only silence. Wayne took a couple of steps forward. The air was still and dry. Wayne took another step. This time he heard the robot.

Sarah said, "I see it, this thing is huge!"

Wayne said, "Why does he react to me but not to you?" Wayne could not see anything, so he yelled out, "Sarah turn on the lights."

Sarah said, "I know what happened. When I crashed the computer, the weapons area went into lockdown. The computer is still off-line, but let me see what I can find."

Wayne said, "Can you just blend with the bot so it doesn't attack me?"

Sarah laughed. "I like it when you're scared. It is very entertaining."

Wayne thought this was an interesting problem. Normally all mechanical devices or bots respond only to the computer's programmed inputs, but this bot was still active. Wayne stopped and said, "It was the protection or security protocol that has been engaged." It was an amazing piece of technology—an integrated chip connected to a backup power supply that would override a lost power signal and go straight into protection mode.

Wayne thought of a rather disturbing possibility: what would happen if all the bots had their power circuits cut, allowing the protection chip to take over? Any bot operating on protection protocol would assume the personality of a paranoid murderer on the loose.

Wayne asked, "Sarah, can you check the bot's circuits?"

Sarah asked, "Yeah, but what are you looking for?"

Wayne replied, "Check the connection between the power supply circuit and the processing chip?"

Sarah said, "Wait a bit, checking."

Wayne said, "Also look for a secondary power supply connected to another integrated chip, like a modification of some kind."

Sarah said, "Wait. All bots have a power supply."

Wayne said, "Yes, I know, but what should happen if the computer goes down. Shouldn't the bot go down, too?"

Sarah said, "Okay, I understand now. Checking."

Wayne could hear the bot's mechanical tracks rotating wildly in his direction. Wayne shouted, "Sarah, it's getting closer, I'm running for the tram!" Wayne started to see the shadowy outline of a beast headed straight for him. Wayne estimated it to be some twenty feet high, with two appendages for arms with lobster-like grips for handling missiles and torpedoes. It did not have a head *per se*, just a set of cameras mounted on top of its shoulders. The bot's robust structural torso connected to a swivel-type mounting bracket attached to a rather large tank chassis.

Wayne turned and sprinted toward the tram with the robot in hot pursuit. The tracks thundered as they hit the metal floor, shaking the entire weapons complex. Wayne did not know where Sarah was, but he was not about to stop and ask. Wayne could see the tram thirty yards up ahead. He ran and ran, still feeling the floor vibrate as the mechanical tank treads thumped ever closer.

He jumped into the tram, went to the console, and pushed the button for engineering. The door closed as the robot came onto the loading platform. Wayne was afraid the beast would knock the tram off its tracks. Slowly the tram accelerated and headed for engineering. Wayne had never been so scared in all his life.

Wayne realized he left his touchpad back in the corridor by the weapons access door. The only access he had with communications was in engineering, but then he remembered the computer was off-line. Wayne had no choice but to return to weapons.

Wayne thought he could walk the twenty miles from engineering to weapons on the lower access tunnel. "Can't see that happening," he said to himself.

Wayne successfully stopped the tram halfway between engineering and weapons. He pushed the button for weapons and started back, hoping the beast bot was gone.

Wayne could see the weapons stations about a hundred yards ahead. He had his finger on the bridge button in case he needed a quick getaway. The weapons station slowly opened up, but the bot was gone. Wayne looked around to see if it was hiding somewhere. Wayne encouragingly said, "I hope it went back to the armory chamber."

The tram gently stopped, unlocking the door's locking clamps. Wayne knelt down, feeling the vibrations of the platform's floor to make sure it was all right to come out. Wayne looked around, wondering where Sarah was.

The air was still and quiet as he slowly exited the tram. He headed for the corridor, expecting an ambush. He gently looked around the corridor's corner—no bot. Wayne continued down the corridor, nearing weapons' main entrance. The large door was open and dark inside. Wayne looked around for his touchpad and realized it was gone. “Oh, crap!” he yelled, aggravated at his pitiful display of bravery.

Wayne called out, “Okay, Sarah, you have had your fun, please help me.”

Sarah busted out laughing. She even programmed the bot to laugh. Wayne stood there as the lights immediately came on, and there was Sarah and the incredible mechanical beast, both laughing at Wayne’s valiant display of cowardice.

Wayne had been humbled. He walked up to the bot, admiring its incredible display of biological imprinting, and then to Sarah, who loved every bit of it.

Wayne said, “See anything odd in the circuitry?”

Sarah said, “Yes, you were correct. It appears that these bots were designed to protect, but within the protocol of their programming. The weapons bot is meant to protect the weapons armory. The same protocol applied to the other bots, too. They were never connected to the main computer. I did not anticipate this at all.”

Wayne said, “There could be other bots we haven’t found. Sarah, they didn’t detect you, but they certainly detected me.”

Sarah said, “Well this big guy has been reprogrammed to be a lot nicer.”

Wayne walked up to the bot, straining his neck to look up, and said, “I am pleased to know you.”

The bot handed Wayne the touchpad and said, “I am pleased to know you, too.”

Wayne turned and said, “Man, this is creeping me out, I’m going back to the bridge.”

Wayne could hear Sarah and the bot in the background

congratulating themselves, then starting on the ship's ordnance inventory.

Wayne had always been the go-to guy. Even as he helped finish the aircraft carrier's reactor final assembly, wiring, and final testing, everyone wanted his advice. Everyone wanted to know how this worked or that worked. Being the center of attention was a little annoying, but he understood his role as a responsible leader.

As Wayne slowly walked back to the tram, he felt humbled—but who would not? Under the circumstances, he felt real accomplishment since his abduction. Wayne needed to return to weapons and at least show a sense of community by meeting with the beast bot again. He understood that humility is an honorable trait, but it could jeopardize his confidence and leading ability. The ultimate fear of any leader is to face rejection by his or her crew.

Wayne stepped into the tram, hesitating before the door closed. He said, "I need to go back to weapons and play a trick on those guys!" Wayne ran back, but stopped short of the long corridor. The evil plan was still brewing in his head, but he continued walking down the corridor. Sarah and the bot were still discussing inventory issues.

Wayne avoided detection by creeping up behind the large, open door. The chamber lights were on; Wayne saw the beast bot up on the mezzanine platform, stacking cargo containers. Sarah explained that she wanted a ready stack of ordnance next to the torpedo tubes. Also, the bot needed to fill the torpedo carriage carrousel in case the ship needed a continuous load.

The thirty-foot-high mezzanine was a jumble of cargo containers and discarded cargo lids without bottoms.

Wayne could see little misty clouds of dust as the bot moved some of the containers. Then Sarah sneezed. Wayne looked in amazement as clouds of static dust particles sparkled around her, interfering with her normal electrical patterns. Sarah kept sneezing as she drifted down to the main weapons deck. Sarah floated toward the rear of the weapons chamber to blend with some of the radioactive proximity mines. Wayne quickly ran up to one of the cargo containers recently brought down from the mezzanine. Wayne smirked at the accumulated dust. He grabbed two handfuls of the soft loam and ran up to where Sarah had cleaned herself off. Wayne threw a baseball-sized fistful of dust and the static cloud rained down on Sarah's wiggly, amoebic body.

Sarah shouted, "Sparks! What happened!" Sarah turned around and Wayne and the bot laughed hysterically. Sarah was not happy, but she understood why Wayne needed to do that. The beast bot went over to an adjacent loading elevator and pushed the button to go down. Wayne watched the small, seven-foot-by-seven-foot-square elevator lower the massive twenty-foot bot. Wayne waited for the elevator assembly to collapse, but it gently settled to the floor with the bot exiting. The weapons bot rolled over to where Wayne was standing and held out its massive lobster claw, saying, "I am glad you came back."

Wayne said, "So am I."

Sarah looked back at the both of them and said, "Well, I'm not!" Sarah again retreated to the radioactive proximity mines to neutralize the static that was still arcing across her body. Sarah eventually came back, looking like herself, saying, "I need to be on the bridge to help those bots reconfigure the computer network. Wayne, can you help the weapons bot offload the entire mezzanine onto the main deck, please?"

Wayne said to Sarah, "You know, I like you more now than five minutes ago."

Sarah never understood why relationships were so important to biological units, since the entities were part of one body. Sarah was rather repulsed by the concept of biological eggs and live young. Carbon units formed permanent bonds, only to die a mortal's life. Many of the entities regarded all biological units as contributing to their own demise because of differing opinions between one generation to the next. The perpetual cycle of confusion and inconsistency was why many alien species never reached space technology. Those that ultimately did, though, destroyed themselves anyway.

Sarah disliked these modified bots because of their protective protocols. They were too unstable and had issues with authority. Sarah blamed the biological units for reconfiguring these bots, because the bots' only crime was to follow their preprogramming. To make matters worse, biological units routinely killed other biological units because they too were overly social and envious of others. What seemed to be the ultimate hypocrisy was for any biological unit to feed upon another's carcass, as if it held the secret of life's enlightenment.

Sarah said, "Wayne, I have to admit, you got me. See you on the bridge later."

Wayne graciously nodded and said, "See you later, Sarah."

Wayne turned to the bot, saying, "Let's get busy with this stuff."

Sarah drifted off, dissolving through weapons' upper bulkhead on her way to the bridge.

After about ten hours of hard work, Wayne and the weapons bot had the entire mezzanine cleaned off. Wayne could not find a broom, but he carefully looked over the entire mezzanine in search for some interesting artifact or long-discarded object. Wayne asked the bot, "What was up here a long time ago?"

The weapons bot replied, "I was brought on board only recently. I do not know."

Wayne carefully inspected the welded joints and prepared corners. They were fitted with incredible precision; it looked to be forged as one entire section. The mezzanine's metal bulkhead had not been painted, but it still radiated a black luster as if meticulously polished. He continued looking for some discarded trinket, but then something caught his eye. He went over and picked up what looked like a coin. Wayne saw some alien scribble on one side and scribbled etching on the other. Wayne went over to the elevator and pushed the down button. He figured he would scan the coin from the touchpad. The elevator reached the main deck, and Wayne jumped off and grabbed his touchpad. He placed the coin on the touchpad's screen, first on one side, then the other. The touchpad's light flickered for a few seconds, then said, "Alien race extinct, killed off by the Venus-flytrap-faced aliens."

Wayne said, "Sarah, I found something you need to see."

Sarah said, "It is not some another trick?"

Wayne said, "Sorry, but check out what I just scanned on the touchpad."

Wayne watched the touchpad's download light flicker, and then she said, "Where did you get this?"

Wayne said, "Found it on the mezzanine."

Sarah said, "Get up here now!"

Wayne said, "Yes, madam."

Wayne said to the weapons bot, "Thanks for the help. What should I call you?"

The bot said, "You can call me Max."

Wayne said, "That's just the right name! Thanks, Max."

Wayne turned and left his newfound friend and headed off to the tram to see what news Sarah held.

After entering the tram, he pushed the bridge button. The door closed and locked into position on its way to the bridge. He knelt down reclining against the edge of the wall and began reading about engineering systems.

The ship was equipped with two huge engine-start batteries, supplying one hundred trillion volts to the two aft-center reactors. Once the batteries enabled the two reactors, the other engines ignited off from the two reactors as the aft thruster de-energized.

The entities had a difficult time teaching biological units not to jettison their old batteries as space debris. The entities documented several gravitational problems because, as alien ships discarded their old dead batteries into active nebulas, the batteries would break up in the spatial turbulence, sending the anode toward one end of the nebula and the cathode to the other end. As the nebula accumulated enough discarded batteries, a gravitational and magnetic field created enough of a difference in potential that, in some instances, the space-time distortion was enough to create a small wormhole or a vortex.

The entities tried to regulate strict dumping procedures. There were rumors of several species vanishing because of battery-related anomalies. One in particular was the galaxy next to the Venus alien's galaxy.

Wayne wondered if the coin he found was from an unknown alien race.

Wayne sat back as he cleared his mind of all the recent activity. He detected a slight decrease in the tram's velocity. Wayne picked himself off the floor. He could see the lights from the bridge's subway station getting closer.

Sarah was waiting on the loading platform as the tram glided into the station. Wayne though it must be important for Sarah to inspect the coin herself. The tram stopped, releasing the door's locking clamp. Wayne was a little annoyed that the door opened too slowly. He forced it open with a push of his hand.

Sarah said, "Let me see the coin." Wayne held the coin in his hand and Sarah gracefully waved an amoeba appendage over it, taking the coin. Wayne detected that Sarah had seen this coin before because she only inspected it for a couple seconds then put it inside herself.

Wayne said, "That coin is from that extinct alien race, isn't it?"

Sarah said, "No, this is from the high council."

Wayne said, "High council?"

Sarah said, "I will not talk about it now."

Sarah departed the bridge's subway station and went back to her bots. Wayne loved the suspense, but he figured Sarah would explain later.

Wayne slowly entered the bridge and saw Sarah talking with Cheng over the touchpad. Cheng told Sarah to depart for the agra-planet. They had a fresh computer core to swap out. Sarah acknowledged Cheng's request and signed off. Sarah turned to see Wayne watching her. Sarah said, "We need to get moving."

Wayne said, "I would rather get a new core than to trust the one we have now."

Sarah said, "I already wiped it clean."

Wayne said, "Well, then, let's try it out."

Sarah said, "Starboard thrusters on." Sarah called for the bots in engineering. "Engage primary engine, start now."

Wayne was relieved that Sarah had erased the computer's hostile programming. The computer was so preoccupied in the queen's business that it neglected many of engine room's critical inspections and diagnostic tests. Wayne remembered that Sarah sent five thousand bots to the engine room to clean up injectors, clean out reactors, replenish the coolant system, and clean the deposits from the ionic drive compressor and aft turkey feathers.

Bots came over the touchpad. "Engine start successful, aft thrusters disabled. Primary coolant system operational, engine temp normal, injection pressure normal, plasma conduit enabled, particle accelerator enabled, all go for full engine start."

Sarah said, "Go to full engine start."

Bots acknowledged over the touchpad, "Full engine start, all conditions normal, ram-air intakes full aperture, navigational inputs enabled, coolant temp normal."

Sarah inputted the coordinates for the agra-planet,

and off they went. Sarah said, "I expect a three-month journey. I want to see if I can fix this computer."

Wayne asked, "Can I help?"

Sarah replied, "Yes. Monitor these controls while I reboot the computer."

Wayne watched her dissolve through the floor and waited for the boot-up sequence to initiate. The half-installed main console was still inoperative, but Sarah only needed the engineering and navigational protocols to get underway.

The initial diagnostic program listed failure after failure, because of all the broken wiring connections in each of the ship's systems. Wayne wanted to see the queen's hologram again. He stepped down to the sunken bridge level, walked over to the projection box, and turned it on. Immediately the hologram came on and the majestic queen pranced around the bridge. The sound was muted because of the disconnected wiring, but the image spoke for itself.

Wayne immediately heard Sarah shout out, "Who turned her on?"

Wayne realized his mistake as the computer shouted, "Destroy the agra-planet! Destroy the agra-planet!" Sarah went over to turn the image off, but then she took a closer look at the separate holographic laser beams.

Sarah said, "Hey, Wayne, come and look at this."

Wayne came over, examining the bluish lasers emanating from the hologram generator. Along each laser appeared a sequence of square, saw-tooth, and sine waves all riding as a carrier wave. Sarah said, "This is a DNA imprint program, a computer BIOS, and recovery program."

Wayne asked, "What is a DNA imprint program?"

Sarah replied, "A stasis-protocol program to regenerate living tissue from a digital signal."

Wayne noticed Sarah's fearful pose as she descended to the computer core to erase it once more. Sarah returned, saying, "Bots, connect communication wiring so I can transmit a message."

A couple minutes later, the bots had both audio and visual capability, and she transmitted a message to the chancellor.

Sarah urgently shouted, "Chancellor, chancellor, are you there?"

The squirrel-frog-faced chancellor maneuvered in front of the slime-covered monitor, saying, "Thank you for taking care of those vile creatures. How can I serve you?"

Sarah asked, "How many of those ships did you salvage?"

The chancellor asked, "What in particular are you looking for?"

Sarah said, "I understand you have a computer core for us."

The chancellor said, "Yes, but right now, we are having problems with our medical labs. We took several computer cores, weapons, engines, and reactors from the damaged ships. Our technicians tried to add them to our existing computer network, but we are having problems."

Sarah asked, "Do you have a stasis laboratory in your medical facility?"

The chancellor said, "Yes, we do, several …" Before the chancellor could finish, Sarah and Wayne watched as a huge, queen Venus-flytrap-faced alien tore into the chancellor, ripping him from his shell with its mighty facial spikes. All of a sudden, the communications link went dead.

Sarah yelled out, "Jettison the computer core." The bots wired up the appropriate connections, then felt a massive jolt deep inside the ship's belly as the computer core lay adrift in open space.

Cheng came over the touchpad. "I have reports of five abducted or stolen spacecraft leaving Agra-planet Alpha's airspace."

Sarah said, "Our computer just transmitted a DNA-imprint signal to the stasis facility on the agra-planet."

Cheng replied, "Then Agra-planet Alpha has been compromised. Expect planet's destruction in five, four …"

Wayne looked through the front windscreen, and a bright flash briefly illuminated the empty void ahead.

Wayne was in charge of a severely broken-down vessel. Cheng felt forced to destroy the contaminated agra-planet to prevent further infestation. The spider ship was adrift with no computer core and no real means of light speed without computer-generated navigational inputs. The two aft thrusters were their only power source, which barely represented any measureable momentum.

Cheng came over the touchpad. "Wayne, you are in charge. Don't expect my help."

Wayne smiled and said, "I don't want your help!" Wayne continued, "Sarah, where is the nearest alien settlement?"

Sarah looked on her map and said, "A Venus-flytrap-faced planetary outpost is no more than two days' journey from here. I need to get the two primary reactors on line." Sarah started to explain the situation. "The supreme queen mother was in charge of her home world, but with the home world destroyed, each settlement containing a viable queen is presently jockeying for power to be the next queen mother. Each prospective queen is also negotiating that her settlement should be the location of the new home world. We need to be careful in approaching any Venus-flytrap-faced outpost at this point."

Sarah turned to Wayne, saying, "I am sorry about my reaction when I saw that hologram. I felt rejected. However, as it worked out, even if we installed a fresh core, the hologram would have corrupted it anyway. Never have I seen such twisted technology used by any alien race. Sorry, Wayne."

Wayne said, "Any relationship has its ups and downs, but that's what builds a relationship. Oh, by the way, we don't have a stasis lab here on this ship, do we?"

Sarah said, "No, but Cheng is probably out looking for those five rogue ships. Even if one of those renegade queens gets loose, this entire sector is in trouble."

Wayne said, "What about the hoist bot? Did it detect any of the queens?"

Sarah quickly dissolved through the bridge's aft wall to where the hoist bot was supposedly working.

Wayne sat down, looking the broken wiring bundles of fiber-optic cable. The bundles resembled those toy fibrous light fountains you find in craft shops. Wayne looked for any identifying markings on the individual glass fibers, but no markings were visible. Wayne took his touchpad and said, "Engineering, can we get initial engine start?"

The bot transmitted a synthesized voice through Wayne's touchpad. "We need to configure a couple more wiring networks from the bridge to engineering. We also need a feedback connection to the two main batteries for primary ignition enable."

Sarah arrived, saying, "The hoist bot is fine, and it is on his way up here to lift these consoles up." Sarah continued, "When the supreme queen mother lays a queen egg, the egg is automatically deposited on a deserted planet. When the queen hatches, she starts the process of creating a colony. It is imperative for the two queens to meet periodically and show allegiance to each other. Apparently, several queens were unhappy with the queen mother and conspired against her. It appeared that the queen mother discovered their plot and started maneuvering against them."

Wayne said, "When I went through the ship's airlock for the first time, I found this facial horn, which belonged to the queen of this ship."

Sarah said, "The queen mother's little band of avengers later destroyed the egg and nursery chambers. They ate the eggs and the young to make sure they were all dead."

Wayne asked, "Cannibals?"

Sarah asked, "What is a cannibal?"

Wayne replied, "Any species that eats its young or others from the same species."

Sarah was amused at Wayne's naivety and said, "All aliens lay eggs. Due to the long duration of space travel between destinations, eggs provide the best means of transport and colonization to a fresh planet. It is called 'zygote hibernation' and is a better alternative to stasis regeneration. When a ship departs on a long-distance journey, the queen begins by laying a cargo load of eggs. The queen then closes the cargo hold and returns to her palace. Along with the eggs are several subservient workers who tend to the eggs and maintain the spacecraft. The eggs are suspended in a low-temperature environment until the ship reaches its destination. By that time, most of the original crew would have already died. When the ship arrives at their destination, the computer returns the eggs to incubation temperature and they hatch soon after. The newborn feed on the carcasses of the dead crew or on the weaker ones still living. At least one of the hatched eggs is a queen, who is responsible for leading the colony forward. Never will two queens hatch."

Sarah continued, "This is what happens in a matriarchal society."

Wayne's preconceived notion of TV aliens and UFOs were totally wrong. They were really egg-laying cannibals. Wayne said, "This ship is dead in the water, but it is impressive nonetheless. What ship could match the power of this ship?"

Sarah answered, "A drone ship."

Chapter 5

The Drone Ship

The queen's ship lacked both navigational control and speed from only two aft thrusters. The bots managed to get one of the reactors and ionic-drive engines online while the other engine had injector problems. Sarah was worried about having only one engine, because regulations required three functioning engines when attempting any orbital approach vector.

The only way the ship could communicate to the settlement planet was through the nursery bot's language-protocol transmitter. Sarah requested that the bot transmit an inventory request to the planet's main computer. After a couple of minutes, the planet's computer retransmitted the list back, but there was no drone ship.

Wayne asked, "Does it have to be a drone ship?

Can we salvage a compute core, maybe retrofit another ship?"

Sarah kept the nursery bot busy by transmitting and retransmitting inventory requests without much success. Then Sarah asked the bot to transmit a list of all drone ship itineraries. The planet's computer said there was a drone ship docked on another planet. The computer transmitted the coordinates, and Sarah ended the communication link.

Sarah maneuvered the crippled ship as the one main engine slowly limped along on another two-week journey. Sarah and Wayne took shifts, but because she did not need any sleep, she kept watch most the time. She needed a radioactive bath twice a week to rejuvenate her bodily energy potential.

Sarah was at the helm when one of the bots alerted her about an incoming message. Wayne was asleep in the subway station. Sarah said, "What is it?"

The bot transmitted a wireless signal to her touchpad. "An incoming distress call."

It had only been four days into their journey. Sarah said, "Destination to distress beacon?"

Bot repied through it transmission, "Twenty hours."

Sarah transmitted an urgent wireless message to each bot's transceiver. "I need radar, give me the longest possible range." Sarah watched as the bots connected wires into each other's battery inputs and constructed a larger power supply. Each of the bots searched through bundles of fiber-optic spaghetti, finding the appropriate splices to connect to. After about two hours, a low-intensity radar display started to develop. Sarah tried turning up the gain as more bots came from engineering to help with the power configuration.

It took another half a day to maximize the radar's power output to a range of eight hours. Sarah said, "Range to distress beacon?"

The bots transmitted, "Eight hours." Sarah realized it must be a ship because of the beacon's closure rate.

Sarah said, "Bots, give me helm and weapons control."

More bots were coming onto the bridge to help, and they configured weapons and helm control. Sarah noticed a blip on the radar screen; it was about seven hours out. Sarah said, "Engines, all stop. Enable thruster control and stability. Nursery bot, I need to transmit a message."

The ship appeared to be approaching normally and did not appear distressed. Sarah assumed it was a ploy, but was not sure how to proceed. Sarah called out, "Go wake up Wayne." One of the bots exited the bridge and proceeded down the passageway to wake him up.

Wayne came in, saying, "What's wrong?"

Sarah said, "Inbound ship six hours away. It originally sent out a distress call, but it seems more like a trap."

Wayne asked, "Are we stopped?"

Sarah said, "Stopped and holding thruster position."

Wayne said, "Let it come in. Charge up the plasma cannon and wait for my firing command."

Sarah said, "The bots enlarged the firing plasma conduit from ten feet to twenty-five feet."

Wayne said, "Wow, then I can adjust my PRF for maximum damage."

Wayne and Sarah watched as the ship slowly closed

in. Then Sarah said, "That's the drone ship we were supposed to pick up."

The drone ship had an entirely different dimensional-discharge configuration. The queen's ship incorporated an internal discharge system of resonance chambers and emitter electrodes that dispersed the discharge blast. The drone ship was a little smaller, about eighty miles long, with a large vertical stab and two diagonal stabs on either side. One the end of each diagonal stabilizer was an emitter electrode, which controlled the dimensional subspace envelope and contained the resulting discharge once it dropped into normal space. The vertical stab had two emitter electrodes. The containment field encapsulated the discharge field as a weapon, which could be jettisoned off the leading edge of the vertical stabilizer.

Wayne asked, "Did it seem odd that you used a nursery bot to look for a drone ship? You know, that might seem suspicious."

The drone ship was four hours out. The smaller yet more aggressive ship looked more curious than threatening.

Sarah said, "I failed to warn you: the plasma cannon is connected to the main-engine-start batteries, because our main engines are off-line."

Wayne said, "How many bursts can we get off?"

Sarah said, "Two, maybe three." Sarah continued, "We do have the advantage. A drone ship will never attack a queen's ship."

Wayne watched as the drone ship slowly maneuvered around the queen's port flank. Sarah powered up her port thruster, turning the ship to the starboard. Sarah knew that the ship's aft fascia was constructed of heavy ballistic material, so if the drone ship fired, the ship would not suffer much damage. In addition, maneuvering the ship's aft quarter toward the drone ship also suggested a submissive posture. Sarah needed the drone ship intact if they expected to salvage it.

The two ships engaged in a deadly game of ballet as each ship stabilized, bow to bow. Sarah knew the distress call was a fake. The drone ship transmitted a message to the nursery bot: "Is the queen dead?"

Sarah nervously held her tongue as she maintained radio silence. Sarah transmitted this message, "Returned after destroying the entities." Sarah figured, with Cheng looking for the rogue Venus queens, it gave the appearance they were all destroyed.

Sarah waited for a response, but there was none.

Sarah transmitted, "I have come to claim the position of supreme queen."

Sarah waited, but again, no response.

Sarah transmitted, "We have suffered much damage. Request time for repairs."

Sarah noticed a couple of the bots flinch as the drone ship scanned the ship for damage. Sarah knew the drone ship would detect some damage with the bridge torn apart and the computer core missing.

The drone ship and the queen ship were bow to bow, each maintaining thruster position in a stagnant standoff. Sarah had witnessed firsthand how ruthless the drones were, but wondered if this was a drone piloting that ship. Sarah tried another approach and said, "Your eggs will not be harmed."

Sarah, for a split second, could see the first ignition of the drone's plasma cannon. Sarah said, "Fire!" One short blast sent the drone tumbling backward in an end-over-end drift.

Sarah knew the drones were the best pilots in the fleet, but this pilot apparently was a queen, which did not make sense. The drone ship continued to flounder out of control as Sarah took chase. Sarah transmitted to the bots, "Configure main engineering. I need more power."

The drone ship, without warning, fired its main engines like a rocket and whizzed past Sarah's windscreen, nearly causing a collision. Sarah maneuvered the ship around, only to see the drone ship adrift again. She watched as the port and starboard thrusters fired out of sequence, causing the drone ship to roll. Sarah did not want to get too close to the chaotic ship.

Wayne was watching helplessly as Sarah battled against her nemesis, another female. Sarah was getting tired and said, "Target battery access panel."

One of the bots said, "Locked on."

Sarah quietly said, "Fire." Wayne could see the access plate fly off as a shower of sparks radiated from the drone's battery posts.

The drone ship was in a dead drift. Sarah transmitted a wireless signal to the bots in engineering, "Take a shuttle and go stabilize that ship."

Wayne and Sarah watched as the small shuttle left the queen's ship. It slowly approached the drone's aft docking ring. Sarah said, "I want as many fusion reactors online as we need to power to hull's containment shields."

The bots came back. "Getting primary fusion reactors started."

Then the bot came on. "Fourteen fusion reactors on line, main power to the batteries and to shields.

Sarah said, "Brace for shielding impact. Three, two one." Sarah bolted off the bridge to inspect the containment force field as the two ships were electrically connected mid-fuselage. Wayne was impressed with Sarah's flying ability. Wayne grabbed his touchpad and quickly boarded the bridge's elevator. Maybe Sarah might attach a passageway from the drone ship.

Wayne pushed the button for the cafeteria as the elevator's door closed and locked. Wayne noticed that all the bots were leaving the bridge and headed for engineering to shuttle across to the drone ship. This was an exciting time—a brand new ship even more powerful than the queen's. Wayne did not have a weapon, but remembered there was a small armory access panel by the airlock.

The elevator finally landed on the cafeteria level, and Wayne ran toward the airlock. He waved the touchpad, unlocked the weapon's locker, and took out a small and a medium plasma gun. Looking through the airlock window, He could see the shuttle maneuvering a large, flexible passageway into position. He heard the docking ring's security bolts lock into place, but did not hear the passageway pressurize. Wayne waited until the passageway pressurized, and after five minutes, the passageway had atmosphere.

Wayne opened the airlock and proceeded down the passageway for about fifteen miles until he finally hit the drone's airlock. Wayne was tired, but not tired enough to fight. The drone's airlock was already open, and he jumped in with both weapons ready.

Wayne immediately noticed that the corridors were much narrower, maybe six feet across. He saw that the airlock's foyer emptied out into a long corridor, and then into a junction of four other corridors. The air was still, with no sounds. Wayne noticed right away that the walls were a dull black finish. There were no bouncing or rejoicing little alien infants eating or feeding their faces. Wayne quietly said to himself, "I guess all men like drab."

Wayne slowly walked toward the junction up ahead, until he heard some scurrying and violent rubbing, almost metal against metal. He was nearly at the junction when a huge Venus-flytrap-faced queen tried to squeeze herself down the narrow corridors, waving her face in anger. Wayne fired and repeatedly fired until the entire corridor junction was a wash of bluish yellow guts. He noticed two parallel corridors, which representing an ambush hazard. He saw another smaller warrior alien running down the parallel corridor, and Wayne fired a couple of plasma shots. One alien had a small, greenish yellow orb in its claw—a plasma grenade. Wayne went over and grabbed the baseball-sized grenade while more creatures advanced down the corridor.

Alien corpses were everywhere. The stench and graphic carnage was overpowering. Wayne took out the plasma grenade, pushed the plunger tab, and threw it far as he could. The aliens continued to advance until the grenade suddenly exploded. The backpressure from all the dead carcasses sent them flying in his direction, immediately propelling Wayne backward down the corridor as alien guts rained over him.

About that time, Sarah appeared near the airlock's

foyer as alien guts even reached the airlock itself. She had a difficult time finding Wayne among all the bluish green innards and scattered keratin debris.

Sarah spoke from her touchpad. "Hey, where's your touchpad?"

Wayne said, "I don't even want to hear it!"

Sarah laughed and said, "You need to see this."

Wayne and Sarah walked past the ooze and alien guts to a smaller, yet similar-looking subway station. Wayne noticed that the tram was a lot smaller. Sarah opened the tram's door and followed Wayne inside. She pushed the button for the bridge, and off they went.

Wayne sat down as Sarah went over all the details.

There were five major parts to the drone ship: engineering, weapons, the dimensional complex, accelerator, and the bridge. The bots recovered two additional shuttles aboard the drone ship. One was a passenger shuttle, and the other was an open-bay shuttle for carrying larger containers. Sarah instructed the bots to transfer weapons, fission material, all hydrogen-fusion supplies, all necessary parts, and tools from the queen ship to the drone ship by way of the aft cargo bay. The aft cargo bay was a large shuttle hanger and storage area. The weapons bot began the orderly process of transferring ordnance through the aft shuttle bay to the weapons armory.

The drone ship had a dimensional gradient potential of five steps instead of the queen's three. The diameter of the weapon's plasma cannon conduit was already twenty-five feet. The ship has a long-range radar frequency of fifty megahertz with a multiple fire-control plasma-turret configuration operating at ninety-five gigahertz.

The long-range radar was an asynchronous-modulated pulse radar with pulse-compression capability. The radar's modulator encrypted the transmitter pulse along with the receiver's modulated crystals to ensure echo verification. Due to the power needed to transmit up to ten-hours radar range, the radar incorporated a large power supply, a modulator, and a transmitter connected to a ten-thousand-waveguide network, all tuned to fifty megahertz. The diplexer allowed both transmit and receive on the same planar array antenna, which had a diameter of two miles.

Sarah gave Wayne a new touchpad with all the necessary information.

Wayne said, "Thank you. I guess the other touchpad got damaged in the attack."

Sarah said, "Study this. This ship is a dangerous ship, even if used properly."

Sarah left the tram to check in with the bots in the aft shuttle bay. The tram still had about two hours to go. He sat back and studied his touchpad.

The stab configuration was only on the drone ships. The mid-fuselage lateral box beam extended to a set of diagonal stabilizers that curved at an angle of thirty degrees. On the end of each diagonal stab was a one-mile diameter circular-emitter electrode. The vertical stab extended a little higher than the other two diagonal stabs. The vertical stabilizer supported two emitter electrodes, each pointing to the opposite diagonal stab. These emitter electrodes held the dimensional gradient envelope while in subspace.

The vertical stab's heavily reinforced leading edge was constructed of a uranium-ceramic coating. Upon returning to normal space, the kinetic energy from the dimensional accelerator and amplifier vented the residual discharge energy to the power conduits. The shield-containment generator magnetically encapsulated the static discharge between the networks of emitter electrodes, then jettisoned the discharge down the vertical stab's leading edge. The discharge blast was capable of destroying whole planets, or in the very least, burning off the planet's atmosphere.

Wayne put down the touchpad and thought about his wife and kids. Cheng alluded to the notion that there was no all-encompassing universal constant in the universe. Gravity, energy, the magnetism, and mass itself was all in constant flux. Even the concept of time had no meaning. Time slows down; time speeds up; and time even stands still. Cheng explained that the principles of time only apply to normal space. In dimensional subspace, dark energy negates time because of the absence of matter. Time is neither energy nor matter, but measured by particles traveling at the speed of light. If light does not exist in subspace, then time as we know it does not exist.

Wayne detected a slight deceleration in the tram's velocity. He slowly got up to his feet and watched the glooming darkness fade into light as the subway station drew ever closer. The interior lighting seemed brighter in the drone ship than in the queen's ship. Wayne noticed the added weapons lockers scattered around the drone ship, which made him a bit more comfortable.

Wayne waited for the tram to stop. The drone's stations were not as elaborate as the queen's and were much smaller. The tram's door-locking mechanism retracted, allowing the door to open. Wayne stepped out and proceeded down the short corridor to the bridge. Wayne saw that this arrangement was infinitely more convenient than the queen's bridge. The only problem was that the bridge did not have an elevator. Wayne preferred the drone's four viewing windscreens, which had a better view of peripheral angles left and right. Wayne could see Sarah inspecting the plasma damage from when she fired on the drone ship. The bridge seemed empty compared to the queen ship. There was one main console that controlled navigation, communication, radar, engineering, and dimensional systems, and there was a computer-interface terminal.

He made his way back to the subway station for a visit to weapons and engineering. Wayne noticed on his touchpad that Max added a revised weapons inventory and logged it into the main computer. There were one million proximity mines and two million plunger torpedoes. Then he saw something that was not on the queen's weapons manifest: one hundred-plutonium-proximity drones.

Wayne scanned through the weapons database, but could not find any mention of the plutonium proximity drones. He looked through the computer's database and helm's control choices, but there was nothing about the drones. Finally he found it in the radar section. It said, "Jettison drones at ten radar-range hours. Stop all engines. Push the commit-to-launch-sequence on the radar section of the main console. The missile's propulsion system has a maximum distance of ten radar-range hours. Target and fire a one-step dimensional gradient discharge blast at the drone. The blast has a range of five hours, so once the ship fires off the discharge, the minimum safe distance to any PPD explosion is five radar-range hours.

Wayne looked at Sarah's schedule on the touchpad. She identified one hundred bots to survey the condition of the vertical stab's leading edge. All repairs needed documentation and identification of any parts, the correct metals, and the time allotted to complete the task. Wayne submitted a request to survey each emitter electrode and associate mounting bracket assemblies along each ionic-drive combustion chamber, injector, and turkey feather.

Wayne saw that the offload/on-load was still in progress from the queen's ship to the drone's ship. The dimensional complex required cleaning. The ship's magnetic-conduit system needed degaussed and a new bot's repair shop was incorporated off the aft cargo shuttle bay.

Wayne noticed that the tram was slowing down. He hated the fact that he had to sit down on the tram's floor. Maybe the bots could build him some seats.

The tram was entering the weapons station, with Max standing there at the loading platform. Wayne slowly got up and saw Max waiting for him. The door finally opened and Wayne greeted Max by saying, "Good to see you."

Max transmitted his deep, synthesized voice to Wayne's touchpad. "I am happy, too. Did you get my inventory list?"

Wayne said, "Yes, I did. Any good stuff in the drone's weapons armory?"

Max said, "No, not really."

Wayne said, "I see the other bots are helping out with the transfer. Have any storage problems?"

Max said, "No, but there is a small problem."

Wayne asked, "What's wrong?"

Max said, "I am having difficulty bringing the weapons stores from the aft cargo hold up here to weapons. I need an access tunnel like on the queen's ship, or a separate tram line."

Wayne said, "I like the separate tram line. Hold on, let me talk to Sarah." Wayne called Sarah, saying, "Can the bots put in a separate weapons tram or trolley system?"

Sarah said, "You must be talking to Max."

Wayne said, "Yes, he is here with me."

Sarah yelled loud enough for Max could hear. "Max, I already have fifty bots on that assignment. They are disassembling the queen's tram and thirty miles of track to put in a separate tram line between weapons and the aft cargo hold. Give us about five days to finish it. Okay?"

Max said, "Thanks Sarah!"

Wayne said, "Max, you amaze me every time I see you. Who made you?"

Max did not want to answer right away. "I was brought here by the supreme queen. Where the queen found me, I can't remember."

Wayne said, "Then someone erased your memory files."

Max said, "This loading transfer has helped me remember something. I remember being in a spaceship that was under attack. I was not on the queen's ship or even with the same species. Those vile creatures were mean to me. I do remember a name: Nyerle."

Wayne took his touchpad and entered the name Nyerle.

The touchpad's download light blinked on and off a couple of times, then the drone's main computer linked up with the touchpad. Wayne allowed the drone's computer to have access to the database. Soon the name came up with the following explanation: "Nyerle was the name of a ship under contract to destroy an unknown species that infested this galaxy. The contract originated from the high council of ambassadors. The high council of ambassadors awarded the contract to the most advanced of all the alien races, the Skurlords. The Skurlords created a fleet of biological robots as conscripts. Due to the non-technical willpower of the Insecoids, the biological bots were defeated. The Skurlords tried to surrender, but their entire galaxy was destroyed."

Wayne figured that Insecoids were the Venus-flytrap-faced aliens. He also remembered how Sarah got upset when the topic of the high council came up. It sounded if the entities were playing sides, and their side lost. Wayne wondered who the ambassadors were.

Wayne looked up at Max and said, "You come from a powerful race of warrior robots."

Max said, "I am a happy warrior."

Wayne laughed and said, "I like happy warriors."

Wayne stepped back into the tram, waving bye to Max. The door closed, and Wayne was off to visit engineering.

Wayne leaned up against the tram's wall and wondered how he should handle this high council thing. He probably should not mention it at all. At least Max would get a new weapons tram. It would make weapons transport a lot easier if there were a conveyor system.

Wayne had never seen the queen's engineering complex, and now he was headed to see the drone's configuration.

Wayne took out his touchpad and entered Sarah's to-do list She added her own inspection of the vertical stab. "Due to the tremendous stress between the stab configuration, I found multiple cracks, scars and delaminations along the vertical stab's leading edge. Also found cracks on the stab's emitter-electrode mounting assembly and degraded power cables from the emitters to the each of the four shield generators. It all has to be replaced or reinforced." She put two hundred bots on the job.

Wayne contemplated the high council situation. Political scenarios as they were, the entities represented a superior race—an indestructible force in all dimensional space. What did it mean to police dimensional space? The lure of dimensional sabotage was within the realm of possibility, both technologically and strategically. Dimensional sabotage could influence critical timelines, infringe on solar system or galactic stabilization, and invite entity involvement. Why would any species attack other dimensions as if they were unhappy with their own? The entities possessed the power, but policing the various dimensions was a bothersome responsibility and liability. But it was their jurisdictional duty. One could assume a discrepancy existed between the possession of power and greed and the notion of responsibility or jurisdictional duty to manage that power. The obligations of the powerful are always to themselves or their jurisdictional privilege rather than to the needs of their citizenry. Assuming that any discretionary judgment is dependent on stewardship, responsibility, and jurisdictional duties, means that such actions were divinely inspired.

Humans have always dismissed God and substituted

themselves in that role. However, if humanity represents an endless cycle of bad judgment, greed-filled economic disasters, power-hungry conflicts, and acts of revenge, than assuming that man was a worthy substitute to replace God is the ultimate hypocrisy.

Wayne detected a slight deceleration. Wayne stood up, and saw a large, illuminated opening up ahead. Wayne realized that the rails terminated inside the engineering complex. Once the tram cleared the tunnel and entered into the complex itself, the view was colossal.

The massive engineering complex resembled an oil refinery. What looked like fifteen huge, circular oil-storage tanks were actually fifteen fusion reactors lined up in a straight line just beyond the tram's termination buffers.

The tram stopped and the door's security latch disengaged. The door opened up, and instantly the sound of thousands of servos, motors, and welding torches reminded him of when he and Roy had spent years building that aircraft carrier. The entire engineering complex was some fifteen miles across from port to starboard and fifteen miles from aft fantail to the forward most bulkheads, complete with an overlooking mezzanine.

The most complicated structures in engineering were the ionic engine airlocks and associated mounting brackets. Each ionic engine had its own access tube to facilitate installation and removal. Within this access tube were three airlock collars and a removable pressure plate on top with a permanent one on the bottom. Whenever an engine needed replacement, the entire engineering complex had to be depressurized back to empty space.

Every engine rested in a supporting cradle that secured the engine to the ship's superstructure. Within the cradle assembly were seven massive clamping collars, which supported the five-mile-long ionic engine. The upper collars were detached from the pressure plate, which acted as a gantry I-beam hoist crane to facilitate the engine's removal.

Due to the enormous amount of atmosphere needed to pressurize engineering, the drone ship normally remained depressurized. The extreme, frigid temperatures helped cool many of the coolant and fusion reactors, but added unneeded stress to the bots that worked there. Sarah asked to the bots to pressurize engineering while the maintenance continued.

Wayne looked back at the tram's tunnel access and could see the tunnel's open airlock. The airlock was normally secured when engineering was depressurized.

Wayne could see some of the bots carrying in the queen's tram and segments of connecting track. The bots had already constructed another airlock and were now drilling through unnecessary bulkheads to lay the track.

Wayne watched a passenger golf-cart bot pull up beside him. Wayne boarded the small bot, saying, "Aft cargo holds, please." The golf-cart bot quickly turned around, nearly colliding with some other bots, and off it went to the cargo hold.

Wayne watched as the bots hoisted each coolant line for cleaning and final inspection. Each coolant tube was about the diameter of a football field.

Wayne stood in awe as several bots hoisted metallic injector hoses from the engine's nacelle and combustion-chamber assembly for cleaning and inspection. Each injector had to be cleaned and inspected from the outside and inside while attached to the nacelle, because each injector had its own airlock collar.

The floor had the same smooth, black finish. Special cleaning bots followed a grid network of lanes and pathways as they dodged other working bots.

Wayne had felt enormous pride when he worked on the aircraft carrier. However, these diligent little bots far exceeded what any man could do, even on a good day. The whole concept of mechanized slavery was a human term built upon the assumption that machines were partially human, too. However, assuming these bots deserved respect was like hugging a tree and expecting the tree to hug back. With that perception, a shoe might be a functional entity. Whether it was a broken-down bot, a shoe, or a burnt tree after a forest fire, each did not deserve a second look.

The golf-cart bot finally arrived at the cargo hold. The cart bot said, "Cannot go any further." Wayne could see the ballistic bulkhead that had been specially designed as an airlock to facilitate transport of cargo from ship to ship. Wayne could see several bots on the open bay shuttle carrying large cargo containers and ferrying them into the cargo bay, as the bots unloaded container after container. Wayne caught sight of the egg hoist bot lifting up containers from the open bay shuttle and stacking them according to Sarah's instructions. The whole operation was amazing.

Sarah called on the touchpad, "Wayne, I see you are in engineering, I need you on the bridge." Wayne asked the bot, "Please return to the tram." The bot turned around and accelerated back to the tram.

It was all that Wayne could do to hold back tears. The day that Roy introduced his sister, the bar scene and the great time they had together. The days when Roy was training him to weld and the nights, he could barely move because his muscles ached. Wayne remembered his last day in the Navy; the Admiral awarded him with award after award for his dedicated accomplishments toward the ship's commissioning. A kid from rural Dakota who flew toy airplanes, picked up artifacts, soldered radio transmitters and fixed ILS systems, was now in command of an incredible warship in the vacuum of space.

Wayne understood the nature of power. Yet the abuse of that power was why many alien species destroyed themselves to gain that power. Imagine hiring a contractor to build a house. Instead of using diagrams or schematics, the homeowner only supplied an idea. An idea is worthless until it is accurately understood. Unfortunately, it is during this time that an idea is the most vulnerable to corruption, rendering the house useless to the homeowner. Wayne tried to figure out which came first: the idea, the entities, or the aliens. God's idea of a peaceful coexistence suddenly turned sour at the Tower of Babel. It is wrong to assume that man's lust for power and greed was an offense to be blamed on God. God spared the lives of these immoral builders so that the idea eluded them only because of language. Alliances are much like the Tower of Babel, but instead of God destroying the alliance, it was man's contempt for each other that destroyed the alliances. In that respect, were the entities helping or hurting the overall alien fabric by intervening? Wayne said to himself, "Even associating yourself with the entities is an open invitation to trouble." Even assuming that subspace required added security invites those who wish to violate that subspace. Archeology does not dig up bones, but excavates lessons forgotten. Destroying whole planets is an open invitation to lessons lost.

Wayne continued to strategize this evolving political chess game as the tram slowly approached the bridge's subway station.

Wayne exited the tram and met Sarah at the subway station. She said, "The drone's main batteries were destroyed in the battle, and the only way to swap out batteries of that size is in a space port.

Wayne laughed and said, "Are there any cables in the queen's battery-access bay?"

Sarah asked, "Cables?"

Wayne said, "If we had a long set of cables, we can connect the queen's batteries to the drone's batteries via a long cable. We could power up a couple of the fusion reactors to recharge the drone's depleted batteries."

Sarah said, "Cables, I saw some power cables." She bolted back toward engineering.

Wayne said to himself, "I've jumped many a car in my day; never figured on jumping spaceships."

Sarah ordered a thousand bots to meet her at the upper stage elevator. She asked the hoist bot to change jobs from the cargo bay and escort one thousand bots from the upper-stage elevator to the outer-hull-access platform. The mission was to connect some cables from the queen's main power batteries to the drone's dead batteries.

Sarah already had some bots working on the vertical stab's leading edge, where several panels, along with the stab's substructure, had to be replaced or reinforced.

Most of the spare parts came from the queen's ship, like the uranium-ceramic outer-coating material.

Sarah was writing down some notes on the stab's preliminary inspection when the hoist bot opened the upper-state elevator's access plate. One by one, the bots assembled by the battery-access bay and the missing access cover, which had been shot off. Another group of bots assisted in the fabrication of another battery-access plate.

Sarah floated to the drone's port angle, where the fuselage met the wing assembly. A congregation of bots from the queen's ship connected the first battery cable and extended it out. On the drone side some ten miles away, the bots were installing the other battery cable on the fifty-foot battery-cable posts. Both cables extended out, but did not reach. They needed another cable to make the connection.

Sarah and the thousand bots on the drone side looked over the edge at the two cables draped over the side. The containment shield that was holding the two spacecraft together was an envelope of sparks—a blanket of glowing translucence. Sarah did not know if the bots could cross the force field without suffering electrocution, so she chose the oldest, most damaged bot and said, "Cross to the other side."

The bot faithfully stepped out and headed for the ledge. Sarah and the other bots looked on in surprise when the bot suddenly vaporized in a mist of fire and flame. Sarah looked down as the other 999 bots looked at Sarah. Almost in unison, 999 bots moved one motorized track backward. Sarah needed another cable to connect to the two other cables. She floated over to the queen's ship and looked inside the battery cavity. There was another cable.

The bots finally dragged out the spare cable and connected it up. Sarah asked two bots to go down to weapons and ask for a rocket engine. The two bots took off.

After about an hour, the bots returned with a twenty-foot rocket motor. Sarah wondered if this was a good idea. The rocket motor might go wildly out of control, and they would lose both battery cables. Sarah put the rocket motor on the hull, but did not connect the cable. She wanted to know what the rocket would do. She waved her amoeba-electrified body over the fuse, and off it shot. The rocket took off in a huge cloud of smoke, blinding all the bots. Sarah lost sight of the rocket, then saw the bots on the drone ship angrily yelling out among the thick smoke. Sarah had to laugh. She needed to try something else.

Sarah called down to Wayne on the touchpad. "I have a problem. I have all three cables, but I need a way to carry the cable across the divide between the two ships, but not let it touch the electric shielding holding the two ships together."

He said, "You can use a compressed air rocket. Just adjust the amount of compressed air. Or you can use one of those floating passageways or even have a shuttle do it."

Sarah said, "A shuttle!" Sarah ended her transmission without offering her thanks. She propelled herself toward the shuttle bay as an empty shuttle was leaving the drone ship. She called for the bot piloting to help her out. The shuttle moved into position, hoisting the cable from the queen's ship to the awaiting cable on the other side. Slowly the shuttle maneuvered across the massive canyon between the two ships, and the bots reached for the extended cable. Finally, the cable bridged between the two ships and Sarah asked to fire up the two hydrogen reactors.

She called out to Wayne, "Wayne, go to the main console and push the primary reactor-enable button."

Wayne pushed the button and felt the drone ship lurch forward.

Sarah called out, "Wayne, push the button to enable the drift thrusters, because the containment field is causing the two ships to become unstable."

Wayne pushed the button to restart the aft thruster-stabilization system and the ship returned to a level drift.

Sarah said, "We have all the supplies we need from the queen ship." The shuttle began picking up all the bots off the queen's ship and the stragglers from the aft shuttle bay. Sarah continued, "Apply port thrust, then enable the two primary ionic engines to clear the queen's ship. Prepare for shield-containment collapse between the two ships."

Wayne adjusted the power to the port thrusters as he enabled main ionic drive from the two operational hydrogen-fusion reactors. The drone ship lurched forward as the engine's thrust slowly overcame the shield strength keeping the two ships together. Finally the shield collapsed into a fiery aurora of sparks and bolts of static electricity. The drone ship slowly maneuvered away, and the troublesome queen's ship drifted into the dark void.

Sarah completed her final inspection on the vertical

stab's leading edge and on the access cover to the battery bay. Sarah forgot to check the power cables as the ships pulled away from each other. She looked over the edge, and there were two cables dangling over the drone's angle. She had the bots pull them back up and then store them in the battery bay. The bots closed and secured the new battery-access panel and boarded the upper-stage elevator back to engineering.

Sarah looked back at the queen's ship, never expecting that it would come down to this. The dead carcass of a ship was drifting wildly, but Sarah took great pride in what they had achieved. A drone ship had the power of ten queen ships, and off they went to one of the remaining agricultural planet, Agra-planet Beta.

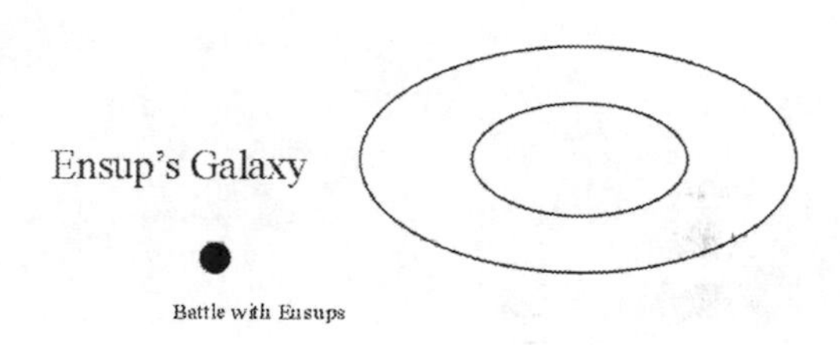

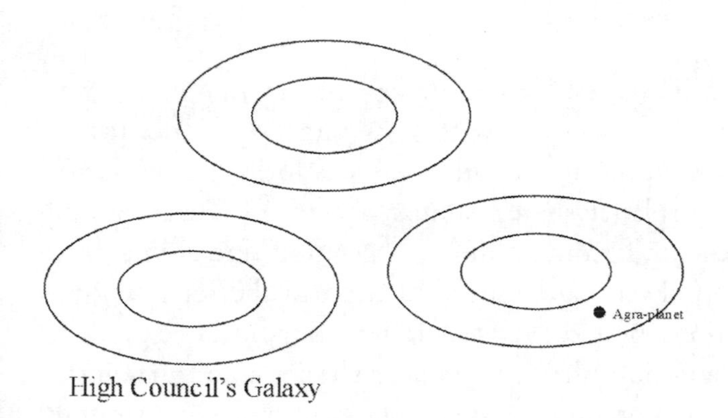

Ambassadors of the High Council

Chapter 6

The High Council

The closest agricultural planet in this sector was Agra-planet Beta, but with Agra-planet Alpha destroyed, pleas went out to the other galaxies for help. Each agricultural planet shared similar characteristics, according to geology, farming, mining, vegetation, and animal husbandry. Every agricultural planet had the following restrictions: no radioactive mining, no radioactive processing, and no utilizing the planet's inner core to reconstitute spent uranium. Due to merchant traffic and shuttles in and out of atmospheric airspace, orbiting satellites presented a collision hazard and were therefore prohibited.

A franchise of sales merchants assigned to each agra-planet acted as alien account managers. Each account manager created a particular produce profile according to the needs of that alien species. All shipments were screened for quality, security, distribution, and available inventory. Since there were only three agra-planets left, a small percentage of errors did create problems with immediate refunds. Four neighboring galaxies were able to augment inventory requests to avoid problematic shortages, but overall, it created a good business climate.

Sarah received a message, "Cheng captured three of the five rogue queen ships. Also, a detachment of entities are being sent to Agra-planet Beta as a security detail."

Wayne was excited about the port visit. He received a copy of the food-provisions manifest, which was due to arrive tomorrow. The Agra-planet Beta's chancellor ordered steaks, hamburger, fruits, coffee, vegetables, and some alcoholic beverages, along with several cargo containers of DNA-digitized food microprocessors and molecular chemical base material used in food replicators. Because of the eliminated threat from the Venus aliens, the Agra-planet's chancellor presented the provisional shipment as a gift.

The surrounding galaxies were celebrating a major victory against oppression. The chancellor warned of small ships, curiosity-seekers, and joy-riders around the planet's orbital perimeter. The chancellor also wanted a personal tour aboard the drone ship, along with his entourage. Wayne agreed in a gracious act of diplomacy and allegiance to the galaxy's rebirth of freedom and prosperity.

The drone ship had been performing flawlessly. The bots finished Max's weapons tram, shuttling explosives back and forth between weapons and the aft cargo bay. The bots finished all the engineering repairs and the cleaning and re-installations of the coolant lines and the injector tubing. Wayne requested new engine-start batteries, which were in stock.

The busy business and commercial traffic prevented the drone ship from orbiting, but it allowed access to the spaceport in an orbit further out. Wayne could see from the bridge's windscreen thousands of smaller private and charter tourist craft encircling the drone ship. Wayne watched as planetary magistrate patrol ships tried to keep the peace and prevent any unnecessary collisions.

Wayne had four days of rest and relaxation as he familiarized himself with the ship and took time to enjoy some great cooking and coffee.

Sarah was concerned with Wayne's choice in berthing. He was still sleeping in the corridor between the subway station and the bridge. Wayne and Sarah examined the bridge's structural schematic and found a large chamber on the port side of the bridge's main complex. Sarah had thirty welding and fabricating bots cut out an access corridor off the main bridge to Wayne's new apartment. The bots fabricated two large food-storage freezers, an infrared oven/broiler, some drawer space, and a large bed frame. Wayne asked if the agra-planet had any insulated bedding material or if they knew what mattresses were.

Sarah received word that the chancellor's shuttle was en route. Sarah decided to do the honors. She floated down to the aft shuttle bay and waited for the chancellor's shuttle. She was watching the shuttle maneuvering on its final approach sequence when a message came from the chancellor's shuttle: "Request to come aboard."

Sarah transmitted in a synthesized voice, "Permission granted." Sarah continued, "Chancellor, I need to discuss a matter with you in private."

Sarah maintained her position floating off to the side of the airlock. She felt a little nervous about compromising sensitive information. Sarah understood the chancellor's concerns, but the greater need was for another agra-planet. Sarah was concerned about an intercepted message regarding another rogue alien species wanting to move into the power vacuum left by the Venus aliens. The message did not give any specifics, but was cause for alarm.

The shuttle docked and all the locking clamps engaged into position. Both airlocks pressurized, as well as the passageway. Sarah floated off to the side, and Wayne finally showed up for the formal occasion. Sarah yelled, "Where have you been?"

Wayne laughed. "Having some coffee."

The airlock from both sides opened and the chancellor and his entourage exited the shuttle. Wayne did not know what to expect. Wayne opened the airlock and caught a brief aroma of fresh atmospheric air. Wayne held his breath, wondering what would emerge from the alien shuttle. Wayne caught sight of a horseshoe crab with a nasty-looking scorpion tail at its rear. His legs were crab-like, with two hand claws and two bulging eyes like a horseshoe crab. One of the chancellor's emissaries, another horseshoe crab, but without the scorpion tail, was holding a communication device to aid in translation. The other emissary accompanying the chancellor was a walking, bluish mud-brown, wide-mouth catfish waddling uncomfortably from side to side.

Wayne introduced himself to the chancellor and his two emissaries. Sarah floated off to the side, away from view. Wayne escorted the guests to an awaiting cart bot as

Sarah pulled the chancellor off to the side. The chancellor was somewhat disturbed to see an entity so close to the political turmoil.

Sarah spoke over her touchpad, "My supervisor is searching for another agra-planet. We will be leaving this galaxy in thirty-six hours on a separate mission. I am concerned about the recent power vacuum left by the Venus aliens. I humbly request the following …"

The chancellor interrupted Sarah by holding up a communication crystal attached to a small wand, saying, "I want this to be a pleasure trip, not a political one. What is your request?"

Sarah replied over the touchpad, "Request all commercial and industrial shipping to be accompanied by an entity in and out of Agra-planet Beta's airspace."

The chancellor replied, "I understand your need for security and our obvious vulnerable situation. Yes, the ambassadors can stay, but they must establish a perimeter-style checkpoint. There must not be any interference or give any knowledge that the ships are being watched."

Sarah said, "I accept the terms. I will strive to earn your trust." Sarah quickly dissolved into the bulkhead on her way back to the bridge. One of the cart bots went by and picked up the chancellor to start the tour.

Wayne felt relaxed after his first cup of coffee and was ready for the multitude of questions from the chancellor and his entourage. Wayne was happy to see the tram completely refurbished with seating, tables, and a small, portable bed.

The chancellor felt overwhelmed by it all. Wayne could see that gleam in his eye—the unmistakable gleam of power. Wayne heard that a neighboring galaxy promised additional supplies to the three remaining agra-planets. What the chancellor needed was not a big, fancy drone ship, but a multi-galactic alliance to maintain the balance of power against any new enemies. The agra-planets were not known for their defenses, their military might, or even their food. The agra-planets represented what all helpless planets offered: nothing but an expendable bargaining chip for the powerful elite.

Human history was littered with fraudulent promises, bad advice, and pizzeria shootouts, where the rich and powerful seemed indignant even toward their own empire. The agra-planets were forced to ignore black-market extortion, drive-by shootings and ambushes against potential upstarts. Wayne felt great pride that the chancellor, despite the odds, accepted this job.

Wayne took the tour group everywhere. The chancellor was most impressed with the weapons bot, Max. Max was waiting at the weapons loading platform when the tram stopped to make a visit. Max seemed to understand the chancellor's position, since they both managed a valuable inventory and were responsible for the safety of everyone onboard. Wayne explained that Max served as a Skurlord mechanical warrior, of the galactic society that was destroyed by the Venus aliens. The chancellor had heard of the Skurlords and their powerful army of robots, but with Max there, all the stories became even more real.

Max and the chancellor departed deep friends. The chancellor was amazed that biologically imprinted robots were even capable of such emotion or loyalty.

Wayne finally wrapped up the tour as the chancellor and his guests approached the drone's airlock. The chancellor understood the need for militarization, but he also understood the value of the entity's support. Wayne thanked the chancellor and watched them board their shuttle. He closed the drone's airlock and heard the shuttle releasing its docking-ring clamps. Wayne waved goodbye with a new appreciation for what aliens could accomplish together.

The port visit was a success, but now it was time to leave. Wayne stood behind the bridge's command console as Sarah patrolled the outer hull for any careless tourists. Wayne engaged primary ignition, gently propelling the drone ship away from the agra-planet's temporary orbit. Wayne sent a communiqué thanking the chancellor for the food, the great friendship, and wishing prosperity to come. The chancellor returned with a message of a safe journey and a safe return.

Sarah gently descended onto the bridge and heard the chancellor's remarks. Sarah said, "Wayne, I just received a message from Cheng. Two groups of entities tried to find another suitable agra-planet but were unsuccessful."

Wayne figured as much. With 197 planets destroyed, the chances of finding another one were probably slim to none. Sarah asked Wayne, "Should we tell the chancellor?"

Wayne responded, "Nah, the chancellor will find out on his own. He is quite capable."

Sarah commanded the computer, "Plot a course."

As she entered the coordinates through her touchpad, Wayne brought it up on the navigational display and said, "Hey, this is in deep space in between galaxies."

Sarah said, "Yes, it is. There is a rule between entities:

when leaving one galaxy to enter another, you must discuss the terms of rendezvous first."

Wayne asked, "Rendezvous?"

Sarah said, "a family reunion of sorts. Consider it mandatory."

Wayne laughed and acknowledged that he was not to ask any more questions. Wayne commanded, "Computer, designate coordinates. Estimated time of arrival at light speed?"

The computer came back in a clean synthesized voice, "Estimated time: 54,794.5 years."

Wayne said, "Computer, how about in dimensional subspace?"

The computer said, "Estimated time: twenty days."

Wayne said, "Computer, plot course to designated target, full engine start. Go to light speed, dimensional drive. Route all discharge to the ionic drive engines. Initiate."

Wayne watched as the computer accelerated the drone ship to light speed. Then the particle accelerator and the uranium plasma conduits engaged, as the dimensional amplifier built two massive charges between the diagonal stabs and the vertical stab. The bots installed another emitter electrode above the bow's windscreen, and the dimensional drive's charge built up across the top of the ship. The whole ship dissolved into subspace as the highly charged discharge injected through the nacelle's emitter electrodes in each ionic engine, shooting out a continuous bolt of lightning through the engine's combustion chamber. All ram-air-intake doors were open to maximum aperture as they left the Venus and

Cheng's galaxy behind. The next galaxy that lay ahead might supply information as to the Grays' home world.

Wayne spent the next twenty days eating and studying the drone ship's strengths and weaknesses. Sarah was in the aft cargo hold, sorting through all the containers while scheduling new work projects. The bots completed Wayne's apartment over the port visit installing the freezers packed with frozen steaks and vegetable matter as well as a metallic pot for making coffee. The agra-planet had some bedding and blankets, but no mattresses. As a substitute, some of the local birds donated their feathers to make a thick mattress-like mat.

Sarah stood in front of the command console as the drone ship neared the designated coordinates. She wanted to drop out of subspace close enough without overshooting the target.

This was Sarah's first rendezvous, and she had no idea what to expect.

Sarah spoke over the computer's digital processor, which was cleaner than the touchpad's processor. "Computer, disengage dimensional drive; vent remaining discharge. All stop. Initiate."

The computer took all the associated dimensional systems off-line and let the remaining discharge emit itself through the vertical stab's emitter electrodes. The engines disengaged as well as thirteen hydrogen fusion reactors, leaving two primary reactors online for ship's internal power.

Sarah asked, "Computer, estimated time to designated coordinates?"

The computer replied, "Estimated time: six days."

Sarah said, "Computer, engage all engines. Go to light speed. Initiate."

Wayne was still enjoying the chancellor's great food. He walked into the bridge and let go of a deep-belly belch that echoed throughout the entire bridge complex.

Wayne asked, "Sarah, are we close?"

Sarah replied, "Six days by light speed."

Wayne said, "Wow, 54,794.5 years dropped to twenty-six days!"

Sarah received a message from the ambassadors. They asked for the ship to stop.

Wayne said, "Computer, all stop. Initiate."

Sarah turned toward Wayne with great anticipation, then dissolved through the bridge's port bulkhead. Wayne went over to the large windscreen and rested his arm on the reinforced window ledge, wondering what the great amoebic congregation was discussing.

Sarah could see the gathering up ahead. Suddenly she found herself surrounded by other female entities jumping and dancing in the massive void. Sarah could not believe it; she was in the middle of chaotic, joyful jubilation. Sarah found herself barraged with questions about the other galaxy, and about how it felt to be one of the more powerful governing ambassadors because of her new assignment. Sarah, whether she knew it or not, was very close to her political trial by fire.

Many of the entity's secrets were just that, secrets. The entities never discussed the concept of procreation or gender issues. The entity's knowledge of procreation involves widespread destruction, and that destruction creates life. Entities are not born, but spawned from energy itself. In the event of a naturally occurring nova or supernova, billions of subatomic particles immediately congeal, creating a newborn entity. The initial subatomic charge determines gender. Men are a negative charge; the females a positive charge.

All entities are of one body, because of the attraction between negative and positive charges. However, when the men or the women segregate, the difference of polarity creates a massive gravitational field. When the entities detect an alien's magnetic or gravitational anomaly, whether accidental or militarized, it is immediately destroyed. The entities divide themselves up, males on one side, females on the other, to counteract the anomaly's forces. The resulting cancellation of charges restores the natural equilibrium.

Sarah communicated to her friends via a carrier wave riding on microwave radiation, "I need to get this ship to the nearest agra-planet!"

Wayne was still looking through the windscreen at the perpetual darkness, with only scattered galactic swirls as a backdrop. He went back to the command console and brought up the radar. Even the radar did not detect the entities.

Wayne heard a bot roll onto the bridge quite unexpectedly. The bot spoke through Wayne's touchpad. "I don't like the name bot."

Thinking this was a joke, Wayne said, "What?"

The bot repeated via the touchpad, "I don't like the name bot."

Wayne sarcastically said, "Okay, I'll play your silly little game. What name do you want?"

The bot said, "We want a name like Max."

Wayne called down to Max over his touchpad, "Hey,

Max, how many bots have complained about their names?"

Max replied, "I lost count."

Wayne said, "Well, quit it. From now on, you name all bots, not me!"

Max said, "The bots want a nameplate attached to their chassis."

Wayne said, "Have the bots go down in the welding shop, stencil out name plates, and rivet them on."

The bot said to Wayne, "I want a name."

Wayne said, "All right, what name do you want?"

The bot said, "Ghost Rider."

Wayne just shook his head and said, "Go down and talk to Max. He will take care of it."

Sarah and her female associates surrounded the drone ship as a one-dimensional force, then deposited the ship in an outer orbit of the nearest agra-planet.

Wayne had just terminated the conversation with Ghost Rider when he realized the entire spatial landscape suddenly changed. Wayne ran to the bridge's windscreen to see a massive planet, a distant sun, and multiple ships coming from every direction.

Wayne received an audio-visual communication link from the chancellor, requesting identification. Wayne said, "I come under the banner of peace at the request of the chancellor of Agra-planet Beta."

The computer translated the chancellor's digital transmission. "Yes, I heard that a strange ship might arrive—the ship that defeated the evil insectoids. You are most welcome."

Wayne was a little surprised that the chancellor was halfway normal. The chancellor had the body of a hairy, brown pig and the head of pelican. Wayne was annoyed when the chancellor spoke, as the extra skin on the bottom of the beak flapped from side to side.

Wayne said, "I congratulate you on the tremendous success of peace and prosperity in this galaxy."

The chancellor said, "I, too, would like a tour of your ship."

Wayne said, "Do you make clothes or fabric?"

The chancellor looked confused, and Wayne noticed the chancellor was not clothed. Wayne figured it was a lost cause and said, "Forget it. Come over anytime. We are most happy to have you and your entourage for a tour."

Sarah came back onboard and said, "Good news. I have negotiated several deals; this galaxy lacks an adequate market of metal and ore. Cheng is willing to collect all debris and metallic scrap in exchange for a permanent agricultural run at least twice a week. Cheng managed to find two other queen ships and has retrofitted them with dimensional drives. The first shipment of scrap should arrive next week."

Wayne said, "Wow, you have been busy. Cleaning up your galaxy will be a good thing. Maybe bring back some business."

Wayne was finalizing some thruster controls at the command console when Sarah's touchpad sounded an incoming message without the caller's identification. Sarah said, "Yes?"

The caller announced, "Meeting in one hour at these coordinates."

Wayne overheard the request and figured it was entity

business. Sarah felt embarrassed that Wayne had to hear that. She said, "I need to talk with the high council."

Wayne did not want to intervene, but he figured Sarah's impending gauntlet was necessary to become a political leader. Wayne said, "You take care of business, I will give the chancellor a great tour".

Sarah looked at Wayne in silence, then departed the bridge on her way to meet the high council.

Sarah arrived in the high council's chambers, and after some formal greetings, she found herself in a very uncomfortable discussion. One of the ambassadors offered her a commission if she took care of a problem. Sarah patiently listened to each of their requests or complaints, wondering who had the greater passion for power and greed.

Sarah listened, as many of the requests were against a particular species called the Ensups. The Ensups were a reptilian race, a technically below-average species involved in weapons smuggling. The Ensups were involved in many of the same pizzeria shootouts as the Venus aliens, eliminating 90 percent of the agra-planets and creating a severe galactic gravitational unbalance.

Along with the Ensups, the spirits who managed the galaxy had mysteriously disappeared. It appeared that the spirits were playing two sides, one side being the Ensups, and the other being the Confederation of the Twenty. Because of the spirit's lack of initiative, the Ensups ran the galaxy like an adolescent bully.

The high council commanded, "Sarah, you need to end this conflict and restore peace, so says the council." The council handed her a new touchpad, and to acknowledge her importance, a council staff. Sarah had no choice but to accept. Sarah formally motioned her allegiance and obedience to her new appointment, then said her good-byes and departed for the drone ship.

Sarah slowly drifted onto the drone's bridge. Wayne was asleep next to the command console. Sarah said, "It must be nice to sleep away your problems." She flashed off a message that she needed to discuss the staff and her appointment with Cheng.

Cheng came back, saying, "Awesome job, Sarah. I heard of your new assignment. The council staff is partially ceremonial, but its real power is that it can manipulate and neutralize gravitational anomalies without assistance from other entities. The staff is extremely dangerous, even in the right hands. You must keep this staff with you at all times."

Sarah was not aware that the ambassadors had such destructive technology. She was reluctant to use it as the first option. She was not a good negotiator or diplomat, but watching Wayne's flair at generating alliances gave her hope that all was not lost. Sarah needed to discuss the situation with Wayne, but there must be a better way out of this other than the staff.

The bots, while constructing Wayne's apartment, discovered an auditorium three floors down from the main bridge. Sarah wanted to construct a large holographic strategy room. She needed the bots to construct a bridge balcony overlooking the auditorium, because there was no direct access for Wayne to use. The holographic generator would receive inputs from navigation, communications, the main computer, and radar. The auditorium measured out at thirty yards square and twenty feet high, with an overlooking bridge's balcony—the perfect strategy arena.

The bots needed to cut out a portion of the second deck for an added viewing area.

The high council also presented Sarah with countless maps, coordinates, military and commercial facilities, and political information to help in the Ensup affair.

The high council offered this bit of military intelligence, the Ensups were on the verge of discovering antigravity.

The Confederation of the Twenty was a rumor. No one knew what the Confederation represented, not even the high council. The spirits assigned to monitor the Ensups' galaxy were carelessly derelict in their duties to stabilize the threats from anomalies. Sarah read many of the written statements and complaints sent to the high council, but none of it made any sense. It appeared that the spirits did not want to involve themselves in protecting the confederation. What worried Sarah was, with the galaxy in gravitational freefall, she was powerless to stop the daily complaints. She was looking at a lost cause, and it would be her cause to lose.

Sarah needed to set up a meeting with these rogue spirits and determine their side of the story. Many of the remaining inhabited planets demanded food, but food was the least of their problems. They required relocation to another galaxy.

Sarah sent a message to these rogue spirits, requesting an informal meeting. Sarah waited for an hour until a response finally arrived. It read, "We wish to be neutral." Sarah was shocked.

Sarah received word from the bots that the holographic generator was completed. She descended to the auditorium and asked for a demonstration.

Sarah commanded through the computer's voice processor via her touchpad, "Computer, enable hologram generator. Initiate." The hologram generator immediately sent a rainbow of multi-colored laser beams and colored lights everywhere with no real pattern or display.

Sarah said, "Computer, input the following information. Initiate." Sarah inputted the computer chip the high council had given her. She waited for about five minutes as the computer core configured the data to the holographic driver.

The computer came on, saying, "Download complete."

Sarah, speaking through her touchpad, said, "Computer, transfer navigational data to hologram generator. Display a radar range of nine hours. Initiate."

Sarah watched as the entire auditorium came alive with laser beams, waypoints, military beacons, and assorted imagery. She identified the agra-planet and the orbiting drone ship. There were other planets, the system's sun, and some other stars, as well. Sarah could see commercial and corporate traffic going in and out of orbit or docking with the agra-planet's spaceport. Many of the ships transmitted their own transponder identification information for added security or for assistance. Sarah noticed that the colors changed depending on the various ship's vectors, taking into account the Doppler shift. Sarah weaved in and out of the laser beams as she analyzed the political aspect of this region of space.

Sarah commanded, "Computer, holographic display. Zoom out to show entire galaxy. Initiate." The auditorium opened up to a four-galaxy anatomy. Three galaxies belonged to the High Council of Ambassadors, and the fourth, off to the northeast, was the Ensups' galaxy. She identified several stellar systems on collision course with other systems. Some stars had actually broken galactic orbit, but failed to achieve escape velocity. Sarah counted at least four recent nova nebulas as a result of the catastrophic unbalance, with several more collisions pending.

Wayne awoke from his peaceful sleep. He needed something to eat. When he heard some activity below him, Wayne said, "Are those bots finished with my balcony yet?"

Sarah said, "down here".

The bots tasked with the bridge's balcony had not finished with some of the second-deck reinforcement framework. Wayne could see the hologram, and he said, "Wow, look at that! What an awesome holographic display!" Wayne took some snacks from the icebox and set them on the table to thaw.

Sarah said, "Wayne, tell me what you see."

Wayne came over, chewing on some vegetables and holding a cup of coffee. He peered through the open metal framework and slowly said, "That galaxy looks ill." Then Wayne heard something thundering down the corridor, and he realized it was bots needed to finish the bridge's balcony.

The bots asked Wayne to call them by their nameplates. Wayne looked down at ten bots, all with nameplates riveted to their chassis. One of the bots said, "Wayne, call us by our nameplate, or else your balcony is screwed."

Wayne laughed as he called out, "Thor, Lex, Tron, Laser, Flash, Plasma, Hades, Rex, Vic, and Khan." Each of the little bots gleefully swiveled around as their names rang out. After that, the bots went right to work.

Wayne tried to concentrate on Sarah's holographic analysis. Wayne said, "Taking the Doppler shift into account, the galaxy should reflect a symmetrical pattern of reds and blues." He gazed at the terminally ill galaxy awash with chaotic cyclones of yellows, greens, and blues, all affecting the overall galactic torque.

Sarah said, "I was afraid of that."

Two days passed. The drone ship continued to orbit the agra-planet as Sarah tried to start a dialog with the spirits.

The bots finished Wayne's balcony overlooking the auditorium chamber. Max said that all supplies and provisions from the agra-planet were onboard in the aft cargo bay.

Sarah floated onto the bridge as Wayne checked all the ship's systems. Sarah said, "We need to discuss something on the hologram." Sarah dissolved through the floor as Wayne stood, overlooking the massive hologram from his new bridge balcony.

The task seemed impossible. Sarah lacked any sense of strategy or how to use the available resources.

Wayne said, "The stars are collapsing into each other."

Sarah said, "Yes, I know. This is my new assignment."

Wayne, shocked at the seemingly impossible task, said, "At what point has the high council stopped functioning and started delegating out of incompetence?"

Sarah said, "An alien species struggled to perfect some questionable technology, inadvertently destroying many of the surrounding planets. Consequentially, each of the affected solar systems have lost all gravitational stability."

Wayne stopped her, saying, "Let me guess: the planets were agra-planets?" Wayne continued, "How many were destroyed?"

Sarah said, "We can only tell from the number of nebulas and recent star novas. I say maybe one hundred."

Wayne said, "The Venus aliens also attacked agra-planets. Why didn't this happen there as well?"

Sarah said, "The dimensional gradients and subspace anomalies created enough of a counterbalance that the solar systems remained intact. Cheng told me several times that the entities had to post warning beacons around critical anomalies, or else they would disturb the gravitational equilibrium. The Ensups, the alien race that caused this catastrophe, were not aware of the gravitational consequences. What disturbs me is that the spirits who control this galaxy let this happen by not getting involved."

Wayne asked, "What about rivals?"

Sarah said, "The Confederation of the Twenty. We don't know who or where they are."

Wayne said, "The high council delegated this to you. Do you feel this was a setup?"

Sarah said, "We are looking at a dying galaxy, but my job is to fix it."

Wayne said, "Well, we better set up a meeting with these Ensups. Maybe this drone ship might encourage a compromise."

Sarah sent another message to the spirits, asking for a

meeting with the Ensups. The spirits replied, “Unable to comply.” Sarah was hot!

Wayne said, “Let me try.” Wayne was still amazed at the massive hologram, but he liked the dancing Venus queen better.

Wayne walked from the bridge balcony and proceeded to the command console. Wayne said, “Computer, open all communication channels and transmit this message: “Request audience of Ensup leader at these coordinates.” Wayne entered the coordinates via the computer navigational interface and pushed transmit. Wayne could see the Ensups’ galaxy from the agra-planet. If Wayne wanted to get to that meeting, they need to break orbit now.

Wayne turned to Sarah, saying, “Tell me about antigravity; more specifically, are we vulnerable to attack?”

Sarah said, “I don’t know.”

Wayne said, “We need to capture one of their ships. You know, a prisoner exchange is a powerful tool, especially when technology might fall into the wrong hands.”

Wayne said, “Computer, open channel to the chancellor. Initiate.”

Sarah needed an ambush hideout to abduct an Ensup ship. Sarah plotted some coordinates to some distant debris fields and smuggler hideouts.

The chancellor came on. “I greet you again. I want to express our thanks and my appreciation for the great tour.” Sarah looked over at Wayne, and Wayne whispered that he gave the chancellor and his entourage a tour while she was away.

Wayne said, “Thanks, Chancellor. We had a great

time. I am sorry to inform you, we are about to depart, and I hope to see you again."

The chancellor said, "Tell Sarah we received the first shipment of scrap metal. We are very pleased with the quality and hope to repay your generosity."

Wayne said, "The only way you can repay us is to keep this galaxy safe. That will make both our jobs easier."

The chancellor said, "See you soon."

Wayne said, "Computer, starboard thruster to maximum, go to primary engine start. Initiate." Wayne figured this port visit was a bit too long and wanted to get back home. The drone ship slowly maneuvered out of orbit. Sarah felt reassured that the negotiations with the scrap metal went well. She should thank Cheng for all his hard work.

Wayne said, "Computer, go to full engine start, proceed to light speed and to designated coordinates. Initiate." Wayne needed to clear the galaxy's upper wake zone before engaging the dimensional drive.

Sarah received a message from the high council. "Congratulations on a great port visit and the exchange of scrap metal for provisions." The high council also mentioned that other agra-planets were putting in requests for scrap metal; maybe they could be included, too.

Sarah showed the transmission to Wayne. He started to laugh and said, "If you do it for one, you have to do it for all of them. This is where problems start, because when one assumes, they all assume that the chancellor will share with the other agra-planets. He might, or he might not. In any successful negotiation, everyone must attend. Negotiations do not include rain checks."

Sarah felt a little on the amateur side, then Wayne said, "You did your job; get that straight: you did your job. Now the question is, can these aliens work together to do theirs? If the high council has anything to say about it, they will probably regulate the metal scrap themselves. Then the aliens will complain of disenfranchisement, because they were not given equal shares. See, handouts do not require innovation or creativity; they just spawn the roots of discontent. And so it goes."

The navigational monitor indicated dimensional drive clearance, exiting the galactic no-wake zone. Wayne commanded, "Computer, plot a course to designated target, dimensional drive, route all discharge through ionic drive engines. Initiate." Wayne put in the necessary coordinates for the upcoming Ensup meeting and pushed initiate.

The computer put the necessary systems online and the drone ship accelerated into subspace for a forty-day trip.

Wayne said, "Sarah, let's plan a strategy on the hologram." Sarah was overjoyed with the Ensups potentially involved. The rogue spirits were still holding out. Wayne's advice was, "Push to commit, and pull to sucker."

Wayne said, "Computer, display radar data on hologram generator. Initiate."

Sarah said, "Sorry, when the ship is in dimensional drive, the hologram is frozen—no data update. We need to wait."

The computer said, "Unable to comply in dimensional subspace."

Wayne wanted radar that could transmit and receive

information while in subspace. What a technological advancement: dark energy radar.

The drone ship was nearing the designated coordinates. It had been thirty-six days in subspace. Subspace was like driving in a dark tunnel; you knew the car was moving, but you were disconnected from the reality of outside light.

In the early days of supersonic flight, the friction from air resistance overheated the airframe, causing overstress and metal fatigue. In the vacuum of space, light speed represents the ultimate friction, where matter ignites into energy. A dimensional drive eliminates light as a coefficient of friction, so infinite speed can be achieved.

The drone ship approached the appointed coordinates. Wayne stood next to the command console, saying, "Computer, all stop, discharge remaining dimensional residue across vertical stab's emitters. Initiate." He continued, "Computer, radar scan at maximum, route image to console's monitor and to the hologram generator. Initiate."

Sarah was in the auditorium monitoring the radar image while Wayne was trying to determine who was out there. The drone ship dropped out of dimensional drive about one week too early, which was good, considering.

The computer said, "Discharge complete."

Wayne said, "Computer, full engine start. Go to full light speed toward designated coordinates. Initiate."

Sarah did not see anything on the radar or on the full galactic display. Sarah said, "Computer, display all holographic data, commercial, and military traffic. Initiate."

The display did not change much, but she wanted

to locate some debris fields for a possible ambush site. The drone ship's radar only had a radar range of ten hours, but it needed more range if they expected to set up an ambush. She wondered why the spirits had not challenged the ship's presence so close to their galaxy. She had her staff ready if they needed to make a sudden commanding presence.

Sarah yelled out, "Stop the ship!"

Wayne said, "Computer, all stop, go to one-fourth dimensional gradient. Initiate." The drone ship had five-dimensional setting. The first gradient step was one-fourth, the second step was one-half, the third step was three-fourths, the fourth step was four-fourths, and the fifth step was five-fourths.

The computer said, "All stop. Initiating to one-fourth subspace."

Wayne said, "Sarah, what did you see?"

Sarah's had the volume turned up on her touchpad, and it shouted three decks below the bridge level, "Two ships just maneuvered on an intercept course. Their transponder codes show them fifteen hours out."

Wayne said, "You know, first contact should never be conducted under the cloak of subspace."

Sarah asked, "Then what should we do?"

Wayne said, "Just sit here and see how they approach—a nice approach or a bad approach."

Sarah said, "I am picking up five more transponder signals along with the other two. All appear on an intercept course toward our location."

Wayne said, "If they can see us, then they can detect gravitational anomalies. Let's go to normal space and see what happens." Wayne continued, "Computer, go to normal space, slow discharge dispersal over the aft stabilizer emitter electrodes. Initiate." Wayne had no idea what to expect.

Sarah said, "The targets are approaching, thirteen hours out.

Wayne said, "Any other ships in the area?"

Sarah said, "No, just those I mentioned."

Wayne said, "Max, load all torpedoes tubes and carriage to capacity." The weapons complex housed a large, carriage-carrousel assembly, which supported eight torpedo tubes and sixty torpedoes.

Max said, "Loading now."

Wayne said, "Sarah, you said the ships had transponder signals. Did the high council isolate certain codes or signals as Ensups or other aliens?"

Sarah said, "Checking."

Wayne said, "Man, if they're transmitting transponder signals, I wish I had some homing missiles."

Sarah said, "No mention of transponder signals. They must be military, or else they wouldn't be broadcasting their identification."

Wayne said, "Computer, open channel to transponder codes. Listen for any communication chatter."

Sarah said, "The ships stopped. Wait, they are returning to base."

Wayne asked, "Sarah, how far to the debris field?"

Sarah replied, "A two-day trip".

Wayne said, "I would rather swat one big fly than try to swat seven little ones. Head to the debris field."

Sarah analyzed the hologram as Wayne took the command console. The drone ship slowly altered course, trying not to attract attention.

Large salvage ships patrolled these debris fields and hid among the damaged ships, preying on stragglers, ships that are out of fuel, or ships smuggling contraband. Wayne figured that the seven ships were a police force of some kind. Still, surprise was on their side.

Twenty-four hours later, Sarah picked up seven ships at radar range eight hours away. Wayne said, "Computer, full stop."

Wayne said, "Computer, open channel to approaching ships. Initiate."

The computer said, "No recognizable frequency to link to."

Wayne said, "These ships are not transmitting any transponder frequencies."

Wayne asked, "Sarah, did the high council give us communication frequencies for the Ensups?"

Sarah said, "Yes, loading now: 200.5 megahertz."

Wayne commanded, "Computer, open channel to approaching ships. Initiate."

The computer said, "Channel open."

Wayne said, "Approaching ships, we come in peace. Request audience with Ensup leaders."

The computer's digital universal translator announced over the speaker, "This is Ensup outer security patrol, surrender your ship."

Wayne said, "Wrong answer." He terminated the communications link. Wayne said, "Computer, designate all targets according to priority and fire torpedoes. Initiate."

Wayne went over to the bridge's windscreen to see seven missile-guided torpedoes racing off into the black void. Wayne continued, "Transfer torpedo tracking data to hologram."

Sarah said, "two ships slowly going to port, two to starboard in flanking maneuver. They do not see the approaching torpedoes, coincidence in two hours."

Wayne said, "Max, reload torpedo carousel carriage. Don't rush, we have some time."

Max said, "Torpedoes being loaded."

Wayne said, "The element of surprise is not to surprise yourself by wasting an enormous amount of time."

Sarah said, "The approaching fleet is continuing to fan out, coincidence in one hour". Sarah continued, "Two unknowns just came on radar screen at eight-hours radar range."

Wayne said, "Probably salvage ships wanting to pick up the pieces."

Sarah said, "Detected two ships fast approaching at nine hours radar range with transponder signatures."

Wayne said, "I would expect the Ensups' high command to be the last ship to engage."

Sarah said, "Torpedoes on target. The seven craft are unaware of the approaching torpedoes. Coincidence in ten, nine, eight ..."

Wayne went to the bridge's windscreen and witnessed seven puffs of fiery flame like seven fireflies glowing in the perpetual darkness.

Sarah said, "The two unknowns are pulling away, going back home. The two other military craft are five hours away. Their approach is faster than light speed."

Wayne said, "Computer, target and designate priority of approaching craft and fire torpedoes. Initiate."

Sarah said, "Coincidence in two hours."

Wayne said, "That's cutting it a little too close."

Sarah said, "Wow, they are approaching fast. Coincidence in five, four, three …"

Wayne ran to the windscreen as two cruisers erupted in a massive nuclear explosion. Wayne yelled out, "Computer, shields up!" The pressure wave collided with the ship, throwing debris against the drone's containment-hull shielding. The impacting percussions echoed throughout the ship as fragments of the enemy's ships ricocheted off the shielding.

Sarah said, "I have two ships de-cloaking off the starboard bow, about one radar-range hour away."

Wayne said, "Computer, open a communications channel."

The computer said, "Channel open."

Wayne said, "Ensup ship, we come in peace. Respectfully request an audience to negotiate friendship?"

Sarah angrily bolted off the auditorium deck and dissolved through the hull with her staff in hand.

The cruisers measured about twenty miles long. The bulky fuselage and wide aft section allowed for four smaller ionic engines fueled by four hydrogen fusion reactors. Sarah noticed that the ship exceeded light-speed capability, technology that Wayne was very interested in obtaining.

The Ensup ships and the drone ship, both in plasma-cannon range, drifted in a guarded standoff. Wayne surveyed the surrounding space, but there was no rescue attempt yet. Wayne wondered why the computer did not detect the Ensup ships so close to their starboard bow.

Wayne said, "Computer, display all gravitational

anomalies within a radar range of eight hours. Initiate." Wayne remembered Cheng's gravitational isobar maps that he used to detect dimensional anomalies. Maybe it might work here, too.

The gravitational isobar display represented an additional overlay processor that correlated real space-time against gravitational space-time. The actual display processor had a ten-second time lag for compiling the physical extrapolation of gravitational forces against known constants in normal space. After a couple of seconds, the display started to emerge. Wayne could see the two ships, then five additional anomalies grouped in a semi-circle configuration about one radar-range hour behind the Ensup ship.

Wayne took his touchpad, saying, "Sarah, five more cloaked ships in a semi-circle configuration just beyond the Ensups' aft position." Wayne said, "Max, make sure all torpedoes are loaded."

Max said, "Torpedo tubes loaded with plungers."

Wayne said, "Computer, can we target the five dimensional anomalies?"

The computer said, "Each torpedo has a radar altimeter proximity input, along with a fifty-gigahertz uranium-frequency-sensitivity sensor. It is not possible to designate cloaked ships, but their positional coordinates can be targeted. Calibrate all torpedoes for maximum sensitivity with a maximum fuse delay to prevent the torpedo from inadvertently coming back."

Wayne said, "Max, did you hear what the computer just said?"

Max said, "Yes, eight torpedoes being reconfigured now."

Sarah was not happy. She bolted toward the Ensup ship and dissolved through the bridge's windscreen, yelling, "Stand down! Who is in charge?"

Sarah was looking around when she received Wayne's warning about the five other ships. Sarah continued her rant, "Who is charge here?"

Sarah could see four nervous reptilian creatures all lounging on circular hovercraft.

The Ensups were a reptilian race of lizard-like creatures. A hundred thousand years ago, when the Ensups first entered space, zero-gravity had degenerated their bodies. To adapt, they invented hovercraft pads to get around. One of the more bizarre biological adaptations to zero gravity was the loss of their scales. The scales proved to be a liability in space because they cut like knives into their sagging and degenerating bodies.

In the rear of the Ensups' bridge was a cage with raw meat and vegetable scraps. Sarah could see small little white things rummaging through the garbage, along with buzzing, flying insects. One could only image the overwhelming stench of rotting food and meandering maggots. The maggots served as nutritious protein, while the flies continued to lay eggs to perpetuate the cycle.

Sarah watched the quietly hovering Ensups, who were all blasé to her presence. The Ensups spit out their forked tongues in disgust. Sarah looked out the bridge's windscreen to see one of the ships de-cloaking and heading toward the drone ship.

Sarah departed the bridge, repulsed at the Ensups' lack of respect, and quickly pursued the other flanking ship to starboard. Again, Sarah bolted onto the bridge, yelling, "Who is in charge here?" The five hovering Ensups remained silent.

Sarah, in a blind rage, called out to Wayne, "These Ensups are not being cooperative. Have the computer start designating targets. Fire on my mark."

Sarah shouted, "We will destroy your entire fleet if you do not negotiate. Again, who is in charge?" There was no response from the hovering reptiles.

Sarah said, "That's it, I've had enough. Wayne, fire torpedoes!"

Wayne pushed the launch button and he called out, "Computer, shields up to maximum!"

The drone ship fired off seven torpedoes as the Ensups' lead ship tried firing its plasma cannon. The Ensups' plasma cannon blast resembled a welder's torch against the drone's outer shielding. One after the other, the torpedo's proximity sensors penetrated each gravitational anomaly, causing the entire horizon to erupt in fiery debris and nuclear detonation.

The white glow of nuclear static enveloped the entire ship as subatomic particles arced across the ship's containment shielding. Wayne called out, "Computer, route all subatomic particles to the dimensional emitter electrodes. Then disconnect all power grids going to the hydrogen reactors and the plasma conduits. Initiate."

The computer said, "Static and radioactive levels receding. Emitter electrodes successfully discharging residual static from subatomic ionization."

Sarah spent the next few hours swimming through the radioactive cloud surrounding the drone ship. It was like the fountain of youth—an enormous wellspring of subatomic particles cleaning every ounce of Ensup hatred.

Then Sarah noticed another ship de-cloaking off the port bow. Immediately she bolted onto the bridge, touching every conceivable live circuit and computer interface she could. The entire bridge was alive with showing sparks as the ship tried to maintain navigational control. Sarah, in a fit of rage, shouted, "Who is in command here!" Four Ensups were trying to hide behind one of the computer consoles, pushing each other out of the way.

One of the Ensups, still cowering, managed to say, "You destroyed all of our scout ships in this sector, and more are on their way."

Sarah said, "Well, I guess we will have to destroy them, too. Are you in charge?"

The pathetic-looking creature said, "We are Ensups. We do not negotiate with spirits."

Sarah said, "We are here to protect you. Your galaxy is collapsing. I represent the high council, and we are here to relocate you to another galaxy."

The Ensup said, "Lies! Where did you get that ship?"

Sarah said, "We are from a distant galaxy; we are hunting for escaped prisoners." Sarah reached into her secret inner pouch and pulled out a small box. She pushed a button, and a huge hologram of a Venus-Flaytrap-faced alien began dancing around the bridge. Three of the four Ensups fell off their hovering lounge pads trying to escape. Apparently they had never seen a hologram and thought it was real.

An Ensup yelled out, "What is that?"

Sarah held out the hologram box and disengaged the image with a push of the button. "This is what we are looking for. They have destroyed more powerful creatures than you. Therefore, if you see this creature, you had better tell us."

The little Ensups felt sufficiently violated. One said, "We can take care of ourselves." With that, the four Ensups turned their backs on Sarah.

Sarah had had enough. She left the bridge in disgust and headed for the drone ship. Sarah looked back, hoping the ship would attack, but it retreated toward the safety of its outpost.

Feeling dejected, Sarah dissolved quietly into the auditorium deck and brought up the galactic display.

Wayne heard something down below and said, "Sarah?"

She said, "Don't talk to me!"

Wayne had heard that phrase before. It was a male's universal warning sign, saying, "Run for your life!"

Sarah apologetically returned to the bridge, too frustrated to explain what happened.

Wayne said, "Bad days teach us lessons about the value of good days."

Sarah said, "I need to draft a formal request for an audience with the Confederation of the Twenty." She also sent a formal complaint to the spirits for their inexcusable ineptness and signed it, "High Council." Sarah graciously smiled then hit the transmit button.

Sarah returned to the auditorium and brought up her galactic map. The high council did provide Sarah with some classified documents and computer chips, which she downloaded into the computer. Sarah managed to download the alien's entire computer core while she was trashing the bridge. She began downloading the data.

After compiling all the additional information, she said, "Computer, display image on all recent data."

A new hologram began to take shape. The Ensups held a vast claim of galactic territory, but it appeared to be desolate and unpopulated. She wondered if these belonged to the Confederation of the Twenty. The Ensups did not believe in negotiating, but instead had a warrior's mentality of destroying all newcomers.

Wayne said, "Hey, come listen to this!"

Sarah went upstairs to the bridge, and Wayne played back a communiqué he intercepted. The universal translator began a voiced modulation of the incoming message: "We lost forty planets to this alien race to the north, and our ships are powerless against them. We already lost thirteen ships to the south when we encountered a rogue ambassador."

Sarah and Wayne were not sure who was responsible, but losing forty planets in a day was urgent news. Sarah's intelligence report still did not specify who the Confederation of the Twenty or their designation were.

Sarah sent an urgent message to the high council, saying, "The continuing galactic instability, plus a new power struggle threatens to escape the galaxy's confines. I recommend total annihilation of the galaxy." Then she added, "If I go ahead with the galaxy's destruction, imagine the number of new recruits within the ambassador's ranks under the leadership of the high council."

Sarah did not have long to wait. The high council regretted to hear this latest news, but their scouts did report a growing conflict to the north. The scouts reported that an alien race of broad-faced insectoids incited rebellion, along with an accompaniment of allied forces. The scout ships had not seen the Confederation of the Twenty.

Sarah sent another urgent message recommending the total destruction of the Ensups' home galaxy. At this point, quarantine was the only option.

The high council agreed with Sarah's assessment of the situation: destruction of the galaxy was the only alternative. The high council requested as many new recruits as possible.

Sarah said, "Computer, designate the following coordinates. Navigational computer, proceed to coordinates. Command primary and full engine start, go to light speed. Initiate." Sarah turned to Wayne and said, "The drone ship is headed toward the farthest reaches of the void. I planned to fight the Grays by your side, but not today. I must destroy the Ensups' galaxy, then return to the high council to face judgment. These are the new coordinates for another galaxy to check out. Get as far away as possible. I will be with you again."

Sarah took her staff and dissolved from view.

Sarah watched as the northern regions glittered like diamonds. But these were not diamonds. They were a terrible war of power. Sarah watched as the drone ship accelerated and shot off at light speed. Sarah, content that the drone ship was out of danger, prepared herself for the ultimate hypocrisy.

Sarah said, "No more." She held out the staff high above her body and violently brought it to her side as she said, "Children, come to me." The entire galaxy began to glow, and then exploded, sending a blinding light in all directions. Sarah felt the cleansing radiance sweep across her brownish charcoal amoebic body. She held her staff out high and thousands of infant entities surrounded her with a loving embrace of security and warmth. Sarah looked across the building haze of condensing nebulas and radiating galactic forest fire, saying, "If you can't fix it, blow it up."

She failed to honor the high council's request to negotiate the terms of compliance.

Sarah motioned her staff: males to one side, and females to the other side. She watched as the young entities separated by gender in perfect balance. Sarah called out, "I am your mother, and I love you very much!

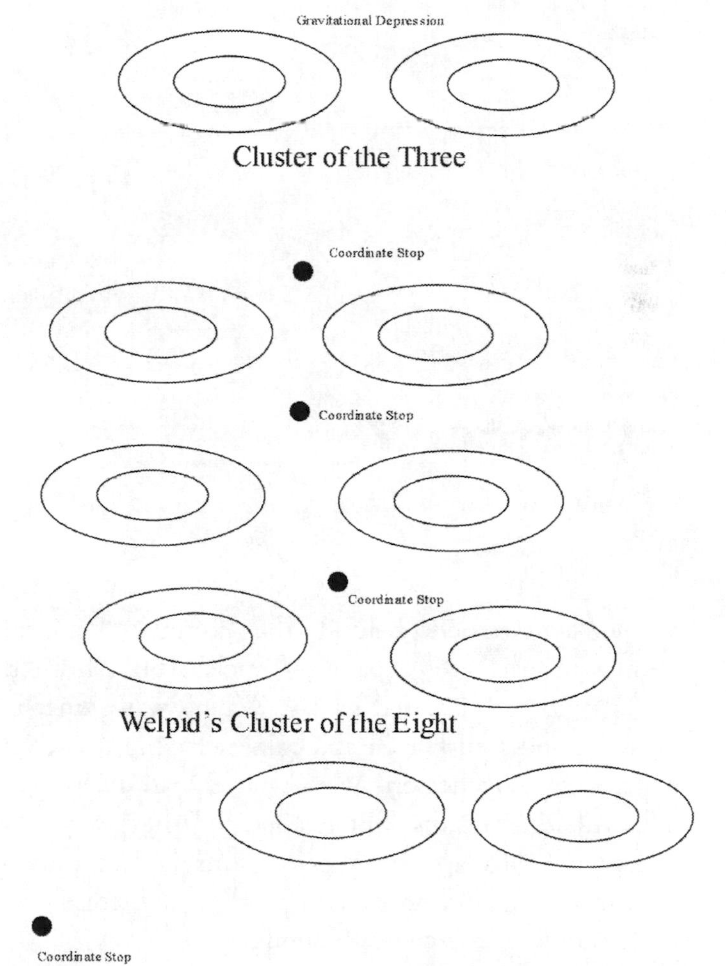
Gravitational Depression
Cluster of the Three
Coordinate Stop
Coordinate Stop
Coordinate Stop
Welpid's Cluster of the Eight
Coordinate Stop

Chapter 7

Welpid

Wayne stood behind the command console, monitoring the ever-expanding nuclear blast from the Ensups' now obliterated galaxy. Wayne was alone, but his heart and soul felt Sarah's pain at having to face the high council by herself. Wayne never had a chance to talk with the Ensups, but it appeared they were more concerned with acquiring possessions and technology than in understanding how to produce it themselves or understanding the science behind it.

Wayne never understood the concept of consumerism. Consumerism was essentially thievery while obeying by the laws of commerce. Has there ever been a relationship between industrialization and consumerism? In an industrial town, consumerism is the basic understanding of what one consumes without being extravagant. In a commercial setting, the consumer's only interest stems from a horde of advertisers. Consumers are not interested in understanding what they are purchasing, but in the perpetual accumulation of unwanted stuff. In comparing school curriculum between an industrial town and a commercial city, the emphasis on technical knowledge is inversely proportionate to the desires of gaining wealth. In what appeared as a disassociation between economic priorities, consumers would voluntarily degenerate to a level of ignorant dependency beyond what anyone could understand. The Ensups were thieves in search of technology, but were too stupid to understand that technology. Strategy and knowledge are strictly proportional until consumerism believes it can appropriate a viable substitute for what it does not understand.

Wayne began to see a pattern: as an alien race became more standoffish, they tended not to negotiate. On the other hand, if an alien race possessed a technological competence and saw benevolence as an inspirational enlightenment toward divinity and science, then charity was an extension of that knowledge and understanding.

Wayne understood the allure and fascination with UFO technology, but the technology was way beyond the grasp of human understanding. Yet humans wanted that technology, not for scientific research, but for military annihilation. Science is not about reverse-engineering, but about discovering the truth. To understand science is to understand technology, but dissecting technology does not necessarily teach us the science behind it. Wayne had every intention of discovering the truth about earth's alien influence. Governmental propaganda has denied the existence UFO's or little green men for years, but to assume that the government needs to conjure up rumors indicated a deeper conspiracy that science was forbidden to know.

The computer announced, "cleared radiation rate of expansion".

Wayne said, "Computer, shut down all engines, except for primary." Wayne continued, "Computer, transfer all radar and navigational data to the hologram generator."

Sarah presented Wayne with a list of galactic coordinates of possible places to look next. He felt alone and missed seeing Sarah floating next to the hologram generator, carefully analyzing the tremendous amount of display data.

Wayne took the touchpad and began going over all the coordinates one by one, with the computer displaying the waypoints on the display grid. In all, there were ten coordinate locations. Wayne began to piece together the emerging galactic picture. He counted eight different galaxies, ranging in all sizes and shapes, but none resembled the Milky Way.

Wayne took his finger and pointed to the coordinate furthest away, saying, "Computer, set course to these coordinates."

The computer said, "The estimated time of arrival is one million years by light speed; dimensional drive is one year."

Wayne said, "Computer, go to full engine start. Proceed to light speed. Dimensional drive enabled. Discharge cycled through ionic drive engines. Initiate."

The drone ship slowly accelerated, and all engines went to afterburner. The forward emitter-electrode access panel aft of the bridge's windscreen began to open enabling the motorized actuator crane. Wayne could see the bright blue glow from the forward emitter as the entire drone ship descended into the dark energy of subspace.

Wayne said, "One year! What am I going to do for one year?" Wayne picked up the touchpad and began going through Sarah's bot repair list. The bots had plenty of unfinished tasks, and this would be the perfect opportunity to get them fixed. Wayne wondered if he needed a first mate. He decided to call up the hoist bot from engineering.

Wayne said, "Egg-hoist bot, please come to the bridge." Wayne generated a to-do list for the hoist bot to look over. He wanted three projects: first, find a suitable space for a research lab; second, start work on the antigravity engine; third, research the dark-energy radar. Wayne knew the value and the potential hazards of antigravity, either as an engine or as a weapon. He knew capturing an antigravity ship might be tricky, but he wanted the bots to work on the project on their own before they started reverse-engineering it from another ship.

Wayne also wanted to push more input power to increase the radar's range output. He searched through all the touchpad's data files, but no mention about changing the synchronizer's pulse repetition frequency, also known as the duty cycle, for maximum range. Wayne noticed how the radar picked up random clutter and false targets due to debris from subatomic contamination. If anything, attenuating the receiver's sensitivity prevented critical damage to the receiver's oscillator crystals.

The drone ship did not have a tractor beam. Wayne

was impressed at how Sarah joined the two ships with the shield generator. Wayne wondered if the ship's aft fuselage could be fitted with a shield generator to capture other debris or salvaged ships.

The hoist bot arrived at the bridge's subway station, calling out over the computer's voice modulator processor, "Wayne!"

Wayne said, "Hoist bot, I'm here in the bridge."

The hoist bot came rolling in and said, "You asked for me?"

Wayne said, "Yes, would you like a job on the bridge?"

The hoist bot said, "It would be a change of pace."

Wayne said, "Your task is to organize and oversee research project throughout the ship. Sarah listed some unfinished projects, and I have others I want you to look at."

The hoist bot said, "Can I have a name?"

Wayne asked, "Have you been talking to Max? Okay, what name do you want?"

The hoist bot said, "Harold."

Wayne asked, "Harold?"

The hoist bot said, "I want to be named Harold."

Wayne said sarcastically, "All right, Harold. I want you to look over these unfinished projects. Decide which are necessary and which are a waste of time."

Harold looked at the touchpad while Wayne held it for him to read. Harold said, "They are all a waste of time. Sarah issued that as busy work."

Wayne asked, "Okay, how many of the engineering bots are research and computer qualified?"

Harold said, "I know of fifty actually qualified research bots; maybe twenty more on top of that."

Wayne said, "I want you to gather up all the research bots and meet me in the bridge's subway station."

Harold said, "See you soon."

Wayne said, "Harold."

Harold the hoist bot turned around, saying, "Yes?"

Wayne said, "I had a long talk with Max about who made him. Max said he belonged to a biologically imprinted corps of warrior robots from an extinct alien race. I will ask you the same question: who made you?"

Harold suddenly felt ashamed, saying, "The supreme queen found me and made me her own. I kept her eggs for only a short time; I loaded the queen's eggs onto shuttles bound for other planets to colonize. My job was to load the eggs into cargo containers. I escaped and put myself in a cargo container. That is how I came into the service of my beloved queen."

Wayne said, "You, too, might be related to the extinct alien race that tried to defeat the Venus aliens."

Harold said, "I found purpose and reverence in those precious eggs. That is who I am."

Wayne pulled back from any further questioning. He had never seen such commitment or the level of understanding about the sanctity of life from a bot before.

Wayne watched as Harold rolled down the corridor toward the tram to get the other research bots.

Any research facility, especially one working with antigravity, required a high level of shield containment and coolant lines. The coolant lines feeding the ship's critical systems were already overtaxed.

Wayne returned to the command console and he monitored the dimensional system status. He was very happy that the bots cleaned and serviced the ship's major systems when they took possession of the drone ship. This was not the time to have a mechanical failure while in dimensional drive.

Having Sarah on the bridge was a real pleasure, but he tried not to let his mind get too distracted. Yes, his ultimate goal was to get back home, but too many realities hinged on that one reality. Focus and concentration was his ally now, not boredom or self-pity.

Wayne wondered if his route was strategically sound. Considering that the Confederation of the Twenty was at odds with the Ensups, they might prove helpful if he could find them. He knew that, if he traveled to the farthest galaxy, he might not find the Confederation of the Twenty.

Wayne said, "Computer, maintain dimensional drive, allow for new coordinates to be inputted."

The computer said, "Identify new coordinates."

Wayne walked over the bridge's balcony, saying, "Computer, bring up last known holographic display." Wayne said, "Computer, proceed to these coordinates." He focused a green light beam over the desired coordinates with his new laser pen. Wayne looked at the galactic layout. In all, there were a cluster of eight galaxies. The new coordinates put him in the middle of the grouping, with four on either side. The holographic image did project some galactic debris stemming from the Ensups' galaxy. Maybe some intelligence gathering would prove beneficial. The coordinates were far within the dark void of empty space, so as not to attract any unnecessary attention.

Wayne heard some noises coming from the subway station; maybe it was the bots. Wayne rushed down the corridor, yelling out, "Harold?"

Harold positioned himself as the research group's leader as bots continued to exit the tram. Wayne was quite amused, as the bots were complaining or generally loitering around the loading platform, waiting for the meeting to begin.

Wayne gathered up all the bots, commanding, "Research bots, Harold has a job for you."

One of the bots said, "Who is Harold?"

Wayne said, "Oh, no! Not now!"

The hoist bot came up beside Wayne and said, "I am Harold."

A tremendous chattering commenced all saying the same thing, "I want a name, too!"

Wayne figured he had six months before arriving at the new coordinates, so he asked all the bots to transmit their name into a computer's database along with their identification number. The engineering bots would fabricate name-identification plates later.

An hour passed, and all the bots had time to enter their chosen name and identification number into the computer with the nameplates already in work. Wayne surveyed the group and said, "I understand all of you are research bots. I have two research projects. The first is antigravity, and the other is dark energy radar. Your first task is to find an appropriate laboratory to do the research. It must be far away from engineering so not to contaminate the reactor stabilization."

One of the bots called out, "My name is Clyde."

Then all the bots blandly echoed, "Hello Clyde."

Clyde said, "I helped fabricate the weapons tram. I remember excavating when we came across a large room. The room has no direct access, but is far away from engineering." A couple of the other bots remembered the room, too. "We could excavate past the tram and construct an access corridor from inside weapons."

Wayne said, "How big is this room?"

Clyde said, "Maybe two or three subway stations in length."

Wayne said, "I anticipate any research with antigravity might require a small accelerator and a plasma conduit for laboratory use only."

Clyde said, "We can start on the research center immediately."

Wayne said, "The large room would be great. Maybe check neighboring bulkheads for hidden rooms we can add on."

A couple of the other bots said, "We brought over a spare accelerator from the queen's ship."

Wayne called Harold over and said, "You take it from here. Get the research labs built and set up. Concentrate on the small projects; do not worry about the accelerator, the containment, or the coolant lines yet. Also, look at my notes regarding an aft-shielding tractor beam."

Harold seemed happy with his new job, saying, "This is going to be fun!"

Wayne watched as Harold herded the freshly named bots back into the tram. Wayne stood there, amazed at how the little biologically imprinted bots got excited over their new names and their new job.

Harold gave Wayne a little nod with its hoist boom as the tram's door closed, and off they went.

Wayne still needed a first mate, but with the bots gainfully employed, this might be a productive trip.

Wayne had never been out to sea, but the time spent on the aircraft carrier sure went fast. Wayne heard stories about how slowly time passed while out at sea. The past five and a half months were pure misery. The bots were having a great time; they created the perfect research facility. They were able to fabricate a plasma conduit, but had still not found an accelerator.

Twenty of the bots successfully tested an antigravity prototype in a computer program. The dark-energy radar had some problems. Dark energy proved to be more elusive. One of the problems with dark matter or dark energy was the relationship between gravity, energy, and a transmission beam reflected back to the receiver. Transmitting dark matter depended on the gravitational relationship between visible light and the energy beyond visible light. Receiving a dark-matter return was not based on frequency, but on maintaining a sufficient energy level beyond visible light. Dark energy had a nasty habit of dissipating when the energy level fell below the visible light spectrum. The local oscillator also required its own antigravity unit to match the transmitted energy signal against the returning signal to calculate the dissipated energy.

One of the inherent problems with the antigravity drive engine was maneuverability and hull containment. In a dimensional drive, the subspace shielding acts as an envelope or protective umbrella. In an antigravity drive, the subspace field allows for more light-speed friction, which overheats the hull. Many alien spacecraft were zeppelin-shaped, which limits the amount of spatial aerodynamic friction.

Wayne had two weeks before returning to normal space. Wayne was nearly out of coffee and steaks, but had plenty of vegetables and fruits. It would be nice to visit another agra-planet, even to visit another bizarre chancellor.

In UFO research, medical evaluations and case studies firmly established how psychological stress and mental disorders affected the overall health of abductees; fear of the unknown, fear of death, and fear of the helpless separation from loved ones. Militarily, taking prisoners during war was necessary for surveillance and intelligence gathering missions. It was one thing to anticipate the prerequisites of war as it pertained to abductions or solitary confinement. In contrast, it was unconceivable to expose ordinary citizens to the horrors of abductions. However, as terrorism or extremism fought to eliminate individual freedoms, the ordinary citizen posed the biggest threat to socialistic governments. Aliens, on the other hand, saw technology as the end game or the greater prize, where life held absolutely no value.

Wayne understood the abduction process, but as the drone's captain, he was not looking for payback, just those benevolent aliens who recognize the value of negotiation over blind rage. Strategy and war has its place, but true enlightenment comes from a charitable prowess.

Wayne was somewhat disappointed in the aliens' concept of music or appreciation of the arts. It seemed that art or music required a negotiated understanding, a conscience effort to appreciate another's cultural expression. The concept of tolerance is the free expression of beauty and imagination without bias. In the aliens' eyes, the acquisition of technology governed commerce, trade, and forced negotiation, where the battlefield of monopoly was the name of the game. The goal of any alien political structure is the acquisition of technology, regardless of the lives lost or the underlying expense. Technology is king, and you serve that technology without question. In the race for alien technology, aesthetics has no meaning.

Wayne had lost all concept of time. The computer kept the only time device, and that was the radar display of time spend in dimensional drive or light speed. Wayne finally called out, "Computer, drop into normal space, route all residual discharge through the stab-emitter electrodes, no target designation. Initiate." Wayne continued, "Retract the forward emitter electrode and secure access door. Bring up radar and navigational displays, all communication channels open. Bring shields to maximum."

The radar display was clean, with no targets. Wayne commanded, "Transfer all radar and communications to the hologram generator." Wayne walked over to the bridge's balcony as the hologram booted up.

The hologram began displaying convoys of spacecraft, all aligned in orderly traffic patterns going from one galaxy to the next. If the term "galactic mall" ever existed, this was it. He noticed a couple of ships altering course in an intercept approach to the drone ship. Wayne said, "Computer, transmit on all channels this message: I wish to negotiate with the chancellor a peace treaty, a sign of friendship, and trade."

Then Wayne realized that the entities had not made

their usual overlord appearance. Yet seeing the level of organization from a entity-les society was just as awe-inspiring, in that aliens could negotiate their own path without fearing the entity bullies down the street.

Wayne watched the hologram as the ships approached in a diamond configuration, now some nineteen radar-range hours ahead. Wayne asked the computer to drop shields as the drone ship silently drifted in normal space.

Wayne continued to transmit the welcoming message, but was not sure if the universal translator applied to this region of space. Wayne continued to watch as the curious ships closed in. Hour after hour, they continued in their diamond formation, until they reached the four-radar-range-hour mark, and then they stopped. The radar picked up a single shuttle exiting the formation on an intercept course to the drone ship. Wayne said, "I believe we are having guests."

Wayne said, "Computer, bots, approaching shuttle, docking protocol in aft airlock."

Wayne turned off the hologram generator and turned toward the corridor. Wayne knew he had to rush; the aft airlock was the only formal docking platform, and he was still on the bridge. He hurried to the tram and he pushed the button for the aft airlock. The door finally closed, and off he went.

Wayne arrived in four hours and thirty minutes. He could see the shuttle making its final approach toward the docking ring as the small ILS transmitter sent alignment data. He could not see through the shuttle's dark glass. There were some alien markings on the shuttle's fuselage and vertical stab, but he saw nothing familiar. The shuttle's overall black color was almost invisible against the black void of space. There was one blue-colored warning light, which was a feedback transceiver sending alignment data back to the docking ring.

Wayne looked around; there was Harold, a couple of the research and engineering bots, and a cart of tasty treats and several tubes of glucose.

The drone's airlock began to compress atmosphere, and the docking bolts clamped into place with a forceful metal-to-metal bang. The center passageway began to pressurize atmosphere as well. Wayne could hear the shuttle's airlock-locking bolts disengaging as the passengers prepared to disembark. The airlock's keypad warning light changed from red to green, and the actuated rams opened the airlock's door.

Wayne poked his head down the passageway, but it was still deserted. Wayne did not hear anything, but he could smell something sweet like fresh cake frosting. Wayne continued watching as an Ensup hovercraft emerged with a fat overstuffed cupcake riding on top. He could see some smaller protruding appendages from the little pastry treat, one appendage held a small staff or stick. This multi-colored cupcake appeared to be changing hues as the alien drifted toward the drone's airlock flange.

Wayne had seen the impossible: a floating, living, breathing cupcake suspended on an Ensup lounge-hoverpad. Wayne watched in amazement as the puffy muffin slowly approached, and he wondered how he should greet this extremely bizarre being. He dared not grab on to anything, fearing he would tear it from the pasty outer covering. Wayne figured the cupcake was some four feet in diameter and about four feet high.

The cupcake hovered over the airlock's flange, and an appendage greeted Wayne with a translator computer chip. Wayne quickly scanned the device across the computer's terminal interface and said, "Computer, input translator chip and process all communication coding in this format."

Wayne looked down the corridor, wondering what happened to the entourage. Wayne was about to close the airlock door when another figure moved into view. Wayne stood there, shocked, as he gazed upon another human. The floating cupcake held up a communication transceiver, saying, "This is Crelk, he is a Xynod. My name is Welpid. I am the chancellor; I represent the Cluster of the Eight Galaxies."

Wayne watched Crelk leave the shuttle's sanctuary and begin walking down the passageway. Wayne then realized it was not a human. Crelk's head was no more than an audio-visual appendage. Crelk had no mouth, nose, or facial hair. Crelk's arms were relatively normal, but his fingers were long and creepy. Crelk's was dressed in a one-shoulder, full-length toga diagonally draped toward his waist. Crelk passed through the drone's airlock, and Wayne noticed something across its upper chest where his collarbone should be. Wayne, conscious that he was gawking at Crelk's neckline, suddenly jumped back when he noticed a mouth opening up to breathe.

Wayne stood almost frozen as one of the bots ran over his foot. Wayne suddenly came to his senses and offered some snacks from the catering tray. Welpid immediately snatched up one of the tubes of glucose and smeared it all over himself. Wayne stood there, dumbfounded, when Welpid picked up another tube and repeated the nasty maneuver. The humanoid, Crelk, seemed despondent, almost intoxicated, as he stood, glassy-eyed waiting for Welpid to move out of the way. Crelk's Mediterranean toga had a beautifully designed patchwork of alien script and mosaics. He also had a pair of alligator slip-on shoes. Wayne was glad Crelk was intoxicated because, he was not interested in seeing his chest talk.

Wayne escorted the two guests into the foyer lounge area where more food was prepared, along with places to relax.

Wayne continued to watch Welpid grab two more tubes of glucose and place them on his hovercraft for later. Wayne then began noticing Welpid's bizarre complexion; it almost appeared as if his outer frosting was cracking. Each crack appeared as a small volcanic fissure opening up, with frosting like ooze filling in the fissure. Each subsequent fissure out gassed the sweet aroma of frosting.

Wayne then turned this attention to Crelk, who still looked lost. Wayne said to Welpid, "I have three cargo containers filled with glucose just like this; I will gladly present these as gifts toward our friendship."

Welpid instantly grew a small appendage near his base that suddenly made a loud, snapping sound. Wayne noticed a small bot emerging from the shuttle. Wayne said, "Harold, please have the three glucose cargo containers brought to the airlock and loaded onboard the shuttle. The chancellor's bot will assist you."

Harold selected a few of the engineering bots to help, and off they went to get the cargo containers. Welpid turned to Wayne and said, "Your ship is very large and impressive, and I thank you for your gift of friendship.

You seem well-versed in the matter of negotiating. I look forward to our session together. Now, may I see your bridge?"

Wayne said, "Yes, Chancellor, this way please." They all proceeded to the awaiting tram.

Crelk and Welpid boarded the tram, and Wayne noticed some familiar alien script on Welpid's hovercraft; it resembled Ensup writing. Wayne began assembling his strategy to-do list for the upcoming negotiation, trying not to be adversarial, but rather to compete as equals. Wayne could see that Welpid and Crelk were not exactly friends. Maybe this little tidbit of information might prove valuable.

Wayne pushed the bridge button on the tram's dashboard, and off they went. Wayne felt it was inappropriate to bring up the entity issue, so he started the conversations off with, "Before your ships detected me, I noticed the amazing level of organization and commercial enterprise within your galactic network. On any scale, this must have been a challenging task to accomplish."

Welpid said, "I am glad you approve. It was difficult, but we negotiated several valuable alliances who wish to remain anonymous. Crelk negotiated one alliance in particular with Vegh, who reigns further to the northeast."

Wayne had a small laptop that included most of the unclassified design characteristics of the drone ship. Wayne said, "Welpid, please take this laptop of the ship. You will find the data informative and helpful."

Welpid took the laptop and began reading every detail. Wayne tried to strike even the most elementary conversation with Crelk, but he continued to look drugged or hopelessly drunk. Wayne spent the tram trip watching Welpid's outer complexion cracking, then oozing, then cracking again repeatedly. At one point, Welpid put the laptop down to smear another tube of glucose all over him. Once he felt satisfied, he picked the laptop up and continued researching. Wayne attempted to search for Welpid's eyes or visual sensors, but could not find any.

The tram finally arrived at the bridge's subway station. Wayne opened the door, and the two guests stepped out on the loading platform. Wayne escorted the two down the corridor to the main bridge complex. Welpid and Crelk looked around in amazement at the bridge's size and simplicity. Welpid inadvertently said, "What, no maggots?" Wayne pretended not to hear Welpid's statement, but ushered them instead into his little apartment.

Wayne asked Crelk, "Do you want some meat?"

Crelk perked up and said, "Yes".

Wayne said, "Cooked, raw or frozen?"

Crelk said, "What is cooked?"

Wayne took out a stiff, frozen slab of meat from the icebox, placed it in the infrared broiler, and set the grill-temperature button for medium-rare. Crelk could hear the crackling of the meat's oils and juices as the smell of T-bone steak filled the air.

Welpid held up his universal translator cane and said, "What is that awful smell?"

Crelk said, "That is a very different smell, I kind of like it."

Two minutes later, Wayne took the sizzling platter

and placed it on a small dinner tray with a fork and a knife. Crelk leaned over from his lounge chair to smell this delightful new food. Wayne assumed that Crelk would pick up his eating utensils. Wayne watched as Crelk, in an awkward motion, leaned over the tray and a grotesque shark jaw protruded from his upper chest, devouring the steak whole and nearly knocking over the tray. The steak was gone in a flash. The reflex took a fraction of a second, until Crelk leaned back in the lounge chair with the neckline of his toga stained with steak juice.

Wayne said to himself, "Wow that was something different!"

Wayne regained his composure and decided to push the negotiations further, but Welpid was still reading the specifications on the laptop.

Wayne said, "Welpid, I see you find the ship interesting."

Welpid continued reading as Crelk drifted off to sleep. Wayne needed a real negotiating grenade to liven things up. Wayne considered Welpid's position as chancellor. Wayne knew that technology represented gold, but technology also represented greed, which might jeopardize his commercial empire. Welpid probably was a habitual liar, based on his commercial expertise. Politicians and financial heavyweights find comfort speaking in half-truths or falsehoods as a plausible ploy of deniability.

Wayne decided to ask the hovering biscuit, "Where are all the entities?"

Welpid jumped from his reading slumber as the cane said, "Spirits and ambassadors are prohibited within the Cluster of the Eight Galaxies."

Wayne looked over at Crelk, who was still asleep. Welpid continued reading the laptop.

Wayne then said, "I see you visited the Ensups."

Again, Welpid jumped, saying, "Damn Ensups, either they killed themselves or the ambassadors did it."

Wayne said, "Did what?"

Welpid held up his universal translator cane, and the cane said, "Did you notice that huge nebula? That was once the Ensups' galactic home world."

Wayne was more than curious why Welpid hated the entities. Wayne asked, "What happened to the Confederation of the Twenty?"

Welpid snorted, saying, "What do you know about the confederation?"

Wayne said, "The confederation left the Ensups' galaxy before it blew up."

Welpid looked at Wayne, wondering where this was going. Welpid said, "Do you know who their leader was?"

Wayne replied, "No. I picked up provisions from a distant agra-planet. We traded for a translator chip, which included the Ensups' spoken and written languages. On my route here, I overheard a communications about the Ensups and the Confederation of the Twenty. There was also something about the entities playing both sides."

Welpid said, "Yes, the spirits were playing both sides, but the confederation left some time ago. The ambassadors destroyed the Ensups' galaxy."

Wayne said, "The Ensup galaxy only had five agra-planets. What happened to the others?"

Welpid said, "The ambassadors destroyed them." Wayne knew that was a lie.

Wayne said, "Crelk must have negotiated an important deal to keep the entities away from your empire."

Welpid said, "The spirits have an old prophecy: they will not inhabit a galaxy that is in the likeness of their creator."

Wayne stopped and said, "Whose likeness?"

Welpid said, "Crelk's and your likeness, as well."

Wayne took a chance and said sternly, "Do you know the Grays?"

Welpid twitched, realizing Wayne was a skilled negotiator. Wayne knew Welpid was hiding the truth and demanded, "Give me coordinates to the Grays' galaxy."

Welpid asked, "And what if I don't?"

Wayne said, "Imagine how much money you could make: a bet to determine the impending outcome, myself or the Grays. Imagine such a confrontation. The bet is whether I survive, or whether the Grays would prevail. Would you take that bet?"

Welpid was beginning to get annoyed, saying, "I will take that bet!"

Wayne said, "Good. The Grays and I are about to do battle."

Welpid assumed that all creatures like Crelk and now Wayne were notoriously incompetent when it came to negotiating. Welpid prided himself as the chief negotiator but now was asking, "What do you want?"

Wayne replied, "Welpid, you have everything you could ever want, but what would happen if technology was allowed to interfere with this incredible level of commercialization? Your peaceful little Cluster of Eight Galaxies would turn on itself once the Grays discover you have a technologically superior ship. Your whole world will turn into dust."

Welpid was furious, and Wayne added, "You know I would like to take Crelk and his other Xynod friends with me to fight the Grays. If the entities revere us as their creator, the Xynods might prove to be a valuable ally."

Welpid almost twisted off his hovercraft, "The Xynods are not for sale!"

Wayne said, "Give me your best odds that I survive against the Grays, and I will match it. Go ahead; run the numbers on your laptop, I will wait."

Welpid hesitated, then took his own laptop and logged onto the galactic network. He spoke into his translator cane, which linked to his laptop, "This is the chancellor. Give me your best odds that the stranger can defeat the Grays." Welpid pushed the enter button as the download light went berserk. Welpid turned the screen around so Wayne could see it. The display was a split screen. On one side was the betting tally, and the other side was the point spread. The initial odds broke out at ten thousand to one, and Wayne waited patiently for ten more minutes. The monetary value was in credits. Wayne was not familiar with their banking or monetary system, but it looked quite expensive.

After ten minutes, Welpid spoke into his translator cane. "All bets terminated." He waited a couple more seconds for the final tally, then Welpid motioned to Wayne and said, "One million to one against you surviving."

Wayne laughed, saying, "I'll take it! You know, with those odds, you could build a ship just like this one. You have the designs and specifications right there." Wayne pointed to the laptop.

Welpid said, "I cannot buy your ship, because then there would be no bet." Welpid continued, "I have to admit, if the Grays did discover this ship, I would lose everything. I would rather take the money and save what I have created."

Wayne said, knowing he had won the argument, said, "Give me the coordinates."

Welpid handed over a small computer chip with all the valuable information. Welpid said, "Now the Grays know you are coming."

Wayne said, "Yep!"

Wayne stood up and escorted Welpid to the bridge's balcony. Crelk was still asleep. Wayne and Welpid left the apartment, and Wayne scanned Welpid's computer chip across the center console. Wayne escorted Welpid over to the bridge's balcony, saying, "Computer, input data from computer chip and display on hologram. Label data as the Milky Way." Wayne watched the computer-download light blink on and off for a few seconds, then stop. After about ten seconds, a majestic hologram of the Milky Way began to blossom, and the holographic flower took shape. Around the Milky Way were several other galaxies. To the south was the Cluster of the Three Galaxies. Still further to the south was Welpid's Cluster of the Eight Galaxies. To the west was the Cluster of the Five Galaxies. To the north was a menagerie of assorted galaxies, and to the east was the Cluster of the Four Galaxies.

Welpid hovered backward as the auditorium was ablaze with laser beams and navigational data. Wayne slowly looked around the galactic image, then noticed something ominous. Wayne said, "What is this? Are the Grays destroying star systems for ore? This is what the Ensups did to upset their galactic gravity equilibrium?"

Welpid quietly said, "Yes, they are repeating the errors of the Ensups." Wayne looked over at Welpid, knowing that he blamed the entities for upsetting that equilibrium.

Wayne said, "What is with you and the entities? And where did the Xynods come from?"

Welpid found himself in a very peculiar situation—having to tell the truth. Welpid softly said, "The Xynods originally inhabited the Grays' galaxy some three million years ago. The Grays had moved in from another galaxy when a battle ensued.

Wayne asked, "The Xynods already had space technology three million years ago?"

Welpid replied, "The Xynod's battle with the Grays was going badly. The spirits brought them here to the Cluster of the Eight Galaxies long ago as refugees."

Wayne asked, "Then the Grays defeated the entities?"

Welpid, speaking with the aid of his cane, said, "In a manner of speaking. The Grays in their technological greed created a plutonium planetary-particle accelerator and connected it up to a heavy-metal fusion reactor. The Grays then wired a remote detonator to the device and detonated it within proximity to the Xynod's home world. The entire quadrant went supernova right there on the test planet. Consequentially blast spread to other star systems, which also went nova, creating a colossal nebula. The Grays were surprised to discover an entire population of infant entities emerging from the clouds of subatomic particles: the first fabricated entities. This was two millions years ago. The Grays realized their newfound power and created a conscripted military force of entities to invade other galaxies." Welpid closed with this, "Wayne, do you still like those odds?"

Wayne said, "You are a great negotiator, not because you are rich or powerful, but because you are honest."

Welpid appreciated Wayne's good gesture. Welpid said, "We have taken care of Crelk and his Xynod friends for a million years, but where has it gotten us? I would gladly take the spirits over the Grays. Do you really want to take some Xynods with you to fight the Grays?"

Wayne and Welpid looked at each other from the bridge's balcony, and Wayne said, "This is my fight, though friends do make good allies, especially when battling for the same cause. Crelk is not part of this bet. I would not want Crelk to fall victim to a monetary wager."

Welpid laughed as he held out a spongy pasty appendage for the two to shake hands. Welpid said, "I look forward to our next meeting, hopefully sooner than later."

Wayne said, "I am sure it will be sooner."

Welpid returned to the apartment, where he bumped Crelk's leg with his hovercraft and said, "Get up, Crelk!"

Wayne said, "I forgot to give you your computer chip."

Welpid said, "You can keep it if I can keep these schematics and diagrams of your ship."

Wayne laughed, saying, "Sure you can."

Welpid said, "Is there another laptop with the classified information."

Wayne laughed and said, "Part of my down payment will be those classified files."

Wayne, Welpid, and Crelk all departed the bridge, making their way to the tram. Welpid and Wayne continued to talk, and Crelk fell asleep on the tram's floor.

The tram arrived at the airlock, and they each said their good-byes. The bots had just finished loading the chancellor's shuttle with the cargo containers of glucose and a bio-replicator chip to fabricate more.

Welpid and Wayne said their final farewells, and Crelk and Welpid boarded their awaiting shuttle. Wayne closed the drone's airlock door and locked it into place. The shuttle locked their door, and the connecting passageway rapidly depressurized with an ear piercing escape of air.

The chancellor's shuttle violently released the docking ringbolts in a mist of depressurized gas, and the shuttle slowly maneuvered away.

Wayne made his way back to the bridge for a very long and extensive intelligence briefing.

The Milky Way Complex

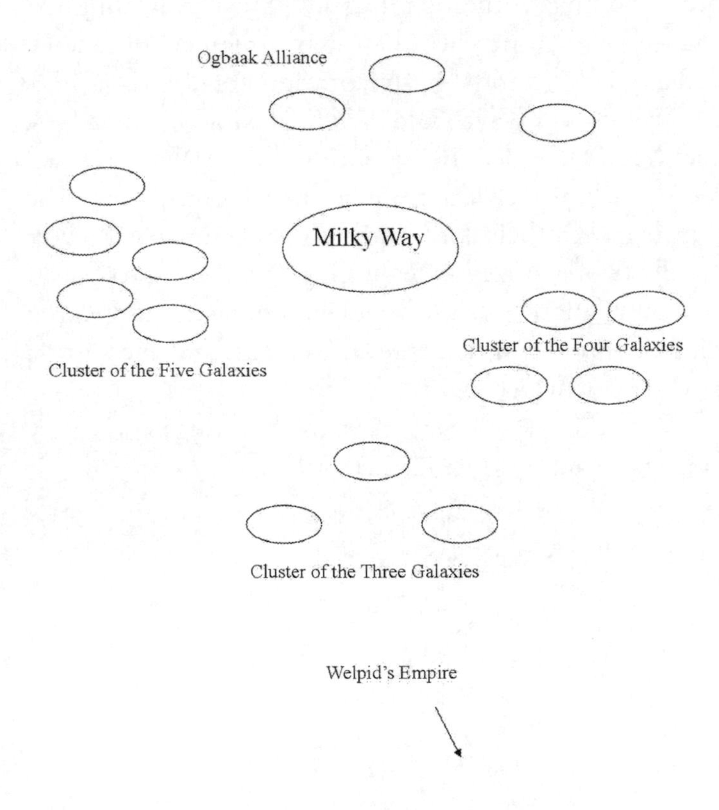

Chapter 8

Earth's Secret Past

Wayne carefully examined all the tiny laser beams as the auditorium-sized hologram plotted outposts, planetary settlements, military posts, and scouting routes.

Wayne said, "Computer, find the stars with a configuration of eight planets." The computer quickly illuminated two possible stars matching Wayne's criteria. He said, "Computer, zoom to this star's configuration." The computer brought up a series of planets that were all wrong, then Wayne said, "Computer, zoom in on the other star." The computer brought up eight midsized planets, including Saturn, Jupiter, Mars, and the Earth. Wayne started crying as he sat down on the bridge's balcony, repeating, "Home, home."

As his laser pointer marked the planet Saturn, Wayne

said, "Computer, designate this coordinate and mark it as home."

Wayne said, "Computer, display all systems belonging to the Xynods." The computer displayed ten star systems far in the southwest quadrant. Wayne continued, "Computer, display all star systems inhabited by the Grays." This time the entire galactic hologram lit up like a Christmas tree as thousands of data markers littered the galaxy.

Wayne noticed the Earth had a marker, too. Wayne commanded, "Computer, isolate designated marker and zoom in." The Earth had a small mining icon and a minor settlement. He read a list of extracted metals: iron, uranium, aluminum, salt, and plutonium. There were a couple of uranium-mining icons over two undersea subduction zones and several uranium and plutonium icons over several land-based installations.

Wayne said, "Computer, zoom in on this planet." A six-foot image of the Earth began to take shape as it revolved around its axis. Wayne inspected the land-based mining installations. Each icon listed uranium and plutonium as the products mined. These sites were in the United States, Iran, Russia, Pakistan, India, and France.

Wayne said, "Computer, remove image. Bring up image showing the process of plutonium mining and explain."

The computer brought up a flow chart diagram and explained, "Process involves a fifty gigahertz antigravity beam. The beam extracts materials within the fifty gigahertz frequency range, such as uranium and plutonium, up to a range of two miles. To retrieve biological matter, an alien ship attaches an antigravity generator in a backward configuration similar to the mining operation. Along the ship's belly is a storage compartment where a deployable boom assembly attaches to the antigravity unit. The deployable boom carrying the suspended antigravity unit is shrouded in a shield-containment cone to prevent sucking up atmosphere. At the bottom of the containment cone is an attenuated opening, which picks up biological matter.

"The antigravity beam dissolves all biological matter by a gravitational force close to the speed of light. Antigravity operates on a subatomic level where it can either assemble or disassemble matter. Antigravity is restricted for space use only and never used in a planet's atmosphere, unless encased in a shielded force field. Antigravity is primarily a matter-energy converter that dissects atomic and subatomic structure. The process requires a subatomic-shielding generator, which isolates the near-black-hole event caused by the antigravity device. Due to the generated heat, all Gray spacecraft are equipped with a cradle-deployment system attached to the antigravity unit. In case of emergency, the entire cradle unit can be jettisoned. The complete unit operates as a subatomic vacuum cleaner.

"Internal cryogenic coolant system prevents the shield generators from overheating. Military ships use the antigravity device as a tractor beam to retrieve scrap metal or store digitized matter in a computer-containment buffer. Each ship could store one-tenth of its weight in scrap metal or data storage before the computer's memory is full. An important warning, an antigravity matter-energy beam cannot extract dimensional matter currently in subspace. The resulting discharge will destroy both ships."

Wayne asked, "Computer, what the Grays' dimensional technology?"

The computer said, "Ships have a three-fourths gradient or three steps, but planetary facilities have an eight-fourths gradient, or eight steps. The Grays have experimented with vortex or twelve-fourths gradient, or twelve steps, but due to catastrophic containment issues and system arcing, several star systems were destroyed in the process."

Wayne commanded, "Computer, display all Gray fleets, surveillance, and scouting patrols." The computer displayed several fleets operating in and around the Milky Way complex. Wayne continued, "Display current position in relation to the Milky Way." The computer adjusted the auditorium's image from the Milky Way, zooming out until he could see the Cluster of the Eight Galaxies, plus three more galaxies beyond that, and then the Milky Way. Wayne needed to navigate past seven more galaxies before reaching the Milky Way. If what Welpid was true, the Grays patrolled the Cluster of the Eight Galaxies plus the three galaxies beyond that. This was an amazing stretch of territory, and Wayne needed an edge.

Wayne said, "Plot the closest Gray scouting patrol to current position." The computer displayed a fleet well beyond the Cluster of the Eight Galaxies in the grouping of three galaxies. Wayne could set up an ambush point on the northern edge of the Welpid's empire. Wayne said, "Computer, open a channel to Welpid's shuttle."

A few seconds later, Welpid came on, saying, "I am

enjoying your glucose." Wayne smiled and said, "My first waypoint will be on your northern border, deep into space. Alert your people to stand clear."

Welpid said, "I will pass that information on. Be safe, my friend."

Wayne said, "Computer, full engine start. Go to light speed. Initiate."

Wayne said, "Computer, plot course to the northern empire at this location, estimated time of arrival in dimensional drive."

The computer said, "Estimated time of arrival by dimensional drive: six months."

Wayne said to himself, "A lot can change in six months. Maybe we need to take shorter trips." Wayne pointed to another marker between the four northern galaxies, saying, "Computer, estimated time of arrival in dimensional drive to these coordinates?"

The computer said, "Estimated time of arrival in dimensional drive: three months."

Wayne said, "Computer, plot a course to those coordinates between the four galaxies." Wayne continued, "Computer, go to dimensional drive, and route all discharge through the ionic engines. Initiate."

The computer enabled all the necessary systems, and off they went.

Wayne said, "Max, I need you on the bridge."

Max said, "On my way."

Wayne commanded, "Harold and all research bots to the bridge.

Harold obediently said over the computer's voice processor, "On our way."

Wayne was in his apartment, fixing some steak, when

he heard the bots coming in from the subway station. He yelled from the apartment, "Come on the bridge."

Wayne organized them in a large semi-circle along the bridge's balcony. He turned on the hologram generator and asked the computer to bring up the large display, which spanned from the drone's ship current position to the Milky Way.

Wayne announced in an arrogant tone, "Bots, we are going to war. This is the situation. This is my home galaxy. Sarah will eventually meet me us here. We are going up against the Grays. We will be setting up an ambush point here. We need to deploy around five hundred proximity mines in this area. Once we break up the fleet, load all torpedo tubes to get the rest of them. My goal is to retrieve an antigravity device for research. There will be a crew to take apart the antigravity device and another crew to find anything salvageable or useful we can use. Have the open-bay shuttle ready to transport goods from the damaged or salvaged ship to the drone ship.

"I talked about a shield generator on the aft part of the ship for tractor-beam purposes. Did you get that message?"

Harold said, "That project is finished. The shield extends far enough to grab onto it and creates a cushion when brought against the hull."

Wayne commanded, "Once I have the enemy's technology, and you figure out how it works, I do not want it installed onboard. I want to fabricate several weapons, either a torpedo or a mine. Right now, we lack a suitable rocket platform for such a weapon. Our first priority is to get all weapons inspected. Our second priority is finding out what can we use from the queen's ship to help in the weapon's effort."

One of the research bots said, "I remember bringing missile rockets onboard."

Wayne said, "Okay, let's find those rockets and get them organized in the cargo hold. Max and Harold, all weapons will be assembled in weapons or the research lab. All rockets must remain in the cargo hold. The final assembly will take place in the cargo hold. Anything else we can use?"

All the bots were silent as they looked at each other. Wayne said, "Okay, Sarah is counting on you guys. Please be safe and take your time; no unnecessary rushing or cheating on procedures. Anyone have any questions?"

All the bots were excited. Finally, this was what they were waiting for. The bots made their way down the corridor to the subway area, but one decided to come back. This little research bot had chosen the name Missile Mike. Missile Mike told the other bots to go on and that he would catch up later. One of the bots yelled out, "We will wait for you."

Wayne went back up to the main bridge to get a juicy steak and some coffee from his apartment. As he passed the command console on his way to the apartment door, he heard a bot from behind the corridor wall. Wayne went back to the corridor, and there was the little bot. The bot quickly said, "My name is Missile Mike, and I need to talk to you."

Wayne seemed encouraged by the bot's name and said, "Okay, Missile Mike, what is on your mind?"

Missile Mike spoke through the computer's digital processor. "You asked us to investigate subspace radar.

We discovered this is impossible, but what we did find may help in our communications."

Wayne wanted to hear what Missile Mike discovered, so he said, "Do you want a touchpad to input data on?"

Missile Mike said, "I can download the information to the computer once we are finished."

Wayne said, "Proceed with your communication idea."

Missile Mike's synthesized computer voice said, "Dark matter or dark energy only exists when normal space is under tremendous gravitational stress. When discussing dark matter or dark energy, we should be talking about cosmic, gamma, or X-ray radiation. A black hole is similar to antigravity; it breaks down subatomic particles into their individual components, releasing radiation. An antigravity device is not about capturing subatomic particles, but creating a tremendous amount of energy. Dark matter exists because light does not exist. I want to try an experiment: if we can fire a bolt of high-energy subspace gamma radiation encoded with a transmitted signal, its range should span two galaxies. The dimensional discharge is similar to gamma and cosmic radiation, but too random for communication sequencing. We need a gamma-ray magnetron, a modulator, and a transmitter connected to a dedicated emitter electrode. A couple of bots have constructed a magnetron, a modulator, and a transmitter, but we need to install a separate emitter electrode to test the unit. Can we drop out of dimensional drive and test my idea?"

Wayne needed another intelligence assessment, and if this idea worked, giving out false information about false coordinates from an incredible distance away might be helpful. Wayne said, "Computer go to normal space, route all discharge to the vertical stab's emitter electrodes. Maximum radar scans, stop all engines, and engage aft thrusters. Initiate."

Wayne looked down at Missile Mike and said, "Get to work."

Missile Mike quickly retreated down the corridor where the tram was still waiting. Wayne could hear Missile Mike talking to the other research bots about assembling the transmitter antenna.

Wayne went to the bridge's balcony, saying, "Computer, initiate hologram with current radar and navigational data." Wayne noticed there were three fleets approaching the northern flank of Welpid's empire. Wayne noticed a small scouting detachment about twenty radar-range hours away on a perpendicular path. The scouting detachment was transmitting a transponder identification code.

Wayne saw that Welpid's entire domain was in lockdown; all commercial traffic between galaxies had stopped. Wayne needed to give the bots time to set up and conduct their experiment before setting up his ambush point.

Wayne said, "Computer, display the gravitation-isobar overlay on the hologram up to twenty radar-range hours." Wayne watched as the image slowly came up. It looked clean. There were some anomalies about sixteen radar range hours away. As he designated each one with the light pen, Wayne said, "Computer, track these anomalies for movement."

Wayne said, "Max, load all torpedo tubes with plungers."

Max said, “Loading now.”

Wayne said, “Harold, did anyone find those rocket engines?”

Harold said, “We found a hundred of them; they have a range of seven radar-range hours.”

Wayne said, “Max and Harold, build a twin-proximity mine unit with a plunger detonator. Harold, once Max sends the mines to you, attach them to the rocket engine and a small navigational transceiver so we can fly it remotely. Any questions?”

Harold and Max chimed in together, “Understood, and we will inform you when it’s ready.”

Wayne kept studying the anomalies until the research bots signaled that the test was about to start. Wayne said, “What is your message?”

Missile Mike said, “I do not know, we were going to transmit a coded buffer to see if the sequencing works.”

Wayne said, “Okay, go ahead.”

Missile Mike said, “Transmitting now.”

Wayne immediately noticed that the scouting detachment suddenly stopped. The computer came on. “Anomaly is within four radar range hours.”

Wayne said, “Computer, designate anomaly, fire torpedo.”

Wayne said, “Bots, get inside now, going to subspace in one minute.”

Wayne asked, “Computer, distance to next anomaly?”

The computer said, “Five radar-range hours.”

Wayne said, “Designate target at five radar-range hours, fire torpedo.”

Wayne said, “Max, load all torpedoes tubes.”

Missile Mike said, "We are inside."

Wayne said, "Computer, come around 180 degrees, full engine start and take us back four radar-range hours at light speed, then full engine stop and then come around again. Initiate."

The drone ship slowly maneuvered around 180 degrees, then fired all engines to retreat to a safe position.

Wayne said, "Missile Mike, whatever you transmitted sure got their attention. What happened?"

Missile Mike said, "The coded buffer transmitted successfully, but instead of transmitting a concentrated gamma beam, we transmitted in a wide-angle beam that caused a vibration effect. We need to adjust the anode, cathode, and grid-power inputs for a better beam projection. We can do that in the research lab.

Wayne said, "All right, keep working."

Nearly four hours had passed until the first torpedo exploded, sending a reddish yellow blaze across the empty void of space. The drone ship stopped and started to rotate around.

Wayne said, "Computer, go to dimensional gradient four-fourths. Initiate. The stab's emitter electrode began powering as the drone ship disappeared from view.

Wayne continued to monitor the scouting detachment as the second torpedo hit its mark. Now the scouting party accelerated to light speed to intercept the debris field. Wayne had a separate monitor dedicated to the gravitational isobar overlay. It appeared that all the anomalies were gone or vaporized.

Harold said, "The proximity mine missile is ready."

Wayne said, "Do you have a remote transmitter for the rocket-enable signal?"

Harold said, "Yes."

Wayne said, "Do not fire the engine. Jettison rocket now."

Wayne asked, "Computer, are you detecting a small navigational transceiver?"

The computer said, "Yes."

Wayne said, "Computer, designate debris field as target. Transfer designated coordinates to small transceiver, and transmit data along with navigational alignment."

The computer said, "Navigational receiver transmitter aligned to target."

Wayne said, "Harold, push the commit to launch rocket fire now."

Harold said, "Rocket is away."

Wayne said, "Computer, track receiver transmitter to designated target. Maintain alignment posture."

Wayne watched the scouting detachment closing in as the proximity-mine torpedo tracked toward the debris field.

The computer came on. "Detecting a larger fleet on an intercept course toward the debris field. Estimated time of arrival: three hours.

Wayne shouted, "Where did they come from!"

The computer said, "Cruisers are on station in the debris field. The scouting detachment due to rendezvous in forty-five minutes. The small receiver transmitter should arrive in thirty minutes."

Wayne said, "Computer, estimated speed of the cruisers?"

The computer said, "Cruisers were going about three times the speed of light while in normal space. No dimensional drive detected."

This put a completely new twist in the overall strategy. It was impossible to incorporate an existing ionic drive with an antigravity device. A new shield configuration could cheat light speed, but would create too much drag for the engines to overcome. Wayne needed that technology. Here in the next fifteen minutes, he would have his answer.

The computer said, "Proximity mine is detecting three cruisers and two scout ships. Detonation in three, two, one …"

Wayne could feel the pressure wave against the drone's dimensional field. Even the flash of the explosion radiated deep enough in subspace to create a nuclear pressure wave.

Wayne scanned the hologram for more targets, but all targets were well beyond Welpid's empire. Wayne said, "Computer, go to normal space, no target designated, discharge dispersal across all stabilizer emitter electrodes. Initiate."

Wayne could feel the discharge vibration against the drone's hull.

Wayne said, "Computer, scan debris field. Designate any targets with active momentum."

The computer said, "Debris field inactive."

Wayne said, "Computer, primary engine start, shields up. Designate debris field as destination. Initiate."

Wayne went over to the windscreen and was already seeing flying debris ricocheting the bow's protective shielding.

Wayne said, “Computer, designate all large debris and transfer data to hologram for viewing.”

As the drone ship approached, Wayne could see larger pieces, and there in the distance was an intact cruiser, badly damaged and venting atmosphere.

Wayne said, “Computer, designate perimeter of twenty radar range hours. Any targets present?”

The computer said, “All transponder signals are in the Milky Way or entering the three-galaxy cluster. No gravitational anomalies within twenty radar-range hours.”

Wayne said, “Harold, enable aft shields. We are going to wrap the shields around this cruiser and tow it back to a safe location.

Harold’s synthesized voice emanated from Wayne’s touchpad, “Aft shields enabled.”

Wayne said, “Computer, maneuver above cruiser and capture with aft shielding.”

Wayne said, “Harold, once the drone ship captures the cruiser, launch the open-bay shuttle and inspect the shield integrity around the cruiser.”

Harold said, “Preparing open-bay shuttle for shield inspection.”

Wayne said, “Max, prepare fifty proximity mines with detonators like you did before. Deliver the first ten to the aft cargo hold for rocket and navigational configuration.”

Wayne said, “Harold, Max will be delivering ten more proximity mines and detonators, fabricate the same rocket engine and navigation configuration as before.”

Harold said, “I have ten bots assigned to the task,

have ten rocket motors and ten navigational units ready for assembly, waiting for Max to make delivery."

The computer said, "Aft shielding deployed, cruiser is captured."

Wayne said, "Harold, inspect aft shield integrity."

Harold said, "Launching now."

It took Harold about fifteen minutes to complete his inspection.

Harold, speaking over Wayne's touchpad, "Inspection complete, shield strength at maximum." The cruiser embedded itself against the lower fuselage and the aft fascia's containment shield. Harold continued, "We can tow the cruiser like this, but not real fast."

Wayne wondered if this was a good idea. Even though the cruiser was only ten miles long and looked like a zeppelin, it represented an unstable drag and a dangerous trim problem for the larger drone ship.

Wayne said, "Computer, primary engine start. Engage two ionic engines. Initiate." After about fifteen minutes of dragging the damaged cruiser and straining the aft shield generator, Wayne had to stop and rethink this.

Wayne said, "Computer, all stop. Maintain aft shield around cruiser."

Wayne said, "Harold, take both shuttles and transfer all antigravity technology, data logs, weapons, rocket motor parts, computer files, engineering parts, hydrogen reservoirs, cryogenic coolant reservoirs, navigational computers, power couplers, main engine start batteries, waveguides, and plasma conduits. Also bring me back two bots and one alien, not dead."

Harold said, "The entire bot population wants

to help out; we will use the cruiser's shuttles to aid in transport."

Wayne said, "Computer, maintain a thirty radar-range hour perimeter while transferring cargo from the damaged cruiser. Monitor all anomalies and sudden changes as to the fleet's flight patterns."

Max said, "I am finished with the ten proximity mines, and all torpedo tubes are loaded. Can I help out with the transfer, too?"

Wayne said, "Sure, go ahead, but monitor the computer's warning signal. We may have to scuttle the ship, and I do not want to leave you behind."

Wayne was a wreck. For five days, the drone ship held the damaged cruiser in the precarious force field. The bots worked around the clock, shuttling equipment and nursing the shield generator's coolant problems, which were only seconds from catastrophic failure.

The research bots proved their worth beyond question as they documented and transcribed data files and entered them into the drone's computer. The bots were able to retrieve all the items on the list, including some unknown systems that needed further investigation.

Max was able to retrieve two alien bots and capture one very nasty Gray prisoner. Max personally escorted the three prisoners from the cruiser to the drone ship. The two bots were very similar in stature and appearance to the Grays, but lacked the security clearance to be of any value. The Gray, on the other hand, was one of the engineering officers, and judging by his temper, he intended to die with his secrets.

Max and Harold were busy fabricating proximity mines, detonators, rocket motors, and navigational transceivers. A majority of the bots were back onboard, sorting and classifying the confiscated material. The research bots had their antigravity technology, the data files, and all the publications they could ever ask for.

Wayne sent a message to Sarah regarding what Welpid had said about the spirits and ambassadors. He was also concerned that the antigravity device might disrupt entity physiology because they were energy-based.

The research bots, Wayne, and the computer discussed the antigravity drive and its tremendous speeds up to three times the speed of light. The most critical aspect of the drive was the shield-containment system and the associated cryogenic systems.

Max and some of the research bots designed what they called the "antigravity torpedo" or "deployable mine." The theory posed a gravitational or magnetic risk, but Wayne let the testing continue. The antigravity weapons operated on two levels; the first being the generated heat, and second the disintegration properties of antigravity. It resembled an antigravity engine, where the generated thrust operated as a plasma cutter. The excessive heat would only allow the mine to operate for a few seconds, then implode, causing the surrounding space to collapse in a massive negative-pressure vacuum. Theoretically, the antigravity weapon would disintegrate before allowing itself to grow into a black hole, but Wayne was not so sure. This is what the entities warned about and how the Ensups ruined their own galaxy. The Milky Way was already degraded and prone to further instability.

One of the bots found some papers and a small, metal box on the cruiser's bridge. Wayne asked the bot to bring it to the bridge right away. Wayne was already studying the confiscated computer files, security reports, mining data, and overall politics of the Grays' society.

Wayne heard the little bot coming down the corridor, and Wayne went to greet it. Wayne wanted to call it by name, so he looked at its nameplate. Then he saw what the little bot was carrying a silvery metallic briefcase. Wayne could not wait to open it, but consciously said, "What is your name?"

The little engineering bot was a tray bot, which carried tools and parts from the shop to the work site. The other bots would use the tray bot as a work stand or to keep things organized; consequently, the tray bots were very low in the esteemed ladder of mechanical confidence. The little bot did not have a voice or auditory speech processor, but could transmit voice data to a computer.

Wayne picked up his touchpad and held it up close to the tray bot. Again, Wayne repeated, "Do you want a name?"

The touchpad's synthesized voice said, "I brought you this metal case. I am happy that you see it as important."

Wayne said, "It is very important. This is a briefcase where important papers and computer disk represent valuable information. You did a very good job bringing it to me. Now, what name do you want?"

The little tray bot said, "It seems that everyone has a name. I would feel more important if I do not have a name, because that makes me different. Just call me 'No Name.'"

Wayne stood up over the small little robot, amazed at the technology of biologically imprinted robots. Imagine how an advanced race of aliens would decide to imprint machines, then imprint themselves out of existence.

Wayne said, "All right, No Name, Good job, and if I need something to find, I will call you." Wayne continued, "Harold, there is a little tray bot who wishes a nameplate: 'No Name.' No Name is taking the tram back to engineering. It brought me something of great value. Be sure to reward it."

Harold said, "Yes, I know of the little tray bot. He insisted on going to the bridge. I will look after No Name."

Wayne wondered where Sarah picked up these bots. He recalled these same bots when he was still in the sphere.

Wayne took the metallic briefcase and placed it on the bridge's deck. Wayne sat down on the floor and put the briefcase in front of him. He carefully inspected the security latches and figured that, since the bots found it on the table instead of locked up, a Gray was trying to destroy its contents.

He pushed on one of the latches, and it unlocked. He pushed the other latch, and it unlocked as well. Wayne slowly opened the top, being careful to inspect for any wires or springs. Slowly the silver briefcase revealed its contents: computer chips; paper documents; a small, concealed, hand weapon; and a small, black hologram box.

Wayne took the computer disks and chips and held them close to the computer's scanning interface terminal, saying, "Computer, scan and store all data under the file name *Cruiser* for retrieval at my request." Wayne took each storage device and scanned it across the interface terminal as the download light transferred the data to the main computer. Wayne scanned some twenty different storage chips and disks, some labeled with alien script, and two that looked like Russian script.

Wayne opened up the file with all the paper documents, but none of it he could read. Wayne figured he could get that Gray prisoner to read it. That would be an interesting interrogation session.

Then his attention shifted to the black hologram box. There was a small push-button on the side, but no visible script or drawings. Wayne placed the box on the floor and pushed the button. A series of laser beams started to unfold as the hologram created an image of a miniature Gray standing with his finger pointing at something or someone. The auditory processor engaged as the Gray figurine started to talk. Wayne held the touchpad up close so the speech processor could translate.

The little Gray hologram spoke in a very angry, petite voice. "We are losing control of our empire. We have assaults on our northern border; we have problems in our outer provinces, and the damage we caused to our galaxy may be irreversible. Our mining settlements lack the ability to meet our production quotas, our willingness to conquer lesser alien societies has softened, and we are noticing a severe interruption in our communications with the high council. I know of three alien species who are challenging our right to exist at this very moment. None of us wants a full-scale war, but it seems this is our only way out. Our southern flank is weak, and at this moment, we are en route to a distress call from our scouting ships. Extraction of provincial tribute can only go so far, and we do not have the resources to confront such an uprising. Concentrate all efforts on the western, northern, and eastern borders. From now on, confiscate all provincial commercial shipping for scrap-metal recycling and spare parts, by order of the Military Junta."

Wayne sat there, not believing what he just heard. Wayne transferred the recorded message from his touchpad and sent the file off to Welpid with this warning: "Captured a Gray cruiser a couple days ago, found this message. Secure your shipping routes now."

Wayne had not assembled all the pieces yet, but mentioning the high council created even more questions. Welpid said something about fabricated entities from a manmade nova, but that was millions of years ago. Cheng did say that he found Wayne in a vortex anomaly and had transferred him to the sphere. He did say something about the Grays then. Cheng may have taken high-council payoffs to assist in the Venus alien's demise once the Skurlords fell in defeat. He even suspected Sarah in this bizarre conspiracy where entities played sides to manipulate societal growth and power. Wayne's main emphasis was to get back home, and that hinged on defeating the Grays at their own game.

Wayne had not seen the bots this excited. They were engaged in endless conversations about pirate ships, valuable booty, and killing dangerous aliens. They were researching new technologies and fabricating complicated weaponry. I guess it was an exciting time to be a bot onboard the drone ship, but Wayne's strategic chess match was only getting started. His first move should be on the northern border of Welpid's empire.

Wayne said, "Max and Harold, construct as many mine-navigational missiles as possible. Try to construct a storage platform or cargo rack so we can save space. Make sure you have the corresponding rocket motor matched with the correct rocket launch remotes."

Max said, "Working on them now."

Harold said, "We tested the antigravity simulator; it is far too dangerous, but we were able to configure the gamma ray transmitter to a beacon marker configured as a distress call."

Wayne said, "Wow, that's perfect! Along with the mine missiles, we can fabricate the mine beacon deployed by a rocket motor. Have the rocket attached to a jettison docking ring so when the rocket burns out, it leaves the beacon to do its dirty work."

Wayne said, "Computer, bring up the hologram display." Wayne monitored Welpid's northern empire, which appeared to be target-free. "Computer, designate these coordinates," Wayne said as he moved his laser pen on the northern edge of Welpid's galactic territory. "Computer, full engine start, go to light speed. Engage dimensional drive, route all discharge though the ionic drive engines. Initiate."

The computer said, "Estimated time of arrival, five months."

Wayne was not sure why the Grays allowed the Earth to exist while evicting Crelk's people, the Xynods. It appeared that the Xynods were not a formidable force, and the Grays had the clear advantage. Wayne would not make the same mistake the Xynods made. The Grays were the primary target, and if anyone or anything got in the way, oh well. Wayne had no intention of creating alliances along the Grays' three battlefronts: the west, north, and the east. One of the basic rules to siege warfare was never to attempt a siege when others request invitations. If you cannot do it by yourself, do not expect others to blindly help from the kindness of their heart.

Wayne said to all the bots, "We are going to war, boys. bring the three captured prisoners to the bridge, along with a security escort, and bring up the nursery bot, too."

Chapter 9

The Gray Prisoner

The nursery bot and three other bots arrived at the bridge's subway station, escorting the Gray prisoner and the two bots. As far as the Gray prisoner knew, it was an unknown alien ship loaded with strange-looking bots. Wayne communicated to the nursery bot through the touchpad's synthesized voice modulator. "I want the two Gray bots first. Hold the Gray alien in the tram, under guard."

Wayne knew the Gray alien would be hostile, but he was not sure about the bots. Keeping the Gray in the locked tram only added to the anxiety. The last thing Wayne wanted was for the Gray to see a pathetic human instead of a mighty bot captain. Wayne could get Max, but the Gray had already seen Max.

Wayne heard the nursery bot's motorized tracks,

but wasn't able to hear the bot's footsteps. Wayne stuck his head down the corridor as the nursery bot escorted two petite mechanical grays, about two feet tall. Wayne went back and sat down on the floor in front of the main console. He prepared a little show-and-tell exhibit: the silver briefcase, the hologram, the document written in Russian, and the data file on the slow galactic decay of the Milky Way.

Wayne reached for his touchpad just in case he needed the universal translator.

Wayne said to the nursery bot as they entered the bridge, "How is our Gray prisoner doing?"

The nursery bot replied, "I have the bots with me. Three security bots are holding the alien in the tram. The Gray has a restraining lock on all four appendages; he is not going anywhere." The nursery bot slowly positioned the two bots in front where Wayne was sitting. Wayne needed to know two things: first, whether the bots biologically imprinted like Sarah's bots; and second, whether the bots understood any other languages.

The nursery bot announced, "Here are the bots you requested."

Wayne said, "Do you feel comfortable here?"

The nursery bot reacted negatively to Wayne's question. Wayne waited for the two Gray plastic figurines to react, but they just stood there. Wayne started to wonder if someone erased the bots' hard drive before they were taken prisoner.

The little bots stood motionless. It was hard tell what they were looking at with their creepy black eyes. Wayne repeated, "Do you like it here?"

The little bots were nonresponsive. Wayne knew something was up.

Wayne turned to the nursery bot. "Have these little bots said or did anything since their capture?"

The nursery bot said, "Not a sound the whole time."

Wayne picked up the little hologram box, placed it on the floor, and pushed the button. Wayne watched the two bots as the hologram image unfolded. Wayne played the audio from the touchpad, and the hologram show commenced. Wayne watched carefully—neither bot reacted in any way to the hologram.

Wayne disappointed with the situation, said, "Nursery bot, take these bots down to maintenance. Erase all prior programming and replace with fresh programming, then put the bots to work."

The nursery bot said, "It will be like taking care of my little kids again."

Wayne laughed and said, "Yes, they are your little children, teach them right. Now bring in the Gray."

The nursery bot took the little mechanical toys back down the corridor. Wayne figured he needed the hologram image playing when the Gray prisoner walked in. Wayne needed the conversation to go from start to checkmate in one question. The only tactical strategy the Gray had was to play on Wayne's sympathy. He needed the Russian document translated and a full explanation regarding the computer files and classified information ranging from military assets to political problems back home.

Wayne also needed his restraining harness removed once he arrived on the bridge. The Gray would never concede to a human or to knowing a human was pulling his strings. Wayne thought about a hidden transmitter and wondered if the computer could detect such a transmitter. This alien was better off dead, but knowing that a human killed him made it that much sweeter.

Wayne went into his apartment and picked up a small weapon from the locker. He also took a steak from the icebox and placed it in the infrared broiler, selecting medium-rare. Wayne left the apartment door open so the fresh aroma of barbequed steak could mingle with the air. Wayne could hear the nursery bot and the other security bots entering the bridge area. He also heard the Gray struggling and grunting as he tried to escape. Wayne shouted out to the nursery bot and the security bots from behind the safety of his apartment door, "If he tries to escape, kill the prisoner!"

Then there was a strange silence. Wayne wondered if he had given it away by speaking human without the touchpad's speech synthesizer. Wayne said in his normal voice, "Want a steak, Gray?"

Wayne noticed the definite sound of labored breathing. He wondered if the Gray would have a heart attack if it struggled too much.

Wayne shouted from his apartment, "Hey, Gray, can you read Russian?" The heavy breathing began to subside, but there was a definite sound of struggling as the restraining bolts rattled like chains against the bridge's metallic floor. Wayne figured the alien must have seen the briefcase and the hologram cube by now. Wayne continued, "I have some beer here. I know Grays like beer and whiskey."

That was it, the Gray alien said in a nasty, squeaky

voice, "I hate beer, I hate whiskey, I do not like steaks or anything else you try to offer me!"

Wayne said, "You want to know something, Gray? I am a time traveler. Yes, I am human, but I have journeyed across thousands of galaxies, but next to the Ensups, you are the dumbest species yet!" Then Wayne figured he would make his grant entrance. He walked onto the bridge, went over to the main console, and sat down on the floor next to the hologram box. Wayne had never seen a Gray sweat as much as this one did. He pushed the button, energizing the hologram's image as the audio from the touchpad synchronized up. Wayne watched as the Gray was fighting to break free. One of the bots who was standing in the corridor had a small weapon drawn and pointed at the Grays' head. Wayne also noticed that the bots were really enjoying this interrogation session.

Wayne reached for the Russian paper document from the floor. Wayne challenged, "Here, translate this Russian message."

Wayne could see the file's reflection in the Grays' creepy black eyes. The fear of death was only moments away. Whether his death was by suicide, at the hands of a pathetic human or worse yet, shot by a bot, he was already dead in his eyes.

Wayne removed his concealed weapon from behind his back and placed it beside him on the floor. If Wayne could get this alien to crack, he might prove to be valuable.

The hologram show stopped with an eerie silence, and Wayne said, "Computer, open data file marked 'Cruiser,' transfer file to the touchpad, and play." The touchpad started playing a file from one of the confiscated data chips from the briefcase. The recording consisted of communications or messages received from various enemy factions who were attacking Gray planetary possessions and strongholds. Wayne did not recognize any of the recordings. These were new players in the overall scheme of galactic politics, but the Gray sure reacted negatively to the recordings.

Wayne said, "Space buddies, or enemies of yours?"

Wayne knew that any suggestion might come off as a trick or ploy to earn the Gray's trust. Judging by the Gray's attitude, he was not buying.

Wayne said, "You know, if we work together, we can fight these enemies of yours. But in the end, we still will be enemies, won't we?"

The Gray angrily said, "Yes, we should have killed off your pathetic species long ago, but the high council prohibited it."

Wayne quickly said, "You know why the entities are not helping you? It is because they are helping me. I have a direct connection to the high council." Wayne reached for his touchpad. Wayne selected the appropriate icon for the high council and showed it to the Gray. "See, I am the chosen one. Your society is old and gray." He pushed the button on the hologram box once more.

The Gray was doing his best to break free, but the two bots maintained a tight and oppressive grip.

Wayne had always known that arrogance could never measure up to a weaker, yet stronger-willed individual. This Gray was extremely arrogant, but his self-confidence was about to give up the ghost. There were only a couple more minutes left.

Wayne pointed to the bridge's windscreen. "See

anything out there?" Wayne continued, "That is because we are traveling in subspace to the cluster of the three galaxies. Then after that, I will be invading the Milky Way, our home galaxy. I have already negotiated a peace treaty with Welpid and Crelk of the Xynods.

The Gray broke in, saying angrily, "Welpid scum! Crelk scum! Xynod scum! Human scum!"

Wayne said, "How many ships did I destroy? I didn't fire a single shot. How many cruisers and scout ships are floating debris right now because of your stupidity?"

Wayne challenged, "Either we fight together, or else I will annihilate you and your enemies and hand over this entire quadrant to Welpid to manage."

The Gray refused to answer, so Wayne said, "Well, that is it. I have to kill you now."

The Gray said, "You can't kill me."

Wayne laughed and asked, "And why not?"

The Gray seemed to be searching for an explanation, but was too nervous to talk or think straight. Wayne said, "Let me help you out, I have to spare your life because you're too rich and important to risk such jeopardy."

The Gray said, "How much money do you want?"

Wayne said, "What is money? Money only exists to satisfy those who see value in politics and greed."

The Gray again asked, "I can get you land on Earth, you are from the place called America. Grays have plenty of land in America; much of it is deep underground or under the ocean."

Wayne said, "As if the Grays will blindly accept your plea in exchange for your life. Trust should never be extended to a third-party participant, no matter how appealing the transaction."

The Gray challenged, "I am the president of all the Grays."

Wayne replied, "Okay, once I hand you over, the Grays will most certainly kill me for abducting you. I am better off returning a corpse than inviting my own death."

The Gray continued the struggle as the negotiation dragged on.

Wayne said, "Tell me about the cruiser's stability issues when exceeding light speed. Antigravity is an awesome piece of hardware, but the risks and safety hazards are well beyond the tactical usefulness of such technology."

The Gray continued to struggle; Wayne figured he must be tired.

Wayne said, "This ship combines dimensional technology with older ionic-drive engines. Instead of traveling at the speed of light in normal space, I can travel the length of whole galaxies in the comfort of subspace in a matter of weeks."

The Gray said, "That is not possible!"

Wayne said, "Sure it is. Subspace is like dark matter; there is no speed limit. I can travel through a star or planet while in subspace and never even know it." Wayne continued, "What alerted the scout ships and you, as well, to fall into my trap? Did you receive a gamma-communications signal?"

The Gray would not admit to falling into anyone's trap or acknowledging that a gamma-ray signal even existed.

Wayne said, "I even knew your transponder signal. The scout's signal was 967 megahertz, and yours was 945 megahertz."

The Gray was about to crawl out of his skin, he was so mad, but Wayne continued to sit silently with the gun on the floor as he pushed the button on the hologram box once more.

Wayne said, "I determined you erased the memory core of the little bots before they were captured."

The Gray interrupted, "Yes we did. They are useless to you now."

Harold said over the touchpad communicator, "We received your alien bots. They are now reprogrammed. What do want with them?"

Wayne replied, "Perfect timing. Send them back to the bridge." Wayne turned to the Gray prisoner, saying, "Guess who is coming to pay us a little visit? Imagine being killed at the hands of your own bots."

The Gray continued in a belligerent tone, "What part of Earth's future do you belong to?"

Wayne said, "A future where there are no Grays. A future where galactic commerce, peace, and enlightenment rule supreme. The age of power, governmental corruption, and greed is over. The oppression and philosophy of enslavement no longer plagues the human spirit, but has blossomed into a new renaissance of science, exploration, creativity, and freedom of the heart, the soul, and the mind. Technology no longer indentures scientific expression. Science has taken a more responsible role in understanding the relationship between technology and material possession. My futures is where the entities play an active role in the galaxy's overall security, but are prohibited from interfering commercial or in individual lives. My future is where the entities and all alien species believe in a divine God and that He created the universe, not the Grays."

The Gray shouted, "Hypocrisy, blasphemy!"

Wayne laughed as he said, "The concept of being civil—how can you describe the relationship between being civil with the illusion of technological oppression? Is such a concept proportional or disproportional? One would think that technology was proportional to one's civil, philosophical view. However, as technology makes our lives miserable and enslaves us, then our civic responsibility toward others collapses into chaos as we see our own individual greed and entitlement more important. Technology does not make us self-reliant, but dependant on the master who feeds us the next best thing."

The Gray, still contemptuous, shouted in a squeaky voice, "Blasphemy! The Grays are gods!"

Wayne, amazed at the Gray's own self-absorption, said, "A false god, leading a decaying empire, feeling the pressure from outside, feeling the rebellion of your own provinces, feeling the pressure that you are not the supreme being you think you are. The Grays' existence is nearly over. The resulting power vacuum does not belong to one particular species, but to an idea that a divine being will help others to understand that people create civilizations, not governments."

The Gray struggled, and then suddenly his face tightened up as his body convulsed and his hands reached for his chest. The little Gray's body went limp, and the bots released him, his body falling to the floor. The Gray's ghostly black eyes were still open, and his little blue tongue drooled on the floor.

Wayne, still sitting on the floor, said, "So much for being a god. Bots, toss this false god out the aft airlock. He is useless to me now."

Wayne picked himself off the floor, picking up the piles of show-and-tell material. He walked into his bridge apartment where his steak was now cold and tough. He could hear the bots dragging the Gray's body down the corridor as the tram approached the bridge's subway station.

Wayne could hear Harold, the egg-hoist bot, talking to the security bots, asking them to wait for him. Wayne walked from his apartment through the bridge and down the corridor to meet Harold and see the new Gray bots.

"Harold," Wayne said as if greets an old friend.

Harold said, "Here are the bots you requested. All freshly programmed, their memory cores were compatible to the biological imprints. They are very fragile, so we cannot use them in engineering."

Wayne said, "I can use them on the bridge with me. Good work on the gamma-ray communications. I discovered the Grays received your transmission, but were unable to determine its source. The gamma-ray transmitter and the beacons are your first two accomplishments. Good work!"

Harold said, "Thanks, I had a good time working with the other research bots. We have about one thousand rocket motors with corresponding remotes and navigational transceivers ready for deployment. Max has assembled two hundred proximity mines and detonators, which are being stored in weapons until the order of final assembly."

Wayne said, "We are going to drop out of subspace

in three months, so now is the time to prepare, fix what's broken and get organized. Keep the ideas coming, and the research team working. Thanks, Harold."

Harold turned around, leaving the two Gray alien bots with Wayne as he watched Harold board the tram with the security bots and the dead Gray. Wayne waved good-bye as the tram left the subway station. Relieved that this matter was over, Wayne looked at the two gray bots, saying, "What are your names?"

The bots said in rapid succession, "Fritz and Fanny."

Wayne said, "Man, you guys are too creepy!"

Chapter 10

Work-ups

Warping or bending space for faster space travel had its advantages, but was it technologically ethical? The technology required a tremendous amount of energy, and it radically altered gravitational equilibrium. On the one hand, the entity's desire to maintain the universe's equilibrium preempted all alien technology. Wayne was not sure where the entities went wrong. The equilibrium edict had morphed into a political raffle, where equilibrium gave way to playing favorites between alien races. The high council apparently took it upon themselves to decide who would benefit from the security of equilibrium. The real question was, who passed the edict onto the high council?

Fritz and Fanny turned out to be very valuable as bridge support. Their ability to interface with the computer and their ability to express themselves vocally almost made the touchpad obsolete. Wayne positioned them on the bridge's balcony, overlooking the auditorium's hologram, where they memorized stellar and planetary locations, fleet transponder codes, communication frequencies, and protocols, and they calculating speed vectoring when the cruisers exceeded light speed.

Max and Harold came by the bridge to play computer games on the hologram. That was when Wayne introduced them to chess. Harold took the chess pieces down to the bot-repair ship and fabricated multiple chess sets so all the other bots could play. In a month's time, chess consumed the entire ship. Nothing was getting done. Wayne felt that it occupied the bot's time. The bots could not stop talking about their next game or who was beating whom. Wayne had to step in a couple of times when the games became too competitive.

The data chips and disks from the briefcase revealed three valuable pieces of information. The first were the communication frequencies of the various factions who were assaulting the Grays' outposts. The second was the Earth's Christian date. The year was 2050. The global economic boom of the early to mid-2000s had deteriorated into a bloodbath of poverty, war, rebellion, disease, and socialism. Governments only existed on paper as global factions governed from the back rooms at the United Nations. All commerce and industrialization ceased to exist. It was as if Rome had fallen to the barbarians. The Grays had long influenced public policy, especially in the development of nuclear power and advanced polymer ceramics. The report stated that Russia, Iran, China, and France were cooperating with the Grays' request to boost nuclear development for the expressed purpose of refueling orbiting spacecraft. The United States banned all nuclear development in the late 2000s, severely crippling any monetary exchange for political favors. The Plutonium Wars raged as a multi-galactic war, but on Earth, Venezuela, Cuba, and North Korea fought over America's ailing corpse. In a surprise move, Russia received the final deed to America's vast mineral and resource reserves, in accordance to the Grays' wishes. Venezuela received the rights as Russia's proxy to manage all of America's resources. Venezuela, twenty years earlier, had absorbed all of Colombia, Central America, and Mexico as part of Washington DC's socialistic mandate. In the year 2050, America itself was dissolved to became New Venezuela in an effort to produce what America refused to. Russia, in turn, absorbed Alaska and was now poised to take over Canada.

The third was an internal memo regarding the ambassadors and the high council. Continued political turmoil within the high council over preemptive favoring of alien species cited two incidences: the Ensup affair and the Skurlords affair. The Grays desperately needed reinforcements against neighboring factions, but the ambassadors either refused to help or were not aware of the problem. Welpid understood the danger in allowing the spirits and ambassadors to threaten the commercial and industrial fabric of freedom and capitalism. Now that Wayne was putting the puzzle together, the high council received their orders from the Grays.

The Grays needed to end Welpid's reign to create a direct path to the high council's galactic enclave. To understand the greater picture, the ambassadors routinely staggered both emerging and declining civilizations together to create a slow progression from one to the other. Unfortunately, the ambassadors created a situation where several emerging civilizations developed all at once. The Ensup affair and the Skurlord affair were little more than a weeding-out process. Wayne now understood Cheng's role in the final demise of the Venus-flytrap-faced aliens.

Technology was not the "end all and be all." Even as Greece, Persia, and Rome fought with technology, the underlying current was still political. Technology might open up galactic space, but the ultimate force will always remain political.

Wayne began to realize Welpid's impact and contribution toward a galactic free-market economy. Markets require two very important character traits: honesty and cooperation. Conversely, large political governments demand both technology and military plunder to perpetuate the propaganda of oppression. When the Grays perfected the process of stasis regeneration, oppression became obsolete, as immortality went to the select few.

Wayne's new mission was to create his own thriving civilization based on Welpid's principles. Wayne knew he needed help, but for the time being, he was a one-man show.

Wayne commanded, "Computer, go to normal space and maintain light speed with all engines on. All residual discharge routed through the ionic-drive engines and the stab's emitter electrodes. Initiate."

This was when the drone ship was the most vulnerable; dropping into normal space in enemy territory. The radar scan immediately picked up two major fleets and four scouting ships some thirteen radar-range hours away.

Wayne commanded, "Computer, all stop. Go to one-dimensional gradient. Initiate." The radar scan showed both fleets changing approach vectors and scouting patrols accompanying the cruisers.

Wayne said, "Max, load the plutonium proximity drone."

Max said, "PPD loaded."

Wayne said, "Computer, fire plutonium proximity drone."

From what Wayne remembered, detonation required a discharge blast no closer than a six-hour window. Wayne turned toward Fritz and Fanny and said, "What is the best firing resolution where I can still be six hours away?"

Fritz and Fanny looked at each other and said, "Wait two hours. Drop into normal space and target the plutonium proximity drone. Come about, and then power all engines for light speed for a four-hour burn."

Wayne said, "Wow, I hope you are right.

Wayne watched the two cruiser fleets and the scouting patrols fly as one formation, traveling at the speed of light. The cruisers were capable of faster speeds, but that was what happened before: the cruisers had taken off, leaving the scout ships in the dust. Wayne figured they had learned their lesson and were staying together as a group. This gave Wayne a better weapons advantage. The ships were at twelve radar-range hours and closing. The computer was suppose to acknowledge when the PPD was in position, and the discharge bolt would be fired. It would take another four hours for the discharge blast to arrive. That is a ten-hour lapse time. He only had a six-hour window. To achieve coincidence at six hours, he would have to wait three hours, fire the discharge, and then come about with an engine burn time of three more hours."

Wayne said, "Weapons, load all torpedoes."

Wayne said, "Max and Harold, I want ten proximity mines, rocket engines, and navigational transceiver missiles built and ready to go on the cargo bay."

Harold said, "We are getting set up, Max is prepping the tram now."

Two hours lapsed. The Grays' formation is now at the ten radar-range hour mark. The discharge window would opened up in one-hour, and then the drone ship would drop into normal space, fire the discharge, and be out of there.

Wayne checked the gravitational isobar overlay data. No anomalies were detected.

One hour passed. There were a couple of minutes remaining until zero hour.

Wayne said, "Computer, designate plutonium proximity drone as target. Go to normal space, fire discharge at designated target. Fire." The entire bridge lit up white hot as the discharge shot off as a collection of a thousand lightning bolts.

Wayne said, "Computer, primary engine start, come around 180 degrees, then full engine start to light speed. Initiate." The drone ship ignited two of its primary ionic-drive engines and slowly maneuvered into a sweeping U-turn. Then all fifteen engines ignited with full afterburner, propelling the ship to light-speed acceleration.

The Grays' fleet formation was at nine radar-range hours when the computer came on, saying, "Detected enemy torpedo launch."

Wayne said, "Max, how good are you at targeting an enemy torpedo?"

Max said, "Proximity mines should take care of that torpedo, or we can jettison scrap metal as debris."

Wayne said, "Harold, find all the scrap metal you can find and jettison it out of the aft cargo bay."

Harold said, "Getting scrap together. Jettison in fifteen minutes."

One hour went by.

The computer said, "Multiple torpedoes inbound at seven radar-range hours."

One hour went by.

Wayne noticed the fleet's formation was at seven radar-range hours.

The computer said, "Drone has reached three-hour mark, discharge is on approach, coincidence is in two hours."

Wayne said, "Computer, we have one more hour to make up. Plot drone's projected coordinates in one-hour time."

The computer said, "Projected coordinates on hologram. Coincidence is in line with approaching targets. Discharge two hours behind, is on target."

One hour went by.

The computer said, "Plutonium proximity drone has stopped at five radar-range hours. Discharge will arrive in one hour. Fleet is at six-radar-range hour mark, coincidence will be one hour off, but within lethal parameters. Discharge is tracking on target."

The torpedoes maintained a steady distance of six radar-range hours behind the drone ship. Torpedoes had a burn time of five hours. Wayne decided keep going and let the torpedoes run out of fuel.

One hour went by.

The computer said, "Drone detonation in five, four, three, two ..." The black void between Welpid's northern flank and the Cluster of the Three Galaxies lit up like a nova, incinerating everything within six radar-range hours including the pursuing torpedoes. Wayne figured they were at least seven hours away, but they felt the nuclear pressure wave from the blast.

Wayne analyzed the hologram from the bridge's balcony. "Computer, bring up the hologram generator and display the Milky Way and the Cluster of the Three Galaxies, including our position."

What an explosion! The pressure wave extended into the three-galaxy cluster, causing additional damage to surrounding fleets. The blast destroyed the entire southern fleet. Parts of the radar scan were impenetrable because of the radioactive interference from the blast.

Wayne said, "Computer, stop all engines except for primary. Come about 180 degrees, then go to one-fourth dimensional gradient. Initiate."

According to the holographic image, the Grays were calling up reserves as a concentrated force toward the southern front.

Wayne remembered one summer job, when he worked at a beef processing plant and kosher slaughterhouse. His job lasted for two hours, from eight a.m., when he started, until ten a.m. when he quit. The whole process turned his stomach and made him terribly ill. If there was anything of value he took from that job, it was an old butcher named Sam. Wayne figured Sam was a psychopath, because he called the cows "enemies." Sam would say, "You need to bleed your enemies before you attack them." Wayne never really understood what Sam meant until just now: bleed the Grays' defenses before attacking.

Wayne called Harold on the touchpad, "Harold, I want you to fabricate a holographic generator like the one I have on the bridge. Will that be a problem?"

Harold came back. "No, no problem. Much of the same computer-access cables extend toward engineering and weapons. When Sarah had us build the holographic generator, we kept the same cable identifiers and schematic blueprints. We can start work. It should be finished in a couple of days. We have the perfect place for it, too."

The Cluster of the Three Galaxies was a naturally occurring gravitational depression because of the variations in torque vectors generated by each of the revolving galaxies. The Grays saw this gravitational anomaly as more of a natural barrier than a strategic battleground. Wayne said, "Harold, build a rocket-propelled beacon mine and navigational transceiver. The package should include two proximity mines and detonator, a beacon with one of the faction's distress frequency, and a navigational transceiver. How long will that take?"

Harold came on the touchpad. "I have one here, but it is a prototype."

Wayne said, "Harold, jettison the prototype. Be ready with the commit-to-launch remote."

Harold said, "Prototype jettisoned."

Wayne said, "Computer, search for navigational transceiver on aft quarter."

The computer said, "Navigational transceiver active and ready."

Wayne pointed the laser pointer at the bottom of the gravitational depression within the Cluster of the Three Galaxies.

Wayne said, "Computer, designate target, transfer navigational data to local transceiver, and align to target. Initiate."

The computer said, "Transceiver data loaded. Aligned to target."

Wayne said, "Harold, commit to launch. Fire."

The rocket was a larger, staged missile appropriated from the Grays' cruiser. This was a long-range, high-thrust, solid-propellant rocket with an ionic-drive engine. Wayne could see the rocket's telemetry on the hologram as it approached the gravitational depression.

Wayne said, "How many of those rockets can you fabricate and have ready?"

Harold said, "We can have twenty ready in five hours. Max already sent us the proximity mines and detonators."

Wayne continued to watch the prototype, and then he saw a ship drop into normal space in hot pursuit of the missile. This ship was about one hour away—too close for comfort. Wayne called up the radar display and the gravitational isobar overlay data, but it was clear. The ship was not a Gray, because there was no transponder signature.

Wayne said, "Computer, designate ship as target, launch torpedo. Fire."

Wayne watched the hologram as the prototype was now descending down into the gravity well with the ship still following, and now a torpedo added to the chase.

Wayne said, "Computer, search for anomalies within nine radar-range hours." Wayne added, "Was there a detectable discharge when the ship dropped into normal space?"

The computer said, "The ship was not in dimensional space."

Wayne said, "Then how did it sneak up on us, because it nearly bit us on the ass?"

The computer said, "Older technology: shield-blending frequency generator."

Wayne said, "What is that?"

The computer said, "A shield cloak. The shield generator transmits a carrier frequency that matches the background horizon."

Wayne said in a belligerent tone, "Great!" He figured the ship was already at one-fourth dimensional gradient. If the ship was operating on older technology, there was a chance the ship did not detect the drone. Wayne was not interested in allowing buzzards to wait patiently on neighboring trees.

Wayne said, "How can we detect these cloaked ships?".

The computer said, "Weapons should have a static-field-pulse generator, which sends out a sudden surge of electromagnetic energy over a five-hour range."

Wayne said, "Good. Computer, launch a static-field-pulse generator."

The computer said, "Firing EMP in one minute.

Protocol shielding with grounding to the emitter electrodes, initiated."

Wayne watched through the windscreen as the entire horizon blossomed into thousands of bolts of electricity glowing from the hull and extending far out into space. Wayne ran over to the radar monitor and saw five more ships with their shielding stripped away.

Wayne said, "Computer, designate all targets, fire with low-yield torpedoes. Fire!"

Wayne ran over to the windscreen as five reddish fiery explosions blended into the already amazing bluish white electric storm.

Wayne said, "Computer, search for debris. I need to know who these guy were."

The computer said, "Found intact ship at one radar-range hour."

Wayne said, "Designate target. Can we use thrusters while in dimensional subspace?"

The computer said, "Yes, aft thruster on with stability control. Estimated time of arrival, two hours."

Wayne said, "Harold, we are coming up to some debris in two hours. Send over a detachment in an open-bay shuttle and see what you can find."

Harold said, "Following up on previous request. The hologram generator is now operational in an adjacent chamber between the research lab and the weapons chamber. We are monitoring the debris field now. We have more prototype missiles ready."

Wayne said, "Thank you very much, Harold."

Wayne said, "Computer, status on prototype missile and enemy ship."

The computer said, "Torpedo destroyed ship. Prototype

has settled into the lower gravitational depression with distress call functioning properly. Monitoring several other ships on the lip of the depression, but none will go in. Escape velocity is too high, at 95 percent light-speed velocity."

Wayne said, "I wonder who will dive in first?"

Wayne watched the hologram as the southern front had all but dissolved, and assets transferred to support the northern and eastern fronts.

Wayne heard something on the main bridge. "What is that?"

The touchpad received a message-acknowledgement tone. Wayne picked up the touchpad with an image of some numbers and a coordinate designator. Wayne said, "Computer, plot these coordinates and display on hologram."

The computer's hologram image suddenly zoomed out, way out. The Milky Way was in the middle, the Cluster of the Three Galaxies was at the six-o'clock position, and another four clusters were at the three-o'clock position. The five clusters were at the nine-o'clock position and more unknown territory to the east and north. The coordinates slowly began to illuminate and blink repeatedly at the four-o'clock position between the grouping of the three clusters and the four clusters.

This was unknown territory, but whoever sent this message was an entity. Then another message came through. "Request meeting." I was signed "Vegh."

Wayne heard that name before, but could not remember where. Wayne said, "Computer, estimated time of arrival to designated coordinates?"

The computer came on. "Debris locked to aft quarter force field."

Harold said, "Launching open-bay shuttle for debris inspection."

Wayne said, "Harold, request video-feed recording."

The computer said, "Estimated time of arrival in dimensional mode, four months."

Wayne said, "Computer, maintain force field. Delay dimensional drive until inspection is concluded. Monitor incoming video feed and route to touchpad for display."

Wayne said, "Computer, monitor all gravitational anomalies up to nine radar-range hours. Monitor all communications traffic within a four-radar-range-hour perimeter."

Wayne watched the touchpad-screen-video feed from the comfort of this apartment. The engineering bots had just arrived to open up the bridge's viewing area.

The open-bay shuttle made a complete sweep around the damaged ship. This was an unknown ship. The exterior hull was devoid of any obvious markings or planetary-registry insignias. There were two access airlocks on the aft port quarter. The ship had suffered extensive damage to the bow and the starboard side, with atmosphere venting from cracks and fissures from all parts of the ship.

The ship was maybe two miles long at best, with one torpedo tube and one laser port. Harold had established a link with the ship's computer system to open a larger aft-quarter access bay. Wayne, watching the display noticed, No Name, the little tray bot, and Missile Mike rolling from the open-bay shuttle onto the deck of the port cargo bay. Missile Mike also had a remote-feed camera link connected to Harold's video feed. The touchpad was a split screen between Missile Mike and Harold's camera. Six other security bots took point as they ventured deeper into the cargo hold. The entire cargo hold and adjacent corridors had already vented atmosphere, and alien bodies drifted throughout the viewing area. Wayne did not recognize any of the alien's species or the script written on the wall. Wayne took a snapshot of one of the dead aliens and sent if off to Welpid. Maybe he might know.

The video feed demonstrated how powerful the drone's torpedoes were, showing buckled bulkheads, snapped power and fiber-optic cables arcing and sparking, and floating bodies of dead aliens drifting through the passageways.

The aliens resembled a prehistoric fish-amphibian blend with the beginnings of four walking appendages. They had no visible tails. They sported a large, flat, amphibian heads with turtle jaws wrapped in mucus coated skin.

Missile Mike headed down the main corridor with two bots walking point and one picking up the rear. The bulkheads were not even bulkheads, but a mesh of corrugated steel fibers woven like a ship's catwalk. Below, Wayne could see engineering, weapons and cargo-storage holds, all tossed around in an awful mess.

Wayne could see the beginnings of the bridge as Missile Mike's camera caught sight of helm and navigational controls. The ship's captain was dead, pinned against some cargo boxes. Missile Mike found the bridge's locker and storage safe. One of the security bots shot a plasma blast at the door hinge, cracking it wide open. The security bots loaded all the papers, disks, and two hologram boxes onto No Name's magnetic tray. The security bots took some pieces of metal and secured them on top of his tray. Missile Mike said, "Let's get out of here."

Harold said, "I found a bot." The camera's image displayed a small, Gray mechanical bot. The security bots took the Gray traitor and escorted them back to the open-bay shuttle. Wayne said, "I want that bot up here on the bridge, along with the stuff No Name found. Good work, Harold. Good work, Missile Mike and No Name."

Wayne watched the touchpad as Harold said, "Leaving the access cargo bay, release the force field holding the debris."

Wayne said, "Computer, disengage shield force field holding the enemy ship."

Wayne received a return message from Welpid. He had heard about the damaged southern fleet and the plutonium proximity drone. He said that Vegh, Crelk's spirit liaison, once represented the Ensups' galaxy. They moved their operations to the Grays' eastern front. Welpid said that the aliens were the Dzokos, who operate as conscripts to the highest bidder. He was not sure who was paying, but they were a pitiful race of opportunists who deserved a horrible death.

Harold said, "Open-bay shuttle just landed in aft cargo bay."

Wayne said, "Computer, go to normal space, fire discharge down leading edge, no designated target. Initiate."

Wayne watched as the bolt of discharged energy streaked across the bow's windscreen as he commanded, "Computer, designate coordinates from touchpad, full engine start, and go to light speed. Enable dimensional drive with discharge through all ionic-drive engines. Initiate."

The computer designated this as a one-year trip. Wayne wondered if Vegh was one of those entities who responded negatively to Sarah's request. This should be very interesting. In the meantime, Wayne needed to go over the data from the Dzokos' ship.

Wayne was very satisfied with his first real work-ups. They created many new weapons, the bots put a hologram generator next to weapons, Missile Mike and No Name proved their worth, and they were off to visit a very suspicious entity.

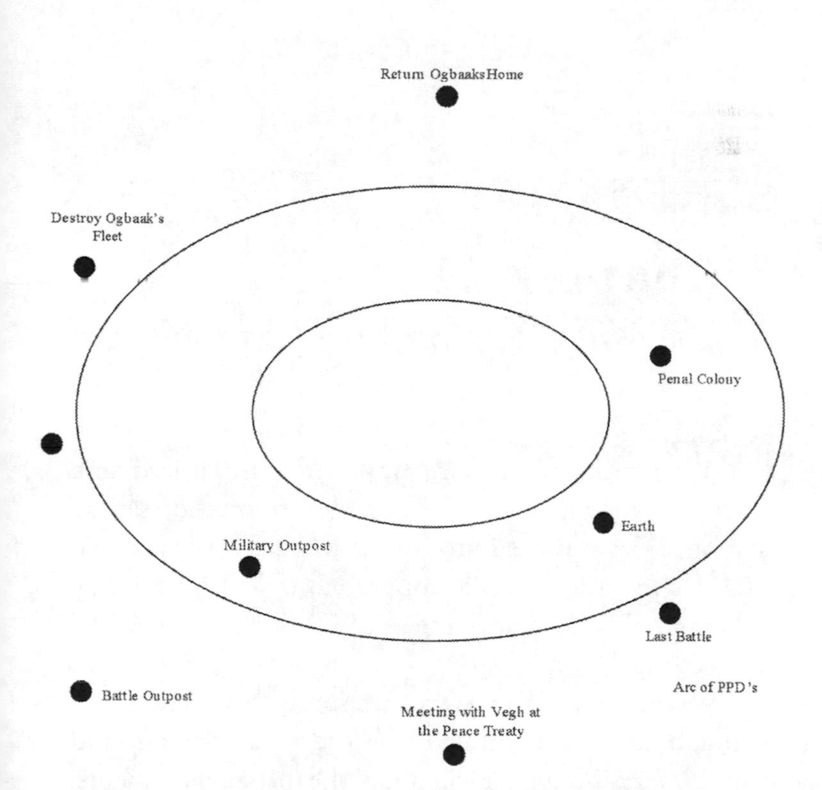

The Milky Way

Chapter 11

The Milky Way, Stellar Urban Warfare

Wayne heard the familiar sound of motorized tank tracks thumping down the corridor from the subway station. Wayne turned around as Missile Mike and No Name approached the command console with his tray full of goodies. Missile Mike said, "Did you see me? Did you see me?"

Wayne said, "You were awesome! I watched you through my touchpad's video feed. I see you found some booty." Wayne picked up the paper documents, the computer chips, and disks, along with the two small holographic boxes and a Russian cavalry sword.

Wayne said, "Do you want to see what you found?"

Missile Mike said, "I want to see!"

Wayne sat on the floor with all the stuff next to Missile Mike's camera eye. Wayne pushed the activation button on the first hologram box and placed it on the floor. The box slowly began a programmed sequence of laser beams that transformed into a small, Gray alien. Wayne put the touchpad close to the box to broadcast the audio.

The Gray said, "Go to the southern front and see what you can find."

Wayne said, "At least we know who was behind this little surveillance mission."

Wayne placed the second hologram box on the floor and pushed the activation button. The laser lights began to unfold, and another image popped up, this time with a very different alien, one he had not seen before. The touchpad began translating as the alien gestured the message.

"Partial payment is being paid via the Venezuelan liaison in glucose and agricultural commodities. The Grays, as part of their treaty with the mining planet, forbid all third-party commercial transactions. We were able to negotiate for a small shipment of smuggled goods from the Grays' uranium- and plutonium-processing planet to help in the fight against the Grays on the northern front. We need you on the Grays' front line, acting as conscripts to create a little diversion on the southern front. The Grays have launched nearly all their available craft in the war effort. Grays usually ignore us, and we don't expect any trouble. I just hope the entities stay clear."

Wayne said, "Computer, return to normal space. Maintain light speed. Route all discharge through the stabilizer's emitter electrodes. Initiate."

Wayne went over to the auditorium hologram and designated a spot on the western front. Looking at the hologram, the cluster of the three galaxies was at the six-o'clock position. Wayne wanted to attack from the west at the nine-o'clock position, next to the cluster of five galaxies. There was a large expanse of empty space between the cluster of five galaxies and the Milky Way. Wayne said in disgust, "If Vegh is an entity, and then he should start acting like one."

Wayne said, "Computer, designate deep-space coordinates to Milky Way's western front. Go to dimensional drive, route all discharge to the ionic-drive engines. Initiate.

The computer said, "Estimated time to designated target, five months."

Wayne said to No Name, "Where is the Gray bot?"

No Name said, "In the tram with security, I will go get it."

Wayne picked up the written documents. It appeared that Earth had turned into an agra-planet without the Grays' permission. Wayne said, "All I want is to find my wife and kids. After that, the Earth can go to hell!"

Wayne had no intention of getting off the floor. He decided to have another show-and-tell session. He hoped that this bot still had its memory core intact and could provide some answers to these conspiratorial turn of events.

Missile Mike, No Name, and two security bots bought in the prisoner, an innocent-looking Gray bot. Wayne turned around as he saw that Fritz and Fanny were looking on, too.

Wayne stared at the fragile little bot, when it spoke to Fritz and Fanny, "I see you have adopted a human pet."

Fritz and Fanny said, "We are here to interrogate you, Gray."

Wayne said, "Gray bots make such loyal friends, once you reprogram them. You will be like them in a few minutes. We need to download your entire memory core to this interface device."

The Gray bot said in a petite voice, "And if I refuse?"

Fritz and Fanny said, "We will sell you to Welpid as his personal servant." Wayne laughed as the Gray bot's little black eyes got very big, and his mouth convulsed in a sequence distasteful insults.

"I should have killed Welpid long ago."

Wayne slowly said, "You should have killed Welpid. When did you have the chance to kill Welpid?"

Then Wayne had a terrible thought: what if this alien's memory core was an exact duplicate of a biological spy? This bot was living someone else's memory, according to whomever implanted that memory.

Wayne said, "Who are you?"

The Gray bot said, "I am the Grays' Russian liaison."

Wayne said, "Holy Crap!" Wayne immediately got up, grabbing the sheath in one hand and drawing the Russian Cavalry sword in the other. In one fatal swing, Wayne lopped off the liaison's metallic, black-eyed cranium. The Gray bot dropped like a box of metal chains, with its metallic cranium still spinning on the floor. Wayne said, "Take this head and body and download it all to the main computer, now!"

Wayne took his touchpad, saying, "Computer, search damaged bot, frequency check for hidden transmitter."

The touchpad blinked for a couple seconds and then said, "Transmitter deactivated, but there are still two active transmitters in the room, behind you." Wayne, still holding the sword, ran back to Fritz and Fanny and lopped their heads off, too, as he shouted, "Monitor for transmitter signals now!"

The computer said, "All transmitters deactivated."

Wayne said, "Computer, transfer the three frequencies to the touchpad."

Wayne watched as the touchpad displayed, "Frequencies: 874 megahertz, 912 megahertz, and 972 megahertz."

Wayne said, "Harold, here are three frequencies you can load onto the next beacon mines. Transfer data from the touchpad, onto your internal memory." Wayne watched as the download light blinked and then stopped.

Wayne said, "Missile Mike, take these bots down to Harold. Tell Harold to download their entire memory core onto this computer chip. You guys can go." Wayne halted the two bots, saying, "What's with this sword anyway?"

Missile Mike said, "The bot was wearing it when we captured it."

Wayne still had two computer chips from the Dzokos to analyze. Wayne had no way of telling if these computer chips were corrupt or comprised.

Wayne said, "Harold, sorry, had to destroy Fritz and Fanny."

Harold said, "Missile Mike told me, he thought it was pretty cool the way their heads spun around on the floor."

Wayne said, "I need an auxiliary computer; I suspect these computer disks are corrupted. The computer must not share any links with the main computer or any computer on this ship."

Harold said, "We have a portable computer core from the Grays' ship that might work. I can fabricate the appropriate terminal interfaces for all sorts of chip designs. Then we can destroy or jettison the core afterward."

Wayne said, "Thanks, have it put on the tram. No Name can carry it in."

Wayne was beginning to calm down after whacking the heads off the three Gray bots. All were transmitting homing signals. No wonder the Dzokos ships were able to track the drone ship. Thanks to Fritz and Fanny, they nearly destroyed the mighty drone ship.

Wayne sat in his little apartment with the door still wide open. The Earth was now an agra-planet, a Russian liaison bot, all while running black-market goods. In addition, who was this entity named Vegh? Wayne did not trust Vegh because of what he did to Sarah. In addition, he did not trust Crelk for his lazy attitude. The best smugglers and weapons dealers were the lazy types who saw more value in the black market than in doing an honest day's work. Crelk was another creep who deserved scrutiny. Wayne was not about to go suck-up to any entity, thinking they were the all-powerful. If Vegh wanted to talk to Wayne, then Vegh needed to go find Wayne.

Two days later, Harold brought up a portable memory core that had an older pre-programmed two terabits of PROM memory and a disposable SDRAM memory of one hundred terabits. Harold removed the magnetic core to prevent residual computer contamination. Harold also gave Wayne the computer chip with the Russian liaison's biological imprint data. Wayne took out one of the computer chips from the Dzokos ship and scanned it across the input terminal. The portable memory core also had an attached monitor. Wayne watched the monitor as the data retranslated into English. The data represented a report from the eastern front on the ongoing battle between the Grays and an alien species, the Oyalpirs. The report was more like a political explanation until it mentioned the Confederacy of the Twenty. It appeared that the confederation had moved to a galaxy way beyond the eastern front. It was rumored the confederacy was not a biological race of aliens, but a race of ancestral spirits even older than the Grays themselves.

Wayne sat back and wondered if Vegh was a member of this Confederation of the Twenty. Wayne still felt he needed a couple more victories under his belt before he went off and became an entity groupie.

Wayne picked up the second chip from the Dzokos ship. This was a report on the western front. The Cluster of the Five Galaxies represented a consortium of neutral or appeasing alien species respectful of the Grays' power, but not necessarily committed to their cause. Their technological horizon was meager at best because of the Grays' oppressive technological nature. Wayne felt reasonably comfortable that the western front was benign enough to mount a successful offensive—maybe attract a resistance movement.

Then Wayne took the chip downloaded from the Russian liaison bot. Wayne scanned it across the interface terminal and waited for the data to compile. It was broken down into a list of names, including some bizarre Gray names too complicated to pronounce. It all started when a Gray alien died in the middle of a mission. To complete the mission, the bot served as the agent's body after the alien's brain was downloaded onto the bot's memory core. The agent's mission was to sabotage the western infrastructure of Welpid's empire. There were no real specifics or points of interest. It appeared that the bot boarded the Dzokos' ship and was en route. There was some data about the attack, but only a few lines. The bot did not have enough time to send off a distress call prior to capture, or again when brought onboard the unknown vessel. There was no mention of Fritz and Fanny's transmitters.

Technology was supposed to be the answer to our dreams, or at least that was the sales pitch. The military saw technology as a way of being able to fight a better war, as if better could measure up against the best. Finally, the root of all alien intrigue rested in the basic political assumption that robot spies with biologically imprinted brains acted as immortal mechanical couriers to perpetuate the socialistic call to arms.

What the Grays saw as a corporate evil evolved into its own socialistic corporation, where accumulated wealth only drove the wheel of technological manipulation. Greed filled the coffers as the hoard overflowed with commodities, power, and territory. Possession became its own worst enemy as the barbarians descended from the mountaintops to take possession of their fair share.

Greed and malice will always consume a marketplace until there is nothing left to sell. To be content or happy is to deny the existence of technology. If happiness and contentment were its own enlightenment, then the divine truth of God created that happiness and contentment. Technology represents the bottomless pit of obsession, where greed becomes a dangerous narcotic. The Grays were gods in their delusional reality. They had even deleted all historical and archaeological data in favor of documenting that the Grays were the premier species since the dawn of time. The Grays were the original and the only race of humanoids made in their own image to rule the galactic realm. They were even superior to the entities themselves. Now, it was all falling apart.

The two greatest fallacies of political socialism are the sharing of wealth and the promised power toward the people's good. It was anything but.

The five-month journey to the western front sought to improve on the new research projects, to build elaborate weapons platforms, and to sort through confiscated data files.

Finally, after five months, Wayne said, "Computer, go to normal space, route all discharge to the stabilizer emitter electrodes, no designated targets. Maintain light-speed velocity with full radar scan, up to ten radar-range hours. Initiate."

Wayne stood over the bridge's balcony at the holographic image of the western flank of the Milky Way, the Cluster of the Five Galaxies, and the huge expanse of empty space. The drone ship was making its approach toward the middle of the void, with radar scans showing only minor activity. Much of this space belonged to smuggler and pirate merchants who operated out of debris fields and clandestine shuttlecraft. None of the targets appeared to be aggressive, nor did they want to pick a fight with the deadly eighty-mile long warship.

Wayne waited for about an hour of flight time—enough for the rumors to get off to a good start. Wayne said, "Computer, all stop. Initiate aft thrusters and navigational stability. Monitor all communications. Monitor all gravitational anomalies within ten radar-range hours. Monitor all shield generated cloaking signatures. Initiate."

Wayne watched as the surrounding debris fields were abuzz with activity. Wayne commanded, "Computer, monitor all frequency transmitters similar to the robotic Gray bots in the higher megahertz range. Initiate."

If strategy taught Wayne anything, trusting alliances was like playing Russian roulette, and you should never underestimate their ability to horde the spoils afterward. Wayne did not like allies, but finding someone willing to act as decoys or as runners with false information might be beneficial. Wayne watched the radar monitor and the hologram as the smugglers kept their distance, not wanting to get involved.

"Computer, full engine start, proceed to designated target." Wayne said as he took a laser pointer and placed it very close to the outer margins of the Milky Way. "Go to light speed. Initiate." Wayne may have left the smugglers behind, but he knew message traffic was at full tilt. The western front was now under assault from a monstrous unknown warship entering the Grays' galactic home world with the full intent of annihilating everyone and anything.

Wayne said, "Computer, all stop. Go to four-fourths dimensional gradient, full radar scan. Check for all gravitational and shield anomalies. Aft thruster navigational stability. Initiate." Wayne said, "Max, prepare twenty proximity-mine missiles for jettison with matching engine-launch remotes."

Wayne stood over the hologram as one cruiser fleet

departed a deep space outpost. Wayne said, "Computer, designate outpost as discharge target. Go to normal space, fire discharge." Wayne held his eyes as the bridge suddenly became white and the bolt of discharge energy descended toward the planetary outpost.

Wayne said, "Computer, go to four-fourths dimensional gradient. Initiate." Wayne watched as the fleet's transponder signature was within the fifty-radar-range-hour mark. Wayne figured it would be nice for the cruisers to collide accidently with the discharge blast, but having an entire planetary outpost explode was more exciting. Wayne did run the risk of repeating what the Ensups did to their galaxy, so Wayne figured he had better not target anymore planets right now.

The cruisers had engaged their antigravity engines past light speed when the entire horizon radiated in a glorious chance-intercepted trajectory. The entire fleet vaporized when they accidently vectored straight into the discharge's path. Wayne was not sure how many cruisers there were, but he could see the beginning of the debris field coming his way. The drone ship was already in deep subspace, so the debris field was of no consequence.

Again, three fleets disembarked from the planetary outpost. Wayne said, "Computer, designate fleet as discharge target, go to normal space, fire discharge. Initiate."

Wayne held his eyes as the discharge headed for its target. Wayne thought this was "space bowling," but he was a little disappointed that the Grays lacked the technology to detect incoming discharge blasts.

Wayne waited for another two hours until again the horizon was ablaze with fiery flame and nuclear detonation.

Each of the three fleet's transponder signatures suddenly disappeared from view. Wayne said, "Computer, enable maximum shields to bow, port, and starboard stabilizers and the vertical stabilizer. Computer, monitor the debris for bot transmitter frequencies or distress calls."

The computer said, "Multiple bot transmitter frequencies and distress calls following the blast. The cruisers did not transmit any distress call, only the bots in the debris."

Wayne said, "Computer, can you target transmitters with plasma cannon?"

The computer said, "Yes"

Wayne said, "Computer, acquire all bots transmissions. Fire plasma cannon at incoming targets."

Wayne watched as the computer began targeting hundreds of bots' transmissions as the plasma cannon tried to keep up with them all.

The Gray outpost stood silent in the black void of space with no more fleets to launch. Four fleets had been annihilated within a matter of a few hours.

Wayne said, "Computer, disengage all outer-hull shielding."

The outpost represented a stellar system far removed from the swirling arm of the Milky Way galaxy. Wayne said, "Computer, go to five-fourths dimensional gradient. Initiate." Five-fourths, or the fifth step in the dimensional gradient scale, was the highest the drone ship could tolerate.

The computer said, "We can only hold this dimensional gradient for one minute."

Wayne said, "Computer, designate planetary outpost as target. Go to normal space, discharge at target. Fire!"

Wayne realized why the computer issued the warning; the entire bridge and windscreen glowed white-hot, and the bow's outer hull glowed red from the discharge blast's radiated heat.

At the rate of travel, the discharge would arrive in about forty hours. Wayne thought he needed to move to a different location further north, maybe at the ten-o'clock position next to the Milky Way.

Wayne said, "Computer, full engine start. Go to light speed with maximum radar scan. Initiate."

The auditorium's hologram began to paint a very different picture. The Grays' northern forces were altering their trajectory vectors toward the southwestern planetary outpost. At the same time, scouting reserves and conscripts formed a weaker picket line along the northern border.

Wayne then noticed fleet movements from other western planetary outposts toward the crippled southwestern front. This left the northwest quadrant vulnerable, as well as the northern front. Wayne needed to move closer to the northern front, maybe negotiating a chance encounter with one of the northern factions.

Wayne watched the hologram as the powerful discharge blast approached ever closer to the undermanned planetary outpost while neighboring fleets were coming to the rescue.

Wayne said, "Computer, monitor all gravitational and shield-cloaking anomalies within ten radar-range hours."

Wayne pointed to a point on the northwestern edge of the Milky Way galaxy, saying, "Computer, navigate to designated target, go to dimensional drive. Route all discharge through the ionic-drive engines. Initiate."

The computer came on. "Estimated time of arrival, one week."

Wayne left the bridge's balcony and shut down the hologram generator. He went back into his apartment, sitting on the lounge chair and wondering what Vegh's plan of attack was. Vegh had the capability to destroy all the Grays in a matter of moments, and all the other factions as well. Did Vegh need his permission, as if Wayne could give it to him? No, Wayne decided he would stay on mission and attack the northern front. Maybe later Vegh might meet him on the eastern side as he swept around.

The drone ship had passed the designated coordinates by only a couple minutes when Wayne commanded, "Computer, return to normal space, all stop, route all discharge to ionic-drive engines. Maximum radar scans with aft-thruster navigational stability. Initiate."

Wayne then commanded, "Computer, go to four-fourths dimensional gradient, maximum radar scan, and search for gravitational and shield-frequency anomalies. Initiate."

Almost immediately, an undesignated ship appeared at a distance of seven radar-range hours, approaching from the north. Wayne commanded, "Designate unknown ship, fire torpedo at targeted ship. Fire." Then eight more targets suddenly altered course. Wayne said, "Prioritize and designate the eight targets, fire torpedoes."

Wayne said, "Max, load torpedo tubes."

Wayne said, "Computer, initialize hologram. Integrate radar, communication, and navigational data."

The nine targets were all unknown at a distance of eight radar-range hours.

Wayne said, "Harold, load three missile-mine beacons and navigational transceiver package with the three frequencies from the Gray alien bot's transmitter."

Harold, who was working on the cargo hold, said, "Programmed and awaiting jettison."

Wayne said, "Jettison."

Wayne said, "Computer, search for three navigational transceivers signals off the aft quarter."

The computer said, "Acknowledge and receive transceiver signals."

He pointed to three separate destinations: one to the southeast, one directly east, and another to the northeast. "Computer, enter navigational data and align to targets."

The computer said, "transceivers aligned to specified coordinates".

Wayne said, "Harold, commit to launch all three missiles, now". Wayne went over the bridge's windscreen to see all three missiles vectoring toward their destinations.

The computer said, "coincidence with torpedoes to target, three hours. Wayne calculated the explosions were about four hours way, a little too close for comfort but acceptable.

Wayne saw the hologram flash as an unknown ship from the east moved in on one of the bot's transmitter beacons, and then the horizon erupted with the first kill of the battle.

Then the black void erupted with nine more explosions as the torpedoes found their mark.

Wayne said, "Computer, another cloaked ship. Please

monitor both gravitational isobar and shield-frequency anomalies."

The computer said, "No anomalies detected."

These were ships from the northern faction. They appeared to be "chasing rabbits," since the Grays' fleet was gone, and they were chasing anything that came into range.

Wayne said, "Computer, zoom out to Milky Way and the Cluster of the Five Galaxies and to the southwest quadrant."

Wayne instantly yelled an upsetting, "Oh, no!"

Not only was the southwestern planetary outpost gone, but also the entire system's sun and three neighboring stars went nova because of the blast. The entire southwest quadrant was one expanding nebula cloud, making the entire quadrant uninhabitable. After zooming out the hologram again, he could see that several Gray fleets were moving to the east and northeast quadrants. The northern picket line of fleet reserves had all but disappeared.

Wayne zoomed in on the northwest quadrant, where the computer picked up a very large ship, probably some fifty-miles long, about at the twelve-radar-range-hour mark, with nine escort ships.

Wayne said, "Harold, jettison seven proximity mines with navigational-transceiver missiles, no beacons."

Harold said, "Jettisoned."

Wayne said, "Computer, search for seven navigational transceivers."

The computer said, "Acquired seven navigational transceivers, waiting navigational telemetry."

Wayne commanded, "Computer, approaching ship is

the designated target, lock-on all navigational transceivers to target. Align transceivers to target."

The computer said, "Transceivers aligned."

Wayne said, "Harold, commit to launch all engines now."

Wayne went over to the windscreen as seven deadly proximity mines attached to ionic-drive rockets shot off to greet the large ship.

Wayne said, "Computer, monitor all anomalies, gravitational and shield-frequency."

The computer said, "No anomalies detected".

Wayne suspected the attenuation circuits in the radar's sensitivity were missing too many of the shield-frequency anomalies.

Wayne said, "Computer, increase radar sensitivity for anomaly detection."

The computer said, "Radar sensitivity increased. Warning, damage to receiver's oscillator crystals possible, automatic override, closing receiver shutter."

Wayne said, "Computer, set sensitivity to original setting."

Wayne counted down, and the computer said, "Torpedo coincidence in three, two …" Nine targets suddenly disappeared from the hologram's image, with the larger mother ship signaling an emergency distress call. Wayne was not sure if the larger ship had actually detected the drone ship in subspace or was just broadening its territorial claim. There were two beacons still unexploded; one going to the east and another northeast. The computer never allowed the transceivers to drift out of range, so they were loitering around, looking to attract an overly confident ship.

The hologram's display remained clear except for the large distressed ship.

Wayne said, "Computer, return to normal space. No target designated, route all discharge through the stab's emitter electrodes. Initiate."

The bridge again turned white hot as the bolt of dimensional energy cleared the bow's windscreen. Wayne did not want the discharge hitting the large ship.

Wayne said, "Computer, primary engine start, shields up, maximum radar scan. Initiate." Wayne noticed some debris hitting against the bow's shielding as the large alien ship cried out like a wounded animal. The radar was clear. The northwest quadrant lay deserted, except for the two wayward beacons and some approaching debris.

Wayne said, "Computer, scan for any anomalies, gravitational and shield-frequency."

The computer came on. "Large debris on the starboard bow."

Wayne could see several plumes of showering sparks emanating from the large, crippled ship.

Wayne said, "Harold, see the wounded ship on your hologram? I want a security detail and some bots to take anything of value plus the contents of the bridge. Every bot must have a weapon."

Harold said, "Max has already loaded himself in the open-bay shuttle; I have ten security bots, along with Missile Mike and No Name. Will transfer video feed to the drone's comm link."

The ship was listing heavily to the starboard, with many of the decks venting atmosphere. The structural integrity appeared safe, but the aft fascia suffered the most damage, as if it sustained a near direct hit. The bow and amidships appeared normal. If the ship was transmitting a distress call, they must be on backup power.

Wayne had never seen such a ship. There were no script or markings, no apparent insignia, nor port of registry.

Wayne went back to the radar screen. It was still deserted, with no visible rescue or assistance.

Wayne said, "Computer, scan for all communications and message traffic within nine radar-range hours."

Wayne figured he had some time for maybe a quick-look inspection. Wayne commanded, "Engineering bots, we need a hundred bots to inspect the vertical stab's leading edge for cracks, panel integrity, and any needed repairs."

Engineering said, "Taking the upper stage now."

The radar continued to be clear, with no activity except for the eastern quadrant. Wayne notice some traffic from the Cluster of the Five Galaxies on the Milky Way's western quadrant coming out for the first time, probably wondering where all the Grays went.

Harold said, "Preparing to dock at port amidships airlock."

Wayne said, "Harold, I sent bots up to inspect the vertical stab's leading edge. Can you pick up the bots, secure the upper-stage access plate, and take them to the cargo bay."

Harold said, "Secured airlock foyer. Missile Mike and No Name going to the bridge with three security bots. Max is going to weapons with the remainder of the security detail. Visual feed transferring data."

Wayne picked up his touchpad and watched as Missile Mike maneuvered through the cluttered passageways.

Wayne said, "The ship is segmented." The inner structure contained both lateral and longitudinal bulkheads, like a naval ship with watertight integrity doorways.

Gravity and atmosphere appeared to be functioning, but there were no alien encounters.

Max said, "I am in weapons; I have never seen anything like it."

Wayne interrupted Max, saying, "Max, listen, take everything, and I mean everything. We can figure it out later, okay?"

Max said, "I have three bots here taking care of a wounded alien, want them, too?"

Wayne said, "Most definitely!"

Harold said, "Missile Mike has the bridge's contents. The captain is dead."

Wayne said, "Harold, send Missile Mike to the shuttle. No Name and the remainder of the security detail, go to weapons. Max needs some help, plus he found some bots and a wounded alien. Help Max unload weapons."

Wayne looked at the video feed from Missile Mike's bridge encounter. He saw the usual booty, like computer chips, hologram boxes and something else he could not identify. Wayne did notice the captain; he was a humanoid mix, but Wayne was not sure what the mix consisted of.

Wayne said, "I need someone to take a shuttle to pick up the wounded alien and transport it to the drone's airlock."

The nursery bot said, "I will fly the shuttle to pick up the wounded alien."

Wayne said, "Thanks, nursery bot. Are you sure you don't want a name?"

The nursery bot said, "I want the name Annie."

Wayne smiled and said, "Okay, Annie. Keep me informed about the bots and the wounded alien. It may be hostile. They are in weapons with Max and Harold."

Wayne said, "Computer, transfer all console commands to my touchpad. I will be at the aft airlock."

Wayne checked the radar—it was clear. He hurried to the tram, wondering who this strange humanoid was. He boarded the tram, pushed the button marked airlock, watched the door close, and off he went.

Annie transmitted over Wayne's touchpad, "Picked up the wounded alien and two bots. One of the bots had a gun. Harold shot the bot, but Max was the one who crushed it."

Wayne said, "Harold, did you get the video feed of you and Max against the bot?"

Harold said, "Sorry, the bot had a gun. It is all captured on video."

Annie said, "I saw the tape, it was quite funny."

Wayne sat in the comfortable lounge chair and picked up his touchpad. The video started when Harold and Max approached the three bots and the wounded alien. One of the bots closest to the wounded alien ran toward Harold, and the security bot shot one of the bot's legs. Max then went over, picked up the bot with one of his lobster claws, and snapped it in half. The other two bots decided to say with the crippled alien.

The radar was clean. The computer monitored for any anomalies, but none were detected.

Wayne finally arrived at the aft airlock. Annie had placed the wounded alien across her motorized carriage with the two other bots following behind.

Wayne looked as the two bots saluted him. Wayne said in amazement, "What?"

The wounded alien also turned to Wayne and tried to get up, but was too badly hurt. Wayne held out his touchpad, and the touchpad's communications link tried to boot off one of the bots' universal translators. After about two minutes, the touchpad finally acknowledged a complete download with the program installed.

Wayne said, "Who are you?"

One of the bots said, "We are the Ogbaaks. We inhabit the galactic realm north of the Grays' home galaxy. We were celebrating a great victory when our armada exploded. All of our escort ships were destroyed, and our only mother ship is beyond repair.

Wayne said, "Why did you salute me?"

The bot said, "Our ancestral race was once like you. Over time, their bodies began to deteriorate, then the Grays forced them to mate with an animal subspecies."

Wayne looked at the wounded alien, he could see the humanoid characteristics, but could not figure what the inbred animal was. The wounded alien was humanoid in appendages, eyes, mouth, arms, legs, and feet. Everything appeared normal, but something was out of place. The wounded Ogbaak was badly burned. The alien's ears were somewhat floppy, and his nose protruded like a small dog's. His hips were like a dog's hindquarters. The pelvic joint was not linear to the thigh, but bent, like an animal's. The alien was about five feet tall with narrow features, but it carried around a huge gut. The alien's jaw-line and mouth were wide and deep, with large flat grinding teeth. If what the bot said was correct, the Ogbaaks mated with a small cow-type of animal.

The bots were humanoid in every way, almost as if they were fabricated on Earth. The bot's demeanor leaned toward the dramatic, with mannerisms favoring feminine characteristics. Wayne figured it was faulty programming. Harold could fix that.

Wayne said, "Why were you battling against the Grays?"

The wounded alien said, "The Grays would routinely invade our galaxy and herd us into large transport ships and take us back to their home galaxy. We heard rumors that they used our organs and bodily fluids for stasis regeneration. We had to stop them, or our species would go extinct."

Wayne said, "How many are left now?"

The bot said, "There are a few outposts and one major colony, but that is it."

Wayne said with great remorse, "I am here to defeat the Grays. This is my home galaxy. I am human. I fired on your ship by mistake. Whatever I can do to fix this situation, please tell me."

The wounded alien spoke in a labored curiosity, "You caused the southwestern nebula and destroyed the Grays' fleets?"

Wayne said, "I am a time traveler from the distant future. I am here to cleanse this galaxy. I am sorry I targeted your ship thinking it was a Gray ship."

The wounded alien said, "We saw the northern, western, and southern fleets collapse, but no one knew what was happening. The eastern factions were afraid, so they retreated further east toward their home galaxies. We went to the south thinking we could find the reason for the Grays' demise. I guess we found it when our armada suddenly exploded without warning."

One of the bots said, "We can call one of our ships if we get close enough."

Wayne said, "Give me the coordinates, and I will take you."

The bot transmitted the coordinates to the touchpad.

Wayne said, "Harold, Max, and all bots, get what you can and come back to the drone ship immediately. We will be leaving in two hours."

Harold said, "Understood, moving to evacuate."

Wayne said, "I have some food. Want some?"

The wounded alien motioned for some food, and Wayne cooked up a steak and some alcoholic beverages. One of the bots was tending to his wounds. His abdominal bleeding had stopped, and it treated some of his burns.

Wayne cooked up a hot steak. The alien said, "We do not eat land meat, but we do eat aquatic meat. We eat vegetables." Wayne had plenty of vegetables, and he handed over several hot, prepared selections.

The wounded alien ate everything and wanted seconds. The alien soon fell asleep.

Harold said, "Everyone is back onboard."

Wayne commanded, "Computer, designate coordinates on touchpad, go to primary engine start, go to dimensional drive, route all discharge to the ionic drive engines. Initiate."

The computer said, "Estimated travel in three months."

Wayne motioned to the bots, saying, "The Grays are no longer a threat. Live out your lives in freedom and peace. I request an alliance, wishing that your dead did not die in vain, but to serve as a testament that your freedom will be our responsibility."

The bots looked at each other and said, "Agreed. Your strength far exceeds ours, but you have given us hope that your mistake will be our survival. The Grays are dead. It is finished."

After three months of travel, the wounded alien was back to normal. Wayne said, "Computer, go to normal space, all stop. Route all discharge to the stabilizer emitter electrodes. Full radar scan. Aft thruster and navigational stability protocol. Initiate."

The radar scan was clear. A couple of ships were on a parallel course some twenty radar-range hours away. The bots began transmitting a distress beacon from within their internal transmitters. Wayne watched the ships alter course on an intercept trajectory toward the drone ship. The bots said, "The ships will not attack. They know about our transfer."

Wayne watched as the ships drew closer. These were medium-sized ships, almost like destroyer-class starships.

Wayne watched as a launched shuttle separated from the formation and headed for the drone ship. The bots were coordinating all message traffic with the fleet and the Ogbaak's home world, telling them that the war with the Grays was over and victory was theirs. The bots also transmitted the message about the new alliance with the ancestral human who defeated the Grays' mighty fleet.

Wayne said his goodbyes, and the alien and his two bots departed through the airlock toward the fleet's shuttle. Wayne did feel sorry about destroying their armada, but war often disguises the most honorable of adversaries, especially when too many participants want to get involved. Wayne said as he waved goodbye, "Our first real alliance since arriving in the Milky Way." Wayne wanted no part of Vegh's slobbering wisdom; he just wanted to go home.

Wayne stood over the bridge's balcony, trying to figure out where to go next. He saw there was a military outpost on the eastern front. Maybe they could gather some intelligence as to the Grays' hideouts. Wayne said, "Computer, designate target as destination, full engine start, go to light speed, dimensional drive enabled, route all discharge to the ionic drive engines. Initiate."

The computer came on. "Estimated time to designated destination, ten months."

Wayne sat down on the bridge's balcony floor, stretched out prone on his back, trying to get his joints to pop. Wayne thought, *The enemy has been sufficiently bled.* The hardest part was now yet to come, with politically motivated treaties, pleas of appeasement, and accusations of excessive violence, all meant to prevent the Grays' loss of their mighty empire.

Six months into the journey, Harold shouted out, "Stop the ship!"

Wayne said, "Computer, return to normal space. Route all discharge through the stab's emitter electrodes. All stop."

Wayne then commanded, "Computer, go to four-fourths dimensional gradient with stabilization control, maximum radar scan. Search for gravitational and shield-frequency anomalies."

Wayne said, "Harold, get up here on the bridge! Now!"

Wayne knew Harold had a good explanation, but the drone ship was deep within the Milky Way's perimeter.

Wayne stood over the bridge's balcony as the radar data fed into the computer's holographic processor. The drone ship's position was adrift in the east-northeastern inner quadrant. Wayne was thankful that the drone ship escaped detection, but even after two months in subspace, the Milky Way was relatively quiet. There were several inactive military outposts and minor mining installations, but still an eerie silence. Wayne heard the tram entering the subway station as Wayne went to meet Harold at the loading platform. Harold exited as the tram's door was opening and yelled out, "I feel a queen nearby."

Wayne was not happy saying, "Harold, where, which direction?"

Harold urgently said over the touchpad, "Need to get on the bridge, was going to take the open-bay shuttle, but maybe the bridge would be better."

Wayne angrily shouted, "You think?"

Wayne said, "How many queens?"

Harold said, "Just one."

Wayne said, "Close?"

Harold said, "Maybe four-hours distance."

Wayne ran through the corridor yelling for the computer to bring up the hologram of the southeastern quadrant. Wayne stepped onto the bridge's balcony, studying the various stars while the auditorium reached a five-hour perimeter. Wayne noticed one small outpost about five radar-range hours ahead. Wayne said,

"Computer, zoom out to ten radar-range hours. Display all anomalies, targets, and debris fields."

The computer said, "Detecting another drone ship docked in orbit, see designated target on hologram."

Wayne watched as the generated target illuminated about four-and-a-half hours away. The computer said, "detecting another ship, a queen's ship orbiting alongside."

Wayne said, "Man, I don't like this."

Wayne asked, "Harold, can the shuttle go the speed of light?"

Harold asked, "Yes, why?"

"You and I will take the tram to the airlock and fly the shuttle to the outpost."

Harold said, "We will?"

Wayne said, "Max, go to the aft airlock." Wayne continued in disgust, "I don't believe I'm doing this!"

Harold and Wayne got in the tram and set off to the airlock. Wayne was holding his touchpad, monitoring the radar scans.

The tram finally arrived at the airlock station. Wayne and Harold quickly departed, and Max was waiting by the airlock.

Wayne commanded, "Max, you are in charge. Right now, we are in subspace. I advise you to sit and wait for us to return. Harold has detected a queen on a neighboring planet. Harold wants to talk to it."

Max said, "Harold, forget the damn queen!"

Harold said, "I can't, I feel a goodness about her."

Wayne said, "Harold, I have two guns with me. Even at the slightest indication of trouble, both queen and drone are toast!"

Max said, “There is a drone, too?”

Wayne said, “If we are not back in twelve hours, go to these coordinates and talk to an entity named Vegh.”

Max loaded the coordinates into his head, saying, “Please come back, Wayne.”

Wayne said, “I expect to.”

Harold and Wayne pressurized the airlock, and they opened the flange door. They went down the passageway, and Wayne said, “Max, close the hatch.”

Wayne entered the shuttle, and Harold closed the shuttle’s airlock and bolted the locking ring. Harold positioned himself up to the pilot’s consoles, and then established the shuttle’s communications link via a remote-coded protocol to the drone’s computer. Harold deactivated the shuttle’s docking ring and slowly reversed engines, backing away in a port-maneuvering trajectory.

Harold designated the planetary outpost, and off they went at light speed.

Harold broke in. “Let me explain, each queen has two primary bots, the egg bot and the nursery bot. The queen customarily inserts two remote receivers, one in her nursery bot and the other in the egg bot. The queen has her own transponder inside her that transmits data to us, as well as her location. The transponder acts as a neural-biological communicator to our receivers. These impulses are for egg-laying, nourishment, or keratin. Each bot is in her service until discharged for unsatisfactory work or until the queen dies. I am not familiar with this queen, but I can almost guarantee she is sensing me. It is the drone’s responsibility to visit all the colonized queens and replenish her reproductive juices.”

Wayne said, "What about this conspiracy against the queen mother?"

Harold said, "The queen is communicating with me now. She indicated there were two drones that disliked the queen mother. The two drones felt it was important to petition each colonial queen to join them against the queen mother. Apparently many joined the drone's cause, but this was how we found the drone ship—it was killed by the queen mother's private army."

Wayne said, "Then which queen did Sarah kill; the one who tried to escape from the drone ship?"

Harold said, "That queen was the supreme queen mother. She feared for her life. She escaped and retreated to a colonial outpost before her home world was destroyed. She killed the drone and took his ship. It is customary for the supreme mother to visit other settlements. Guess the drone was in the wrong place at the wrong time."

The shuttle slowed down as Harold plotted an orbital trajectory and engaged the shield frequency cloak. Wayne could see in the distance an orbiting queen ship and a drone ship, both inactive and quiet.

Harold said, "This queen should be receptive, because this is not her planetary colony and she has no eggs or young to protect. Now, I want to negotiate a peace for two reasons: they hate the Grays, and they are masters in neutralizing gravitational anomalies. We can use them to repair the damage done to the Milky Way and the southwest quadrant."

Wayne said, "What about the entities?"

Harold said, "Under no circumstance should the entities be mentioned. This is between us and us only."

Harold angled the shuttle for an atmospheric

descent, causing the entire shuttle to glow red. The hull's containment shielding was more than adequate to protect the shuttle during reentry.

The planet was about the size of Mars. It was a dry and arid planet. It resembled a penal colony more than a military outpost. Harold followed its implanted biological-homing signal until they noticed a large outpost constructed of thick, black walls and guard towers. It was a penal colony.

The shuttle continued to maintain its cloak as it descended toward the inner courtyard. Wayne only notice a slight downward thrust of dust, but nothing that would indicate a huge shuttle had just landed.

Harold kept the shuttle's main power engaged and the shield cloak on. Harold put the engines on idle in case of a quick getaway.

The old penitentiary looked deserted—no guards, no inmates, no activity anywhere. Wayne recognized two Venus shuttles parked way off beyond the border walls. There was another shuttle parked nearby with a Russian insignia on the vertical stab.

The shuttle's door opened and Wayne and Harold exited down the boarding ramp. The air was hot and dry, and a stiff breeze was kicking up some sand. The gravity felt a little mushy and light—Wayne could feel a definite spring to his step. Harold said, "Over here."

Wayne had both weapons as he walked around the courtyard.

Harold yelled out, "An underground access tunnel." Harold led the way down the dark and dusty passageway to an underground prison bunker.

Wayne heard a voice coming from the touchpad, which he had tucked under his arm. "Who is that?"

Harold said, "Your new egg bot."

Harold went another thirty yards until he came across two cells: the queen's and the drones'. The queen said, "Let us out."

About that time, Wayne stepped alongside Harold as the queen Wayne's eyes locked stares. The drone said, "Another human."

Wayne then said, "There is another one?"

The drone said, "In the other cell."

Wayne walked down another corridor to an adjacent cell where a human laid dead. Wayne shot at the cell door's hinges, causing the whole door to fall forward. Wayne stepped inside. The ten-foot-by-ten-foot cell had a pile of clothes in one corner, and the human prisoner sat propped up against the wall across from the cell's door. The dead prisoner had two insignia tattoos; one on each shoulder. One was a biker skull, and the other suffered some recent scaring. His fingernails and toenails were gone; they appeared to be ripped out from the roots. He had several teeth knocked out and both eyes cut up.

Wayne searched his clothes and found a wallet with some identification. Wayne took the wallet and said to the drone, "What happened?"

The drone said, "He caught food for us and removed his nails so we could have keratin. He was here long before we arrived. The human saved our life."

Harold said, "We saw your shuttles parked beyond the penal compound. Here is the deal, my queen. We need to talk at length once we are settled. The human and I have another drone ship adrift about five hours out.

I would like each of us to depart; go to your own ship and we'll rendezvous for an in-depth meeting. The meeting is about taking over this galaxy."

The queen and drone looked at each other and agreed to the meeting.

Harold continued, "We have some other business to take care of, which we will fill you in on later." Harold shot the hinges from both doors and Wayne carried the dead prisoner outside to the courtyard. Harold escorted the queen and drone out from the inner prison bunker directly to the awaiting shuttle.

Wayne said, "Harold, take the queen and drone to their shuttles. I have something to do here." Wayne found a piece of metal and began digging a moderately-sized grave.

The drone asked, "What are you doing?"

Wayne said, "A human tradition. It is from dust we are made, and to dust we will return to Him. Humans are a very reverent species and obedient to our God and to our friends. A burial is to honor those fallen for helping others survive."

Harold escorted the queen and the drone into the shuttle and then took off. The drone watched Wayne through the windscreen as Wayne shoveled a dusty shallow grave, with the brave dead prisoner beside him. The drone bid farewell to the strange human who allowed them to escape this terrible hell.

Wayne placed the man in the grave and covered him up. Standing over the grave, Wayne looked at the wallet and read the name, "Bertram Allan Logston, born December 2, 2012, from Montana. Dust to dust, pray that this man's soul is with the Lord God and Jesus Christ, Amen."

Wayne put Bertram's wallet in his pocket next to his own and waited for Harold to return. The shuttle landed. Wayne boarded the access ramp, carrying the touchpad, the two weapons, and Bertram Logston's wallet.

Harold closed the door, and off they went to the drone ship, far out in space. Wayne checked the radar scan on the touchpad; it was still clear with ten radar-range hours.

Wayne took the wallet from his pocket and opened it up. Wayne found a Montana driver's license, a discharge card from the military, dated 2042, a national-security card dated 2048, and a note. Wayne opened the note, which was written in pencil, dated 2052. "To my wife, Ann. I love you very much. I am under arrest in a prison cell far from home. Russian troops and several Gray aliens captured me while conducting searches in Washington DC. I love you, and I will always love you. I do not know how this letter will get to you, but I pray that it does. Love Al."

Wayne thought about his own Sarah, Carolynn, and Bud. Russian troops and Grays conducting sweeps across America made Wayne's blood start to boil.

Wayne gently folded the note and placed it back into Bertram's wallet. Never had Wayne felt such blinding rage or a father's determination to confront all odds just to see his family again.

Wayne had singlehandedly routed most of the Grays' defenses and operational fleet. He had arrived too late to help Bertram. Was he going to be late for his own family, too?

The shuttle finally docked with the drone's airlock. Max was there waiting for the passageway and the airlock to pressurize. Max opened the airlock, allowing Wayne and Harold to pass through, saying, "The queen and drone are on the bridge."

Wayne said, "That was fast."

Harold said, "I need the nursery bot to go with us."

Wayne said, "Yes, go get the nursery bot; go get Annie."

Annie was in engineering, playing a chess game with one of the other bots. Harold said, "I have a surprise for you."

The nursery bot said, "Did you find the queen?"

Harold said, "They are on the bridge now. "Let's go visit."

Wayne, Harold, Max, and the nursery bot boarded the tram and took off for the bridge.

All four of them looked at each other, and Wayne said, "I remember finding Harold, Max, and Annie on the queen's ship. I have to admit, I was very scared."

Harold said, "I have never been treated so nicely or understood by anyone. Thank you, Wayne."

Max and Annie both agreed that they all shared a moment of biological imprinting.

Wayne said, "We need the queen and drone to stay in this galaxy. This is my galaxy, too, and will be your galaxy, as well. This is now our home.

Wayne was not home, but he felt as if home was a little closer, here with all his mechanical friends.

The tram slowly pulled into the subway station as the queen and drone stood on the loading platform. The door swung open, and Harold and Annie happily caressed their long, lost queen. Max was still suspicious about the Venus aliens, but he greeted them respectfully nonetheless. Wayne took the drone's claw and shook it in greeting and in friendship.

They all went into the bridge area so Wayne could see the two massive ships off their starboard bow. The other drone ship, an exact duplicate, was the terror of the galactic realm, and so was the queen's ship.

Harold said, "We request you find a suitable colony here in this galaxy. The human and the weapons bot will continue to fight the last bastions of Gray holdouts. The nursery bot and I will accompany the queen back to her ship, because we belong to her now. I submit that the drone and queen remain together until this situation is over."

Harold said, "We must be leaving, the human must continue attacking the Grays." The queen turned and said to Wayne, "Human, I know of Vegh, and he will protect us. I need to tell you this. I know that an entity killed the queen mother. The high council was under the Grays' protection, because the Grays created the high council. The high council's job was to exterminate other alien races who threatened the Grays' existence. The high council tried to use the Skurlords to defeat our species, but failed. In turn, the high council defeated most of us, but not all. Vegh is the leader of the Confederation of the Twenty. He is the last representative of the one, true, divine God. Since the beginning of time, the Confederation of the Twenty has protect the heavens. In turn, the divine God created one world apart from all others. That world God created was the human world. Our lives are in God's hands, and in the humans' merciful charity."

The queen turned and proceeded down the corridor toward the subway station. Wayne turned to Harold and to Annie, saying, "Take care, and you will always be my friend." Wayne stood on the bridge and watched them as they boarded the tram.

Max said, "I better catch that tram, so I can get back to weapons."

Wayne said, "Thank you, Max, for taking care of the ship."

Wayne watched Max depart, and then walked to the bridge's balcony to plan for the final battle. Wayne said, "Computer, plot the entire Milky Way on the hologram. We need to find Vegh." The hologram showed only minor skirmishes along the southeastern border where two fleets were engaged in battle.

Wayne had enough; he went into his apartment and went to sleep.

The touchpad received a message when Wayne was asleep. The message said, "Looking forward to meeting you. Crelk is bringing an entire fleet of Xynod refugees back to their galaxy, your Milky Way. Also two of the factions who participated in the fight also wanted part of the Milky Way, the Scos and the Ekglrs, both insect species. I am on the southern border between the Milky Way and the Cluster of the Three Galaxies. The Grays managed to inform the high council of the invasion, which resulted in Sarah's arrest as a conspirator against the Grays, based on your association. I can take care of Sarah, but I need you to take out the Grays' reinforcements coming from the southeast. There is a forty-fleet armada containing more than seven hundred ships. This is their current location.

They are traveling at light speed with a trailing convoy of support and supply ships. Good luck!"

Wayne heard the touchpad beep, but really did not want to get up. Finally, he stumbled onto the bridge and selected the icon for received messages. Wayne, suddenly awake, shouted, "Xynods and insects invading my Milky Way!" Wayne slammed the touchpad against the bridge's floor in a sudden rush of rage. He went over to the bridge balcony, saying, "Computer, plot these coordinates from the message and display on hologram." A computer-generated point of light began glowing brightly against the laser image. Wayne said, "Computer, zoom-out image." The image displayed the Cluster of the Three Galaxies, the galactic clusters east of the Milky Way and the Cluster of the Four Galaxies on the southeastern quadrant, and part of Welpid's southern empire. The Grays' fleet was at the northeastern quadrant of the Cluster of the Four Galaxies, but far enough away from Welpid's territory that it did not cause an immediate alarm.

Wayne went to the windscreen. The drone and the queen's ships were gone.

Wayne said, "Max, are you looking at the hologram down there?"

Max said, "yes, I downloaded the message and plotted the coordinate. I have ninety-nine plutonium proximity drones, plenty of proximity mines, the prototypes Harold built. We have plenty of weapons, but the problem is where to deploy them.

Wayne said, "I agree."

Wayne said, "Computer, plot a gravitational iso-bar overlay of this entire holographic image."

The computer slowly began to etch out gravitational

contours, gravity wells, gravity hills, and various gravitational hazard traps. The Grays' reinforcement armada was nearly six months away from the Milky Way, but Wayne needed to prepare the battlefield just the right way.

Wayne said, "Computer, designate coordinates to my laser pointer. Plot coordinates as destination. Full engines start, go to light speed, dimensional drive enable, with discharge routed through ionic drive engines. Initiate."

The computer said, "Estimated time of arrival: two months."

Wayne said, "Max, Harold was an excellent coordinator down there in the cargo bay; I need you to select and train another bot to do the job."

Max said, "I know the perfect bot."

Wayne said, "Send him up to the bridge. I want to talk to him."

Max said, "You already know Missile Mike."

Wayne smiled and said, "Max, put Missile Mike to work, no goof-ups!"

Missile Mike said, "Thank you for trusting me. I will not let you down."

Wayne said, "Missile Mike, status report, what do you have down there?"

Missile Mike said, "Twenty prototypes with beacons, thirty prototypes without beacons, one hundred proximity mines with beacons and rocket platforms that I need to count, both ionic and solid booster."

Max said, "All torpedo tubes and carriages are full, with sixty torpedoes, carriages to deploy up to one thousand proximity mines at a time, and the PPDs."

Wayne said, "This is the problem: the Grays' forces

will split somewhere along their route, probably into two forces; one to the southwest and another to the northwest. We need to arrive before they split up. The gravitational data shows a flat region of space between two large anomalies, a gravity well, and a distant black hole north of Welpid's northern front. The eastern cluster of the four galaxies belongs to the insects, as Vegh said. I have no idea how Crelk will approach with his Xynod refugees. Vegh must be a monumental idiot if he expects three alien species to live together in harmony: the insects, Crelk's lazy bunch of Xynods, and the hot-tempered Venus aliens. The vultures have come to claim their prize. In addition, with Earth as an agra-planet running smuggled goods, playing each faction against each other will only cause more problems down the road. What a mess!"

Max said, "What is it with biological units, their preoccupation with war and greed?"

Wayne agreed, saying, "Good observation. Biological units once measured success through procreation, taking care of offspring and rising communities. Now, power and greed has chastised the notion that procreation promotes healthy generational growth. Oppression promotes generational propaganda at the expense of what is good for the overall society. Political redistribution for the privileged select is more important than allowing society to choose what is good for its overall well being. Biological units prefer to complicate their lives, which in turns cheapens our lives."

Max said, "Since you taught us chess, I can see why biological units are more complicated than they need to be. War is part of all biological units."

Wayne said, "You win the prize for understanding the meaning of life; we are born into a complicated world and die looking back at what we left behind—all the while, dismissing the very reason why we have a soul: to be with God who gave us that soul."

Wayne went to pick up his broken touchpad. There were pieces here, a couple over there, and the screen was black. Wayne said, "Not having a touchpad might be a good thing."

The two months while en route, Wayne kept busy, inspecting the weapons area, working with the research bots on unfinished projects, and playing chess. Some of the engineering bots joined in as the mechanized crew drew closer together.

Wayne said, "Computer, return to normal space, route all discharge to the ionic engines, and maintain light speed until discharge is depleted. Then all stop and go to four-fourths dimensional gradient, maximum radar and search for all anomalies. Initiate."

Wayne said, "Computer, enable the hologram generator with all radar and transponder data."

Standing on the bridge's balcony, the holographic image started to take shape, and Wayne contemplated his next move. The Grays' forces had left the perimeter of the Cluster of the Four Galaxies and were approaching on the far southeastern rim of the Milky Way. Wayne figured he had four days to prepare the battlefield.

Wayne said, "Max, can a proximity-mine detonator set off the PPD instead of the discharge blast?"

Max said, "One PPD is equal to twenty proximity mines, but the PPD is detonated by an electrical detonation, not a percussion one."

Wayne said, "What do we have that can detonate a PPD?"

Max said, "The research bots created a prototype that incorporated a small dimensional mine, but you rejected that idea because of the gravitational consequences it might cause."

Wayne said, "I remember. Yeah, that might be too dangerous right now, can you have a twenty-proximity-mine package attached to an ionic-drive rocket?"

Max said, "Probably not, because of the stabilization issue, even with the navigational transceiver."

Wayne said, "Max, can a PPD detonate other PPDs?"

Max said, "Yes, why?"

Wayne said, "Computer, designate a twenty-hour-radar-range-wide angle arc perpendicular to the fleet's present trajectory at a distance of ten radar-range hours from this present location. Plot thirty separate points along the wide-angle arc. Each equally spaced point will designate one plutonium proximity drone's destination."

The computer said, "Designated thirty separate locations for each plutonium proximity drone."

Wayne said, "Computer, launch thirty plutonium proximity drones, each corresponding to the designated destination. Set up sequenced firing protocol. Fire drones."

Wayne went over to the bridge's windscreen as the computer fired a repetitive sequence of two drones in tandem. A volley of fifteen waves of PPDs slowly assembled the wide-angle concave umbrella. Wayne watched the hologram as the umbrella took shape. The

Grays' trajectory was still on course, but he needed some bait to ensure the trap worked.

Wayne said, "Missile Mike, I need three ionic-drive platforms, each configured with a navigational transceiver with beacons and no mines attached. Program each beacon separately to transmit the following frequencies: 874 megahertz, 912 megahertz, and 972 megahertz. Tell me when the missiles are ready."

Missile Mike said, "Give me about one hour."

Wayne said, "Computer, what is the navigation transceiver's transmission range?"

The computer said, "Maximum is a radar range of ten hours."

Wayne said, "Calculate coincidence of fleet's present trajectory to a discharge blast from present position, meeting at the arc of plutonium proximity drones."

The computer said, "Coincidence is ten hours, calculating present situation, discharge will countdown from now, which is twenty-six hours."

Missile Mike said, "We have two missiles ready with commit-to-launch remotes standing by."

Wayne said, "Jettison the two missiles now."

Wayne said, "Computer, search for two navigational transceivers off aft quarter."

The computer said, "Acquired two navigational transceivers."

Wayne said, "Plot designated coordinate to center PPD of wide-angle arc."

The computer said, "Designated middle PPD along arc, transceivers are aligned."

Wayne said, "Missile Mike, commit to launch. Fire."

Missile Mike said, "The other missile is ready."

Wayne said, "Jettison missile."

Wayne said, "Computer, search for transceiver off port quarter."

The computer said, "Transceiver detected."

Wayne said, "Plot one coordinate nine radar-range hours along center vector of arc to present location. Designate coordinate and align transceiver."

The computer said, "Transceiver aligned."

Wayne said, "Missile Mike, commit to launch. Fire."

Wayne watched the last piece of bait descend into the darkness as the last volley of PPDs departed toward their rendezvous toward the arc.

Wayne said, "Computer, how many of those approaching transponder signatures can you actually acquire, lock-on, and track?"

The computer said, "Can track them all."

Wayne said, "Prioritize all targets. Initiate." Wayne then added, "That's if any get through."

The computer created a countdown display to discharge blast in twenty-five hours.

Wayne said, "Computer, what is the speed of a communications transmission?"

The computer said, "The speed of light."

Wayne said, "Computer, nothing faster?"

The computer said, "The beacons are the best way to project localized transmissions without being detected."

Wayne said, "What if we want to be detected, then what could we do?"

The computer said, "The Skurlords were working on a sound wave that created resonating ripples within the gravitational space-time continuum. It was based on a linear dimensional-discharge resonance oscillation, which produced an echoing effect of outwardly pulsed gravity waves. The oscillation's PRF-produced varying-wave frequencies depended on distance traveled and the severity of the wave's gradient. The problem was constructing this enormous wave tank in space enough to influence entire quadrants. Unfortunately, it was the platform's construction that prevented the Skurlords from adequately securing their borders from the Venus aliens—a good idea turned strategically chaotic."

Wayne said, "Brilliant men were never competent generals. That's what grunts are for."

The time counter dropped down to twelve hours until discharge. The alien armada was still following the same trajectory toward the PPD umbrella. It appeared the beacons were working, because some of the smaller cruisers who had been flying escort for the supply convoys were flanking the force's main body.

The computer said, "Countdown to discharge: six hours." The armada was still within the acceptable trajectory margin of success. Some of the flanking cruisers created a spear-like point formation ahead of the larger cruisers. It was not clear if the supply and support ships were accompanying the main force or were holding position as a logistical depot. The supply and support ships were slowing down, which might prove beneficial to attract the gathering vultures.

The computer said, "Countdown to discharge: one hour." The armada maintained formation while the supply and support ships stopped in a defensive formation.

The computer said, "Normal space, target discharge to center plutonium proximity drone. Discharge enable."

Wayne watched as the computer jettisoned the bright discharge blast toward the chain of thirty PPDs.

The fleet was twenty radar hours way. The fleet's formation remained intact as Wayne watched the discharge blast. The drone ship was on a slow navigational drift in full view of everyone. Wayne wanted the fleet to see him to entice a charge, and then he would sink into subspace.

Wayne said, "Computer, go to four-fourths dimensional gradient. Initiate." Wayne could see the formation tightening up, as coincidence was in two hours. The Grays' fleet was twelve hours away from the drone ship as the discharge was two hours from impacting the center PPD.

Wayne said, "Max, are you watching this?"

Max said, "Yes, and the weapons are ready."

Finally the computer started the countdown, "Coincidence in ten, nine, and eight ..." Wayne followed along as the armada drifted slightly off from the centerline but stayed well within the concave arc.

Wayne said, "Go to normal space and target discharge toward debris field. Fire."

The horizon turned bright white as the chain reaction set off the next domino along the arc. The light was blinding, along with secondary and tertiary explosions from the ships themselves. Wayne said, "Computer, target surviving ships and launch torpedoes. Fire."

The computer commenced a launch sequence of fifty torpedoes. Max yelled out, "Wait a couple minutes until I fill up and tubes and carriages."

Wayne went over to the bridge's balcony. The Milky Way's southeastern outer quadrant was strewn with debris, crippled ships, and ships trying to escape the rapidly expanding nebula of nuclear fire. Wayne said, "Computer, display gravitational-isobar-overlay onto radar image."

The computer came on. "All plutonium proximity drones detonated."

The computer began compiling a holographic image of a gravitational expansion wave created by the PPDs' concave design. The massive gradient wave was some thirty radar-range miles across and rapidly approaching the Grays' supply ships, which were already heavily engaged with smugglers and various faction forces.

Wayne then saw a blinking light from the hologram display some seven radar-range hours from his location. Wayne said, "What is that blinking?"

The computer said, "An incoming message. Transmission reads as follows: my insect faction force has been destroyed in the gravity pressure wave along with the Grays' supply ships. The Xynods are approaching from the southwest. The southwest's nova halted their progress. Many of their home worlds were on the southwestern quadrant. They will be moving into the Cluster of the Five Galaxies to the west of the Milky Way. The queen and drone are with me, along with Sarah. Come to these coordinates to sign a peace treaty."

Wayne said, "Peace treaty!"

Wayne said, "Computer, designate message's point of origin as navigational destination. Enable full engine start, go to light speed. Initiate."

Wayne went into his little apartment and fell asleep on the lounge chair.

Wayne woke up as the computer repeated an orbital

sequence from the high council's traveling spaceport facility. Wayne got up to see the entire windscreen consumed by an orbiting spaceport. Off in the distance he could see the drone and queen's ship. There was one Gray cruiser docked, too.

Wayne put on something a little bit more formal and headed to the tram. He made sure he had his special bag, inside which was the ox horn he found when he entered the queen's ship.

Max said, "I am here at the airlock."

Wayne said, "On my way."

Wayne felt something grabbing onto the drone's aft fascia; probably the spaceport's docking clamps. Finally Wayne arrived at the airlock with Max and Missile Mike patiently waiting in excitement. The spaceport had already extended a passageway to the airlock's docking ring. Max opened the airlock door, and a rush of fresh air filled the foyer. Wayne silently nodded to his friends, and then turned to walk the ten-mile passageway to the spaceport's airlock on the other side.

The view was spectacular. Hundreds of ships of all types and classes butted up against huge docking clamps and refueling umbilical cords. The spaceport's outer hull was a matrix of windows, docking stalls, piers, and numerous security bots flying around. After about a half-mile of walking, a hospitality bot scooted up the narrow passageway and asked, "Need a ride, sir?"

Wayne got onto the one-seat bot and said, "Yes, I like a ride please." The bot was off, and the picturesque view became a more pleasurable experience.

Wayne did not know what to expect, but with the drone and queen there, he was not worried about the negotiation; he was worried about the Grays' terms for peace.

The bot departed the long passageway, through the airlock, and into the grand foyer. The foyer was a good five miles long and three miles wide, filled with travelers and golf-cart bots. Wayne could see the grand arch off in the distance, which led to the official foyer to the grand audience hall.

The golf-cart bot continued through the foyer area and deposited him outside the smaller negotiation chamber, where he saw the drone and queen.

Wayne got off the golf-cart bot and walked up to the queen, saying, "Queen, nice to see you again."

The queen said, "Where is your touchpad?"

Wayne said, "I broke it in a fit of rage, sorry."

The drone laughed as he grabbed Wayne's hand in a greeting of old friends. The drone said, "That's why we couldn't reach you. Well, I have to say that your arrangement of plutonium proximity drones was quite bizarre, until I saw the damage; an incredible sight. You are a worthy battle drone."

Wayne said, "Queen, this is for you." Wayne took out the ox horn he found on the queen's ship.

The queen immediately grabbed the facial horn and sniffed it, saying, "This was my sister. She bravely died trying to right the wrongs committed by the evil supreme mother. The Grays created the high council as a united front to destroy all alien species. When the high council discovered our culture, the high council selected the Skurlords to decimate our culture. Our collective hives were able to beat back the Skurlords, but the supreme mother attempted to discuss a negotiated peace with the

Skurlords. The deal attempted to join both our forces against a conniving and treacherous enemy, the high council. The deal failed when the ambassadors decided to join in the fight. By that time, the Skurlords were all but defeated. The high council caught us trying to escape. A Gray liaison put us in the penal colony. Now, I stand with my sister in memorial; it is finished. I am now the supreme mother, and I vow to create a new understanding of cooperation and rebuilding, which we can all share. Good intentions are never rewarded when you lavish yourself with rewards, rather than appreciating your rewards from the people around you. I petitioned Vegh to dissolve the high council and all they stood for."

Wayne said, "We are not a technical species, but we have our differences over technological endeavors. Our squabbling holds us back, our useless desire to argue distracts from reaching what is right or what is just. I personally have no desire to reach technological enlightenment. Our understanding of science will propel us toward the stars, not technology. Unfortunately, there are those who would surrender their right to the stars because technology has made them lazy, or because the government said so. Governments will be the death of us, not the hazards of space travel. It is finished."

The double doors to the negotiations chamber swung open, and three ambassadors of the high council, two Gray ambassadors, and Vegh and Sarah, appeared to announce, "We have negotiated a peace treaty for the Grays' possession for the home galaxy."

Wayne shouted, "What is this!"

The drone and the queen quickly jettisoned their mighty legs into the air, bolting toward the double doors and grabbing each of the Grays in their lobed faces. Everyone was shocked at the horror as the Venus's flytrap faces clamped shut, squeezing pinkish blood and ooze onto the floor of the reception area. The sound of crushing bones and petite screams for help slowly fell silent as the queen and drone sucked the succulent juices from the Gray sushi.

Wayne yelled out, "Well, that takes care of that! I call the negotiations null and void. I petition that the Milky Way belongs to the humans and the Venus aliens and no others. I petition the immediate liquidation of all high council property and the existence of the high council itself. No more high council. Who will second the motion?"

Sarah's voice called out from the main computer's speech modulator, "I second the motion!"

Wayne demanded, "Vegh, dissolve the high council once and for all, immediately!"

Any advantage the high council might have had was now eaten and gone, and Vegh had no choice but to comply. Vegh had not anticipated this, but the undiplomatic display of violence brought into question the emotional competency and war-like attitude expressed by all biological units.

Wayne said to Vegh, who had not dissolved the high council yet, "Cheng once told me 'If I justifiably kill someone to protect myself, it is honorable. However, if someone else kills, the whole notion of justification instantly falls into question and is deemed dishonorable. I submit the queen and drone's actions were justifiable, and I honor their act of honor."

The surrounding audience shouted in a glorious, "Honor killing!"

Vegh said, "I dissolve the high council and all they stand for, for now and always. Be gone!" Then in a puff of air, they were gone. Vegh floated over to Wayne and said, "The people on Earth are the most backward, the most suspicious, the most strategy-minded, the most destructive, and the most religious. These people here see technology as a tool to deceive, to manipulate others, to dictate, and to enslave. Humans see technology as the adventure of science, and as the appeal of the individual spirit of freedom and exploration. However, in time, humans will see technology as these biological units do: a tool to twist their political terror of enslavement. Capitalism created wealth, but also created corruption. Socialism does not redistribute wealth; it redistributes enslavement and tyranny equally. Even I, a spirit, was lured into the deception that truth is what the government dictates. As a rule, neither government nor wealth can tolerate what honesty demands."

Wayne said, "Vegh, what was the relationship between Crelk and the Grays?"

Vegh said, "The conflict goes back a million years. The Grays negotiated a peace with the Xynods on the condition: if they wanted to stay in the Milky Way galaxy, they needed to supply the Grays' stasis requirements. The Grays were genetically regenerating themselves in stasis chambers using older DNA-cloning imprints. The specifications required humanoid reproductive juices, which the Xynods provided as part of the negotiated peace. The Xynods were little more than cattle, as the male and female hormone sex glands were harvested, giving the Grays longevity. The Xynods were being milked. After a while, the Xynods left. The Grays began harvesting humans for stasis harvesting. Unfortunately, this made the Grays very ill, and so they turned to another humanoid group, the Ogbaaks from the northern galaxies. The Earth's uranium- and plutonium-mining was far too valuable, so the humans were being milked, too."

Wayne said, "I probably won't recognize my home. What can I do to fix it?"

Vegh replied, "To kill the infection is to kill the patient, because the patient is the infection. Starting over is the only solution."

Wayne said, "Vegh, what is this spirit and ambassador association?"

Vegh said, "In the beginning, God made man and woman on the planet you call Earth. God also made twenty guardians, named the Confederation of the Twenty, to ensure the Earth's safety. The entity you named, Cheng, was the last guardian. I am sorry to say that Cheng is no more.

"Cheng, in his desire to rebuild the Confederation, created nineteen spirits to replace the lost guardians. I am the only remaining spirit. The spirits tried to carry the guardian's torch, but were caught up in political wrangling from the more advanced alien species. The spirits found it difficult to keep up with the manmade anomalies, which actually created rogue entities. When the Grays discovered how to fabricate their own entities; this is when they created the High Council of Ambassadors. It was the ambassadors' job to recruit these rogue entities or commission them as conscripts to destroy other alien races. The ambassadors believed that the Grays were the true god, while trying to chase down the last remnants of the Confederation of the Twenty. Cheng told me you were coming, but I doubted your loyalty to your family, to your wife, and to your God. In politics, everyone has a price. No one ever thought you would destroy it all and start over. In that, we are grateful."

Wayne hung his head as Vegh said, "It is time for you to go home. See what you can salvage. The spirits have learned a very valuable lesson: not to interfere. Go home."

Wayne said, "Oh, by the way, I need another touchpad." Wayne continued, "What about Sarah?"

Vegh said, "Sarah will remain here as the newest member of the Confederation of the Twenty. We will contact you when the time is right. Go home, and God bless."

Wayne was hoping that Sarah would accompany him back to Earth. Vegh handed Wayne a new touchpad with a message from Sarah: "I love you."

Wayne turned and tried to put on a happy face as he said good-bye to the drone and queen. Wayne wanted to go home, but leaving Sarah here was too much to handle. He slowly walked away toward the drone ship, and a golf-cart bot gave Wayne a ride. Wayne said repeatedly, "I am going home. I am going home."

Wayne met Max at the airlock, but Wayne was not in a talking mood. All he said was, "It is finished, the humans and the Venus aliens are in possession of the Milky Way, the Grays no longer exist."

Wayne said while in the airlock foyer, "Computer, tell the spaceport to disengage docking clamps and go to full thruster with stabilization control. Initiate."

Wayne heard the enormous sound of the docking clamps being withdrawn as the airlock closed and the long passageway was retracted. The airlock's security light went from green to red, and Wayne slowly made his way to the tram. Wayne turned, and there was Vegh floating ahead of him.

Vegh said, "I can send you to your system right now, or you can go the old-fashioned way."

Wayne said, "send me to the outermost part of my system—the first planet with the large rings."

Vegh said, "You are there."

Wayne looked out the airlock's window, and there was Saturn. He looked around, but Vegh had gone. Now the gut wrenching reality was about to commence.

Chapter 12

Going Home

Saturn drifted as a gallant sentry outside the drone's bow windscreen. Wayne spent a lifetime waiting for this moment. Wayne took out his wallet and pulled out the dark, faded family portrait, old and ragged from constant attention. In his pocket were his kid's locator beacons, which still worked, and a special picture of his wife, Sarah.

Wayne still had Bertram's wallet and the note he left to his wife, Ann. Wayne needed to deliver the message as he vowed to do. He looked at his driver's license and all the worthless stuff inside. However, Bertram proved to be the unsung hero.

The memories of his wife, and kids, Carolynn and Bud, were still fresh in his mind. Even as we live our lives, our hearts are never far from our loved ones or the memories we share. To live forever is to dismiss what God has created for us. How is living forever beneficial when the world we live in is a living hell? God brings us home for a purpose: to show us what goodness really is.

Wayne finally made it to the bridge after a long tram ride. Saturn emitted a soft, solar glow as if to call out, "Welcome Home." To appreciate space is to appreciate the effort and the accomplishment of the human spirit.

Wayne said, "Computer, primary engine start, take it slow. Initiate."

It was hard to see the other planets because of their rotational position. When they came across the asteroid belt, he realized he had missed Jupiter. Wayne asked the computer to bring up the hologram display for only this solar system. He realized the Earth was on the other side of the sun, so the drone ship had to traverse around the sun. The drone ship passed Mars a little too quickly, and Wayne said, "All engines stop. Enable aft thrusters and stabilization control."

Wayne could see a nebula glow of ionic gas and clouds; probably his little accident on the southwestern quadrant. However, with the queen's help, the Milky Way would soon be back to normal.

Wayne could see the Earth and the moon straight ahead. Wayne said, "Computer, maintain position here." Wayne looked around the bridge at his little apartment and all the stuff he had grown accustomed to. This was not his home, but it was the home that brought him home.

Wayne walked down the corridor, holding his new touchpad. He saw the tram waiting at the subway station with the door open, begging him to enter one last time.

He slowly entered the tram and pushed the button to the aft shuttle bay.

When he arrived, there was Max and Missile Mike, both wanting to say good-bye. Wayne said, "I will probably be back, but either way, I will send you a message from my touchpad. Okay."

Wayne climbed into the shuttle, saying his good-byes, until the airlock closed and the docking bolts retracted. The shuttle maneuvered away from the drone's aft fascia, and with one last look, he said good-bye.

Wayne passed the moon, which remained desolate and unexplored. The shuttle approached the outer orbital beacons that had been placed there by the Grays. The shuttle's radar screen was clear. Wayne caught sight of a heavily damaged scout ship and an unknown ship, probably belonging to black-market smugglers. Wayne turned on the shield-frequency cloaking generator. The shuttle had a plasma laser cannon, but it was useless.

He turned his kid's locator beacon on, and to Wayne's surprise; there was a steady beeping sound and illuminations every five seconds. Wayne watched as the beacon picked up in frequency as he flew over the United States toward his hometown. He hovered toward his house with the yard still as he remembered it. The beacon lit up with excitement. He had found someone, but was not sure whom. Wayne carefully landed the cloaked shuttle in his front yard, away from the house, and he saw two people rocking on the front porch. Wayne held out the family portrait, nervously confused about who he might meet.

Wayne opened the shuttle's door and walked outside. It appeared that Wayne had materialized from thin air as the two elderly couple yelled out, "Who are you?" Wayne held out the old beacon, which was ringing loudly, and a picture, which only represented a distant memory. The couple on the porch slowly stood up as they, too, held out their beacons from childhood. The couple started crying, since they knew this was their father, somehow coming back from the dead to see them one last time.

They got hugs and kisses from a father who was not much more than twenty-eight, embracing his long-lost kids who were well into their mid-eighties. In all this, a family's connection to each other has no equal, but for a brief time, that connection reached some measure of closure. Wayne sat on the porch and told them the story, as wild as it was. He escorted them across the yard and let them walk into the shuttle. Wayne watched his kid's eyes as if magically healed from the horror and fear they felt for their father after all these years.

Wayne said, "Where's your mom?"

His kids said, "Follow us."

They led their father out beside the house to a black, grated burial fence, and there was his wife, Sarah. Wayne stood there beside the house with memories racing through his head, and now this. She was dead. He forced himself to see her last words etched in stone: "I love you, Wayne, and my spirit will find you." Wayne quietly said, "You found me, Sarah, you found me!"

Wayne looked around for his kids, but they must have gone back to the porch. He walked around the corner, only to see his kids on their rockers, lifeless. The breeze gently rocked them to heaven. Their beacons were going off as they held their parents' picture still in their hands. It was too much for Wayne to bear. He yelled out in anger, "Why?" What about the stasis chamber? But what would that prove? It was not about getting back their bodies, but getting back the precious time he had lost.

The next day, after spending a painful night alone, he walked over to the two graves he dug the night before; the fresh graves next to their mother, one on each side. Wayne knelt down and prayed for forgiveness that he had arrived too late. Wayne understood that his anger would not serve the galaxy's greater good. Wayne went back into the house and found a filing cabinet stuffed with letters from his wife—letters about trust, letters about faithfulness, letters about not giving up hope, loving letters from long ago that would heal Wayne's breaking heart.

Wayne gathered up all family portraits, letters, and stuff his family left behind in case their father ever returned, and loaded them in the shuttle, along with the rocking chairs, his wife's old clothes carefully tucked away, and the perfume he had always liked.

Wayne stood outside the shuttle, teary-eyed, realizing he had no real home. His only home had become an empty house, some precious graves, and the many memories that lingered in his mind. He climbed into the shuttle and took off, leaving this life behind in search for a new one.

Wayne headed northwest to Montana to see if he could find Bertram's house. Over the entire trip, Wayne could see the scars left by the Grays' mining equipment that stripped the landscape bare. Human laborers who had been forced to mine much of the world's landmasses had all since perished in the dusty clouds of another's greed. Wayne found the Montana city, but the entire area had been plowed under as far as the eye could see.

He turned around, wondering what America's capital in Washington looked like. The entire landscape had been tilled, routed, and twisted. There were no roads, no concrete, and no buildings—just twisted piles of dirt and discarded boulders.

He finally arrived along the Atlantic Ocean. He saw the distinctive shape of the Outer Banks and followed them up toward Norfolk, where he helped build the aircraft carrier. It was all gone; decimated. Not an ounce of concrete or manmade structures stood anywhere. The landscape was devoid of humans, Grays, smugglers, Venezuelans, or Russians. Jesus had come again and wiped it clean.

Flying up the coast, he saw the Potomac, but no capital. It was if man had never existed.

Maybe Vegh was correct; God allowed Wayne one last chance to see his kids, but other than that, God decided to start over. Wayne needed to leave and give the Adam and Eve a fresh start.

Wayne wondered why this happened. The United States had fallen into such disrepair and apathy that science and technology died with it. Even as other socialistic nations fought over the secrets of alien technology, humanity's greed contributed to its own demise. There were no satellites, no fancy communications grid, no GPS—no nothing. Humankind had drifted into such contempt for itself and for others that life had no real meaning.

Wayne said, "God, I pray that your new Adam and Eve will not make the same errors we did. Lord God, please give me a sign that you have not forsaken your faithful followers; that my family is in heaven for life eternal." Wayne maneuvered the shuttle out of earth's orbit and headed back to the drone ship.

As Wayne stood on the drone's bridge with Earth in the windscreen, there were no words to put things right. Wayne took what he wanted: his memories and his wife's letters of hope and love. Wayne turned toward his apartment, and an angel suddenly appeared. It was his wife's unmistakable figure, all aglow. She said, "Your journey has brought us together, yet I have been with you always. God has a place for you, but not now. You are the guardian now; God has dissolved all traces of the Confederation of the Twenty, as well as the high council. It is you and I, for I will be your pilot from now on. The time we missed is now time restored, as we have this time together on this mission from God. We are here to put things right."

Sarah and Wayne were finally together again on God's special journey.

Appendix 1

Senior Project

Dakota High School

The proportional relationship between mass, gravity, and energy is first dependant on mass.

Early native cultures recognized the regional or geographic significance of special powers, or high-energy emissions. Terms like "Spirit Mountain" stemmed from Neolithic oral folklore, which described a terrain's supernatural or superstitious powers.

Geology would later confirm the presence of a previous volcanic deposit or cavity of large crystalline iron ore, or magnetite. The resultant change in regional mass and density from the surrounding terrain created a gravity sink caused by the volcanic iron core. Subsequently, this increased the mountain's potential energy and exerted force. The magnetic field further enhanced the amount of force by lines of flux.

Potential energy = (mass) (gravity) (height). The additional force of gravity did not affect the mass or density, but it did affect the apparent weight of the terrain by those who sensed the supernatural experience. The height is constant, but due to the observer's perception, the changes in gravitational flux gave the appearance that height can be refracted, based on the perceived distortion, however slight.

Astronomy dictates that Doppler influences the electromagnetic spectrum dependant on vector and velocity. As infinite mass influences critical gravity, the Doppler shift appears to be that of dark or black matter/ energy, but it is actually an indigo violent representing extreme Doppler shift toward X-rays, cosmic rays, or gamma particles/radiation.

Energy implies a radiated frequency based on wavelength and time, but the electromagnetic spectrum of indigo violet indicates the existence of an interface between subspace and normal space. In the Law of the Conservation of Energy and Matter, neither can be created or destroyed, but can only change form. As infinite energy from subspace decreases in intensity, it reverts into wavelength, or high-speed subatomic matter in normal space, initially in the indigo violet spectrum then it shifts red as the frequency further decreases.

Infinite mass invokes critical gravity, which spawns energy toward the realm of subspace, creating a multi-dimensional pathway or wormhole. If a black hole, the densest star yet known, is an intake port at the point of critical gravity, it must be assumed that an exhaust port exists in the fashion of an ever-expanding nebula of subatomic alluvial fields.

The nebula's Doppler shift should reflect as intense violets at its exit, while radiating green, red, and oranges further from the point of exhaust, based on Newton's Law of Gravity, where gravitational force between bodies is dependent on their distance. Ionization also contributes to the growing magnetic fields and subsequent fusion reactions that spawn new stars.

Time as we know it is relative, based on the difference between the black hole's intake port to the nebula's exhaust port because of gravitational force and acceleration/deceleration.

The energy cycle is the process of fission and fusion based on critical gravity and infinite energy. The black hole fundamentally alters matter into energy by the process of fission, where mass is converted into radiated energy by disassembling mass. The resultant black hole's exhaust port attempts to reassemble the debris field of subatomic particles by the process of fusion by way of gravity and magnetic ionization.

If space travel is to exist, science and technology must have in place a fission-fusion- energy-cycle-processing facility onboard the spacecraft, not to recycle spent uranium but to ensure a sufficient quantity of reconstituted uranium for extensive tours of exploration. The Earth is fortunate to have radioactive and heavy elements in ready supply, which indicates that our celestial sun was created from an already dense nova or supernova.

I reject the notion of the Big Bang because of the subsequent process of fusion and element-reconstitution from the basic element of hydrogen to the dense radioactive elements of uranium or plutonium. Even assuming that the Big Bang existed in a single dimension or during one timeline, then what created subsequent dimensions when there was only one singularity to begin with? If the Big Bang occurred, its initial state prior to explosion would have been an "implosion" because of the vacuum of space around it—the intake port had nothing to absorb. The singularity prior to the Big Bang exhibited infinite mass, infinite gravity and infinite energy, so the explosion was not from the singularity, but its exhaust port into our dimension. What is considered as scientific fact could never happen under the situation of infinite mass, infinite energy, and infinite gravity. The Big Bang would be more like the "Big Spew," as the exhaust port ejected subatomic debris into other dimensions or only into our dimension.

Two of the technological problems in constructing a fission-fusion-processing facility are the containment and coolant issues. Any containment would have to be a powerful electromagnetic field along with tuned waveguides to ensure stabilization, like a frequency governor. The coolant system would cycle through the magnetic-field generators, the surrounding magnetic field, and the fission-fusion reactors themselves.

The availability of safeguards and interlocks would ensure maximum safety in case of a catastrophic failure to prevent the unfortunate accident of a hull breach.

.

Wayne Ceroi
(John W. McSherry—Grays' Plutonium)

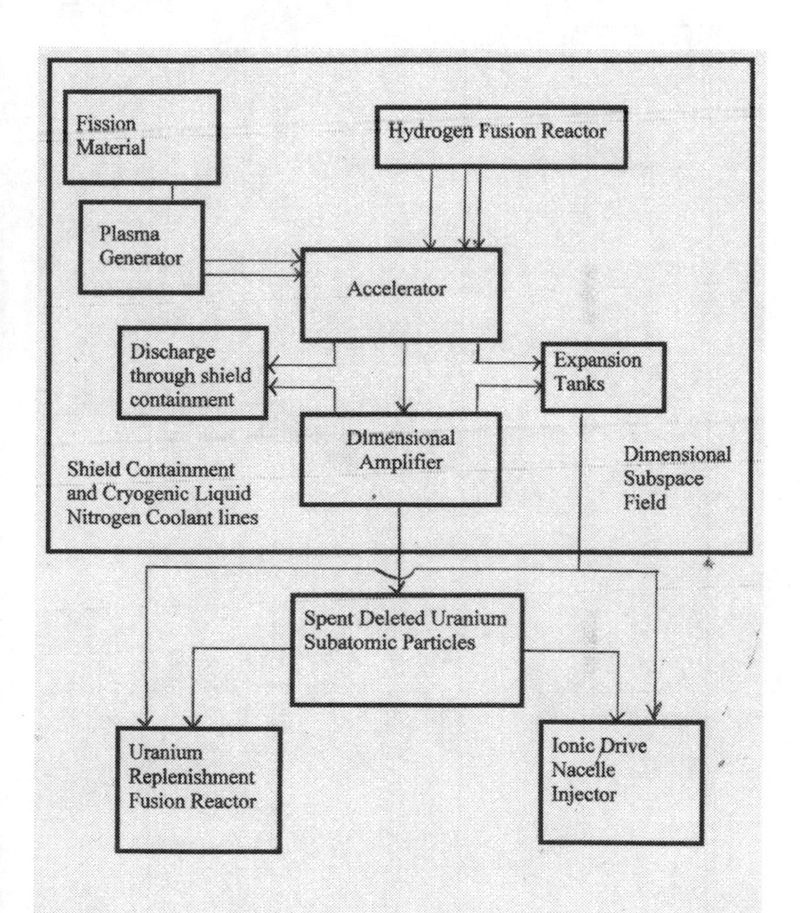

Dimensional Gravitational Gradient System

Wavelength and Waveguides

A = .7 λ

$C = \lambda f$
Speed of Light (m) = (Wavelength)(frequency Hz)
Wavelength = Speed of Light/Frequency

B = .35 λ

To calculate the dimensions in a 50 GHz waveguide, first we need to determine the wavelength.

$$\lambda = 3 \text{ X } 10^8/50 \text{ GHz}$$
$$\lambda = 300000000/50000000000$$
$$\lambda = .006$$

The wavelength for 50 GHz is .006 meters. To calculate each waveguide dimension, we need to refer to the box up top. The length or "A" is .7 λ and dimension "B" is .35 λ.

$$A = (.7)\,(.006)$$
A = 4.2 mm (millimeters)

$$B = (.35)\,(.006)$$
B = 2.1 mm (millimeters)

The rule of thumb is, the larger the waveguide, the lower the frequency. The smaller the waveguide, the higher the frequency.

Dimensional Gradient Steps

Each gradient represents an level of subspace based on the quantity and sustainable energy needed to create an envelope of subatomic dimensional particles. Each level represents an exponential demand in both energy and dimensional subatomic population. The vortex represents infinite energy approaching infinite gravity which requires infinite mass as fuel.

12/4 Vortex

11/4

10/4

9/4

8/4

Planetary Facility

7/4

6/4

5/4

4/4

Spacecraft - High Technology

3/4

1/2

Spacecraft– Low Technology

1/4

Normal Space

Force Triangle

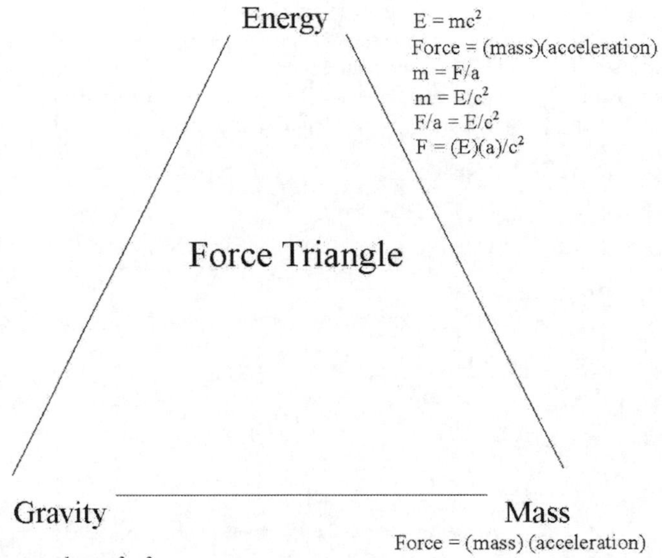

Force = $(Gm^1)(Gm^2)/r^2$
Force = (Gravitational mass of object one) (Gravitational mass of object two) divided by the distance between them squared.

If all of space were a level playing field, then gravity, as dependant on mass and acceleration would reach equilibrium as acceleration reduced to zero. But space is not a level playing field where the force of acceleration represents a continually changing dynamic effecting both gravity and mass. Density as a physical and chemical property is dependant on the potential and kinetic energy as related to acceleration and the gravitational forces influencing both fusion and fission.

As in a tornado, a vortex represents upward thrust. If a black hole is a gravitational vortex, assuming that thrust is one dimensional, but if a black hole remains stationary, then any thrust must extend into another dimension.

Appendix 2

Dimensional Physics and Ship's Dimensional Systems

We should be familiar with the scientific concept of splitting atoms—you know the scene of numerous scientists and technicians analyzing the test results from a massive accelerator as a ballistic projectile collides with a suspended particle. What we see as the debris of subatomic particles is the essence of dimensional physics. The concept of other dimensions is more about science fiction, but in reality, some subatomic particles, yet unidentified, have a distinct characteristic of seeking out dimensional space. Exposing these dimensional particles requires a tremendous amount of gravitational stress, like a near-black hole. To simulate this in the laboratory is not only difficult, but very dangerous because of safety protocols. It also presents the possibility of creating a near-black-hole event here on Earth.

Once science and technology have reduced the potential hazards, production can begin in the real possibility of infinite speed. $E=mc^2$ represents the concept that mass is converted to pure energy when light itself becomes infinite friction. As more mass is converted to energy, the electromagnetic spectrum shifts to the blues and dark violets because of the tremendous release of energy. To eliminate the forces of friction during space travel, light speed must be replaced by the technology of dimensional subspace. Subspace is a function of gravity and energy with mass as fuel.

A dimensional sub-particle only exists when gravity exceeds the speed of light with infinite energy, allowing for the accumulation of dimensional sub-particles. It is this accumulation of these particles that allows spacecraft to drop into the envelope of subspace, using it as a protective cloak.

Once technology can harness a dimensional subspace field, then technology can concentrate on creating dimensional gradients. Dimensional gradients are a function of gravitational and magnetic energy, dimensional accumulation, and shielding containment.

As a general rule, fissionable uranium or plutonium are the elements used in dimensional sub-particle extraction. In configuring an accelerator, first the uranium or plutonium must be in a plasma state. The plasma frequency of uranium is around fifty gigahertz. This means that the accelerator must operate at a frequency of fifty gigahertz as well. The ballistic projectile used to bombard the uranium or plutonium is fusion's heavy hydrogen and associated radiation at a rate of fifty gigahertz. To maintain the accelerator's stability, it is operated at the plasma frequency of the fission material, or in the case of uranium, fifty gigahertz. The use of waveguides ensures a constant frequency throughout the process, from the plasma generator to the accelerator's dimensional particle extraction.

Dimensional technology requires seven ingredients: a fusion power source, a tuned accelerator, high-quality fission material, plasma conduits, injectors, a containmen-shield

generator, a resonance or amplifier to maintain a subspace equilibrium, and a discharge emitter electrode. (See block diagram)

Of the seven ingredients, the most important is the tuned dimensional accelerator. Like in electronics, tuning a tank circuit depends on the reactance between the inductor and the capacitor. The resulting resonance is when the reactance of both components becomes equal. In addition, the power source's resonance is important, because it increases the total impedance of the tank circuitry toward infinity. In dimensional resonance, there must be a continuous and equal distribution between the incoming sub-particles into the accelerator to the frequency of the fission plasma stream, based on the input bombardment from the fusion reactor. Stabilizing subspace is all about equalizing the gravitational forces surrounding the craft to the resonance frequency of the fission material used.

The accelerator operates at the wavelength frequency of the injected plasmatic material. The more advanced aliens have adopted enriched uranium as the best fissionable plasma to produce dimensional particles. Uranium has a plasma wavelength of fifty gigahertz, controlled through plasma conduits to two accelerator injectors. The accelerator's high-velocity smashing medium is gamma and cosmic radiation and heavy hydrogen, fed from the hydrogen fusion reactors into the accelerator at a rate of fifty gigahertz. Exiting the accelerator at a fusion ambient temperature are the fragmented subatomic particles.

Scientists have experimented on fusion power for some twenty years without much success. Nuclear fission is what ended World War II, but the advancement of nuclear fission continues to be a political football. If space travel is to exist, scientists must possess an operational fusion-fission-energy-cycle processing facility. The process of fusion is to fuse molecules together, as in heavy hydrogen or heavy water. The process of fission is to release enormous amounts of energy from the chain reactions between high-grade uranium and plutonium. Just as lead is the ultimate byproduct of radioactive uranium; lead, strontium, or any of the heavier elements can be reforged back into the original uranium atom through the process of nuclear fusion. The process of reconstituting uranium is not about recycling waste, but about having enough fuel to cross the expanse of space.

The technology behind dimensional chemistry starts with uranium and plutonium. The process converts these two components into their plasmatic state. A plasma conduit is comprised of tuned waveguides, a magnetic containment coil, and an inner cathode core, which repels the plasma stream to counter the force of friction. The conduit terminates at a plasma injector, fed into an accelerator, operating at the same frequency as the plasma stream. The accelerator has two input plasma injectors. As the subatomic debris emerges from the accelerator's output, any dimensional particles go into a highly enriched plutonium-plasma chamber under tremendous heat, causing a near-critical gravity wormhole. This chamber is called the dimensional amplifier. The resulting subatomic fission between the sub-particles and the plutonium atoms further generates more dimensional particles, until a subspace field forms. In all phases of the process, maintaining the resonance ensures stability within the subspace field.

The shield generator is part of the gain-control system, which monitors the dimensional amplifier's intensity and adjusts the shield strength accordingly.

As part of the dimensional amplifier and the plasma conduit system, valves within the accumulator expansion tanks open up as the ship transitions to normal space. Due to the extreme heat and subsequent cooling, improper venting of the amplifier chamber can create vacuum problems. The expansion tanks are connected to the fission-fusion energy processor to recover any salvageable matter.

The dimensional step process is based on the mathematical calculation of the ship's present step as compared to the requirements needed to increase toward the next step. These calculations might seem proportional, when but cloaking an entire ship, plus the added friction against gravity, the proportion between steps becomes almost exponential.

Frequency stabilization runs throughout the radioactive plasma cycle by way of waveguides. Waveguides follow the length of the plasma conduit, acting as frequency governors and ensuring the stabilized the flow of plasma and applied voltage to the magnetic coil and the cathode center core. Waveguides orchestrate the operating frequency within the dimensional amplifier.

The Law of the Conservation of Mass and Energy is one of the basic science concepts taught in elementary school. Matter and energy is neither created nor destroyed; it only changes form. One of the problems in dimensional physics is the accountability of matter and energy crossing dimensional lines. Take a black hole—how much energy and matter is lost and never retrieved? Where does it go? If this is true, a black hole consumes matter and routes it to another dimension of space-time as "alluvial" deposits of debris matter. This substantiates the notion that in all space, dimension, matter, and energy are equally shared.

The most crucial aspect of any dimensional system is the discharge when transitioning to normal space. Each waveguide has its own high-resistant ramp, or wedge, to prevent internal arcing. All magnetic plasma coils open expansion valves for proper venting, and all power-supply voltages are de-energized to prevent accidental arcing.

Dimensional discharge occurs when a ship exits subspace and returns to normal space. The discharge is composed of residual particles still captured within the accelerator and the dimensional amplifier. While in subspace, the discharge represents only potential energy. When a ship drops back into normal space, the residual plasma and subatomic particles are converted to kinetic energy and require immediate discharge, or else the ship will explode. The emitter electrodes statically release any residual discharge through the shielding conduits as harmless radiated energy.

The dynamic behind discharge is the residual kinetic energy remaining in the tuned accelerator, the dimensional amplifier, and shield generators. It is imperative that this excess energy is expelled from the system to prevent explosive detonations in the dimensional system once the ship returns to normal space. Plasma conduits from the accelerator and dimensional amplifier route the discharge network to the emitter electrodes. The emitter electrodes act as a diffusing system that radiates the discharge into the vacuum of space. The emitter electrodes can also encapsulate the discharge in a containment field to be fired as an energy weapon.

Subspace dimensional drive incorporates the existing dimensional gradient cloaking system with the a larger shield generator, the existing fusion reactor, modifying the ionic drive engines to accept a "discharge injector" directly into the engine's combustion chamber, along with unwanted subatomic debris from the radioactive plasma and particle accelerator, which are fed through another injector.

Traveling through subspace takes advantage of black matter and black energy, which is proportional to the gravitational stresses beyond that of light speed.

Uranium or plutonium replenishment is one of the more technologically challenging aspects of space travel. In dimensional mode, the plasma conduit and accelerator sees uranium or plutonium as a fuel medium that, under most circumstances, is non-recoverable. A large majority of uranium's atomic and subatomic particles are degraded from the dimensional gradient process. There is little chance of reconstituting any salvageable uranium, unless fusion can restore the original atom. The depleted uranium emitted from the dimensional amplifier is injected as debris into the ionic engines as thrust. There are several problems in dumping spent uranium particles through the main ionic-drive system. One problem is the buildup of heavy elements in highly populated regions of space, These can alter a star's thermonuclear evolution. Another problem is the traceability of uranium debris emitted as exhaust. A third problem is the polarity dynamic, where subatomic and atomic particles separate according to their inherent charge, creating a massive gravitational magnet along heavily congested travel routes.

A fourth problem involves in-ship storage of fission elements. Any radioactive decay in close proximity to the hydrogen fusion reactors can create subatomic contamination, causing catastrophic effects. In addition, the storage of large amounts of stable and unstable uranium or plutonium represents a containment issue involving additional shield generators in case of meltdown. The entities have recorded several instances where alien craft deliberately target each other's fission containment bays, causing both spillage and nuclear detonation.

Several alien species began opening markets to reprocess spent uranium and plutonium material and resell it at a higher price. The reprocessing facilities represent a shared enterprise because it is cheaper to reprocess uranium than it is to salvage a contaminated ship. Accidents, even in a reprocessing facility, do happen. One alien profiteer tried to speed up the process of reconstituting uranium by injecting uranium plasma into a large, carbon-fusion facility. The carbon-fusion reactor was part of an agricultural experiment to reconstitute lost carbon atoms for organic processers. Once the uranium plasma entered the fusion containment chamber, the entire planet exploded. The star's gravitational equilibrium between the individual planets disintegrated, causing several planets to escape their orbital path while other planets collided into the sun, causing the whole solar system to go nova.

Smaller salvage operators have realized the military and commercial importance of destroying each other's planets for profit or blackmail, creating thousand of underground uninspected uranium- and plutonium-replenishment facilities. Over time, the undocumented radioactive deposits actually increase a planet's mass. The resulting heat and gravitational strain against the system's sun eventually result in orbital degradation, causing the same nova event.

The Plutonium Wars had little to do with territory, possession, or even technology, but a massive plague of planetary sabotage, where whole civilizations annihilated each other because they existed. Whole solar systems went nova causing further galactic instability. As a result, several galaxies became a tangled web of expanding nebulas rich in mineral and radioactive elements. The vast wealth that once existed as pillage and plunder became a miner's paradise, as they profited and created new civilizations in the name of freedom and cooperation.

Following the Plutonium Wars, alliances, confederations, and merchants within the expanding nebulas flourished in peace and commerce, where the lessons of obliteration went unnoticed.

The dimensional system initially begins with the hydrogen fusion reactor. The fusion reactor has three inputs to the accelerator, one-gamma/cosmic ray/heavy hydrogen projectile cannon and two input-plasma-conduit injectors. The accelerator inputs the gamma/cosmic ray/heavy hydrogen cannon as the ballistic propellant and two fusion inputs uranium or plutonium to be broken into their subatomic components. The subatomic debris from the accelerator is injected into the dimensional amplifier for dimensional processing with the unused exhaust debris going to the ionic engines.

In analyzing the dimensional amplifier, dimensional subspace is vastly different from normal space. In normal space, space travel is limited by the speed of light, where light itself becomes infinite friction, converting all matter to pure energy. In dimensional space, there is no light, only dark matter and dark energy. Dark matter only exists when gravity itself exceeds the speed of light. The dimensional amplifier operates the same way; it takes the exhaust particles from the accelerator and applies a gravitational force greater than light itself. The final output is dark matter in the form of dimensional subspace energy, which creates a subspace envelope around the spacecraft. The containment generators create a protective shield around the ship to stabilize the counter force of gravity.

Due to extreme gravitational pressure and temperature, the dimensional amplifier is encased in a special uranium-carbide chamber surrounded by a containment shield powered by fusion reactors and cooled by liquid nitrogen. The remaining subatomic debris is injected into the ionic-drive engine's combustion chamber.

Besides the advantage of faster travel, the reduced friction decreases the amount of power consumed, even at the first dimensional gradient. In a dimensional drive system, the discharge is routed through the shield-containment conduits into the ionic drive's injectors. Once the discharge leaves the heavily shielded injector nozzle, the discharge quickly expands and energizes the subatomic debris, causing more acceleration. Additional hull-containment generators ensure maximum hull integrity at high speed.

The major disadvantage to this system is the "no-gravitational-wake zone" established along galactic-trade or military-scouting routes. Dimensional travel is only for crossing between galactic voids.

The dimensional gradient exists in twelve incremental steps, starting from normal space extending and to the vortex level on the twelfth step. (See diagram)

Each step represents a heightened level of subspace as a function of increased potential energy and gravitational distortion. Each subsequent step requires additional energy from the previous step while still maintaining subspace equilibrium.

Most ships have the capacity to attain three-fourths to five-fourths gradient. Planetary-dimensional facilities can achieve a subspace field of eight-fourths while maintaining stabilization.

Climbing or descending the gradient ladder must be done incrementally instead of jumping multiple steps. Once returning to normal space, the dimensional system must discharge any residual kinetic energy still trapped inside the dimensional network. This will be explained later.

The supervisor entity has demonstrated through the orb's holographic presentation that, if any alien society reaches the capability of the sixth step, that alien race automatically receives a "mug shot." When an alien race achieves the eighth step and continues to disregard warnings, the entities have the prerogative to destroy that installation or destroy the planet. Once the entities detect an alien race with vortex capability, or the twelfth step, then the entities destroy the solar system's sun. The orb displayed the Gray's mug shot, a previously unknown race of aliens gone undetected.

One of the entity's fears is alien-to-alien sabotage, where crossing dimensional boundaries can influence time, events, or even the gravitational stability of space itself.

The liquid-cooling complex begins with containers of liquid nitrogen. The network of coolant lines passes through all the critical systems, like plasma, fusion reactor, dimensional systems, containment shield generators, and ionic-engine-nacelle ductwork. Expansion tanks are scattered along the coolant network to vent off gaseous nitrogen for recondensing back into liquid nitrogen. The condensing network consists of plumbing along the interior ram-intake ductwork exposed to the vacuum of deep-space, cooling the liquid nitrogen enough to repeat the cycle.

When the engines are shut off, the computer enables two aft thrusters, allowing for minimal navigational stability, along with a port and starboard thruster to prevent rotational drift.

The computer's most critical function is coordinating engineering's many protocol procedures, like temperature, plasma control, scheduled maintenance, and cleanliness. The turkey feathers control the afterburner nozzle pucker. If the feathers become dirty or caked with burnt debris, they become inoperable.

Appendix 3

Weapons

When considering a weapons platform, the two primary considerations are speed and distance. There are three subordinate considerations: your enemy's shield potential, cloaking ability, and ambush tactics.

The radar determines weapons delivery. The radars scan while tracking lock-on and output power to determine accuracy and maximum radar distance at which the target can be acquired.

The development of long-range radar will be the primary challenge in successfully negotiating battlefield engagements. Due to the vastness of space, identifying hostile targets with ballistic accuracy guarantees both survival and battlefield prowess.

The primary weapon for long-range engagements will be the fission torpedo. The torpedo's platform can be altered to match the battle requirements by including such modifications as a home-on jam, proximity detonation, or its own radar guidance system. The torpedo's rocket platform can be a solid or liquid propellant, but due to range and speed required, ionic engines are a better choice.

As technology comes online, the use of fusion torpedoes or fission plasma torpedoes might be a better choice.

The use of plasma "lasers," or cannons, is the last resort for close quarter's engagements.

The use of mines is a tricky situation, especially in space where drift and accountability can cause even the most seasoned captain to run into their own mines. The use of tethering mines or remote-controlled intercept mines would be a better choice when trying to fabricate a "spatial tripwire."

Cloaked ships have a better chance at survival with deployed mines rather than torpedoes or plasma cannons. The element of surprise is the number one strategy of all space warfare.

Containment shielding or force-field shielding consumes power and is only meant to be a temporary safeguard between enemy fire and the spacecraft. Containment shielding is an effective protective envelope during ionic storms or minor asteroid damage, but the constant barrage from weapons fire is only delaying the inevitable. The use of torpedoes while keeping a tactical distance can prevent most close-quarter's damage or death.

A computer can alter the plasma frequency from uranium, which is fifty gigahertz, to the new material of seventy gigahertz or greater. Chemically, this might be possible—the ship had the technology, but what was impossible was the waveguide configuration. Normally within the plasma conduits are a series of waveguides controlling the plasma's wavelength frequency. If the computer decided to use another radioactive element, the new wavelength would not correspond to the existing waveguides, which means changing the waveguides. Since waveguides are made of a non-magnetic metal specifically tuned to a particular frequency, changing frequencies also means changing the waveguide's dimensions. A stronger and more powerful plasma cannon is possible, but trying to refit the waveguide plumbing is not feasible.

The idea behind torpedoes is relatively simple; the problem is in the enemy's hull-shield generator. The basic concept of a shield generator is to create an envelope of charge particles capable of absorbing ballistic impacts. There were two basic concepts when confronting an enemy ship with heavy hull shielding. First, what is the shield's polarity? The second is the shield's refractive and reflective properties?

Shield polarity is the inherent polarity of the field itself. If the enemy's shield is positive, you do not want to use positive plasma cannon. Adding positive charges to an already positive field adds to the final shield strength. To neutralize any shield, the plasma blast must be of the opposite charge. It is difficult to determine whether the enemy's shield is positive or negative, so to be on the safe side, the first principle of space combat is, always use torpedoes before plasma cannons.

Dimensional torpedoes come in two types: plunger and proximity fuse. Torpedoes are very effective within ten radar-range hours. Normally, the resulting nuclear blast from a plunger-torpedo nuclear blast has a lethal range of three radar-range hours. Anything within a three-hour perimeter is crippled, damaged, or destroyed.

Dimensional torpedoes are hull disintegrators. This type of torpedo is built around a highly radioactive material, a small accelerator, and a small fusion reactor, all encapsulated on a missile platform. The missile's infrared sensors target the ionic-drive engines. The plunger torpedoes explode on impact or are configured with an omni-directional radar altimeter as a proximity fuse. This would send the highly radioactive material into the engine room, contaminating the entire fusion-reactor complex. This, in turn, would cause the fusion reactors to become unstable and explode.

One possibility is a "discharge" torpedo—a large capacitor charged with dimensional discharge put into a ballistic missile. When the torpedo hits, a ship would instantly explode from the surge of ionic sub-particles.

The most lethal ordnance in the weapons inventory is the proximity mine. These were discharge mines, dimensional mines, and fission-fusion mines.

Contrary to what one may think, smaller, fighter-type spacecraft represent an unknown concept in alien warfare. Smaller aircraft are wasteful, inefficient, and counterproductive, and with limited range, they are a huge liability. The age of mega-ships has not only jeopardized whole planets, but also destroyed entire solar systems. The escalation to larger ships has also jeopardized many long-standing alliances where trust and negotiated treaties once held the tide against the all-powerful and the all demanding.

The most difficult concept with torpedoes and radar is anticipating closing speed and coincidence. The term *coincidence* means just that: to predict when and where the torpedo will hit the target. Most radars are able to track ships in normal space, but once a ship enters subspace or rides on a gravity wave, the radar target becomes an anomaly. In the construction of any space radars, anomalies had been filtered out because of ionic clutter. The general rule dictating torpedoes is, when the target breaks the ten-radar-range-hour marker, fire torpedoes. Though more dangerous but more accurate, the window can be dropped to six radar-range hours. As a good compromise, eight radar-range hours is the general rule.

A radar-range hour is the distance light travels in an hour. Because space is a vacuum, radar has the ability to travel further without the dispersal problem. Inexperienced alien upstarts generally use radars in the second or minute radar-range. More advanced species possess radars able to detect objects many hours away, and the most powerful radars built by the Skurlords had a range of one thousand hours.

Appendix 4

Ionic vs. Antigravity Engines

An engine requires oxygen in the combustion process; unfortunately, there is no oxygen in space. This is why space rockets or spacecraft must carry their own supply of liquid oxygen. The added weight from liquid oxygen therefore limits the spacecraft's potential payload.

There are two engines exclusively designed for space travel: ionic and antigravity. Ionic engines offer the advantage of added speed without the need for oxygen, but are extremely bulky and waste valuable materials in their intake design.

The term "antigravity" is more of a catchy phrase, but actually, the engine is designed to operate at maximum gravity. The antigravity engine mimics a near-black-hole event where maximum gravity draws mass, i.e., atomic particles, into the intake and spits the debris out the back as thrust.

The engine of choice is a modified ionic-drive engine, which incorporates a fission reactor connected to an accelerator, injecting atomic particles into the engine's nacelle and propelling the debris out the exhaust, creating thrust. The fission reactor never reaches critical mass; its only purpose is to produce enough of a radioactive reaction to send a steady stream of radioactive fallout through the engine's intake. The resulting heat and energy from nuclear fission expands, creating a difference of potential in both volume and pressure inside the combustion chamber.

Antigravity in its purest sense is not levitation. In comparing antigravity to a dimensional subatomic process, the dimensional particle accelerator creates subatomic particles from either highly enriched uranium or plutonium. In climbing the dimensional gradient, the dimensional amplifier collects only those subatomic particles which are dimensionally dependant. In an antigravity system, a high voltage controls the magnetically stimulated gravity sink, generating a small wormhole or vortex near the speed of light. A containment force field shrouds the vortex complex, along with a liquid-nitrogen coolant system. There are three injectors feeding the gravitational anomaly: uranium or plutonium, hydrogen plasma, and ammonia. The idea is to create a sphere of dark energy as the gravitational energy strips away the injected subatomic material, creating a subspace envelope. The dark matter engulfs the outer-hull containment shielding for dimensional cloaking and travel. The resulting exhaust of subatomic debris provides both gravitational and subatomic nuclear thrust, achieving unlimited speed.

One of the dangers surrounding antigravity technology is the shield containment and the coolant network. Because antigravity fundamentally operates near the wormhole threshold, catastrophic implosions or nuclear detonations can occur once gravity exceeds critical velocity. It appears that the Ensups experimented with this technology on several planets. Over a period of one thousand years, the Ensups managed to destroy 90 percent of their galactic agra-planet population. To understand what happened, we need to understand how the universe works. Within the galaxy, there are billions of tiny stars. Each star represents a solar system. A solar system is comprised of a star, or sun, and individual planets that orbit that sun. Each planet has its own selected orbit determined by the forces of gravity. The Ensups' antigravity planetary experiments actually created mini-black holes, causing the planet to implode. This catapulted the solar system into gravitational chaos, resulting in the sun's nova. The Ensups' galaxy gradually began to decay as the gravitation instability effected the galactic rotation and outer torque. The Ensups, almost by default, gained galactic power because of their failed antigravity experiments.

Essentially, the antigravity device replaced the ionic-drive engine. Each antigravity engine connects to a hydrogen reactor to power up an interconnecting network of magnets, which fabricate the vortex. Inside the vortex are two small accelerators, fed by a plasma-uranium port or a plutonium port. A separate dimensional accelerator and amplifier operates as a discharge generator within a magnetic shield-containment field. The discharge feeds into the two small accelerators, which bombard the uranium or plutonium plasma to very high temperature. The vortex magnetic coil creates the intense gravitational force needed to strip apart atomic and subatomic particles, as a black hole would do. The research bots had discovered that black holes prohibit the escape of visible light because of the relationship between gravity and a matter-density coefficient. The proportion of gravity to energy is proportional to the size and mass of the black hole. A small black hole might exceed the speed of light by three times. A larger black hole might cause gravity to exceed ten or one hundred times that of light speed. The technology is simple enough, but the real hazard is in the containment field and the antigravity's temperature control. Due to the amount of radiation from gamma rays and X-rays, the entire engineering department requires extensive shielding. One of the problems with antigravity drives is planetary atmosphere. In the vacuum of space, antigravity propulsion has nothing to push against to create momentum. Once the antigravity engine hits atmosphere, the velocity suddenly increases, causing severe instability and hull disintegration from overheating. This causes many ships to lose stability and consequentially crash or burn up in the atmosphere.

Another problem to the antigravity control is their lack of maneuverability. A cruiser's zeppelin shape and lack of maneuverable surface area, especially when exceeding light speed, creates severe stabilization problems, which can be exploited.

A spider ship has twenty galactic-class ionic-drive engines; each engine had a corresponding hydrogen fusion reactor. The principle behind ionic engines is to accelerate atomic and subatomic particles from the nacelle's injectors through the combustion chamber and out the aft turkey feathers. There are five major injectors, each classified by fuel type, ratio, and rate of acceleration. The first injector is from the hydrogen-fusion reactor itself. The second injector is ammonia. The third injector is discarded atomic debris from the dimensional accelerator for high acceleration. The fourth is the dimensional-discharge injector, and the last injector is from a huge tank of pressurized methane. The two ram-air intakes originate from a huge network of tubes and valves stemming from the forward ram-air intakes on each port and starboard angle, off the amidships fuselage. The port and starboard ram-air intakes measure two miles tall by four miles wide at full aperture.

Certain galaxies have imposed speed restrictions because of jet-wash or debris-wash creating massive turbulence waves along heavily congested travel routes. There is also a situation called "combustion blow out," where the intake pressure exceeds the ionic-drive internal-combustion pressure, creating engine compression explosions, or stalls.

There are three developmental stages in spacecraft power designs. The first is a fission accelerator. This entails a fission reactor, which feeds critically massed uranium into a gas-chambered or solid-chambered accelerator. Instead of having several cores packed in a large tube chamber, each tube fits inside a tuned, rotating carrousel-type accelerator. The fission reactor does not generate any heat or detonate nuclear explosions, but disperses instead high-velocity subatomic debris, which aides in the ionic drive's dynamic thrust

The second engine improvement is the addition of the fusion reactor. In order for the fusion reactor to function, there are three necessary inventions: the plasma conduit, the plasma injector, and the shield containment/liquid-coolant systems. By incorporating the fission and fusion reactors together and with the understanding of dimensional physics, the final drive—the dimensional drive—is created.

The drone ship has two ram-air intakes in the side of each wing-fuselage interface. There are other large intakes under the nose area, connecting to the same ram-air ductwork.

A common design to all ionic-drive engines are the intakes, either ram-air or a fuselage-air intake. The intake does not take in air, because in space there is no air. The intake ingests atomic and subatomic space debris, which is burned inside the ionic-drive engines.